DARKNESS
After the Fall

Elle and Fiona Simpson-Edin

Dedicated to all those with love for the worlds that might be,
for those that see beyond,
for those that endless dream.

For Love.

To Hel and Fenris,
may our paltry offerings of wet food stave off the end of the world.

Table of Contents

ACKNOWLEDGEMENTS

A massive thank you to those who read this, gave us feedback, and made us better. A first novel is hard, and believing you can do this alone is hubris, no matter what you've done before. So, thank you Marc, Quinton, Anna, Kassandra, and thank you to all of our beta readers.

After the Fall Timeline

- **-11052 EE** — Foundation of Göbekli Tepe
- **-1009 EE** — The second stone of Gripholm
- **-15 EE** — First nuclear weapon
- **1 FE** — Launch of the first manned spacecraft
- **157 FE** — First manned expedition to mars
- **192 FE** — First manned expedition to embla
- **482 FE** — Terraforming of embla
- **1969 FE** — Terraforming of mars
- **2020 FE** — Creation of Sphere
- **2170 FE** — Liberation of Mars
- **3045 FE** — The ravaging of Earth
- **32 AF** — Expansion to Sphere
- **62 AF** — Light Mage exodus
- **581 AF** — Birth of Naos
- **2988 AF** — Return to Earth
- **8957 AF** — Creation of Tube
- **11566 AF** — ?

DRAMATIS PERSONAE

Apteryx

Wallang Sam: Senior teacher, member of the Ring

Argent Miskara: Rector and artisan, member of the Ring

Hugh Wasal: Spymaster, member of the Ring

Hira Hirsh: Artisan, member of the Ring

Cormac Vadden: Head of security contracts, member of the Ring

The Speaker: Chairperson of the Ring

Kiste Arang: Operations and logistics, member of the Ring

Keshara Arabris: Early career guild member, artisan

Salvador Infecit: Agent, special operations

Mia Hestion: Agent, infiltration and information gathering

Rinna Fergus: Apprentice

The Astion

Lin Imposs: Ship engineer and pilot, former Kras employee

Beral Regre: Engineer and mechanic

Mohammad Silk: Lieutenant and XO of the Astion

Kitt: Prospective settler

Light Mages of the Tribe

Frid: Light Council representative

Masan: Light Cadre commander

Meg: Mage and tech expert

Freya: Early career light mage

Kaleb: Early career light mage

Gere: Head of security
Sinn: Logistics expert

The Tribe

Milani: A member of the tribe.
Aman: A member of the tribe.

City Six

Sandra Salvarin: Dark Mage, guildless, affiliated with Apteryx
Calanda Salvarin: Dark Mage, guildless, affiliated with Apteryx

Tube

Anne Sirah: Apteryx Agent

Other

Leanne: A mage with no guild

ACT I

35TH DAY OF 11551 AF

IT was thirty standard days since the sun was seen; darkness engulfed the city. Glowing streetlights and storefronts were fighting to claw something back from gloom. A constant din of activity rose from the unseen depths of of the ancient realm. The activity of millions upon millions going about their lives in this hive ensured that it was never silent.

High on the wall of an ancient fort stood a proud figure taking in the view. The man measured six feet, adorned with a long black beard and a heavy cloak. The cloth swirled around his impressive body, hinting at a younger self who'd been built by hard physical work. His pitch-black eyes glistened in the faint light of the city.

Tonight, Wallang felt elation at having abandoned that path in favor of his pursuit of knowledge. He had high hopes for the latest shipment which was currently being delivered to his workshop. Still, he lingered, it had become a tradition for him, particularly during the many cycles of night in City Six, feeling the Darkness and watching the city. A calm over the whole scene, this ancient city, layer upon layer of civilization built on what came before. Somehow the spirit of Embla made it all feel weighty and important, made the dancing and partying and bustling seem like a ritual that appeased the soul of the place; or maybe I'm just a fanciful old fool, Wallang thought to himself.

He walked down wide stone steps, a winding spiral into the depths of the mountain. Every full turn he passed a heavy door made from dark solid-looking wood. All of these doors had been installed thousands of years earlier, never rotting or decaying. Wallang was very impressed by the ingenuity of the original settlers here. He hadn't found a complete set of documents describing the creation of the fort, but he had found enough to know that it had originally been built by a mere handful of builders. They had all been Dark Mages, and they'd carved it from stone and wrought details in magically grown wood. He'd love to get his hands on the spells they'd used for that wood, trees that were as eternal as diamond. What beautiful building material. He didn't dwell on these thoughts for long; he had much more significant things to occupy his mind today.

Wallang arrived at the lowest floor of the building. He pushed open the heavy door and wandered along the corridor to his workshop. He had been forced to pull a lot of strings and do a lot of favors for the other members of the Ring to secure this room. He'd had to do much seedier things to secure the large coffers that were now waiting for him on the floor. He didn't like threatening and extorting, but sometimes the ends did justify the means. This time it surely did, he thought. These secrets belonged with no one but him.

Wallang entered the huge stone chapel that now served as his workshop and office. Most of the room was empty but the inner wall was lined with bookshelves and a large desk. In the middle of the room stood the two large coffers that'd been delivered a few hours earlier. Spread around them was a small mountain of books, memory crystals, and other storage devices, the general detritus of a mage at work.

Wallang sat down on a pillow he'd left next to the books and picked up the next crystal in the lot. He scanned it using his wrist neural link, and the index flashed on the small screen on the back of his hand. Then he sighed and moved the crystal over to the pile of books and crystals designated as the useless pile.

Hour after hour passed, sometimes he'd just scan an index, other times he'd be burrowed in a piece of writing for a long while, trying to find the next thread. His useless and almost useless piles kept growing.

As the screen flared to life for the fiftieth time, Wallang held his breath. This is it. The screen read: Rituals of the Dark Plane: Practical Considerations and Warnings.

Wallang went over to his desk and placed the crystal on the right side, in a small groove made to hold it. Silver letters flowed across the table as it loaded the data from the crystal and organized the contents like the pages of a book. He grabbed his chair and started to read.

The first chapter felt trite and deprecating; such grandiose wording and overwrought warnings. As if anyone who'd be interested in the content wouldn't be aware of the dangers of powerful magic. He skimmed the next few pages until he hit what seemed to be real information. An explanation of the research that had led to this work; discussion of mages Wallang had never heard of, all of whom must have lived before the Fall. It occurred to him that he hadn't checked the date of the crystal. Wallang flicked a finger towards the corner of the desk and a list of information lit up. Written 12551 before the current date, 2060 First Expansion.

Wallang stared at the date. Well, that explained why the language felt a bit different.

The text had a strange syntax. The common language had not undergone any large official shifts since The Fall, but it had slowly warped; it was no longer the same as what had been spoken before The Fall. There was something else here though, something that couldn't be a coincidence; Wallang had seen some of these idiosyncrasies before, the grandiose choice of words and run-on sentences, which were often as long as paragraphs. Some older mages that had been careless developed patterns like this. The signs were subtle but definitely pointing to advanced mental corruption. This could be enough of a reason to take some of what was written here with a grain of salt. Wallang skipped forward even further, flicking through the bright lines of text on his desk. When runes started appearing he stopped. He went back to the beginning of this section and read.

These pieces made sense. The same findings he'd made. The dark plane couldn't truly be explained as an elemental force, it acted as if it had layer upon layer of complexity, almost like something that was alive. He knew many others had forwarded the idea, but here it was so clearly mapped. Experiment after experiment led to a clear conclusion: the dark plane has a will. Wallang figured it was some sort of pseudo intelligence, an emergent property spawned from simple rules; even so, it was a very different idea from what was most commonly taught. As he read on, he found more and more sections he didn't follow; the text discussed spells he'd never heard of as if they were trivial. So much of their history had been lost in the Fall. Some runes were noted down that he didn't recognize. He found a mention of great runes that most definitely were not ones that he'd been taught. Massive help that is. Can't use a rune I've never seen, he thought. A later passage made him perk up: As described in Hand of the Planes. Wallang immediately got on his feet, he'd seen that title, it was here.

He rushed over to the pile of unread and unsorted documents, he rummaged frantically until it lay before him — Hand of the Planes, the words inlaid in a black leather binding. Opening it exposed the crystal inside, a design he'd very seldom seen before, but he'd recognize anywhere. The blue glass held veins of molded diamond: a design for storing actual runes.

Wallang returned to his table, and in a few rapid touches he instructed the system to store all information of the first crystal locally. He placed the second crystal in the reader and watched the new information flare onto the surface.

His body tingled with chills as if he were in one of the towers and not the deepest dungeon. He glanced at the date indicator Year 53 First Expansion. He'd never run into an arcane tome that old. This was from a time when humanity was barely space faring, and three thousand years before the Earth was sterilized. He flicked forward, this work was even harder to decipher. There had been many languages before the Fall that had merged into the common language in the last fourteen millennia. Wallang wasn't even sure this could be considered a version of the common language. With a gesture, he asked his system to add language assist. With help from the machine brain, the document made more sense. The first chapters described who the book was for, and it really boiled down to; adepts with ambition past what most thought safe or sane. Great, I guess that describes me just fine. At least if one would listen to the Ring, Wallang thought with more than a little anger flashing over his face.

Minutes turned to hours as he poured over the sections. This was no simple history book, it was a grimoire. Page after page of detailed instructions on how to craft each rune. The anchor runes alluded to were all of the Dark school, but the other runes detailed were of all types. Patterns were described for great spells, the scope of which would be considered 'rituals'. They were mentioned in several places. He went line by line, not wanting to miss anything, and fought the urge to jump to the things he really craved; then all of a sudden it was there, the actual schematic of jēra-ūruzúr. A great rune.

Wallang hadn't heard of a great rune being uncovered or discovered in hundreds of years, and he'd never even heard a mention of this one. With these tomes, I can do it. I can build a permanent bridge. I can create a gate to the Dark. A chill, this time of excitement, flowed through him.

63RD DAY OF 11551 AF

THE rain cleared the oppressive dust that normally hung in the air of City Six. Even so, it was no nicer a day than any other. An odor of dilute sulfuric acid, and of numerous sulfuric compounds greeted all on the streets. It was a rain that smelled like it should have color though it didn't.

A group of three, dressed in deep green raincoats and protective face masks were picking their way across the chaotic walkways of Mirktown, a less than affluent trading district of City Six. All three were walking with some bounce in their steps, particularly the short figure in the middle, as she hurried along at a trot to keep up with her parents.

The sun had risen just a few cycles ago and did little to light the streets, instead, they had to rely on the purple glow of large fluorescent bulbs hanging from fixtures above the walkway. The shimmer of the raindrops in the light is beautiful, Kesh thought as she rushed ahead of her parents to wait for them at the next intersection.

She was so excited; she hadn't been allowed to see the 'project' that her parents had been working on for so long. Finally, she'd get to visit this marvelous place where all the fantastic drawings and schematics, that usually littered every surface of her home, came to life. In her head, metal horses ran through the glass corridors of a castle reaching all the way into the sky. She knew reality wasn't ever like that, but she didn't care, and she half believed her mom could create something that magical.

Kesh's father stepped onto a large elevator platform and motioned for Kesh to follow.

The party rode up to the highest level. As the group came to a stop at the top-level walkway of the structure, dark and rusted metal details and exposed ventilation shafts gave way to greenery. Vines crawled across the cage protecting the elevator shaft and the lights of the murky brown sky were reflected in brilliant green from the enormous garden that was the rooftops of Embla. Kesh loved it in these gardens, but living up here was expensive, or so her parents told her. She still took every opportunity to sneak away with her friends to visit the green spaces when she had any unsupervised time to play. In many places dark towers pierced the foliage, Kesh knew most of these to be private docking bays for both planetary shuttles as well as for smaller spacecraft. Oliver, one of her best friends, had been off-world once and he bragged about it all of the time. He had left from the large dock however; Kesh knew that was somehow less fancy. She was tugged along by her parents, it seemed she'd been daydreaming again.

After a few minutes of walking, the cleared path took them out to the massive bridge to the west part of the Ushas Mons. A terminal building with a rounded roof painted in red rose on this side of the bridge. They entered a line to the shuttle.

Kesh didn't visit this part of town very often and was taking it all in with wide eyes. Everything was cleaner here. No glaring angry neon signs; instead tall, expensive-looking ceramic towers holding large globular bulbs illuminated the street. The path was wide, and even though the outfits people wore here were different types of rain clothes, they all looked fresh and more varied in style than what Kesh saw in her home block. The buildings here weren't constructed from stainless steel, but rather it was all stone, clay, and ceramics. Houses and mansions lined the sides of the street, at almost every street corner there was at least one grocery store or convenience store, but no other types of shops. Kesh felt like a small alien in a new world.

The trek through this affluent neighborhood only took a few minutes, and then they were there. The manor Kesh had seen so many images and drawings of stood before her. A well-trimmed, blueish-green hedge encircled the courtyard. The lawn was dotted by large trees, each different and curious looking, Kesh knew they'd all been selected from breeders of rare plants, a heritage from Old Earth; species of plants seen nowhere else on Embla. Plants imported from the gardens of Sphere. It was beautiful, but she was impatient. The thing that excited her the most was kept inside the manor. She pulled on her father's sleeve. "Come on slowpoke, I want to see what mom made!"

Kesh's Dad looked at her with a smirk. "No praise for my work? See that building! I designed all of that."

Kesh looked at the building again in a demonstrable way, nodding. A massive doorway, a four-story wall with no windows, two high towers, dark colored stone, each brick half as high as a grown man. "It's fine Dad, but it looks sort of angry. Like you weren't having any fun."

He nodded slowly, "I guess you might be right. Keen eye. I'm still proud, it fits its owner well." Again, he smiled. The party crossed the massive garden, the vivid fragrance of a thousand flowers washing over Kesh. The door slid open as they came close, and Kesh entered before her parents.

"This must be Keshara! Welcome to our home, we've heard so much about you!" The voice was loud, happy, and youthful. The woman who had spoken stood at the bottom of the wide stairs at the other end of the hall. She was tall, dark-skinned, with a large black halo of hair; next to her stood a slightly shorter woman with long blond hair flowing across her shoulders. Both women were beautiful, the tall one in her black floor-length gown, and the blond woman in an all-black suit. The dark-haired woman held up her arm and the other placed her hand on it and the pair came to meet the new arrivals.

Kesh's parents removed their masks and bowed their heads briefly, and Kesh's father said, "Keshara, these are our patrons, Sandra and Calandra Salvarin."

Kesh, who had removed her mask as soon as they entered the building, suddenly felt shy, overwhelmed by the presence of the two tall, beautiful ladies. She curtsied. "Lady Salvarin, and Lady Salvarin?"

Sandra smiled. "You, my young lady, may call me Sandra."

Sandra was taller than Kesh's dad, and her skin was as dark as Kesh's, or her mother's.

Her shorter, plumper, but just as pretty partner curtsied. "And you can call me Calandra. It's lovely to meet you. Feel free to explore, we're just here to do the same today. I've been looking forward to this project being done for so long." Her voice was hypnotic, and Kesh was distracted enough to forget all about the hall and the purpose of the visit for several moments. Greetings complete, an unobtrusive servant collected their outerwear. Kesh stood there fidgeting as the adults talked. Her father noticed and gave her a nudge.

"Kid, explore a bit, this is what you've been giddy about for weeks. Have a look at the statues your mom worked so hard on."

Like that, she knew she'd been dismissed. Adults that want to talk business. She frowned; but in a moment she was smiling again, remembering all of the art she wanted to explore. Her mom was famous enough that she never had time to sculpt at home, only at projects, many of which didn't allow public viewing. She walked through the room looking up at pillars and spirals, abstract shapes of black and white wrapping around themselves and each other. Mostly stone, but sometimes warping into semi-transparent glass. The statues were all still but gave an impression of motion, like the waves of the seas Kesh had seen in films.

As she walked through this forest of stone, time slowed, and finally she came to the focal point of the pattern created by the smaller works in the room; a large clear glass sculpture, reaching half way to the roof of this cathedral dedicated to art. The piece drew Kesh in. The size made it look like it could collapse at any moment, and the angles that the glass spun at seemed impossible, as if laws of geometry had been broken.

She walked around the circular base. As her eyes wandered, she noticed deeply etched symbols encircling the piece. She knew she shouldn't touch anything, but she wanted to feel this pattern under her fingers. As her hand came close to the base, a tingling sensation rose inside of her, starting at her feet and working its way up through her body, out to her outstretched fingers. The room grew noticeably dimmer. Darkness swirled in the sculpture, dancing in the vessel.

It was the most enthralling thing Kesh had ever seen, and she hardly noticed when the tingling started to morph into pain. Time started feeling sluggish, and now the darkness of the room permeated her eyes. The periphery of her vision was dimming and shrinking. It felt like her head was enveloped by something fluffy, something that muffled both hearing and sight. Cold, sharp pain shot through her feet, as if she was standing barefoot on icy metal, and the sensation spread up through her legs. The statue in front of her was all she could focus on. Statue? It doesn't look like a statue. It looks alive, like a sea creature made from black ink, she thought.

"Kesh! Keshara!" She didn't know who had been shouting. Her mom? Everything was fuzzy.

"Get back," Calandra pushed the panicked mother out of her way. She placed a hand on Keshara's arm, and in an instant, the darkness in the statue was gone.

Kesh looked up at the woman, the pain was gone, and she felt empty, "What happened?"

Calandra stood up and removed her hand from Kesh's arm. "It seems you're like me, a Dark Mage; and you just almost killed yourself."

Calandra turned to Kesh's parents, her eyes cold and voice stern. "Did you know?"

***

CRATES were being loaded, and workers were collecting and sorting tools, everyone was moving in a deliberate way, to make sure they lost nothing as this was their last day of construction.

In the middle of the din, a man stood apart from the rest. Masan wore a gray robe in one of the synthetic materials favored on Embla, heavy, sturdy, and resistant to the harsh chemical makeup of the rain. While he was average in many ways, he was just a little too flawless in every aspect, a soft friendly face framing gray ageless eyes. His handlers said he perfectly imitated an average human, while his charisma drew them in. Even though the workers were from one of the stations, and thus used to Light Mages, he was given a wide berth.

Masan surveyed his kingdom. Home for the next several decades. It may have looked like a pile of shipping containers in a vast warehouse, but the disorganized cluster concealed a state-of-the-art communications and surveillance center.

Construction had taken a team of Light technicians and builders over a year to complete, moving personnel, equipment, and building materials slowly to prevent detection. He didn't mind all the favors he'd had to hand out, it was the grueling wait times that was the soul-killer. It was of course critical not to arouse the suspicion of any of the Dark Guild leadership, but that didn't mean he liked the slow pace. This also meant he had to spend more time managing the community of misfits living in the space. They had needed to install shielding, sound insulation, and in some cases magical wards on the work areas to dissuade the inhabitants from noticing the construction. It was slow, tedious work, but it would be worth the investment to have a permanent base of operations in their enemies' home territory.

The Light Mages could have established an open outpost, but the unique planetary circumstances of Embla made that unwise. It was day or night on Embla for 60 wake cycles at a time. Light Mages were at a severe disadvantage here. They were denied the bulk of their power for so many cycles at a time, while the Dark Mages always had the dark and the shade somewhere close by. Defending a public location from Strix, Asio, and Apteryx would have been almost impossible, Masan's people would always be weakened half of the time. It was a profound source of pride: never before had there been a permanent Light Mage outpost here on the planet. While the Light Council had their space stations in the constant Light of the Sun, Embla was a province of Dark and mundane guilds. Until now.

In his early years, he'd wanted to be a Combat Mage, not an academic or an artisan. He'd wanted to defend his people and their way of life against those that would destroy them; to make the whole system safe for those of the Light. The young Masan had envisioned himself descending from on high with the Light Mage combat teams to cleanse dens full of Dark Mage corruption and iniquity. With age came a little more wisdom, and he had realized that the bulk of the work to defend the Light and its Council was performed not by soldiers, but by the organization's vast intelligence apparatus.

Masan had trained on the stations and done his Journeyman work on Mars before the Light Council deemed him ready to head up the new site in City Six. Mars, very much a corporate planet, was full of dangers for the Light Council, but none quite so existential as the threat posed by the Dark Mage Guilds. Where the Light brought calm, order, and serenity, the Dark brought hate, crime, and evil. The Dark Mages could not be allowed to grow powerful enough to displace the Light in the system. There was enough darkness from the void of space. The Light needed to protect the Sun and the warmth and brilliance that emanated from it.

Masan was here with two other subordinates to initiate the mission. His spouse, Sinn, was a Master Mage and an expert in logistics. They had planned and built this facility with the Council, ensuring that the cadre would have a secure location.

The other teammate was Gere, a Master and a skilled Battle Mage. He also happened to be powerful enough to be considered an Adept. Gere was a taciturn man, but a beast in a fight. Masan felt assured that he'd do a fantastic job in the role of security chief.

Masan was in charge of intelligence gathering and growing a community of outcasts to act as a front for the operation. He was already pulling in rejects from the Guilds, mages of marginal talent who had been rejected as Journeymen and cast out. He has also found old-school 'spiritualists' who chased long-forgotten religious practices from Earth to add to their sense of both otherness and foolishness. The people in the nearby markets had already christened the lost souls who flocked to their new ecosystem with a derisive nickname. They were called 'The Tribe'.

45th Day of 11551 AF

THE Apteryx guild sat atop Ursas Mons, on real stone, not the pre-fabbed platforms that held so much of City Six. A sign of their power and permanence, it showed that the guild had been in the city since the beginning, long before the gravity defying scaffolds of newer constructions began to take shape.

Kesh hadn't been allowed to bring many possessions with her. Fledgling Mages were expected to conform to guild norms by dressing in their uniforms and leaving their past lives behind. Kesh didn't want to seem like a baby, so she left her stuffed animals and dolls at home. She had a couple of her favorite books and some fancy common clothes for celebrations and that was it.

A member of the Rector's staff picked her up from her hom, after she said a tearful farewell to her family. Families couldn't visit the guild house until the Mages had "acclimated" to the facility to prevent outbursts from either students or family members. The staffer walked from her family home to the gates of the Guild grounds in silence. Kesh was bursting with questions, but when she turned to look at her escort the words died on her lips. He was as no-nonsense as they came and the expression in his eyes above his breathing mask said that she would learn nothing from him.

The guild house was ineptly named because it was really a fortress. The surrounding terrain had several large apartment complexes that Kesh knew were built to house some of the journeymen. The actual guild complex, however, was a massive fort of black, brutalist stone that rose from lush, jungle-like gardens towering over Kesh and her escort. A large area surrounding the fort was entirely devoid of buildings, and the ground was completely flat and slightly reflective. It looked like black glass.

Kesh finally dared to speak up, "Why is the ground like this?"

Her escort looked around as if he had to consider what she meant, "This? It's what it looks like. Glass. It was made like this when the compound was built. It's to ensure a free view, and to make sure nobody can sneak even the tiniest device in."

"Glass makes it hard to sneak things in?"

"We've got cameras everywhere, and automated defenses. If anything the size of an ant or larger moves here that we don't approve of... Well, look at this." The man produced a piece of candy from a pocket and threw it hard towards the fort. It sailed through the air, and then there was a dark flash, like a shadow had passed by it, and it was no more.

"What happened?"

"That's what happens to anything that crosses here that isn't pre-approved. Important for you to remember, no sneaking out from the building without telling an adult."

Kesh shuddered. The two walked the rest of the way in silence.

He led Kesh into the large building, past a room full of serious-looking adults in front of screens, and up a curved stairwell. Her escort nodded his head to indicate that she sit on a bench in the hallway.

"Give me your raincoat and bag and I will see it taken to the dorms," he said. "Wait here quietly until the rector's secretary comes for you. She interviews all new students on their first day."

Kesh acquiesced, stripping off her mask and coat and handing them over with her small bag. She sat on the large black bench, clasping her hands in her lap, trying to look small and biddable, so the looming, silent man would be on his way. Finally, she might speak to someone who would tell her what was about to happen to her.

Kesh didn't know how long she sat in the hallway before being greeted by a diminutive young man with brown eyes and black hair, not so different from Kesh's own. He was wearing gold-rimmed spectacles and a black suit with gold trimming. "Hello, Keshara. Come with me, I'll show you to the Rector's offices."

The two walked through a long straight corridor that was lined with heavy wooden doors but lacking windows. The walk seemed too long for Kesh, why don't they have auto transporters in a place this large? She thought. She was ushered into a large, waiting room. Dark Mages took their affinity into all of their decor, who was already beginning to miss the vibrant colors of her family home.

The young man opened the doors placed next to his desk, leading into an office.

"Go on in now." He said and nodded towards the entrance.

Kesh timidly stepped into one of the largest offices she had ever seen.

Decorated in dark wood to look more like a library than an office, the walls were lined with books. A large, ornate desk dominated the space with two armchairs in front.

Behind the desk perched a middle-aged woman in a black dress of severe cut. She too had wire-framed spectacles perched on her nose. As she looked up from the papers in front of her, Kesh caught a glimpse of runes etched into the frames and periphery of the glass. So, these glasses were a magical tool, not just a vision corrector. Kesh stared at them intently, because she had never seen an object imbued with such magic before. Both beautiful and intricate, she thought they must have cost a fortune. She immediately corrected herself, an important guild mage wouldn't pay for such things.

The rector turned her gaze onto Kesh, who started in surprise. Behind the lenses were black eyes, without whites with a milky haze swirling around their centers. Kesh cocked her head, trying to figure out what that meant.

The woman indicated to one of the armchairs. "Sit down child. We're going to have a little chat. I want to make sure you understand why you're here with us." As soon as Kesh had gotten into the chair, the Mage cleared her throat.

She started speaking in a stern voice, "I am Adept Argent, Rector of Apteryx, responsible for the education of all of our apprentices. Today is the beginning of a new chapter in your life.

I'm told that you have an unusual affinity for Dark magic. This may be either a blessing or a curse depending on your character.

I want you to understand that magic is more than a force that exists in the world to serve us as a tool. It is a dangerous, capricious thing of its own that lets humanity access it to open up our world for its infiltration. Being a channel for an elemental force is a skill that requires excellent judgment and constant vigilance, as the more magic you channel the more it corrupts your person with its essence." There was a short pause in this stream of words, and Kesh took this as an invitation to speak up.

"I understand mam, I did.." before she'd gotten further the woman slammed a hand down hard on the table.

The rector cleared her throat and continued, "Be wise and be quiet, I'm not done talking. Many a young person has sat in that chair and nodded, feigning to understand the implications of this burden. I want you to look at my eyes,

Keshara, and see that magical corruption can change your very senses, warping and changing you in ways you will not truly understand until months or even years later." The rector paused and brought a cup of tea to her lips. Kesh had been too overwhelmed to even notice the cup and kettle. The intimidating woman put the cup down and continued, "My eyes are the product of a spell gone wrong, a channel to the darkness left open a few moments too long, leaving me in the darkness forever.

You might think that we are going to teach you how to use magic to do great things, but that is not true. We are going to teach you to avoid great magic at all costs. To hone and sharpen your skills to use as minimal magic as possible. Great Dark Mages live short lives and are cursed for warping the fabric of our reality, damaging our collective existence, and opening us all to greater and greater corruption. Their lives burn out as they channel the Darkness into our reality, leaving nothing but ashes and regret."

Kesh squirmed in the chair, made uncomfortable by the barrage of words, and the brutal nature of the rector's speech. It seemed that her dreams of princesses and dragons, running about to do great deeds, were not to be. She wondered if a normal life as an artisan would be preferable to being able to access the Dark. This seemed far more scary than exciting.

The rector pierced her with an unsettling, cloudy gaze.

"I do not expect you to understand the full implications of what you are, of the dangers of magic today. I do, however, expect you to follow the Code of the Academy to the letter because if you fail to accede to our wishes, your quick death is the best you can hope for. If you unleash corruption on yourself and others, you will wish you had died in the process.

Stand and come forward to the desk."

Kesh rose and approached the desk, seeing a metal block inscribed with runes sitting at the edge.

"In order to be an apprentice at this school, we bind you, so that you cannot use magic outside of the presence of an instructor, for everyone's safety.

Place your hand on the block."

Kesh reached out and touched the block. She was a little surprised when nothing happened. The rector placed her hand on the other side and the runes dropped into shadow. Kesh felt a small mental tug as the shadow enveloped the runes, but little else.

The runes returned to their original form and the rector removed her hand.

"I've blocked most of your access to the Dark. Do not fight or attempt to unravel the binding, it will not end well. In time you'll learn the method for undoing this. You may go. Liam will see you to your dorm and explain the process of apprenticeship on the way."

Kesh removed her hand and exited the office. She was too unsettled to realize that she'd hardly spoken through the entire encounter. The young man with the spectacles, Liam, was waiting for her in the corridor.

"Follow me," he said, gesturing to the corridor with his head. "I imagine you would like to know a little more about this place."

***

THE slabs of the floor were cold, but the old mage didn't mind. After weeks of work, the streaks of his silver-coated brush now stretched wall to wall. He wiped the sweat off his forehead. Looking at the sleeve, he realized he'd gotten silver colloids all over his face, his dark beard, and now on his clothes as well. A slight shrug, and then he was at it again. What felt like minutes, but was actually hours, passed as he kept adding finishing touches one after another. Finally, he got up, his knees and back aching, his hand cramping from countless hours of writing without break. Wallang looked over the massive spell he'd crafted. It was the largest pattern he'd ever attempted by orders of magnitude.

Oh well, one shouldn't get complacent. What's the point of all this power if I'm never using it.

With that, he reached down, deep into the black stone, into the depths of the planet, feeling the darkness. He pulled it up, into the room, into the pattern. He let the stream flow into jēra-īsaz kaun, his anchor rune, chained to three others of the same type. Steam rose from the runes, and a light absorbing aura emanated from the lines.

Wallang let the energies branch out to flow through the adjacent parts, towards jēra-ihwaz reið. As magical current reached the master rune the entire pattern came alive at once. All the energy Wallang had collected was pulled in, a maelstrom of uncontrollable power seared through the silvery lines. Darkness poured through every channel, but now they were also glowing red and white as the air around the streaks ignited. Wallang choked down his panic, he felt magic being pulled in through him as well as from his source. He could feel the grim fingers of corruption clawing on him from within.

And just like that it was gone. The room smelled of ozone, burnt minerals, and melted metals, but the patterns had failed and with them the current had been disrupted. Wallang swallowed hard to stop himself from retching. He could feel the nauseating crawling of corrupted flesh in streaks under his own skin. Looking down, he saw sickly black streaks across his arms, the same markings would be covering most of his body. So careless!

Wallang shed his robes, he'd been right. While he couldn't feel any pain, there was a grinding swelling sensation as tendrils of half-formed magical constructs swam in the space between skin and muscle. Where they passed the skin darkened temporarily, looking translucent; it was almost the opposite effect of when a bright light is held to tissue, which illuminated the structures beneath the skin. Only here it was darkness radiating, sketching the outlines of veins and scars, as self-formed magical constructs squirmed their way through their new home.

A wave of despair washed over him. He'd experienced the effects of corruption before, but never like this. He knew there was little to do, corruption born couldn't be unborn, only managed. As he calmed himself, he could swear he heard a faint voice at the back of his head. Laughing. What was there to laugh about?

＊＊＊

THE tall figure of Wallang hurried along the walkways towards the nearby brewery district. Usually, the long periods of darkness on Embla were a soothing balm to him, as they were to all Dark Mages. Today though it just made dealing with the corruption he'd inflicted on himself more painful. He was still determined to make the date he'd set up; Ambrose had such a temper.

He came down the last flight of stairs that left him on the walkways of the Famous Five strip. A small oasis of tidy bushes and flowers lined the metal catwalk between the titular five competing beer halls, each with its own brewery in the back. Wallang was close enough to the owners of these places to know that any competition was for show, the drinks and food were some of the best in the city, and there was never a seat empty for more than a few minutes in any of the dining rooms.

As Wallang stepped into Ambrose's Embrace, he snickered, as he always did, at the narcissism of the man.

The young host, whom Wallang thought was called Will, waved at him. "Welcome, Prior. The manager's table is set up for you, please come with me."

The Embrace was as busy as ever. It was a wonder that Ambrose's people managed to keep this place so clean considering the pure density of people. The thought was interrupted as elevator gates closed and cut off the sound of the room. When he emerged Wallang stood in the familiar lounge above all of the bustle, soundproof glass making the room feel like an isolated bubble. A low melody was playing using a wide range of natural sounds as instruments. Wallang looked at Ambrose who had drawn his chair close to the window to observe the goings-on down in the dining room. Golden locks fell around a face that Wallang often thought could have been chiseled from granite. "One of your new pieces?"

"Yes, yes, it is. I finished it this morning. What do you think?" Ambrose smiled, and the music took on a warmer tone, several new harmonies made themselves heard.

"You know I think everything you touch turns to gold." Wallang winked, but only part in jest. Ambrose's seeming perfection was infuriating.

Ambrose waved at him to come over, and as soon as Wallang was in arm's reach, the beautiful man pulled him down by the lapels of his jacket to give him a deep kiss. "You're late, you oaf."

Wallang, still looming close to Ambrose's face, grinned. "Work. You know how it is."

"Ash. What I do is work. Magery is a bunch of masturbatory handwaving."

"I remember you having done more than a little 'magery' in your day."

"It's overrated... Wait. What's that?" Ambrose's eyes had gone wide as he stared at Wallang's neck.

Instinctively the Dark Mage moved a hand to cover the spot. "It's nothing. I had a bit of an accident."

Ambrose stood up, half a hand taller than his lover. "Show me!" His eyes were icy cold.

Wallang obliged hesitantly, unbuttoning his shirt to expose the upper part of his chest. "It's not so bad."

"Not so bad? It's crawling all over you! Does it hurt? What did you do to yourself?"

"I. It doesn't hurt much. I think I can suppress most of it with time."

"You idiot! You could have died."

"I'm sorry… I know. I'm really sorry."

Ambrose pulled the older man in close, holding him, tears welling up. Wallang could feel him shaking.

"I'm really sorry, Ambrose, I promise I'll be more careful." He meant it in the moment, but a tiny voice in the back of his head seemed to be giggling at him.

340th Day of 11551 AF

A boy lay on his back in the grass, listening to the birds playing in the treetops above. Hundreds of meters above those treetops were another set of treetops rotated upside-down, and another park surrounded by pragmatically designed structures.

The buildings looked like the edges of blades, or pyramids. All aligned in long rows surrounding large gardens, some were beautiful flowery parks for walking and recreation, and others were plantations built to maximize food production. The station was built with both function and aesthetics in mind, with personal transportation made easy by a suspended rail system, and transport of wares by subterranean tube systems.

The boy, Salvador, smiled; the realization hit him often, how strange to have only known this, never having visited a planet. He'd seen enough media to know that the Marsborn were fascinated by the strangeness of Tube. To him, this was normalcy, centripetal gravity, two discs of black void in the distance, living under a sky that was ground to someone else. Normal to him but so alien to most of humanity.

It was early in the morning and the grass was still damp from the sprinkler system. Spheres of floating artificial light were bobbing along, heating the park, and causing a mist to rise as water evaporated.

Salvador loved this spot, nobody to disturb me for hours, no kids, no chores, he thought, only to have that thought interrupted by the murmur of conversation moving towards him. He frowned and looked over in the direction of the sound.

A group of four young adults were wandering through the park in his direction, not having seen him yet. Everyone in the crowd spouted some visible augmentation, and they were dressed in dark blue suits. Salvador realized that they were station techs and at least one of them was likely to be a fellow Mage. Sal frowned harder.

Station tech Mages were not like the ones in his guild, treating magic as a science, using it to maintain station systems only. Sal's father had ranted to him about these people enough that it had been thoroughly impregnated into his mind—they were a lesser class of Mage: traitors and sellouts. Sal's father had a lot to say about their augmentation too, weakness, excuses to not be better at magic. Who needs implants to improve themselves? Sal wasn't sure he entirely agreed. He'd seen some amazing things being done with augments. He wouldn't admit it to anyone in his family or guild, but he thought the mixture of magery and technology was intriguing. The group of people wandered past, not noticing him before they were almost on top of where he lay. The woman of the group, a petty officer from the symbols sewn on her collar, winced when she saw him but hid her surprise with a smile and gave him a little wave as she passed. The other three of the group just ignored him.

Salvador sat up and teased out his dark hair with his fingers. He'd been relaxing longer than he should, and a lot of chores were not yet completed. He rolled up on his toes and sprang to standing. Up and at 'em!

***

THE two round cutouts of black space separated by the dim red light of the so-called night of Tube were beautiful to Salvador's young eyes. Floating orbs illuminated the thousands of trees and flowers below. The voidward side had more of a draw on him than the solward, but both were still so enticing. Letting his imagination run free, he envisioned gods and magical creatures making their way across the star-speckled ether, playing and fighting, creating worlds and destroying them. He'd gotten much of his imagery from his father's notebooks. Sal didn't understand them all, or even much of them if he was honest, but the ideas written there were so fantastical that they burrowed deep into his psyche.

He knew that this was what the guild was researching, what his father's obsession was all about, though he hadn't been told much of the details. Something about ancient beings, and how their nature could allow the strongest of the guild to ascend. It was all quite wordy and sounded a little bit like superstition or religion to Salvador, but he wouldn't say that out loud of course.

While Salvador liked spinning fantastical tales in his head, he was much more serious about the other parts of the guild Smuggling and piracy were exciting and would let him make a name for himself. He would be a great smuggler, and a great adventurer, as soon as he got a proper chance to prove himself. He'd been promised that he could join on a real assignment when he turned fourteen; it seemed so far away though. Why don't they realize I'm ready? I've even got the tattoos.

Noise filled the room behind him as two of his older guild mates, Gil and

Sam, stumbled in trying to catch their breath and speaking over each other. Salvador's father gestured at them to slow down. "Hell boys, one at the time."

Gil glared at Sam, and spoke, "They've caught Elliot, I think she talked. They're gearing up as we speak."

The guild leader paled. "Damn. Well, we knew it might happen. You know what to do. Send the word to everyone who's fighting age. We'll hold them off, and we'll get out of here alive. No materials are left behind at any cost though." He stared at the two young men.

"Understood master," they replied in unison.

Both were on comms within seconds, spreading the word.

Salvador looked at his father feeling a heavy lump in his stomach. How serious is this?

"What do I do, guild master?" Sal asked.

"Get to the gathering point below Anne's office and drag along all the kids you can find. Protect them. If you see anyone from Kras carrying a weapon, run. If you can't run, kill."

Sal nodded. He was brought up to always be ready to respond to emergencies, but this was the first time the training was truly tested. He only hesitated for a moment before he grabbed his jacket that had been carelessly tossed over the back of a chair, and then he was on the move.

***

SAL was walking as quickly as he could without losing any of the five kids—two boys and three girls—that he was trying to shepherd in the direction of the voidward garden district. Greenery brushed against him over and over again, as he kept to the shadows under or close to the large bushes and trees that filled this district. They were moving quickly in spite of the youngest two, a girl and boy of only five, sniffling and asking questions that Sal couldn't answer.

"Where's mom?" The girl tried again.

Sal sighed. "I don't know. Dad, I mean, the guild master, will make sure she's safe."

"Safe from what?"

"Please be quiet," Sal responded. "We're getting close, don't let anyone see or hear you." Sal signaled to the kids to stay put as he made himself as small as he could and edged up the last little hill toward the meeting place. He was moving close to a hedge surrounding a small artificial waterfall, hoping the rush of the water would obscure any sounds. He was careful and slow, wanting to have a look at what he knew to be the most exposed part of the route. Hairs stood on his neck as a man's voice made it clear he hadn't been careful enough.

"Hey! Identify yourself." The Kras guardsman was standing on a walkway some twenty meters to Sal's left. He cursed himself for not having looked up. "I asked you who you are, boy. Why are you sneaking around? Don't make me come down there."

Salvador turned to face the man. "I'm so sorry, sir. I'm getting home past curfew. Please, I don't want my dad to be mad." Sal wasn't the best liar, though he thought he was pretty convincing. The guardsman paused and made a small movement that gave away that he was listening to something Sal couldn't hear. His comm, Sal thought.

A minimal movement of the guard's hand caught his eye. The man was going for his gun. Sal felt a surge as he drew dark energies into himself. Pushing his hands out towards the guardsman, nerves fired across the lines of his tattoo. Dark focused flames flooded the air between them.

There was a gut-wrenching scream, but it almost drowned in the crackling sounds of metal and glass expanding, twisting, and finally exploding. Heat seared Sal's hands, but he knew he wasn't taking any damage. Seconds went by as the roaring of flame and crackling of twisting metal continued, seconds that felt like hours to Sal. His gaze was fixed on the point where the guardsman had stood as he released the darkness, and the flames disappeared as quickly as they had come. The man was gone, and so were several meters of walkway as well as much of the wall behind him. Liquid metal still dripped with an angry red glow from the melted grating of the destroyed walkway.

"Run! This way!"

He recognized Anne's voice, and he ran towards it, hoping running could shape this evil feeling that pulsed in his brain.

Sal looked behind him, and the kids were all on his heels, rushing through the grass. He slowed his pace to let them close in. No one got left behind. The immediate rush had passed, and the subsequent fuzzy brain was clearing again.

Sal realized that while he needed to run, he also needed to be ready for another attack. Those guards always had implants with vital and location tracking, the rest already knew something had happened. While he couldn't protect his family, he could protect his younger guild mates.

The group hit gravel and Sal scanned for Anne, he found her at the edge of the path at a maintenance door in deep shadow. She urged them to get in. Sal stopped at the entrance allowing the kids to pass him, making sure they were all accounted for.

Anne's face was poorly lit but gave away both fear and anger. She looked at him as the last of the kids passed into the doorway. "Is that everyone?"

Sal nodded, "Yeah, everyone else is busy clearing the guild quarters."

"Fools." A frown, and sadness.

Sal wondered why sadness, he knew they'd be fine, no way that the inept station guards could do much damage to a whole guild of Dark Mages. No time to waste thinking of this, the kids needed to get to safety. Sal set off again, through the door pushing past pipes and electrical panels to get ahead of the children. Anne was right behind him.

"We'll continue this way. Keep voidward, I have a crate ship stashed at the very end, it's protected. No station security will detect it, and even if they would, they'd look the other way."

Sal nodded and continued in the direction they'd started. The tunnel was narrow, made for a single tech to wander through to get to all of the electronics that were required for the environmentals below, and rails above. It was dark, but that was to Sal's benefit, he saw better in this dusk than he did on a bright day, and the same couldn't be said for any guards they might run into. He thought that he heard sounds up ahead; footfalls and voices. He raised his hand, and signaled to those behind him. Anne had noticed it too and she made the children stop dead in their tracks with an icy look.

Sal made his way forward slowly, but before he'd taken two steps, he felt Anne's hand on his shoulder.

"We're trying to stay undetected right," she whispered in a tone that made it clear that that wasn't a question.

Sal nodded, but his mood darkened; does she think I'm an idiot? He continued ahead while Anne stayed back to keep the younger ones quiet and calm. He made his way to the next intersection, and through an open hatch he heard talking.

The man paused to listen to his comm. He answered out loud, "Understood, I don't think they'll pass here, but I'll keep an eye out."

The man started turning and Sal struck, this time he wasn't going to kill. No more attention. Darkness flowed from Sal's outstretched hand, a choking black dust, that enveloped the face of the man before he had a moment to react. He fell to the ground flailing, struggling to catch his breath as the dust turned into a slippery plastic-like film coating every orifice. In the thirty or so seconds before the man stopped moving Anne had caught up with him.

"What the hell did you do, you little shit? They'll know!"

Sal motioned with his hand and the black film around the man's head disappeared. "Take it easy, they're set to only send emergency alarms if the heart stops. He's just unconscious." He did a double-take. "Well, there might be some brain damage, but I'm pretty sure his heart is still beating."

Anne looked furious. "Fine." She set off along the corridor where the downed man lay. "Come on then, we need to hurry. And stop it with the constant lashing out, you'll get us all killed."

***

SALVADOR gripped the edge of his seat hard as the ship shuddered and leaped into space. The ship was old and in dismal repair. Rust was visible in almost every corner. His younger guild mates made little noise, but he could see the confusion and terror. After what they saw in the garden the fear was as much of him as it was of whatever had forced them to flee. Anne was looking at him, studying him, he thought.

At his hostile glance, Anne pulled herself upright, her face serious, "You did what you had to do. No shame in that."

Sal was confused. "Shame? About what?"

"Killing never gets easy, but the first time often scars. I just don't want you to be too hard on yourself."

Sal laughed. "Oh, that? Don't worry Anne, I think I'll be fine. I wasn't trained to be sentimental."

A shocked expression passed over her face before she could hide it under a flat serious expression. "Good. Good, I'm glad." She took a breath and continued, "We'll get to a way-station in a few hours, a colleague of mine will take you from there."

Sal filed Anne's reaction away on his mental list of subjects he needed to be more careful about. He had a hard time keeping up with what other people found disconcerting. Either way, he wanted to stick with safer subjects for now. "I thought you were taking us to Embla. Who's this person? How can we trust him?" he asked.

"He's a friend, he's from my guild. Your guild and ours have been allied for a long time. You'll have to trust me on this. As for me, I need to get back before I'm missed. I've got obligations, and if the Corporation finds out I helped your guild they'll probably space me."

Salvador wasn't convinced he could trust this person they'd be paired up with, as he didn't even feel like he could trust Anne. He did understand though, Embla was weeks away on all but the fastest ship, and he knew Anne worked intimately with Kras. While he didn't want to admit it, he did admire her a bit. Being a spy sounded so exciting. He shook his head, and tried to clear his brain. His family was in trouble, maybe even dead. He knew he should be more upset.

Salvador schooled his face into a blank expression and leaned back in his seat. The children were safe for now and he would need the control that came from solid rest if he had to deal with any more unpleasantness. Since he didn't know what was to come, he did what any good soldier in his position would do. He slept so he would be ready for the next step.

367th Day of 11551 AF

DETAILS on the incarceration of the patient are lacking. It would seem this young man was forcibly taken to holding by an off-duty Embla Custodian officer. No notes exist on the supposed infraction that led to this. Written records begin after an altercation between the officer on staff at the holding facility and the patient. The facility physician reported "The boy is dead, but his body still writhes. The same black tendrils that sliced Officer D still extend from the body lying face down before me. We've been unable to move the body, and are awaiting a disposal crew from one of the local dark guilds"

— Case study 184, Suin Lahn, Professor of Necrology, 11564 AF

***

KESH scampered down the stairs to the subterranean levels of workshops. After becoming a student of dark magic, she discovered that only the smallest fraction of the compound was above ground. Most of the classrooms, workshops, and personal workspaces had been dug deep into the mountain where light could not penetrate unless it was deliberately lit. The caverns of the mountain sloped gently down in a serpentine linking the various levels and allowing the transport of large items throughout the compound. Smaller stairs linked some of the rings allowing for quicker passage between the layers of workshops.

Today was an exciting day; the first day of metal-smithing. Early apprentices were only allowed to work in temporary media, like paper and ink, limiting the size, complexity, and danger of their work. These materials were consumed after a single spell and were incapable of holding more advanced runes due to their physical limitations.

Kesh had long admired complex workings like the rector's glasses and couldn't wait to use heftier materials like metal and glass to hold her magic. She knew better than to broadcast that eagerness too much, as an overly eager apprentice was often perceived to be a danger to themselves. Too much enthusiasm might get her training delayed until her teachers felt that she was mature enough for higher workings. Dark apprentices had to master covering their eagerness with studied disinterest or appropriate levels of reservation if they wanted to be allowed to learn more dangerous forms of magic.

She knew this was because of fear of corruption, but she always found the practice self-defeating; the only thing the teachers succeeded in was to make the overly eager hide it better. Still, she had never been permitted into any of the fabrication workshops before and she was eager to get to be among the magical artisans.

The apprentice silver-smithing workshop was brightly lit, one of the first indications that no magic was practiced in the space. It was a relatively small space with six workbenches. Each workbench was set with a plethora of hammers, pliers, and sanding tools. More tools hung in tidy rows along the back wall, above containers of various pieces of metal and wire. Kesh itched to go and touch them, but their teacher awaited them at the first bench.

The solemn-looking man, Hasan, acknowledged the arrival of the last of the cohort with a smile and began speaking. "Today we will briefly review the safety procedures for this workshop and the tools of a metalsmith that you can find in this shop. I know that you are all used to following a lesson and practicing each step as it's shown by your teacher, but metalsmithing is an individual art. I will coach you on best practices and answer your technical questions, but it is up to each of you to determine how you will approach the pieces that we make in this class. Each bench has a vid screen, so you can look up videos of how other smiths have approached similar work to get inspiration. They will also show you how to use some of the more specialized tools."

The four apprentices nodded solemnly, although inside Kesh squealed with glee. She was finally going to get to make something of her own!

"First, it is mandatory that you wear closed-toed shoes, pants, and safety goggles at all times in this workshop. If you are using chemicals or sanding metals, you must also wear a face mask to protect you from breathing in fumes or particles that can damage your respiratory system. Protect your fingers! This shop is full of torches, saws, drills, and other equipment that can hurt you. We trust you to use magic, so I am also trusting you to make careful choices about how you interact with dangerous equipment."

Kesh stared attentively at the teacher, counting down the seconds until she was free of this lecture. She had been watching vids on metalsmithing nonstop in her free time, just waiting until she got the chance to try it for herself. She was so caught up in imagining her first project that she almost missed the teacher's final instruction.

"For your first project, I want you to make a ring with a bezel-set stone.

You can design and embellish it any way you like. Plan your design in advance and make sure you have a drawing of the desired outcome before you start. There are stones on the supply wall along with the metals needed to craft your design."

Kesh's classmates all dutifully headed to their benches and started drawing, but Kesh went immediately to the wall of supplies. She wouldn't know what her ring looked like until she had selected the stone.

The stones were organized by color with no particular thought for the style of cut. Kesh pulled the container of black stones looking for a large cabochon or irregular stone to act as the centerpiece of her ring. She returned faceted gemstones, choosing to lay the smooth surfaced stones on the workbench. Kesh ran each one between her fingers, looking for something that was not too big or small. She wanted it to attract attention without overwhelming her tiny hand.

She finally found what she wanted in a piece of jet, an oval cabochon, marbled with pyrite inclusions. It was the perfect stone for a dark mage's ring.

Kesh carefully replaced all of the gems on the back wall and sat down to sketch her ring. The stone was simple, and she planned to set the gem with its width across her finger. She drew an unfurnished, thick silver band with small flanking pieces of metal scrollwork to accent the gem. She scrunched her nose, unsatisfied. Maybe it should have a textured bezel?

Kesh returned to the back wall to check what kind of already textured metal was available. She found a small box of bezel wire scraps that were obvious cast-offs from one of the guild's real workshops. She sorted through the pieces, looking for something with visual interest that was large enough for her stone. She found a piece of gallery wire with a fleur de lis pattern that was thick enough for her purposes. She then re-drew her design with the wire. Satisfied, she returned to look for the other metallic components of her ring. She was so deeply ensconced in her explorations that she almost missed the teacher signaling the end of class.

Kesh tidied away her project pieces, wishing she could stay and keep working. She hoped that soon, she would get to make metallic magic, and no one would be able to tell her when her workday ended. Then again, the teachers didn't seem to keep good track of the students outside of study hours, and she'd seen a couple of the older students sneak to the lower levels. Maybe they'd be willing to share their tricks?

278TH DAY OF 11554 AF

SAL'S face twitched slightly as the tattoo needle pierced his skin. The room was dimly lit, the only illumination coming from the spotlight in a stainless-steel fixture that was directed at his arm. The surgical chair Sal sat in was old and worn, but clean. The three other seats were unoccupied, as Ben had opened after hours for him. While Sal was impatient, he was also a perfectionist when it came to his tattoos, and he really didn't want anyone to interrupt and cause some error to sneak in. This was his most intricate work so far. While not meant for excessive power, the spell was complicated and effective. He wouldn't give up such nice real estate for less.

The spell was one he'd been working on together with his current mentor, Fredrik. They'd started with an old inefficient version of a lull spell that had been designed for use during riots. This version was far more focused, however, and much faster to cast. Their main innovation was a swap from the unpredictable obala-jō dagaz with a much more orderly and focused obala-alaz laguz, combined with a less costly anchor. This version had proved invaluable time after time when Sal had found himself in tight spots, it might have even saved his life once. It was past time that he'd affix it to himself permanently instead of carrying it on a bulky inscribed bracer.

❊❊❊

THE large screens of the security center showed an unusual sight to the two mages carefully scrutinizing them. Sinn, sitting alone by the fire in the middle of the cavernous space that they now called home. Gere was at Masan's side in their ascetically decorated room, illuminated to a level that would leave non-mages blinded for hours. Between them, on the glass table, sat a large bowl of assorted treats. Gere snatched up a small hard candy and tossed it in a wide arc, catching it in his mouth. "I still think you should have let me do this…"

Masan let out an exaggerated sigh, "We know they won't do anything to us when we're there. When I say we, I mean you. It doesn't take a genius to detect the danger of attacking you."

"Meh, so just because I'm big Sinn gets all the fun?"

"Yes, exactly," Masan affirmed. The problem with battle mages was that they were petulant if you left them out of a fight.

"I guess we'll at least get a show," Gere smirked and flicked another candy into his large, grinning mouth.

"Seems very likely," Masan agreed, gesturing at the screen. Three figures had shown up on the detectors outside the compound and were now hacking the lock of the main entrance with some cheap contraption.

"So, this is why you asked me to shut down all the extra security?" Gere asked unnecessarily. He already knew the answer, he just didn't like it.

"They need to get in for us to take the confrontation, no chaos on the street."

Even though only the old code lock installed decades earlier was the only active security measure, the men took several minutes to breach the gate. Masan was getting worried they wouldn't succeed at all.

As the door swung open, two of the men moved in towards Sinn's position, and the third disappeared from the sensors. The screens flickered between different cameras, constantly finding a perfect angle to keep the two men in sight. On a different screen, Sinn sat, back turned to the entrance in a seemingly casual and relaxed pose reading a book by the fire. A shimmer on the monitor gave away the activation of a shield.

Blonde hair flowed in an almost liquid way through the air as Sinn spun around on their seat to face the intruders. Sinn gave a small sarcastic salute at the two men draped in shadows at the edge of the room. "Welcome, I thought we had locked up, but I must have been mistaken."

The men walked into the open space with confidence in their steps, both in what could generously be described as armor; their multicolored rifles held at their sides painted with what Masan figured was some sort of gang decal.

He gave Gere a meaningful look and the huge man smirked. "I feel like there's some sort of lion's den comment that would be appropriate here."

Masan thought for a second. "Sinn always reminded me more of a mantis or scorpion than a lion."

"I guess you would know." Gere winked at him.

Masan made a hand signal at the screen to increase the volume as the pair turned their attention back to the scene.

The older of the two intruders spoke first in a gravelly voice, "You people have been doing business in our territory. That's a really bad idea."

Sinn looked him in the eyes across the open space. "Why would that be? Last I heard this is a free world, for free trade."

The same man replied, "The world might be, but you know damn well that the neighborhood isn't." He raised his gun and pointed it at Sinn's face. "We'll send a message here, and hopefully those other assholes you hang with will get the point."

Sinn couldn't contain themself and burst out laughing, they almost slid off their seat as they folded over in stitches.

"What the hell is so funny? You're about to die you bitch!" The words came from the younger man.

Sinn looked up at him. "I am, am I?"

The older man must have seen what they had planned and opened fire, but as the hail of bullets came, Sinn was already moving. A few rounds made contact, but at an angle, and they were easily deflected off the silvery mesh that coated the laughing mage. They ducked and got into the cover of the heavy makeshift bar made from stone slabs that had been dragged out from surrounding access tunnels. They were still laughing. "See this, Gere? This is why you're not allowed to come out to play, I'm no threat you see."

Gere swore over the comm, but there was a clear hint of sarcastic joy in his voice. Sinn was putting on a good show.

Metal splintered and cracked the stone that was protecting Sinn, the railgun-make of the rifles lent a lot of destructive power. Over the bursts of bullets, Sinn's silky voice taunted the attackers. "Really? Ganging up on a poor defenseless mage? Such bad form!"

As Sinn taunted the men, Masan saw the third one return on the outside sensors, now in a much more intimidating form. He was wearing an old model of Kras power armor. Masan got on the comm, "Incoming, we were right, they're sending in the one with the armor."

He saw a smile on Sinn's lips past the stone dust on the monitor, "Excellent! Then it's go time?"

"Absolutely," Masan replied and flipped a switch which ignited the hundreds of floodlights of the compound.

Sinn rolled out in the open, moving quicker than any 'dim' could have expected. They lifted a hand in the direction of the two men across from them, and fire exploded from the ground, engulfing both figures with what looked like a bright shining tornado. The firestorm only lasted for a second and as it fell silent all surfaces of the structure went back to normal. The intruders who'd been caught in it, however, kept screaming. Every inch of their skin was ablaze as if covered in burning napalm. Their weapons lay useless on the floor and the men crashed down next to them, rolling around to try to extinguish themselves, hands covering their faces. Any relief they found this way was momentary, as any movement exposed previously covered skin, setting it on fire anew. Sinn frowned at the screaming and gestured twice in rapid succession. Stone shards leaped from the floor next to the destroyed counter and darted straight through the skulls of the two men. The screams were abruptly cut off and the bodies twitched a few times before going still.

Without warning, an explosive shell hit Masan's lover and flung them across the floor of the giant room. Masan jumped out of his chair, in a futile attempt to get a better view, but there was so much debris and dust that the infrared was scrambled from the fires and explosion.

Gere put a heavy hand on his shoulder. "Sit down, chill, they can take care of themselves." As if that had been the cue, a loud roar shook the speakers.

Sinn lit up like a beacon as they threw themself out of the path of the next explosive round, most likely due to the confusion of the power armor wearer. Dodging rounds wasn't a feat seen often, even by battle mages.

"They activated their experimental shit didn't they?" Gere's question was obviously rhetorical, but Masan nodded. He didn't like when they took risks like this.

The giant figure of the armor-clad man scanned the room with his large launcher, looking for an opening. Sinn darted from behind some crates that had concealed them and the gun boomed as another grenade came flying. Sinn was moving quicker than he'd accounted for and again he missed.

The shimmering mage didn't get back behind cover as a sane person might be expected to do in the face of an overwhelming enemy. Instead, they zigzagged in the direction of the mechanized suit weaving between bullets and grenades. They slammed into the hulking beast with a loud slam and brought it to its back. The man inside the suit was obviously panicked at this point, servos whirring as he tried to get the wiry mage off his chest. As the robotic arm came up Sinn grabbed it in an impossibly strong hand, the fingers digging into the metal, oil, and hydraulic liquids spurting out of severed lines.

Masan caught a glance of Sinn's face on one of the monitors and shivered, so beautiful, and so terrifying. Wild eyes shone as miniature suns, and the face was distorted in a violent grimace. Their normally impeccable hair rode streams of leaking magic, forming a bright, blonde halo.

The moment passed.

Sinn got a hold of the second arm and ripped something loose in the armpit, making the mechanisms pull it into a strange and painful-looking position.

They then started slamming fists down on the chest of the disarmed intruder.

240th Day of 11557 AF

THE jagged dark structures of Reas Misalin, with their angry outline of bright red lights, were getting smaller on the screens. The cockpit of the freighter Dio's Sled was cramped in contrast to the overall size of the massive hull; now empty after a shipment of megatons of grub had been left at Reas Misalin.

In the Captain's seat sat a young woman with shoulder-length auburn hair and a face that was all sharp edges. While the ship was a lease from Kras, Lin considered it hers. She'd been captaining these runs for almost two years now and she'd gotten really attached to the metal giant. This was her favorite part of the trip, and she reclined after having set all the parameters needed to reach the halfway point to Sphere.

"Mios! Coffee!"

An exaggerated sigh came from the cots in the living module. "You'll take root in that chair eventually Cap."

Lin laughed. "Whatever, mock me young one, just as long as you also fetch me some fresh brew."

Mios was only a few months younger, but she enjoyed pushing him around a bit. He was hardly the most skilled or experienced hand she could hire but a fellow academy dropout would always get a seat in her vessel over the boring and mossy experienced ones. She found something sad in the idea that someone would have chosen to be a hand on a freighter as their first option in life, the rejects and misfits were much more her tribe.

In the background, she heard the clinking of glassware and bubbling as steam heated her brew. Moments later the young redhead ducked through the hatchway and held out a large glass mug of coffee. The smoke trailed in a strangely serene way in the reduced gravity, and the room filled with the aroma. It was a particularly dark roast, Mars made. Lin knew that there wasn't actually anything innately better about Martian coffee. No difference from Sphere grown really, other than the price tag. It was, however, one of the few luxuries she afforded herself, and she always took a few moments to take in the sensations at that first sip.

"Joining me?" She asked Mios.

"Wouldn't miss the stargazing part of the trip for anything, ma'am." He gave her a wink and sat down in the Second's seat, also reclined, with his own mug in hand.

"That was a good run, it seems the exchange rate is better these days."

Lin nodded and smiled. "I knew it would be. Production is down everywhere except Sphere, and Misalin has managed to make enemies out of most traders from Sphere lately."

"I heard something about it. Some deal they made with Mars?"

"Yep. They struck an exclusivity deal for several component classes for hauler and yacht repairs. So now all the Sphere traders who used to diversify in stock are having to entirely rethink their strategies. Lots of them just gave up on this route."

"And now Mars can't supply enough food…"

"Yep!" Lin grinned a huge grin, she knew she looked a little deranged but didn't care. "So, thanks to my amazing intellect we can squeeze them for an extra fifty percent!"

"Fifty? I thought you said you got thirty over?"

"Did I…. Huh… Must have been thirty then." She winked at her companion.

Mios sighed. "Sometimes you're such a bitch Cap."

Lin waved the insult away and drew heavy on the aroma of the coffee as she stared out towards the green reflected tint of the space ahead, the faint light of Sphere.

The hours passed, and they both went about their routine tasks. In the middle of going over some numbers for the next pick-up, a vague sense of dread started sneaking up on Lin. She threw a glance at the control screens. Something was wrong.

At first, it only registered on gravitational sensors, but within moments alarms flared up as the systems recognized emission patterns. Lin was on the controls within a fraction of a second, and her fingers flew over sensor controls. The ship system had every scheduled flight path updated on the fly. There should be nothing unregistered this close to Sphere.

Mios almost jumped into the chair of the second. "What's up Cap? Why did everything light up?"

Lin hardly registered the voice and made a gesture toward the screen indicating the heat signature.

Mios swore under his breath. "Pirates? They're bloody insane!"

Lin already punched her codes in the emergency systems. Every available interceptor would be on their way, but they were still almost a light minute from the nearest port. Even at max acceleration, help would be half an hour out.

Lin flicked her wrist towards a metal panel at her left, and it opened with a low whirring sound. A metal rack extended from the space, presenting two pulse rifles, sleek efficient machines made to only damage organics, and weaponry developed specifically for onboard combat.

Lin grabbed the first one and handed it to Mios. "I trust you remember school."

He grabbed the rifle, looking a lot more self-assured than Lin knew he was. "Of course, I won't let us down."

She grabbed the second rifle and armed it with a thought and a pulse through her implants. "They'll catch up in two minutes. It's a yacht with military-grade upgrades. No heavies, so it won't blow us out of the sky. They won't have any problems boarding us though. If they think we'll be easy prey, we'll show them otherwise, right?"

"We'll rock and roll, and all that Cap." Mios managed to sound composed, but she doubted it was a reflection of how he really felt.

She moved into cover behind the bulkhead of the cockpit, Mios did the same on the other side of the door. The seconds ticked by slowly, as there was little to be said. They both knew the standard procedures for boarding a vessel like the one they were on, Kras had taught them both the defense and offense for a situation like this. It was unfortunate that they were the defenders; offense was always the preferred side to be on because the advantage goes to the prepared.

She hoped that it was an independent and not a guild or corp rep. She figured that the former was more likely; they weren't high-value targets. The guilds and corps didn't do small fish.

A thought struck her. "Mios, you don't happen to have an inkling of why we're about to be in a shootout?"

Mios looked pale, but Lin couldn't tell if that was due to the question or their current circumstance. "No Cap. No idea."

There was something in his voice. Usually, she'd trust him, but something was wrong. "If you lie to me again, I'll put a round in you myself and hope that'll satisfy our opponents."

Now Mios paled even further. "I'm sorry Lin. I think they're after me. I fucked up…"

"Talk fast. Why are they here, and who are they?"

"I think it's about a bet. I played some people, some people I shouldn't have played."

"You lost?"

"I won, but I cheated. I think they noticed afterward; my surveillance bug never came back."

Lin felt deflated. "You're about to get us killed over a stupid game?"

She didn't have time for another sentence. It only took a moment, a click from a seal on the airlock, and a moment later the hatch swung open.

Lin moved to take aim at whatever came through the door, praying that it wasn't going to be a grenade.

It was a grenade.

Lin tossed herself backward as hard as she could, towards the relative safety of the nook behind the bulkhead. Her eyes were pressed shut as hard as she could, and she managed to get an arm across her face just in time.

The sound exploded through the space and was accompanied by a red-hot flash that lit the world through Lin's eyelids. Behind this initial flash was something else, a humming sound; Lin recognized it and fought her pain in a panic. Her muscles cramped and the world felt like it distorted around her. She'd been exposed to a pain grenade before during training, she'd been puking for days; this was worse, so much worse.

Time slowed, agony burned in every muscle and every nerve. Her jaws were cramped shut and her lungs wouldn't let her draw breath to scream.

Then abruptly the pain stopped. Lin lay collapsed on the floor, but still conscious. The world was blurry, and she couldn't open her eyes fully, she'd fallen so that she didn't have Mios in eyesight. Her gun was next to her, within reach, under the captain's seat. Her muscles weren't responding. She couldn't grip it, couldn't move.

Heavy footfalls on the metal walkway told her that the boarder was just around the corner.

A woman's voice sounded. "There you are, Mios. Thought you could run from me?"

Mios let out a grunt, it wasn't a word, just a noise. The woman came into sight; tall, well-built, long blonde hair, older. The details registered to Lin but she felt emotionally disconnected—a deep nausea made thinking hard. The woman only spared Lin enough of a glance to ensure she'd taken a full hit from the grenade.

The woman spoke again, "Fine, I guess you don't need to speak, just stay alive until I've breached your comms and bank." She brought out a hardline and connected it to her wrist jack.

Lin was furious in her impotence, *Ignore me on my own ship? Rob my hand? You bitch!* The thought brought her slightly more into her own mind. *Stims? Stims help,* she sent an electronic signal to her chem implant, and an almost imperceptible tickle in her chest indicated a valve opening. The rush came within seconds, it wasn't much, but being familiar with the after-effects of a pain grenade it was enough. Her fingers closed around the grip of her rifle, and with a jerk, she got the lightweight weapon high enough to aim in the general direction of the pirate. The pulse rifle sent bolt after bolt of charged matter into the woman and she crashed against the wall howling in pain and confusion. Lin counted at least five direct hits, possibly less than lethal, but no longer a threat.

Getting to her legs proved extremely difficult. She first rolled to her stomach, grabbed the chair at her right, and got on a knee. Then she doubled over with deep heaving cramps, her stomach rejecting her earlier cup of coffee. Anger fueled her, enabled her to collect herself, and try again. This time she got all the way up, rifle dangling in its strap off her right arm. She turned and half dragged herself over to where the woman lay twitching next to a semi-unconscious Mios. *Good, you don't need to see this,* she thought. She came down to a knee again and drew her knife.

"You think you get to fuck with me and mine bitch? Only I get to fuck with mine!" With the last word her long thin blade shot across the woman's throat, a trail of blood spraying across the bulkhead. The body convulsed a few times, blood rapidly pooling under her. So messy, the thought was distant; the fog that had been fought off by the stims was starting to invade her mind again.

Lin reached over and slapped Mios over the face hard enough to make his eyes focus for a second. "Mios, I need another cup of coffee."

325TH DAY OF 11557 AF

THE workshop was mostly abandoned this late at night. Only two apprentices were using the large space this particular evening. The high roof was something that could have been found in a place of worship, but whatever it had originally been, it had been thoroughly transformed to accommodate the artisans and artificers of the guild.

Row after row of workbenches filled the space, holding tools ranging from mundane drills, lasers, and saws to the arcane focuses and drains that were all placed at the back of the room. Kesh was occupying the bench of one of the superfine plasma cutters. Working methodically, she was etching a pattern into a hand-width-sized golden circlet. Next to her lay a half-assembled contraption of glass and copper with a series of branching arms in the central chamber that were designed to perfectly hold the circlet.

Kesh was so focused that she hardly noticed the sweat running down her forehead. When it hit her eyes she blinked to clear her sight and continued the meticulous work without skipping a beat. She had begun with jēra-īsaz kaun, to act as a focus, and to anchor the spell. This made her creation a dark mage's tool.

This was why she was working late, no projects for personal use were permitted during the waking part of the cycle. She had continued with the spindly flowing shape of wunansuz lögr, a rune she truly hated placing. It was so easy to get this rune wrong. Today it looked absolutely perfect. She had felt a surge of pride as she lifted her torch. Now though she was truly struggling, sōwehwaz dagaz was powerful, a chaotic rune from a chaotic element; fire had never been her forte.

The cutter was fighting her, the flame acting as if it didn't want to follow her path. She let a small stream of magic flow through the runes of the tool, something not usually needed, but always a great help when it was necessary. The plasma tip stabilized as it was enveloped by a field of dark magic, allowing her to place the last few lines of the willful rune, representing chaotic fire.

She lifted the ring and carefully placed it in its holder, on the copper arms, and closed the glass shield. Kesh looked over the runes once more to make sure there were no mistakes. She nodded to herself and directed a minuscule stream of dark energies from the shadows of the floor into the lamp. It ignited with a loud thump and then stabilized to have a clear, yellow, ball-shaped flame in the center of the golden ring. Kesh had never grinned so big in her life.

It's perfect, she thought.

200TH DAY OF 11558 AF

MASAN rubbed his temples and stared at his subordinate's reports. Reviewing documents was tiring, this was all about transit through City Six's main shipping lanes, as well as personal transports. A headache had been brewing for a long time, and it was bad enough that not even basking in the bright light of his sanctuary of an office was lifting it. He found himself missing the corridors of the stations, a space so bright that the non-mages often had to wear protective gear to not burn their retinas out. There was nothing quite like it, particularly not here on Embla.

He looked at the timepiece on the book shelf to his right, it was time to head out, the others would almost certainly beat him to their target at this rate. Masan grabbed his purple cloak and exited his brightly lit sanctum. As the heavy security doors slammed shut behind him a few of the Tribe members looked in his direction and he gave a polite wave before heading past them and out into the streets.

As he wandered up the dark and grimy walkways, his mind kept going back to the vastness of his task, and the minuscule resources he had at hand. He was keeping track of the movements of three major mage guilds and innumerable small guilds, as well as the rest of tech and trade on Embla. It was an exhausting job. His team was well-trained, but not necessarily as seasoned as he would like. There was a certain ability for judgment calls that only came with experience and couldn't be trained into operatives. His people were sharp and talented, but the culture shock of the mess and mass of Embla often overwhelmed his newest recruits. He was all for trial by fire, but in this case, their inexperience threatened not only their lives but his operation. He had a much easier time dealing with the potential of them getting killed, but this outpost just couldn't be allowed to be compromised.

The travel only took him ten minutes or so, but he had passed through eight superblocks and ten times that in stories. From the dank bottom levels, through worn old traders' blocks, and finally into the much shinier upper levels, mountainside of their hideout. He'd swapped out of his purple and into a well-fitted grey overcoat on one of the three rapid transit carts he'd been on.

The exterior of the building was covered in green climbing plants, some distant variant of hops, and it was lit in blue neon lights making up an intricate pattern that Masan understood to be the place's name. He felt a bit sick at the thought of someone being pretentious enough not to even give their venue a proper name. As he entered the restaurant he spotted the two newest additions to his crew first. Only arrived from the Stations six months ago. Opposites in both talent and headaches. Firstly, Freya, a stunning honey-tongued devil. Full figured with perfect dimples and abundant cleavage, and a face framed by natural blonde hair. Beautiful, personable, and charming. A shame about her mage talent, barely been enough to let her attain Master status. He thought. Thanks to that one weakness however she didn't need the cosmetics that he, Sinn, and Gere had to employ, and probably never would. She made up for the lack of power with remarkable interpersonal skills. Many lips had been unsealed by her charms. Freya led first with old-school, interpersonal intelligence-gathering techniques supplemented by tech and magic. She was also humble as far as Light Mages went, open to feedback, and ready to ask for help when needed. She was an ideal team player. Thinking of her always brought a smile to Masan's lips.

With this his eyes landed on Freya's counterpart, Caleb, now he was another matter entirely. So much raw power, bundled in that imperious, overconfident package, and so assured of his own immortality. Magic first, then tech, and finally, if he had to, he might try interpersonal skills. Masan and Sinn had tried, on multiple occasions, to make him understand that magic needed to be used sparingly. If they weren't judicious, they'd soon be dead.

Masan sat down at the head of the table and winked at Sinn in a less-than-subtle manner. Gere greeted him loudly while the two younger mages were so enveloped in their own conversation that they hardly noticed his arrival.

Maybe it was their origins. Freya had come to the Light Council from a well-to-do family on Sphere where appearances and social skills were valued in a magicless society. Caleb was a third or fourth-generation Light Mage, born and raised on station with a lifetime of indoctrination regarding the superiority of the Light Mage way of Life. Whereas Freya still considered magic to be well… magic, Caleb considered it his birthright and had always planned a life saturated in magic. He was also not used to the variety of humanity present in an anarchistic society like Embla. People from all walks of life and avocations existed cheek by jowl here and diversity was enmeshed in the very fabric of this city. Freya had proved to be adaptable and adept at appearing to be a beautiful, but otherwise unremarkable Emblan. Caleb struggled not to walk around like one of the young Emperors of legend, cloaked in his Light.

Sinn brought Masan out of his reveries and into the present with a light touch on the back of his hand, "How about you? Anything you're in the mood for tonight?"

Masan realized everyone had already ordered, and looked distractedly at the waiter, "What's the special?" Caleb laughed at this, and Masan got the nagging feeling that he wasn't the first to ask. "If you don't mind, I was somewhere else entirely."

The waiter repeated the details patiently, with the tone some would adopt when speaking to a child, or a particularly slow foreigner. While half paying attention Masan wondered who in the Sun's name had determined that Caleb was suited to life as an undercover agent in one of the solar system's most inhospitable locations. Probably his beloved family, grooming him for a Council seat. The scheming idiots…

"Yes, yes, that sounds fantastic, one of those, and some white wine."

While there was no active conflict between the Light and Dark in City Six, it was a certainty that any Light Mage who revealed themselves would be hunted down by the Dark Guilds like a rabid dog. This lesson had difficulty penetrating poor Caleb's inflexible brain. He claimed to listen to warnings, but Sinn was convinced that he was telling them what they wanted to hear; he hadn't really internalized the message or the danger.

There was little Masan could do about that unless he showed overt signs of disobedience. He could punish outright insubordination, but he didn't want to start behaving like the thought police. He needed agents who were capable of independent thought and good judgment. He couldn't beat that into them, much as he might want to some days. Masan had resorted to gluing Caleb to Gere's side, hoping the taciturn Adept's hostile worldview would at least convince him to act with restraint. Gere never adapted to City Six, but he knew the dangers present and treated it like an active war zone at all times. If Masan and Sinn couldn't convince Caleb to blend in properly, hopefully, Gere could convince him that City Six was a dangerous place for their small, outnumbered cadre of mages.

Caleb wasn't showing signs of accelerated corruption, so Masan hoped Gere had convinced him to dial back on the magic use and focus on developing his other skills. For once, Gere's gruff, disapproving demeanor might work in Masan's favor. Gere wanted teammates who were exceptional across the board and used their brains, not just their powers. He was not shy about letting them know when he felt that they were acting like dolts and endangering them all. It made him a good security officer and battle mage, even if it limited his capacity as a covert agent. Fortunately, he was a man of few words, and that worked in a certain type of establishment here in City Six. Everyone found their niche eventually.

As food was brought out all the strategizing and mulling over banal details fled his mind. The smell was fantastic, and the meal looked like a masterwork painting in its composition. With his first bite, he had the thought, maybe this bastard deserves to be a bit pretentious...

366th Day of 11559 AF

FOUR young students, and the slightly older Sal, sat in the deep green grass of the small courtyard. Mia, Adam, and Kiran were all one year older than Kesh. Mia was the star student of her year and she had already been allowed to select a specialty for her training. Kesh was often transfixed by Mia's features, a slight girl with her always impeccable newly cut short black hair and her deep hooded eyes; Mia's skin was slightly lighter than Kesh's own.

Kesh had been getting darker over her years of magic use, though Mia seemed to be fading, not getting lighter in skin but less material. She was somehow hard to keep in focus. Kesh's older peers told her that this sometimes happened and was a very useful trait in those who chose to go into clandestine work. Mia was the reason they'd managed to drag Sal along, as he was one of her mentors in spycraft. Mia picked an out-of-the-way spot on campus for this little conclave, where they were unlikely to run into one of the Masters or Adepts.

The group hoped that Sal could better explain the Dark Plane, as Prior Wallang, who was supposed to teach them, had been even vaguer than usual. They weren't having much success and Kesh was getting annoyed.

"So it's where power is channeled from, but also it's not? How does that make sense?" Kesh was trying not to sound whiny, but she could tell that Sal was losing his patience.

He gestured towards the shadow of a tree. "Look there, for example, there's a shadow, but the shadow isn't just the absence of light. There's something there instead of light. Light is matter in a way, and so is darkness, though darkness flows more passively. It fills whatever isn't lit. Wherever it flows it thins reality in the direction of its home, the dark plane. As far as I can tell from talking to other mages, this is similar to all the elements. Of course, the mundane elements are more dilute, but still, where they are, reality thins in a specific direction, out from this plane, closer to theirs."

Adam interjected, "But what about Death? It's not a thing, how can the absence of life be a thing?"

Sal rubbed his temples as if he thought the question was frustrating. "Death is a bit special, I don't think they've told you much about it. It doesn't really matter for you lot, unless you pursue some path that will put you at odds with Death Mages."

He leaned back against the rock he'd picked out for a backrest. "I guess it matters to Mia, even if the rest of you brats are unlikely to ever do anything exciting."

Kesh glared at him.

Sal continued, "So, Death is different in some ways, it's true. I love my magic; I live for the Darkness. Death, however, is sometimes far more powerful. It's a density thing. It's actually exactly as you put it Adam, the absence of life. The rarity of the ethereal elements changes the force they put on this plane. Light and Dark are everywhere, and a skilled mage can draw from a huge field or push through to their plane with sheer will. A Death Mage can only find a path to their plane where something once lived, but the focus, or density, of the death plane pushes hard in those places. The effort we need to bring in a trickle of magic could result in a torrent of energy for a Death Mage who's in a place of Death. Never ever screw with a Death Mage on their terms, in their element so to speak; they'll destroy you without blinking."

Kesh looked at the shadows of trees and statues, taking the lesson in; she'd never truly contemplated fighting a mage. Battle, killing, and such had always been a thing of fiction for her. She knew some of the mages of the guild, particularly the spies, were trained to fight. She now wondered if this was more common than she'd imagined.

Mia was nodding along with everything Sal said. Kesh had the feeling that Mia was a bit too impressed with the older boy. Sal was technically a Journeyman, but Kesh heard he didn't get to that status like most students. It sounded more like he'd been made into a Journeyman so he wouldn't bother the regular teachers any longer. She had however also heard that he was one of the most promising spies to advance up the ranks in several decades.

Mia was next to speak, "Did you ever fight someone like that? A Death Mage?"

Sal shook his head. "No, but I've seen what happens when they get into it. Some ass on Mars jumped one on a street when I was there. I don't think he was a mage; he was dead even before his fist reached the mage. Looked like he was hollowed out in an instant. Nasty stuff."

Kesh thought she saw a smile on Sal's face, but that couldn't be right. She still wasn't satisfied. "Ignoring your fascination with Death Mages, could you try not to sound so metaphysical and fancy? You sound like the Prior." She rolled her eyes to punctuate the comparison.

She wasn't entirely sure if Prior was Wallang's official title or a nickname so old that everyone now considered it his title. It was fitting for his esoteric, academic outlook on magic. The only problem was that his theories were a little too out there for her pragmatic outlook and practice of magic.

Sal nodded slowly. "I guess you're right. I guess I've been listening to these old philosophers for too long. This isn't how I learned about this stuff. My old man was ten times the mage any of these dusty skeletons are, so I'll try it in his words: Darkness is like a god, it's one of the things that made people believe in gods. It has a will, but it can't reach into this world and do what it wants. Darkness, shadows, the void, these are the places where you can find it. We mages have a relationship to it. It likes us. It uses us to exert its will; but only if it can reach us. In the shadows, in the dark, whenever we use our magic, that will of the dark plane is what allows us to do so. The dark plane is a god that lends you its power. Is that clearer?"

The students were stunned. This wasn't at all what they'd learned. Kesh's head spun. Darkness is just a force, she thought. She did have this sinking feeling that Sal had revealed something that she'd known deep down, the Darkness had always felt like it wanted things. Some runes didn't want to be in a pattern, sometimes the force didn't want to flow through the spell she'd crafted. Is this why? Darkness only flows easily when it wants to? The whole thing made her uncomfortable. The teachers always treated magic as if it was a skill, a dangerous one sure, but just a skill among others.

"I was taught that corruption is the price and the reward for borrowing that power. It brings you closer into alignment with the goals of the darkness." Sal seemed to realize he'd given away too much, but he doubled down. "I know it's not what they want you to hear. I'd prefer it if you didn't run off repeating what I told you. It's true however, I saw so many things these intellectuals would deny even before I was your age. There are other guilds you know, ones that aren't so go-damned scared." The way he'd said intellectuals made it sound like a swear word.

Mia raised her hand, before realizing they weren't in class, and then looked embarrassed about it. "I'm sorry Salvador, but you really don't sound like you believe what they teach."

"I wasn't taught here." He smiled. "I came here when I was almost done with my training, my old guild was destroyed. Mom, dad, all of them. They don't make them like me here, they tried to indoctrinate me for a while, but I think they gave up. They won't allow me to teach though, even though I know a hell of a lot more than even their so-called masters." Again, he had that sneering intonation.

What had started as a lesson now devolved into the young students being enthralled by the strange mage, whom they had thought was just another journeyman of spycraft. Kesh could tell that Sal was reveling in the attention and reverence he was getting. He was usually so charming, but now he was making Kesh feel a bit uneasy.

A change in demeanor came across Sal. He waved a hand and smiled a disarming smile. "Enough with this, I'm just being dramatic. Take all of this with a grain of salt, what do I know?" He got to his feet. "Listen to Wallang, he's not as thick as the rest of them. Even though he talks in a mossy way you should be bright enough to get his point most of the time. I need to be off." With that Sal turned around and walked away in the direction of the front exit.

Kiran looked at Mia. "What the hell was that? He's one of your mentors? He's got something wrong in the head."

While the jab was meant for Mia, it was Kesh who reacted. She blushed in anger but put on a cool face.

Mia leaned close to Kiran, and her voice took on a sharp tone, "What do you know about anything? He's a bit strange maybe, but he's a lot more experienced than any of us. What's wrong with having a different perspective?"

As Mia said the words, Kesh convinced herself it was true. Sal wasn't bad or mad, just a different perspective. She knew he'd lost his old guild; she hadn't realized they were also his family. She couldn't help but feel sympathy for someone who'd gone through so much misery.

***

SAL stepped out of the compound and took a deep breath. He smiled, the kids always forgot how much augmentation active agents like him were imbued with, including his hearing. Keshara was well on her way to being on his team, and he'd need her in the future. Such a bright mind; he didn't think she knew it, but the guild hadn't seen such a natural for spellcrafting in centuries. It was important to be honest with those you wanted for allies, but not too honest, reel them in slowly. While Sal had a hard time really wrapping his head around why, sob stories were very efficient.

Fuck this guild, I'll make it something better. Sal wandered towards the closest bar; he deserved a drink. Mia and Kesh can join me when I move on. Light take the others.

***

MASAN was infuriated but also perplexed. He sat with Sinn and Gere around the desk in his office, debriefing about Gere's last mission. Except the focus wasn't on the rather intriguing results of his outing, but on their youngest member's direct disobedience.

"What do you mean, when you say that Caleb attempted to cast a spell of invisibility in a crowded shopping center?" Masan tried to hold himself back from growling. After all, it wasn't as if Gere had condoned his pupil's actions. He was, in fact, angrier than Masan.

"Well," started Gere. "It's pretty much exactly how it sounds. We were out doing surveillance on one of the Fusion Forge executives, a Fire Mage, hanging out in the background of his favorite dining establishment. Our objective was just to see who his business contact was, so we could determine if he merited future surveillance."

"I approved their mission. We're still mapping out the full network of contacts and contractors for the Fusion Forge," added Sinn. Sinn was present to ensure that this was a proper debrief and discussion of discipline, and not just two angry mages venting their rage at their inept colleague. They always were the calmest and most rational member of the team—it was why they were in charge of logistics. They were hard to ruffle and behaved as though the word panic never even occurred to them. But, today might put their equanimity to the test.

"The contact was not who we expected. Instead of being a corp functionary or another mundane Mage, we're 95% sure that it was a high-ranking Dark Mage."

"What brought about that conclusion?" asked Masan. His patience was running thin, but he did want to hear the story in its entirety before he tore into Caleb.

"We couldn't see their face. Honestly, with the sweeping robes and the obvious magical obfuscation, we couldn't identify very much about this person at all. Only a high-ranking Dark Mage would feel comfortable displaying that much magic openly. It means that they are both powerful enough not to be attacked and that they don't anticipate repercussions from their Guild for the open use of magic."

"Continue."

Back in the early years, Masan had known Gere resented that Masan was appointed the director of this mission. But eventually, they had reached an understanding. Gere didn't want anything to do with the charm and interpersonal warmth that was required to lead the Tribe. He didn't have the patience or the charisma for the job. Masan didn't have his sheer magical prowess of Gere, in the end, it was clear that field-work was where the massive man shone. At this point, Masan trusted him to perform his functions to near perfection. One of the responsibilities of Gere's was to train any new colleagues thrust on the group from the council. Had Gere had his way; Caleb might have been chopped into pieces when his misconduct became apparent.

"I instructed Caleb to follow protocol, observe, and take notes. Look for defining features the Mage might have forgotten to camouflage. Note the unexpected occurrence in our mission logs for follow-up."

"I take it that Caleb didn't feel that that was enough?" asked Sinn, well aware of standard intelligence-gathering protocol.

"No, he wanted to get in closer, to see if we could hear them or to plant a tracker." Gere's annoyance was evident. "No matter how many times we tell him that this mission is a marathon, not a sprint, he still wants to know everything now. No matter that a Mage of that class is likely carrying significant personal shields and wards that could easily detect a bug, particularly when in a conversation they were conducting incognito."

Caleb had become the proverbial thorn in all of their sides. Too eager, too self-assured, and far too confident. The downside of a lifetime filled with affirmation and assertions of Light Mage superiority. He was so convinced of their divine preeminence that he couldn't understand that high-ranking Dark Mages were, not his equivalent, but Gere's equivalent in power. Light superiority was measured in culture and community, not necessarily in terms of sheer power.

"I thought I had convinced him, and that he was following orders," Gere continued. "Then he went up to get to the bathroom before we left. He was still following protocol, the aim was to exit before the end of the conversation, to allay any suspicions that we were eavesdropping or observing the table. Then assume positions where we could observe their possible route for exit. I had planned to surveil them on their way back to their Guild if possible, but assumed it was unlikely."

"And Caleb never came back."

"Yes. He disappeared. I got a comm message telling me not to worry, he would handle it." Gere grimaced as he said it. He had no doubt watched his life flash before his eyes when he got the message.

Sinn put their head in their hands. "How? How did it get this bad? That's not just exceeding your weight class magically, that's practically suicide by Dark Mage."

"I paid the bill, calmly. Smiled and made pleasantries while I left, found the nearest alley, and keyed his tracking beacon. And then, I overwrote it with a coercion spell and marched his ass home."

Masan made a quiet note to himself that he had been unaware that Gere could do that. They shared a look and Gere shrugged.

"Look, it's not a spell I use often, or without carefully considering the consequences. It probably wouldn't even work on a strong enough mind. But, when there's an emergency and I can't physically drag an invisible lump out of a terrible scenario that he caused. For something like this, I'm gonna pull out all the stops."

"Did you get an explanation for why he thought he could pull off a tail on a Dark Mage using an invisibility spell?" asked Sinn.

"He said he had been practicing larger magics and wasn't experiencing corruption, so he should be able to do something of that magnitude. And then insinuated that we should trust him and give him more responsibility since he was obviously more powerful than we thought."

And just like that, the anger drained out of Masan and was replaced by curiosity. That spell was definitely at the top of Caleb's practical range back home. It required control of light, sound, and even matter. Why the hell wasn't he experiencing corruption from his magic?

***

MASAN stalked through the facility to the container where they'd stashed the coerced Caleb. Sinn and Gere flanked him. Masan never had cause to discipline one of his team before. Sinn and Gere were always professional and diligent, even under stress.

"Release him," Masan commanded Gere.

Caleb slowly came to realize that he was no longer in a public setting, but instead face to face with a furious set of Light Masters. He blanched at the sight.

"Do you know why you're here Caleb?" Masan asked in a low, dangerous voice. He would give him enough rope to hang himself. He was utterly fed up with the constant aggravation of minding Caleb. Cameras embedded in the facility would record this meeting so that it could be reviewed by the Council after Caleb was disciplined.

"Where, how… what happened to me?" Caleb responded. Masan nodded at Gere to explain.

"You disobeyed a direct order from a superior Mage in hostile territory, endangering you and me specifically, and the team as a whole."

Caleb went even whiter.

"Given that you had rendered yourself invisible and I could not safely extract you from the scenario personally, I activated your tracking beacon and overwrote it with a spell of coercion to send you home," Gere finished.

"Do you remember the penalty for insubordination?" Masan asked.

Caleb remained silent, so Sinn interjected, "It ranges from corporal punishment to death."

Masan could not afford to show leniency to Caleb. He half suspected that Caleb had been sent with orders to act disruptive, in order to assess Masan's leadership. The Council were leaders of the 'trust but verify' variety. Masan needed to follow both the letter and the spirit of the Council's directives because plant or not, they would be reviewing any disciplinary actions. Especially given Caleb's influential family.

"What punishment do you recommend, as Caleb's direct commander for this mission?" Masan asked Gere.

"Caleb was lucky today and his actions do not merit execution. I suggest a form of corporal punishment." Gere was playing his role as the stoic battle Mage to a tee. Masan couldn't have orchestrated a better scene if he tried.

"Sinn, what is your recommendation?" Masan asked.

"I have a question first if you'll allow it," Sinn said. Masan nodded at them to proceed.

"Caleb, how did you cast the spell? No one issued you a copy of a complex spell like invisibility for the mission."

Caleb looked at each one of their faces, grasping for any signs of leniency. He found none. He swallowed and answered, "It's one of my tattoos."

Sinn turned to Masan, "I recommend that you remove the tattoo as punishment."

Caleb gasped in shock. Light spell tattoos were sacred ornaments, given in rituals to mark significant levels of Mastery of the Light. To have one stripped was to lose status and honor. It wasn't just a punishment; it was an utter humiliation. Caleb would shame not just himself, but his family. It also wasn't without precedent as a field punishment for insubordination. It removed easy access to dangerous magic and acted as a form of corporal punishment.

Masan stood and considered the suggestion. He left Caleb watching and waiting while he made a show of considering the suggestion.

"I concur. Any objections, Gere?"

"No, let the punishment remove the means and temptation to repeat this particular offense."

"Where is the tattoo, Caleb?" Masan asked. When Caleb hesitated to reply, Masan added, "We can force you to strip and inspect your entire body to determine the location, or you can just tell me."

Finally, Caleb replied, "It's on my left delt." He turned and removed his shirt.

"Good. Brace yourself." With that, Masan let light flow into him, through the runes for one of his battle spells, just a trickle, just enough to create a beam of laser light that'd burn rather than cut. He let the beam play across the skin of the young Mage and stripped every particle of pigment from Caleb's flesh. The room filled with the smell of singed flesh, as Caleb's skin bubbled and blistered, releasing the ink. In order to force the entirety of the tattoo out, Masan cut wounds deep in the dermis. The scarring would prevent Caleb from replacing the tattoo until Masan authorized someone to heal the skin, not that he thought the boy quite that stupid. Sinn and Gere stood as silent witnesses. Caleb, to his credit, didn't scream. Silent tears ran down his face, as he sobbed through the pain.

When he was finished, Masan stepped back. "Turn around Caleb. This is your one and only warning. Future insubordination will result in your execution, either by your superior officer here if the situation is dangerous enough, or as the result of a full court-martial back home. I trust there will be no more errors in judgment."

Caleb nodded silently, still weeping.

"Go bandage yourself. You may take antibiotics, but no pain medication. You're relieved of duty for five cycles. I suggest you spend that time meditating on the gift of your Light and contemplate your future. Dismissed!"

With that, Masan, Sinn, and Gere turned and left a dazed Caleb to deal with his medical treatment. Masan had sent a critical message; he would not be undermined in his stewardship of this mission, and he was willing to use the full authority of his station to enforce Council directives. Hopefully, that would reassure the Council that City Six was well in hand.

235TH DAY OF 11562 AF

TODAY was the day. After years of hard work, Kesh was finally going to find out who her mentor would be for her Journeyman period. The little girl who had entered Apteryx so many years ago would barely recognize the young woman who was on her way to the amphitheater today.

Gone were the sweet chubby cheeks of a child, replaced with graceful cheekbones that highlighted the golden gleam of her dark brown skin. Kesh's irises had darkened from a dark brown to a deep black; the early stages of corruption starting to show. Since today was a formal occasion, Kesh wore an intricately patterned black floor-length dress with a high neck and long sleeves. By convention, Mages rarely showed any skin between their wrists, ankles, and collarbones, ensuring that their runic tattoos couldn't be observed and countered or co-opted by an enemy. Gold decorations glinted in her long black hair complementing the rune-covered gold jewelry that she bore on both wrists and around her neck.

The biggest change was internal, not in attitude, but in tech. Over the years Kesh had acquired significant neural implants. Apteryx didn't skimp when it came to equipping its students with top-of-the-line tech. Every student had comm implants to communicate without a wrist comm, as well as for transcribing speech. Kesh had extensive memory banks to hold books, research, and blueprints; standard augments for many of the Guild artisans. She also had an ocular implant enabling her to see UV and infrared. This opened up a whole new world of experiences. Being able to see the heartbeat of the person sitting across from you had been an amazing experience the first time it happened. It could also deliver visual information from her comm, and record and transmit video recordings of her work, the actual reason why Apteryx had been so keen on getting that particular tech for her. Getting the implants hadn't been forced upon her, rather it was a personal choice; it helped in observing and refining her process when crafting new spell forms. She hoped to eventually get the dermal and spinal implants that would allow her to wear fully integrated battle armor, not because she wanted to fight, but because battle armor design was her great aspiration.

Today, the students in her Apprentice class would discover if they were promoted to Journeyman and assigned an individual Master. Kesh didn't doubt that her full class would graduate, but she was anxious about her Mentor. You were an Apprentice for a fixed time period, but you could be a Journeyman for an indeterminate period of time that could last from several years, and possibly indefinitely. The requirements for the tests for Mastery was at the discretion of your Master.

Kesh was hoping to be assigned to Master Lucas. She knew that she could be assigned a Master anywhere on Embla, but Master Lucas was their preeminent expert in magical smithing. She had worked extremely hard in her courses to show that she was ready to be assigned to a true Master of the form. Kesh had high hopes; she'd been top of her class in the subject, but rumors also said that she'd outperformed every single artisan apprentice of the last decade.

Arriving in the hall with her classmates Kesh took her seat in the front row. Held in the vaulted ballroom of the fortress, the setting was grand to convey the importance of the moment. The hall was hung with Earth-style tapestries and lit with dull mage lights, to provide just enough illumination for the weaker Mages among Apteryx. This graduation was a public affair, so the rest of the Guild who were on site and off duty were present to see the fate of the Apprentices. It was an annual tradition for the Journeymen and Masters to bet on their placements, and the odds were indicating that Master Lucas was likely to snag Kesh.

The Apprentices were seated right at the front, next to the dais, so they had to be on their best behavior. Pranks were strictly forbidden today unless you weren't planning on a future, period. Kesh sat patiently through Rector Argent's speech waiting for her to finally get to the point. Fortunately, with the surname Arabris, she was up first in her class.

The rector moved to the important part, at least to Kesh's mind.

"Keshara Arabris, please rise."

Kesh strode up towards the dais to stand beside Rector Argent. Each step sent her dress swishing, producing both a gentle sound and the glimmer of the golden threads woven into the pattern of the dress. "Keshara, effective today you are promoted to the rank of Journeyman within Apteryx. Your mentor during this time will be Prior Wallang."

The room gasped and Kesh fought hard to keep her composure in front of the rest of the Guild. The Prior rose to the dais. They exchanged the customary bows of acknowledgment and then returned to their seats. The room exploded with furious whispered conversation. Well, that was an utter failure of the odds, Kesh thought.

"Rinna Fergus, please rise," the rector continued in the background, her voice hardly audible to Kesh in her confusion.

The room continued to be full of whispered conversations. Rinna's moment was effectively lost in the chatter. The surprise was palpable. Members of the Ring rarely took Journeymen. Most commanded large sections of Apteryx's operations and couldn't spare the time to properly supervise and guide a Journeyman. Kesh would never even have dreamed about being assigned to a Ring member; to think one was that important was sheer hubris. Even Mia, one of Hugh's favorites, has been assigned to Sal. Being assigned to anyone in the Ring would be cause for surprise and speculation but being assigned to Prior Wallang was unheard of. The Prior was a scholar and a recluse who wasn't running any specific branch. He taught some theory classes when the rector badgered him enough, but otherwise remained apart from the day-to-day of the Guild. He hadn't taken a Journeyman during Kesh's entire apprenticeship. What in the world does he want with me?

Kesh barely heard the rest of the ceremony, clapping along with everyone else.

"Congratulations to our new Journeymen. You will get information to rendezvous with your mentors sent to your comms. Now we celebrate."

A lavish dinner followed the ceremony. Another incentive for Apteryx's errant operatives to return to home base. It seemed like everyone who hadn't been there before the ceremony had materialized to gawp at Kesh and gossip about Wallang's motivations. Any change to Ring operations had the possibility to affect them all. Kesh fought through the crowd congratulating her, looking for the Prior, but he was gone. He must have slipped away immediately after the ceremony. Her comm pinged with an incoming message. "Lowest workshop, 253 at 10:00."

Thwarted, Kesh turned back to congratulate her classmates. She might as well eat, drink, and be merry. Her future had just changed dramatically.

***

MASAN got up, his mind was slightly foggy and the tea hadn't really made a dent in the deep exhaustion he felt. He hadn't slept right for days, or maybe weeks, he couldn't remember. Something about this whole ordeal felt deeply wrong. The city felt wrong. Everything was dimmer than it used to be. It was as if someone had walked through the city and just slightly adjusted every voltage relay to output slightly less. The clouds and fog were thicker. Masan scratched his stubble, the sensation reminding him that his weird hours had made him forget to shave. Gotta shave, Sinn is no fan of the tickles, he thought absentmindedly.

Masan shook his head, cleared his thoughts, and returned to his reports. Apteryx just had their promotion ceremony and the bookies had had a field day. Betting on the ceremony was always a useful source of information on their structures and long-term plans. There had been a disturbance this year, but Masan had had trouble identifying the reason and the Guild mages were unusually tight-lipped about their complaints in public. He knew that mages betting on the spread had been unsuccessful, so he assumed an unanticipated pairing occurred. He wished he could tell what exactly had happened, but the result must have been unusual enough that it was treated as confidential. And it wasn't like Apteryx mages placed their bets with outside bookies.

He was going to need more intel to untangle this knot. He rubbed his temples, then keyed his comm, paging Sinn and Freya into the office. This was a job for the beautiful and charming to sort and there were few better than Freya and his spouse at ferreting out this sort of information.

***

KESH was impatient through the next two days. No one had any more information on Prior Wallang for her, although Apteryx swirled with rumors, some of which were making unkind jokes about virgin sacrifices. Little do they know... Kesh thought. She was either the perfect or the worst virgin sacrifice ever since she exclusively liked women and had known that since fooling around with Matsuki when they were 12.

The first hour of the cycle struck and Kesh headed down the levels of the fort. It was a long journey to the base of the fortress. Spiral staircases gave way to smooth, sloped black floors, as she traveled further and further into the warren that were the workshops. She had never been this deep in the mountain before, few people wanted to walk that far to get to their workrooms every day. Kesh found the final wooden door and knocked.

"Enter."

The Prior's office smelled like incense and looked like a bunch of scrolls had exploded. Beneath the incense was the smell of ink, metal, and ozone. All signs of a mage at work. If it smelled great, it probably wasn't a Dark Mage's place of work. Books and diagrams covered most available surfaces.

Prior Wallang was unlikely to have neural implants for memory storage as he routinely used so much magic that he would have damaged the interfaces. He had to do his reading the old-fashioned way.

"Sit, sit." Wallang pointed her to a nearby black leather armchair.

Kesh sat down, waiting and assessing. The Prior was a huge man. She had been told stories of his youth when he was still one of the most feared battle mages on Embla. His eyes were pitch black and his skin was wrinkled with age. Veins of black pulsed under his skin, hinting at the corruption he carried. His nails were more like claws than human nails, glistening like black opals; yet another sign of the mutations and warping brought about by years of channeling the Dark. The man stood leaning with his back against a stone wall, hands folded over his chest, observing her intently.

His voice was just as intimidating as his stature. "I imagine that you're curious why I wanted to train you?"

"Yes, sir." Kesh kept her voice under strict control, not letting any doubt or anxiety show. She kept a tight rein on her emotions and her actions. Now was not the time to fidget or lose focus.

"We're going to help each other out. I have heard that you are the best metalsmith and artisan to emerge from the Guild in decades."

Kesh blushed at the flattery. It was true and she knew it, but it was still incredible to hear from someone as important as the Prior.

"The magic I work these days is beyond most materials we deal with day to day, and the patterns are so great that even the small amount of energy that normally pulses through them as they're crafted can warp and distort them. To put it plainly, I need help. I know the patterns I need to create, but they rip themselves apart as I put them down. I'm hoping you can solve that problem for me." Wallang pulled out another chair, the twin to the one Kesh occupied, and sat down across from her. He continued, "In return, I will teach you every rune I have ever encountered, some of which no other living human seems to know. I will push the limits of your craftsmanship to get the spells for my research to work and in a few years, you'll be ready to take the test for Master. Is that a good deal?"

"Yes, sir."

"There's no need to 'Sir' at me Kesh, you can call me Prior or Wallang."

Kesh nodded and thought it would be a long time before she had the temerity to call him by his first name. "Now, I have a list of runes I want to etch into several concentric rings of platinum for a spell. Shall we have a look at my diagrams and see if you can craft this?"

Right to the point, Kesh thought. This might actually be fun. My classmates would kill to know every rune that the Prior knows.

Act II

221st Day of 11566 AF

THE shipyard was full of life. The clinking of tools and hums of welding equipment filled the air. Massive interplanetary ships loomed over the personnel in the dockyard.

Lin was hunched over a pile of electronics that were removed from a forward engine block. She knew that the issue that forced the shutdown of her transport ship the day before was caused by a component in this section. That was as close as she'd gotten. Everything looked fine, and she hadn't been able to find any shorts or severed connections using her kit.

A chip failure then, she thought. Sometimes these escaped notice from the automated diagnostics. The control module for the exhaust energy field seemed like a likely culprit, so that's what she went for. The controller was heavily shielded, but with a few quick clicks of her magnetic disassembly tool, she had cleared the bolts that kept the unit intact. As soon as the shielding was removed, she found what she was looking for, one of the four chips had a small black spot, a spot she recognized as an impact site. Whatever had hit this unit had done so from behind, a tiny highly energetic particle had pierced several layers of plating and exited through this chip.

The pilot was lucky it hadn't been a more crucial component, or they might have gotten stranded out there in the void. She checked the make and model of the unit. There were plenty of spares for anything that wasn't super exotic at hand, so she could replace the chip and close everything up in the next few minutes.

***

A small craft was making its way through space, having just passed its halfway mark on the trip from Mars to Sphere. The void of space was becoming radiant as the craft approached Sphere, which was almost a lantern in the dark of space. Gildim seldom took jobs off-world, Mars treated him well, and bounty hunters were treated well there, the corps seeing enough use in the profession that they afforded them a certain level of protection.

In the rest of the system, it was a very different story. The young blonde sported several scars on his neck and face, each of which had been acquired during previous off-world missions, and none of which had been at the hand of his quarries. Security on Sphere and Tube did not wear silk gloves when dealing with independent actors on their respective stations. He rubbed the part of his jaw that still occasionally flared in pain, right where his jawbone had been crushed by a baton and nerves severed. Normally he'd just have had a thing like that fixed up by a local medic; in the case in question though he'd been tossed on a slow boat en route for Mars. Two months of healing without proper medical oversight had not been kind.

The ship he'd chosen for his current mission was an unremarkable one. Blue paint had been layered over the last coat, peeling in some spots. It was built for fuel efficiency and carrying capacity, not speed. A very unsexy vessel. When looking for a ship to charter for this trip, Gildim had chosen this ship for all of those properties. Inconspicuous was the operant word, nothing like the sleek yacht he normally piloted. He didn't normally do business on Sphere, which meant he didn't usually need quite this level of cloak and dagger.

Gildim was hanging out in the cockpit with his pilot, Dianne, a beautiful older woman with short dark hair and chiseled features. She exuded confidence and a serious mindset at all times, which was another one of the key reasons he'd chosen this ship. The price tag had been substantial, but that was to be expected; it was a long trip, and Sphere security was known for being far more diligent than those one would run into planet-side.

He cleared his throat. "You mentioned earlier that you only ever do transports to Sphere, tell me about the place. We have a lot of time to kill and I'm entirely new to that station. It's a very hostile place to people of my profession."

Dianne stared thoughtfully out into space, looking at the gigantic structure that loomed in the far distance, still several light minutes away. "Sphere, well, it's just that; a sphere. The greatest construct made by humans, perhaps the greatest anywhere in the universe." She sounded thoroughly impressed. "We no longer have the schematics or blueprints, all of that was lost during the fall of Earth. There were people living on Sphere at that time, but the information was compartmentalized, so none of the engineers or early settlers on Sphere knew the details outside of whatever subsystem they were working on. The managers and directors of the project were all on Earth in their cozy fortresses when the planet was purged of life. What remained was a station that was ninety-nine percent functional, with no one in charge."

Gildim grinned, apparently his pilot was a bit of a historian. "I hadn't actually heard of this, I thought information about construction was lost to the ages"

Dianne nodded. "Well, a lot of this is conjecture on my side. But I have pieced a lot of things together. I read a lot, and that place is a bit of an obsession. Such a strange place. You did interrupt my flow though. There's a lot more to say about the place."

"I apologize, please go on."

She continued, "None who had any sort of grand scheme or understanding of the project were left standing, and almost all of the people who had intended to move to Sphere were killed on Earth. It took over thirty years before corporations had restored any semblance of order on Mars. It took a long time before they found resources to support all of the people who had lost their homes on Earth and even more time before they agreed on treaties for expanding some of their activities to Sphere.

"There were of course a couple of million people already living on Sphere, the former workers on the project. At this point, they had been forced to become stewards of the station, and experts when it came to its maintenance." She stopped for a sip of steaming coffee and looked off in the distance ahead, where the Sun flickered in and out of sight between the multitude of individual interconnected mega-structures that made up the gargantuan Sphere.

"The expansion from Mars to Sphere was mostly orderly, or so the history books tell us. After the war died down, the surviving corps had to play nice. The corporations of the time tended to at least work better with each other than our current ones.

"A few decades after this expansion started, Sphere's population hit a billion. It's been slowly but steadily increasing since then, and now they number more than 30 billion."

Gildim interjected, "How about corporate interests there these days? I know they still operate there, how much sway do they have?"

"Sphere is no longer in any way under control of the corporations of Mars. Rather, they answer to a board of twenty individuals chosen by vote each time one of them steps down or passes on. It's a strange system as one would expect it to succumb to nepotism and rot quickly; however, this doesn't seem to have happened. While all members of the board are people of means, they seem dedicated to peace and the prosperity of Sphere and have always had a policy of minimal interventionism. They're very careful not to raise anyone with too close connections to the corporate heads."

"So, I shouldn't expect my connections on Mars to help me much if I get in trouble?"

Dianne looked at him, one eyebrow raised. "If you get in the type of trouble I assume you mean you'll be dead. The head offices on Mars have absolutely no say when it comes to peacekeeping on Sphere. There's almost no criminal activity on the station, and it's not because its such a happy-go-lucky place."

"Point taken. I'll be on my best behavior."

Dianne seemed reassured. "Alright, I guess I'm rambling a bit. Anyhow, it's a beautiful place, more space than any other celestial body. There are gardens there that are as large as the surface of Earth. There are skyscrapers that have perpetual day on the upper floors and perpetual night on the lower ones. Sections that can rotate with the hour to allow for night-day cycles for the plants and animals that need that. There are species of flora and fauna that exist nowhere else in the universe, some of which developed there, evolution having gotten a hard kick in the butt by the strangeness of the place.

"Behave yourself, take in the sights. Don't mention my name to anyone when you decide to disregard my advice about behaving."

***

A tingle indicated that she had an urgent message. Lin was busy working on a complex part, so she made a motion that played it back as audio. A woman's voice came alive in her ear, "Sender: Arum Dimitry. Message: My people found an off-world bounty hunter, he's in custody but we found the file with the bounty. It's for you, and it's high. Insanely high. I don't think you're safe. It's a capture order, not a kill order, so at least there's that.

"We could put security on you, but that's at best a band-aid. Be smart; run."

The voice went silent, and Lin stopped working mid-motion. A bounty, but why? Her heart was beating hard. She could feel her saliva get thick; sweat was breaking out. This is insane! She had been around enough criminals in her life to know how this played out. They always got their mark sooner or later, even here. She didn't understand; she had no large debt, very few enemies, and definitely no enemies with deep enough pockets to do this. All of those things mattered very little, if there was a bounty on her she'd better run now and figure out what was going on as she was running.

She got up, put her tools back quickly, and grabbed her kit. Tidiness was less of a factor than speed. If Aurum says run, he's already excluded simple solutions, she thought. The warrant would have been filed off-world, but there were never easy ways to trace these without getting in touch with the filing party. Fuck! Lin exposed her comm and touched the skin to activate the neural interface. While walking towards the commercial docs, she scanned the feeds she had access to. Another hunter had been captured as he was landing. There would be several more on their way or already here. She couldn't afford to return to her apartment. Her heart sank as the realization dawned on her, I'll need to scrap this identity. She abandoned the feeds; she knew enough now that she could make a decision. The numbers that had been tossed around were ones you normally only saw in corp coups, and she was in no way well connected enough to that to be the case here. She triggered the comm text function and shot a message to Mohammad. Such a happy coincidence that I have a friend who's just about to leave for the one place where everyone gets a clean slate, the thought had a tinge of sarcasm and sadness.

The reply was almost instantaneous, "Sender: Mohammad Silk. Message: I'm transferring an access code. You'll need to hurry though, we're only in for restocking, and all passengers are already aboard. You have ninety minutes. Get here in one piece Lin!"

250TH DAY OF 11566 AF

A woman, later to be identified as 22-year-old Magret Lee, was found barely conscious in the exhaust tunnels connected to the walking paths north of Media. The person of first contact noted bleeding from her eyes and wounds on her face. Emergency personnel were alerted and were at the location within 14 minutes. The emergency nurse wrote: "Both eyes show signs of heat damage, no objects can be found lodged in them. There is a peculiar white glow at the center of each, indicating a magical component to the injury. The wounds of the eyes are not self-inflicted, at least not by any means apparent to a non-caster. The face has numerous deep lacerations, these however are a result of the patient clawing herself. The wounds number in the fifties and cut deep. In one of the facial lacerations, a nail remains lodged deep through skin and muscle. The long nails, reinforced by some polymer gel, seem to have ripped off the beds rather than break. The patient has lost three nails on her left hand and two on her right."

The patient succumbed to her injuries in transport, further details were gleaned from the autopsy report.

Excerpt from pathologist notes: "Internal examination found numerous small (1-2 cm) lesions throughout dermal and subdermal fat layers. Some lesions contained material reminiscent of darkly tinted glass. Examination of the pleural cavity found some of the above-mentioned shards penetrating the outer membrane (parietal pleura). A very large volume, in excess of one liter, of reddish-orange liquid was collected from the space...."

— Case study 137, Suin Lahn, Professor of Necrology, 11563 AF

***

THE lights were bright as always, walls and roof covered in luminescent panels, seams between panels hardly showing. This was the one place where the Light Mages were in their own environment on this murky planet. A space built by them and for them, but only barely hitting their normal standards; it wasn't like the radiance of their stations. Masan and Sinn sat there for a while trying to troubleshoot an ongoing problem. The cadre of Light Mages were all complaining of spells fighting them more than usual. The Council instilled a strong sense of duty to the community and reverence for their magic from a very young age, so they had a finely tuned sense of their own powers. Some of the younger members of the team had struggled with magics outside their expertise and capacity, but right now the difficulty extended to experienced mages like Gere and Meg.

Masan rubbed his temples, as his tension headache was getting worse. "Summarize the reports from all of them for me please."

Sinn pulled up the holographic interface on their wrist comm to check all the reports from the team. "All of our mages are having more trouble than usual inscribing runes and ongoing, passive magics have been going out intermittently. It seems like access to magic is more the issue rather than it being uncontrollable."

"Does this affect specific types of spells or runes?" Masan asked.

"You're asking for a lot of introspection from the team, are you not? Most of them are field operatives, not Adepts or even crafters."

"It's their responsibility to provide full, detailed reports on their activity. Especially if they are having difficulties."

"I don't know that it would have occurred to them to look for a rune-specific pattern, but I'll request the information, and I'll ask them to note any runes that cause specific difficulties when casting."

Masan sat and pondered the problem, while Sinn sent the brief immediately. Why now? What has changed? They had been far from the Council's stations near the sun for a long time and night lasted for many 25-hour cycles here on Embla, but those were routine difficulties. Maybe the problem was more mission-oriented.

"Are we sure that our magic hasn't been picked up by the Dark Guilds, who might be selectively toying with us?"

Masan didn't think the leadership of Asio, Apteryx, or Strix would take a laid-back approach to the detection of Light magic, but he couldn't be sure. Maybe they were more aware of their activities than he thought and considered this amusement during their surveillance. A depressing thought, but probably not the worst outcome. They could find and disable dampeners.

"None of the team reports unusual activity at any of the Dark Guilds that would indicate that they've detected our presence here. Central Council Intelligence thinks that Asio and Strix are focused on determining the source of new spells coming out of Apteryx. Apteryx has been moving high volumes of intoxicants and spying on the Martian corporations, so it seems to be business as usual. I also doubt they'd be so subtle or skilled. It'd be easier for them to put together an assault and wipe us out if they had enough information to do this."

"The Council hasn't sent any system-wide intelligence briefings on other magical anomalies or disturbances?" asked Masan.

"No, whatever is affecting our team seems to be local. It might be happening in some places in the other cities here on Embla. The other cadres here are just as secretive as us, if not more, they might just not have reported anything yet."

Normally, Masan took advantage of these meetings to marvel at his spouse's grace and intelligence, but today's topic was too serious. The Council had sent them here to stay on top of the Dark Guilds in their stronghold and prevent them from interfering in Council business.

His team weren't all incredibly powerful mages, they were chosen for a variety of espionage skills. They weren't handpicked by him, but over time they had become a well-oiled team. They were all too proud to do anything less than their best. They couldn't fulfill their Council mandated duties to protect the Light, if it was being actively tampered with.

"Have you experienced the same difficulties as the rest of the team?" Sinn asked Masan. It was an entirely reasonable question that didn't have a good answer.

"I haven't, but then I've been so busy 'ministering to the flock' that I haven't been practicing a lot of magic."

Masan hung his head in regret. Growing up on the Light Stations he had felt as though Light magic was his lifeblood. His younger self would be appalled to find out that they had given over the daily practice of magic to organize and oversee minor mundane Mages and regular people. He honestly hadn't been performing much magic at all because he had been so busy coordinating the Tribe and the cadre at the same time.

"Do you think you should try?" asked Sinn pointedly.

Masan looked them in the eye as he let the Light of the room flow into him, and a large ball of plasma appeared above his hand. "While I haven't flexed that muscle in a while, doesn't mean it's weakening." He did feel something odd though. The conjuring of the sphere had been slightly slower than he'd anticipated.

"I see your point though. I should do something that's usually more of a challenge to me, anything short of that wouldn't really be informative."

"What then?"

"I can always set up a private retreat to 'contemplate the nature of the universe' and try to perform some ritual magic. It has been too long since I have practiced properly."

"Careful my dear, your 'contemplations" come dangerously close to heresy." Sinn smiled as they said this to lessen the implication that they were serious.

The Light Council took doctrine and ritual very seriously. They were the longest continual Mage Guild in existence, having survived the expansion and the fall far from planetary bodies. Unlike the Dark Guilds here, there were no Light Guilds, plural. Just the Council who controlled all educated Light Mages in the system. They mandated complete devotion to the Light and would not find the rituals his faux fire Mage persona conducted amusing.

"I'm just playing the role they assigned me to cover real ritual magic, but you're right as always." Masan reached over and stroked Sinn's cheek. "What would I do without you?"

"Struggle, a lot." Sinn winked at him, breaking the tension of the meeting. They flicked their platinum hair over their shoulder. They were really blessed that white was their color. "Let's map the disturbances out based on location and see if we can find a pattern. We may be affected by dampeners from the mundane or the Dark Guilds. I doubt it's a targeted attack on us, but something of that nature is the least convoluted explanation I can see. If we can isolate their locations, we can take them out and go back to business as usual."

"Wise, as always, my love."

Masan stood and stretched. "I'd better get back to the Tribe, there's a lot on the schedule. Who knew that leading a group of magical rejects as cover would require this much work?"

"Well, no one does magnanimous leader as well as you, my beautiful overlord." Sinn stood and gave Masan a quick kiss.

251st Day of 11566 AF

MIA squatted in a dark service corridor, carefully inserting electronic surveillance equipment into the Vanguard Tower security system. She had been tasked to conduct surveillance on Kristof Park, a high-ranking executive in the City Three Fusion Forge. She was supposed to follow him for a month and record any information or activity that could be used against him. Mia had no idea who had ordered the surveillance or why. It could be anything from a jealous sambo to corporate due diligence to ensure he didn't have too many skeletons in his closet.

Mia had followed Kristof all over City Three and concluded that he was a boring, mundane man. He traveled to his job, appeared to work diligently on his projects, then went home to his family. Mia had inserted spyware on his work systems on the first day of the job, and it didn't show any evidence of espionage, favoritism in his treatment of employees or suppliers, or malicious treatment of anyone at the Fusion Forge. The cameras she placed in his apartment didn't show anything more interesting. He had been married for seven years, had two children, fucked his wife every Thursday night after taking her out to dinner. He was kind to his kids, took them to lessons, and helped with their homework. In short, your prototypical family man.

Mia almost gave up on finding any dirt on Kristof, when he had taken a detour on his lunch break. She was surveilling him on the hovertrain, expecting him to head to a favorite lunch spot to eat in solitude as usual, when he had stayed on the train for three extra stops and exited at the Vanguard Tower station. Kristof was usually a top-tier man, rarely descending lower than a few levels into the subcity. But today, he had found one of the high-speed internal elevators and headed far down into the building.

Mia was excellent at avoiding detection, but she hadn't risked following him into the elevator. He was carrying a tiny magical spider construct on his person that carefully moved between his clothing and personal items, to ensure that she could always trace his whereabouts. She caught the next elevator down and followed the magical signal to a nondescript entrance into one of the tower's private suites.

Mia smiled viciously, on the inside, as it wouldn't do to be caught on digital surveillance with an out-of-place expression. Now, this was getting interesting. It was an empty corridor, and she was dressed like a young tradesperson, so she had no business being there. She acted like she had been distracted by her comm and suddenly realized that she had gone too low. She keyed the elevator to open for five consecutive floors, starting twelve levels above, and began her plan of attack.

Mia exited the elevator on the first floor with a lot of people and moved towards the building exit to the exterior walkways. Once she vanished into obscurity a few blocks away from the building, she shucked her everyman garments to reveal the high-tech suit below and activated her cloaking spell. She slipped back into the building, a combination of the temperature control of the suit and the light interference of the spell, rendering her invisible to the cameras. She didn't know if they had infrared cameras, but she wasn't taking any chances. From there, she accessed the service closet and made her way into the building's service corridors. She carefully descended to the correct level and keyed her comms to pull up any information that Apteryx had on the building structure. It wasn't much, so Mia made a quick decision to hack the network. Setting up a disinterest field to protect her while she worked, she tapped into the building's central camera system. She hoped that there would be cameras inside the units, but this low in the structure they had long been destroyed. Mia pulled the feed from the elevator camera to analyze later. Now, she had to figure out how to see inside the unit Kristos had entered.

Mia's magical specialty was shadow constructs. She pulled out one of her mage cubes, internally thanking Kesh for her ingenuity, and spun off a construct. She sent it out into the hallway to seek its way into the unit by whatever means it could. Fortunately, poor lighting in the lower levels meant that it had very little problem entering the corridor and slipping through the cracks in the doorframe.

The unit had a nondescript reception, where several people sat assiduously ignoring each other. The place could be anything from a drug den to a brothel with that clientèle. Mia's construct followed the shadows into the private rooms beyond the reception area. She closed her eyes and activated her neural implants to record the shadow's observations.

The first two rooms were a bust, Mia only figured out that it was an implant clinic. And quite a high-tech one at that. The equipment in the empty rooms was state-of-the-art and entirely out of place at the bottom of a tower. That intensified her interest because it meant that someone was up to no good.

The shadow hit pay dirt in the third room, sliding into the shadow behind the light illuminating the surgical field. Kristof was lying face down in a surgical chair, his skull open to the robot above. A very cute catgirl, with some of the best ear and tail implants that Mia had ever seen, was operating the robot. Mia tried not to be too distracted by the catgirl's luscious black fur and to focus on what Kristof was saying as she probed.

"I can't carry this much longer, the anxiety is eating me from the inside out. Even the combination benzo and amphetamine drip isn't going to mask it much longer," he whined.

Mia was very intrigued. She carried infusion implants herself, to keep her going in dangerous situations when she couldn't afford to feel exhausted or be distracted. She did her best not to use them because getting them refilled was gross.

"I'm refilling the drug cocktail, but you need to focus on your training and keep your thoughts away from the implant. It doesn't need your input, and you can't afford to have it distracted."

Well, that was certainly damning. A neural implant that didn't need the carrier's input was a strange item to be carrying, indeed. It smacked of high-level interference in Kristof's life, something that was far beyond his pay grade at the Fusion Forge.

The catgirl finished up her procedure and the robot replaced Kristof's skull and sealed him back up. Mia had a hard decision to make. The client was going to want this information stat, but this operation was too interesting to pass up. Mia sighed, turned off her recordings, and made a game-time decision that she knew she was going to regret energetically later.

She pulled out a spider construct the size of her pinky fingernail. This construct was far more advanced than the little spider she had with Kristof. It was bespelled with runes to render it invisible. Internally, it also had spells to counter tech and magic surveillance, making it completely undetectable. She focused, feeling her energy sag a little before her infusion implants flooded her system with amphetamines. She opened her channel to the dark plane and activated the spider, sending it to monitor the catgirl. She could almost feel her body retreating further into the shadow as she filled the construct with magic. Apteryx would undoubtedly have questions and uses for an operation like this, and she could always use the brownie points that came with finding them an intriguing resource.

She keyed her comms to send the recording of the surgery and the location of the clinic to her supervisors at Apteryx. Then she set about erasing all signs that she had ever been in Vanguard Tower, so she could return to her routine surveillance. She might have come across this encounter based on dumb luck, but she didn't think that the client would need much more. No, she fully expected a capture or kill order for Kristof Park in the next 25 hours. Because unless the client was his jealous wife, he was about to face a hideous interrogation and certain death at the hands of his employers.

***

THE aft observation deck was small and sparsely decorated, particularly now that they were so far out in the system that the Sun looked a lot like just a bright star. The crew and passengers had piece by piece moved chairs and benches out from this space into the other public spaces as the deck turned less and less bright. Lin stood leaning against the glass, imagining that she could see the Sun get smaller as she was propelled towards the abyss of extrastellar space.

She knew deep down that running had been her only option. Things like this didn't just go away, and with no way of tracing the source of the bounty she couldn't stop this at the source. It was hellish though; she'd built a life she enjoyed on Sphere. She'd heard stories of Ask, but she knew nothing was all that reliable when it came to that place. The distance meant that any news that made it to the Sol system was already four years old when it arrived, and there had been several large conflicts there over the last decades. She had no idea if she was going to be arriving in a thriving community or a warzone.

So, the enemy I don't know or the other enemy I don't know, a wealth of great choices. Even the voice in her head was dripping with sarcasm.

She didn't really realize she'd been staring off into space and gnawing her lip before a voice broke her out of her internal pity fest.

"I figured I'd find you here!" Sal sounded almost jovial in tone, as he often did. "Beral is finishing some paperwork, but he wanted us to meet up for a game in a few. I assume you're in, can't be more miserable than whatever put that frown on your face."

Lin's shoulders sank as she forced herself to release some of the tension that had been building. "I guess you have a point, and don't pretend like Beral didn't organize this just because he doesn't like it when I'm left alone."

"You know him better than me. You're probably right though. Who can blame him, you turn into a walking rain cloud whenever you have too much time to think."

"Fine, fine." Lin looked out at her home star once more. In her head she whispered, I'll miss you.

Out loud she said, "Let's go then. That big oaf gets grumpy if I don't jump when he tells me to."

Sal smiled at her, and she wondered if he had some inkling of what sort of games she and Beral were up to when they managed to find alone time. She felt her heartbeat just a little harder and had to focus not to blush. "Stop smirking and hurry up!"

***

THE upper observation deck was one of the few parts of the Astion that had been designed with any type of aesthetic in mind. A large egg-shaped window served as a roof, with the heavy blast shields hardly visible in their pockets just outside the glass. Two large aquariums flanked the long sides of the room, interesting plants waving in the light currents.

At this point of the trip, it was apparent that the person who had selected the animal occupants of the tanks was no biologist, as only one creature remained in each tank; both of which had been significantly less alone, as well as less fat, at the start of the journey. Lin thought she must've been imagining it, but she could swear the animals at the opposite sides of the room were now eying each other.

Sal gave her a light kick on her shin. "Come on, stop daydreaming, it's your turn."

Sal the charming rouge. Lin bet he was a favorite with the ladies or gentlemen back home. She hadn't really figured out what his tastes were, he was however very easy on the eye however you looked at him. Black, well-styled hair, with just a hint of curls falling down below his ears, and irises a dark brown that some would almost consider black.

Lin looked at the table. Beral had played an aggressive set of chips. "Really, you old oaf? You set me up like this so the wolves can take me down?" She smirked at him as she said this and followed up with, "Well, no such luck." She tossed in a chip which made her opponents groan.

"You're intolerable, Lin. Always such defensive play, we'll never finish like this!" Sal shook his head, but he sounded amused.

"Got somewhere to be?" asked Beral.

Sal shrugged. "I guess not before we all do. Alright, I lose a marker, but I won't go quiet." He placed a marker with a dark red sun engraved on it in the middle of the table and removed one of the black sticks that served to keep score.

Now everyone turned to Kitt, the youngest of the four. Lin mused that even though there were only two years between them it felt like it could have been several decades. A sheltered daughter of a family looking to Proxima as a new frontier where they'd make something great out of themselves. Naive, the thought passed her mind and it had a sneering tone. Lin corrected herself internally, it wasn't Kitt's fault that she had no life experience, but it made her really hard to sympathize with.

Kitt grinned. "Don't worry, I'll make sure this is over fast and painless." She rolled three tokens in succession to the middle of the table. One that made the move legal, one that doubled the round, and one that ate a marker.

The three older players groaned. "Impressive, been sitting on that for a while," Beral said. He flicked his remaining three markers to the middle of the table. Lin and Sal followed suit.

"Merciless." Sal was smiling as he complained. "All right, boys and gals, let's pay up." He made a movement across the com on his left wrist, and a buzz from the one Kitt was carrying indicated transfer received. Two more buzzing sounds followed as Beral and Lin made their transfers.

Lin turned to the girl. "I feel tricked. The innocent thing is just an act, no? You're some sort of game shark or a runaway gangster."

Kitt laughed, "What, a middle-class kid can't be good at chips? Dad always said family game evenings would come in handy."

***

THERE was something meditative about keeping an hour out of sync with the rest of the ship. Lin enjoyed the quiet. She also enjoyed having the showers to herself. Too close to the times where others showered and the water temperature wouldn't get up past lukewarm; now it was pouring over her steaming. The trip was wearing on her, the longer they lingered the more likely someone figured out where she was going. A timer let out a ding from close to the door of the room, and the stream of water stopped. Time to go to bed, she thought.

Lin sighed as she padded damply down the hallway. She just wanted to go to sleep and wake up in Proxima Centauri already. No more monotonous space travel. Just a clean start far, far away from all this madness.

Large hands shot out from the darkness grabbing her shoulders and pulling her back into a large hard surface. One hand snaked around her stomach while the other grabbed her breast, squeezing her hard. Lin yelped and tilted her head, so the large, bearded man behind her had better access to her neck.

He took advantage of the space and nibbled and tickled her neck with his beard sending tingles of sleight through her. Lin leaned back into his solid warmth, grinding her ass against his considerable erection.

"I didn't think you'd find me tonight, Beral." Lin traced her finger along the outlines of the muscles in Beral's arm. Beautiful. He was so different from Lin's normal choice in lovers, almost a mirror image. In most cases she enjoyed being the protector, the strong one, the one who fixed things. Right now she needed someone to be that for her instead. It really helped the illusion that Beral was a giant compared to her, something about being close to him just made her feel safe. She craved safety right now, the world was crazy, and she was hunted for no reason she could think of, but in the moments when she was in Beral's arms the emotional impact of that lessened somewhat.

"You shouldn't wander around dim hallways half-dressed then. It gives poor men like me ideas."

Beral spun Lin around kissing her while he picked her up off the ground. Lin wrapped her arms around his neck and her legs around his waist, allowing him to carry her off into his quarters. She nipped at his neck, distracting him on his mission to get her somewhere properly private. His smell was all encompassing, an earthy and full musk, as she drew a deep breath of him her heart beat a bit harder and slower, and her mind felt wonderfully cloudy.

Once in his cabin, Beral tossed her onto the bed. She smiled, appreciating his broad shoulders and ripped abs as he pulled off his shirt and pants.

Lin's towel hadn't survived the trip to the bed and had fallen to the side when she hit the mattress, so she waited there naked and appraising, watching his hard on strain his shorts.

"Are you gonna lay there like a little princess or shall I put you to work?"

Lin wriggled in protest, flipping over and crawling to the edge of the bed.

She pulled Beral's underwear down indicating that he should step out of them and went to work.

She started by licking him all over, getting it nice and wet with her little pink tongue. Once she felt he had been properly warmed up, she took him into her mouth, swirling the head with her tongue before starting to bob up and down.

Beral's hands tightened in her hair, encouraging her with their urgency. She loved being used like this, like a toy, capable of molding herself to his every whim.

"Such a good girl. Flip over will you?"

Lin paused in her sucking and rolled, now on her back with her head against the edge of the bed. She opened as far as possible, letting Beral take over.

Lin closed her eyes and relaxed into the sensation. She gave herself over to sensation, hands rubbing over her body.

Beral, watching the show intently asked, "Did I give you permission to touch yourself? It seems like you're getting ahead of yourself."

Lin stopped her self-ministrations and refocused on Beral. Suddenly, he let up, pulling out of her mouth.

"There are penalties for misbehaving on this ship."

While Lin gasped for air, Beral got up on the bed beside her. He took one nipple in his fingers, rolling it between them before pinching it mercilessly. Lin tensed and tried not to squeal with pain. She had been trolling for a punishment, but Beral was inventive and never punished her in the same way twice.

Beral flicked both her nipples, sending more pain arching into her.

"What are you supposed to do?"

"Ask nicely." Lin smiled a mischievous smile. She knew this wasn't the entire answer he was looking for, but it was no fun being too compliant.

"Ask nicely to be...?" Beral asked.

A blush spread over her, as he said it. She loved and hated this little game of his at the same time. It was role-play that made sense to Beral, but she preferred action to talk. Still, if he's having a good time, I'm having a good time, she thought.

"Good girl. So?" He looked down at her with a stern face.

Lin screwed her eyes shut, enjoying holding out him, even as her whole body yearned to be compressed by his weight and lost in sensation. Beral tortured her by positioning himself between her legs and beginning to rub the length of him up and down.

"Please. Pleeeease. " Lin panted as he continued to rub himself along her, pausing occasionally to tease her entrance.

"Hmmm, well I have been very good, even if you haven't."

Lin shifted her hips and opened her legs wider to accommodate Beral's hips.

He groaned as he slowly pushed himself into her. Lin lifted her hips urging him deeper. Beral took his time, moving slowly but forcefully. He was laying much of his weight rest on her, the pressure of him, and the feeling of his skin against her allowed her to float away in her mind further, enjoy the experience more fully. Each stroke sent pulses through her whole body, tingles traveling up her spine, as her whole body arched.

His breath on her neck made her hair stand from the tingly sensation, further helped by his bushy beard. His teeth scraped against her collar bone, a sharp sensation, mixing with the cozy but ticklish experience of his beard sweeping across her skin. She smiled and closed her eyes, reveling in the sensations.

Beral built in force and speed. And finally said the magic words.

"Now you can play with yourself."

Lin's eager fingers found their target, running circles around it as Beral's body drove them into her in the perfect rhythm. He was practically lifting her off the bed with the force. She could feel him hardening inside her.

The image of his pleasure and her steady ministrations took her over the edge. She screamed a little as she came, clamping down uncontrollably. The sound and sensation drove him over the edge as her climax sent her vision full of stars and heat.

He collapsed with his full weight on top of her, squishing her and driving her into the mattress.

Lin's head spun with the freedom of release. There was nothing better than sweaty, intense sex to pull her out of a funk.

After a few moments, she tapped his back and he rolled off.

"You know I just got clean."

"Oh please, you prefer smelling of sex to smelling of recycled water and cheap soap any day." He smirked.

"True. Can I sleep here?"

"Mi bed are su bed, or something. Come lie on me so we can get some sleep."

Lin swapped direction on the bed, curling up into the crook of his shoulder to use the broad planes of his chest as a pillow. She went to say something, but it was too late. She fell asleep mid thought.

256TH DAY OF 11566 AF

THE room was cold, but the old man sitting on his knees in the middle of the obsidian-black floor showed no sign of discomfort. A metal construct with spidery legs stood a few meters ahead of the man, covered in runes that connected to ones on the floor at the base of each leg. Four of the seven oil lamps on the walls, lit many hours ago, had run dry. The room was in a flickering half-dark, shadows chasing each other across the floor around the frantically scribbling figure.

Wallang could feel that he was close. Months of work, months since he found the last writings that had informed this work, months of failure. He was so close he could taste it. Quite literally, I can taste it, he thought. An electric taste, something that is almost ozone, but not at all at the same time. He rubbed his temples, his eyes were tired, but his mind was on fire. The runes were almost right, almost, just a little more, a few more changes. Wallang intently focused on the section ahead of him; this part was where he'd made some mistakes. He was too honed in on details to notice the changes around him.

The previously reddish gray of the ink inscribing walls and floor, and even the door, had changed and now had an oily, shimmering nature. If anyone had been there to observe it, they couldn't have explained what color they saw. Some lines moved ever so slightly as if the runes were righting themselves, fixing minuscule imperfections.

"I've got it," Wallang exclaimed under his breath as he put down one last line of reddish ink in front of him. This was when he saw it. The change was sudden, from red to, well something that wasn't red; it took just a moment before he understood why. A surge charged through him as his unconscious mind let dark energy flow from the depth of the planet, through his body, and let it spew into the room. Deep in the back of his mind, in the part that wasn't consumed by concentration, an elated internal laugh welled up. The last lights went out, but he could still see, someone so used to the darkness as he didn't need light.

Wallang marveled at how easy it had been to channel the energy needed to activate these myriads of runes, a pattern larger than he'd ever heard of anyone creating. Though he had achieved something, he knew that he hadn't made it all the way. The world was thin here now, but he hadn't traveled to the plane that called to him in every dream, in every unguarded moment. He was still in the material world. Something was off though, reality didn't feel right.

He looked up and noticed that there were no walls around him any longer. The floor he sat on felt solid enough, but it seemed like the room extended infinitely in all directions. While he felt confused, he wasn't afraid. This wasn't the first time he'd brushed up against the dark plane. A thought came to his mind, What if I have made it; maybe the dark plane is less esoteric than I've been led to believe. Have I made it this time? How can I know? He traced his hands over the runes in front of him. They now glowed with something that could only be described as the opposite of light; not darkness, at least not in any way known to humankind, as far past the absence of light as a star, but in the opposite direction.

The Prior saw that the runes he'd written weren't as he had left them. Some were intact, others had reformed to similar, almost familiar shapes, and some again were entirely alien to him. The ones he didn't know didn't look like anything he'd seen before, several of them had magnitude and complexity reminiscent of master runes, but that couldn't be. He only knew a handful of master runes, and he'd only used a single one in this maze-like spell.

Panicked, Wallang closed himself off from his magic, wiping his work in a frenzied manner, trying to destroy it. The shimmering, slick, oily lines stained the black stone as if they were part of it. It was nothing like the powdery residue left by the metal ink he had painted them with. He trembled at the thought that, though he did nothing to keep the spell alive, it was as strong as ever. Somehow the spell had become self-sustaining. The infinite darkness of the impossibly large room was made from nothing but dark energies, impossible to harness or control. He opened himself up again and tried to direct his own flow to cut the flow within runes, to no end.

The normal world was remote as if he was in a space removed from everything he had ever known. His body was starting to feel like it wasn't all his own anymore, as if the matter in him was being exchanged for something different, something new. Wallang's view of this strange pseudospace was narrowing, and he was moving away from his own viewpoint, his eyes seemed like windows that his soul stared out through. His self was moving backward, away from the view of the external. Something made waves at the edges of the image of the room, not a movement at the edge of his view, instead, it was something that made the perspective itself waver. A distant feeling of droplets of sweat forming, and the realization came; something was moving across the very edges of his pupils, crawling across his eye and iris, crawling inwards. Wallang wanted to feel afraid, he thought he was supposed to be, the physiological signs of fear were all there, his heart beating hard, sweat beading on his temples and forehead, and his chest tightening, but his conscious mind was removed from all of this. A wall was forming between what he considered to be himself, and this body he was trapped in.

A voice entered his mind unbidden, chilling him to his bone. Thank you, it thought without intonation or timbre, without anything that made it a voice really.

What had that voice been? He was under any type of assault. He was just helpless, unable to comprehend what had happened, and unable to stop it. He laughed a weak and pathetic laugh, one of the most powerful Mages on this planet, and the measly magic he could conjure was like drops of rain, immediately lost in the waterfall of power that coursed through the lines of these runes. The irony of his self-inflicted predicament left a sour taste in his mouth as his laugh petered out.

The door opened with a loud creak, dragging reality back into place with a jolt. Wallang looked up, startled. Kesh was looking at him, looking a bit bored.

"Good morning Prior. Got any work for me today?" There were streaks on the floor, where the door had dragged across the floor severing all the lines he had painted there.

Wallang looked up at the young journeyman with tears in his eyes, the relief of being alive washing over him. "Let's take today off Kesh. I need a drink," Wallang managed in a cracking voice.

✵✵✵

THE two Mages hadn't exchanged many words. It was clear that the old man was shaken up by something, but he had refused to explain what. It didn't seem like he wanted to be left alone, however, so Kesh had little choice but to indulge the old coot.

She felt a slight bit bad about thinking of him as such. He was in fact a very skilled mage; someone she knew she could learn much from if he would just let her. He was just so hard to get to know. They sat on one of the low balconies overlooking the garden; a space normally only occupied by more senior members of the guild. Though the masonry was flawless, it was the same sterile style as the parts of the fort that she was used to, just with fancier décor.

Kesh subtly sniffed her wine before drinking, letting the rich smell wash over her. The chairs were definitely nicer up here, she noted to herself. She looked across the small glassy black table at her mentor. He seemed lost in thought, staring into his glass, seemingly having forgotten that it was for drinking. Kesh cleared her throat.

A little startled, Wallang seemed to remember, all of a sudden, that he was in company. "I'm sorry dear, just a little tired, that's all." He didn't sound convincing. Kesh looked at him knowingly, and he continued, "Fine! Fine. Not tired. More like out of it. I discovered something in my work today. But I don't understand it."

Kesh was surprised at the openness but wasn't about to let the opportunity slip away. She invested many hours into figuring out why the Prior had her crafting obscure runes from every class of magic, but he had been elusive on the subject until now. "Maybe if you speak about it. You know, out loud, it might help. I often find talking while I think helps."

Wallang demurred, "I don't want you to fall into the same mistakes as I have. You're too young for that kind of burden."

Kesh waited patiently, sipping her wine, hoping that Wallang would fill the silence. It was a technique that worked on him occasionally.

Wallang took a deep swallow of his wine. "You might be right, maybe a young brain can give a different perspective as well." Kesh carefully filled up the Prior's glass, waiting with bated breath to see if he would finally let her into the secret.

Wallang continued, "I know you're bright, you've almost certainly figured out that my work concerns the dark plane itself."

Kesh nodded.

The Prior went on, "I've been trying to probe the plane. Find a way in. I have a theory that the shamans of old myth had discovered things about the planes that we have yet to re-discover. I believe it's possible to hear echoes of the material world inside of the other planes. It would open such doors of knowledge."

Kesh suppressed a smirk. "Spy-craft? Is that the use you'd put a world-changing discovery to?" She had almost kept her contempt out of her voice, but not entirely.

Wallang stared at her, his blackened irises burning into her. Kesh was reminded that he was probably the most powerful Dark Mage on the Ring and possibly on Embla. Sometimes familiarity made her forget that the man in front of her, warped by decades of corruption, was as close to a primal force as she would see in her lifetime.

"Is that really what you think of me? That I'd be so unimaginative? No, I'm not talking about spying. I'm talking of echoes of souls, of the ability to understand the very nature that allows us to tap into magical energy. To be able to study the human soul from outside of reality is to no longer be bound by physics. I could finally be able to answer the great metaphysical questions! What is life?"

Kesh was momentarily stunned. That was in fact a pretty magnificent plan for a scholar. Or an insane one. She collected herself. "I admit, that's an admirable goal. This doesn't at all explain why you're so out of sorts though."

Come on, come on, take the bait. Tell me the whole thing.

Wallang emptied his glass again. "I think I almost succeeded." A hounded expression in his eyes, he put his glass down for a refill. "But I didn't do it alone. Something helped me. Something on the other side..."

Kesh felt cold to her core. She emptied her glass. This time it was Wallang's turn to refill her glass. She had always known that some whispered of the darkness having desires; but she had always shrugged that away as being a figure of speech, a simplification of some poorly understood force, or just old-fashioned superstition. Now this Adept, a veritable encyclopedia of current and long-forgotten Dark Magic, was telling her it might have been literal.

Wallang sighed. "We're all just children, playing with a gun carelessly discarded. So little knowledge, yet we call ourselves masters. It would be funny if it wasn't so terrifying."

Kesh still wasn't satisfied with his answers. This was all too strange. Why now? Guild Mages had been poking around, doing insane arcane experiments for thousands of years. Surely, she would have been let in on something so massively important. She decided to see if she could get the last pieces of the puzzle while Wallang was in a talkative mood. "Why now?" she offered. "Why would this be the first you hear of something like this? You've read more on the subject than anyone I've ever known. Wouldn't something like this have happened before if there was really something alive on the other planes?"

Wallang shrugged. "Possibly, but so many adepts keep their knowledge to themselves. Some go mad. What if all who dig into this go mad? They won't continue writing about it after that point now would they? I know I'm not supposed to tell you lot, not even half of what I know. I'm most certainly not supposed to tell you this. I'm drunk. I blame the wine."

***

A crack opened. It was a slight thing, a fraction of a hair, but it was letting air in; air carrying moisture and dust and heat, things that hadn't made it into this space in millennia. There was a faint shiver through the space, something massive was shifting, pressing against its boundaries. Around the crack, a wall was becoming thinner. The mass that lived here felt the outside, licked across the crack, pressed against the wall. A world much larger than this space was out there. A world waiting for this unlife, unlight, to spread out and engulf it. Anticipation bore another shudder, but then the crack closed as fast as it had opened, and now the whole space shook from rage and hatred and longing.

***

MASAN sat with his eyes closed, within his circle of runes, breathing deeply to anchor himself. Equanimity was one of the most important elements of Light magic. Remaining calm and logical in the face of all obstacles was one of the primary tenets of the school.

Masan sat bare-chested in the circle, clad in only white, plant-fiber pants. His body was covered in a swirl of tattoos from his collarbone to his ankles. Each spell had been hard-earned during his apprenticeship, the physical manifestation of his mastery of the Light.

This ritual was usually performed in pure sunlight on the solward face of a Council station. Here, Masan had to make do with bright, white artificial Light, both because of the lackluster sunlight on the always cloudy Embla, and also because a Mage performing a ritual in the sunlight could be a death warrant here.

Masan wasn't doing anything complicated, merely energetically expensive. The runes inscribed on the floor created a dome of pure Light, the initiation of many ritual workings, and he was relaxing and enjoying the sensation of the magic. The meter-wide bright cool imitation of a sun hovered a few hands widths in front of his closed eyes. He had no idea how long he had been in this state, but time was unimportant. He needed to do this right. A clear mind and pure connection to the Light is a must for a leader of a Light cadre.

Suddenly, the dome sputtered out of existence as Masan's magic collapsed. From a place of calm detachment, he tried to re-initiate the circle, but he could no longer even sense the anchor rune of the circle. Reaching out with his senses he realized that he could no longer sense the anchor runes for the passive wards on their stronghold or any of the decorative spells used to beautify their space; neither those that were supposed to act as wards to hide and shield their electronics and security equipment.

Masan set his panic aside and concentrated on only the anchor rune. He opened his eyes and looked at the inscribed stone circle and realized that the engravings were still present, but inactive. They hadn't burned out like a minor spell on a piece of paper, they just didn't do anything. Masan had never experienced anything like it.

His breathing became ragged as he fought for control against panic. Was this what his team had been experiencing? He felt like a mere Apprentice, struggling to open his channel and bring Light energy into the world. No, worse, he felt like a person without magic, who had no pathway to a magical plane. It was as if the Light plane was gone. The panic he'd been suppressing started morphing into horror, and pain shot through his chest. Worthless, mortal, weak, words he'd heard so many times about those not gifted, words he'd often used himself in his youth on the stations. This is not permanent, he steeled himself and calmed his breathing.

There was still light in the room, so obviously he wasn't experiencing the spontaneous heat death of the universe. Just a complete cessation of Light energies. He wanted to stay and wallow in the foreign feeling of magiclessness, but duty called, he had to know if this was happening to them all.

As he stood, the energy came back into his tattoos. He breathed a quiet sigh of relief. They would not necessarily have to face their new adversary without magic.

Masan pulled himself together. He was a commander, and his troops must be experiencing unimaginable chaos and self-doubt. He needed to recall the team, calm them, and put them back to work fixing whatever had caused this.

Masan stood and keyed his comm to call every mage back to headquarters.

***

THE team assembled in the Lounge, looking poleaxed. Any remaining color had drained from their faces, and they looked worn and anxious. The Light had returned, but they had all keenly felt its absence and their vulnerability without it. It was time to prove his mettle as a leader.

"Report."

Sinn started, "We all lost our contact with our wards. It seems that this has killed every autonomous Light spell running in the City."

That scared him to his core. Only a profound shift in magic or some spell of absurd scale could have produced an outage like that. He doubted that whoever and whatever had caused this was something he had the resources to meet head-on.

"My tattoos felt like they were just ink decorations. There's no life or energy in the Anchor runes," added Gere.

"I have lost all of my passive listening spells. I had time to check one on the way in. Tthe runes are still there, but they didn't reactivate spontaneously. I'll have to re-activate them all," reported Meg.

"I feel like Gere, my tattoos were empty, and I wasn't able to cast even the simplest of spells," said Caleb.

Freya was also visibly shaken but was keeping it together. Masan had at one point questioned her suitability for field work, but she was proving herself time after time. "It was similar for me, just this profound feeling of emptiness, of being cut off. It was almost as if I could feel the other side, the opposite of our power. It's the Darkness, isn't it? It's getting more powerful here," Freya said with more than a trace of disgust in her voice. Masan leaned against a wall and looked Freya in the eyes, "I think you might have it right. This is likely the most serious challenge you will ever face in your careers. The Council has trained you to be prepared for almost all situations, but it seems that no one can explain how it feels to suddenly be without our guiding Light."

The group all nodded at this. Masan took a moment to let his words settle, he had to make this challenge seem routine, so they could ditch the panic.

"I don't know what has caused this outage, but rest assured we will find and correct this.

"Our easy days are over. Somewhere in the city a Mage, probably a Dark Adept, has just issued a challenge to the powers of the Light. I have already called in reinforcements from the Council. Adept Frid will be here in two days to take action.

"I need you to spend the next 48 hours pulling every piece of intel you have on who could have done this and why. Leave no stone unturned. We may already face severe consequences for our failure to identify an Adept who could do this. We do not need to compound our failure in Adept Frid's eyes. We can't stay uninformed about the situation, we need something tangible before he lands."

The team nodded solemnly. He could see that Sinn and Gere had already anticipated punishment for this occurrence, but the younger Mages had not. The Council wasn't kind in the face of failure, and this was existential failure of the utmost severity. He hoped they understood just how serious it was that they greeted Frid prepared.

He caught Sinn's eyes and saw that they were already planning to corral the youngest to make sure they understood that there'd be no relaxation or sleep before they had the most complete briefing possible for Frid. Two days, we can make it in two days. Masan thought. As for him, he turned to his private quarters, he needed to get back on comms with the Council for a full debrief. He hoped he'd live to see the end of this offensive. Frid was a hardened battle Mage and a zealot, known for extreme scorched earth tactics, with him in charge neither friend nor foe was safe.

257TH DAY OF 11566 AF

"IF I just didn't have to endure this infernal snoring." Lin pulled her pillow down hard over her head, of course in vain as that was in no way conducive to sleep. Grumpy and tired she got out of bed and into her very fluffy, very pink slippers. She would have preferred an hour or two longer; she shrugged, time for coffee.

The restaurant was still not open, but coffee machines never sleep. A dozen others were already sitting at one of the long tables; the atmosphere was such that it was apparent that no-one would have chosen to be here had circumstances been different. Beral waved at her unenthusiastically.

"Morning... Guess you didn't hear the good news yet: we'll be a week delayed due to 'miscalculations' in processing times of visas." Beral's tone was thick with sarcasm.

Lin grunted, disappointed. "Why do they do this? We already knew that they'd tank our priority for entry. And why can't they just confess that it's due to letting industrial shipments jump ahead in the docking queue?"

They both knew the answer, Lin mainly wanted to vent her frustration. Being packed into this claustrophobic antique, floating way too slowly through the system was weighing on all of them; fifteen hundred smelly, grumpy souls, all running away from their old lives.

A member of the small crew, James, if Lin's memory served her, entered, and was starting up the kitchen. A low humming indicated that the ovens were up and running; the smell of baking bread made her mouth water. Even though it wasn't in his job description, the young ship-hand happily brought out his bread and some quite passable jam to the small group of passengers. Lin, being the only woman of his age there, received some light flirting to go with her breakfast; he got a smile and a wink in return, meaning his day was pretty much made.

Lin shot Beral a jokingly hostile glance as he snickered. Just because James wasn't exactly Lin's taste in men didn't mean she wouldn't indulge his advances just a little bit. No harm in giving the guy a confidence boost.

***

THE flight deck, a small unaesthetic protuberance on top of the rust bucket Mohammad had had the displeasure of calling home the last two years, was bustling with activity. Station management at Tube had, as expected, pushed their docking queue position way down. Everyone was annoyed but trying not to show it; Mohammad was doing a worse job than most of that.

"Again? That fucking cesspool needs a cleansing. Corrupt the bunch of them; can't trust a Kras Officer for shit." Remembering Captain Tamrol's previous employer, he hastily added, "On Tube I mean, not in general, obviously." He got a blank stare in return. She looked tired; however, no matter how hard he tried, he couldn't get a read on her. "Do we tell the passengers the real reason for the delay or just forward the bullcrap they sent us?" he inquired.

"James handled it. He sent a ship-wide memo a few minutes ago. It contains a copy of the communique from Tube."

Mohammad stared out the huge dome window above them. "Alright, I guess we can't do much but wait then." He sighed. "Lieutenant cut eighty-five percent of the propulsion system power." The command was acknowledged, and an almost unnoticeable shudder went through the ship. A few seconds passed, followed by some very surprised faces as gravity failed and the crew were flung forcibly against the glass roof, the light in the room flickered once, and then it was out.

The next thing Mohammad experienced was being woken by a large creaking and a throbbing headache. He tried to remember what just happened, where he was, and why his head felt like the day after New Years Eve. His eyes started to adjust to the low light emitted by the emergency exit sign and the dull starlight. The captain was trying to get back to her console, the lieutenant was fumbling with a torch but was having some major problems. Quite likely the lieutenant had suffered a light concussion, Mohammad touched his head and felt sticky warm liquid, realizing that he was most likely quite concussed himself; that would explain the silvery shine around everything, and why his eyes wouldn't quite look in the direction he was telling them. The creaking sound stopped abruptly and was replaced by the captain's shouting, "Don't just fucking float around, make yourselves useful! Propulsion is entirely fucked, and it looks like one of our steering batteries is broken."

Mohammad was confused. "How can you tell without power? Isn't that station dead?" Thanks to the darkness and his less than fully functional eyes he entirely missed Tamrol giving him an unamused look.

"Turn around. Look out the window." Even in low light, it wasn't hard to make out a forty-meter rocket, the aft starboard steering block, floating past a few arm lengths away.

"Holy shit."

***

TUBE: a station and place to live for millions, but also the most advanced marvel of human engineering, and arcane research. The rapidly rotating megastructure had, in its construction, required the scouring of a large portion of the system's asteroids. The costs had been astronomical, and many would argue absurd. However, it was completed now, just a century back. The command post of the main solward hangar bay was chaotic as always; however, the commander was focused.

He put down the tablet with the docking manifest and turned to his XO. "We had arranged for docking of ten ships had we not? Where's the Astion?" The XO was staring at the same list, he pulled up a chain of transcriptions next to the list. "It seems they went dark sometime around twelve hundred hours." The commander stared at him, feeling dread, but not letting it show. "Send out patrols immediately, how the hell did we miss this till now?"

Hiko returned to reviewing the manifests, sending a neural pulse to sign the ones that needed his approval, and rapidly scanning the rest. He didn't let his upset show, it would be out of character, and he couldn't have anyone poking into his interests in the matter.

Internally he swore, he knew that this was the doing of the guild, of Salvador specifically; it was the only explanation for him leaving his yacht here for months, only to have it take off on a pre-programmed path two days ago. The bribes were not enough to justify these risks, if this was truly piracy as Hiko suspected, the punishment for abetting could be death. Kras were not known for their leniency, especially not when it came to their officers: A recruit could usually be forgiven some slight transgressions, at worst they'd face expulsion or jail, but for a commander, the only way out of the corporation was feet first, on a slab. Hiko was reconsidering a lot of his life choices. Maybe he could barter with the guild, they might let him out. He didn't really believe it himself. The guilds didn't let you go once you were in, very similar thinking to the Kras corporation in a lot of ways.

After the shift was over, Hiko hurriedly made his way towards the highest levels of residences overlooking the voidward part of the gardens. The small, automated pod he was riding silently slid along the metal rail, jumping from path to path without any noticeable jitter or bouncing. What usually was a relaxed trip, with a beautiful view of the jungle-like garden, lit by millions of small floating globes, was now a gut-wrenching wait. Leaning against the railing of the front window, he wished he could will this thing to go faster. He just wanted to get this over with. Not reporting what he'd figured out could be perceived as treacherous, and he really didn't need the guild representative conspiring against him. He needed to make it clear that he knew what was afoot, and that he would remain loyal.

***

HIKO crossed several large patches of grass and in some cases flower beds while hurrying towards the contractor offices. In one case, he passed straight through an active sprinkler and got soaked. He hardly noticed the water, his thoughts occupied by the distress call he'd just intercepted. He was well placed in the hierarchy of Tube just for occurrences like this, but he would prefer to never carry news like this. He took a deep breath as he came up on the office doors of Anne Sirah, the local point of contact for Apteryx agents, though that was hardly what the plaque said.

"He did what?!" Anne was cooking from rage and looked like she might take Hiko's head off. "The ship was left here? And you didn't tell me? How the hell are you this thick?"

Hiko tried to sound professional and self-assured. "I assumed it was guild business, that you had signed off on it." He regretted having sat down, Anne was standing too close to him in the cramped office, and being trapped in the chair looking up at her made him feel claustrophobic.

"I most definitely did not. We don't need this kind of attention!" Anne was pacing now, seemingly having redirected her anger to Sal momentarily. "He won't get away with it this time. I'll burn his fucking ability out of him myself. Damned idiot. And damned the fucking Ring for letting him become so cocky."

Hiko had heard of the Ring, but they were so far removed from him that they might as well be a tall tale, a select handful of incredibly powerful mages who had the others under their thumbs.

Anne abruptly turned to Hiko. "You'll do everything you can to sort this out, if your people find Sal it's your job to make sure his connection to the guild doesn't come out. Go to him as a friend if you can, but if he doesn't let you, put a bullet in his head."

Hiko swallowed and nodded. "Yes ma'am. I'll do my best." Internally he swore. This is not how he'd hoped this meeting would go down.

"You'll do better than that. This is life and death for both of us. If we're discovered, Kras will space us, and if we get away from them, my people will do us even worse." Anne's anger had turned to exasperation, and Hiko could even hear a hint of fear in her voice.

A deep dark thought kept popping up, if she was this afraid, he should probably be even more so. He'd always been in awe of Anne, what the hell did the Ring do to the ones that betrayed them, what in the world could be worse than spacing?

***

SALVADOR, one of the few people that Lin genuinely enjoyed the company of, just entered the mess hall when everything went pear-shaped. As the light came back to the room, after what felt like around ten minutes, Lin stumbled out of the pantry where she had landed. Sal stared at her for a moment and then broke down in laughter; she glared at him, everything felt sticky, crushed plastic bags of jam and marmalade were falling off her.

"That funny? You really need to grow up…"

She only managed to keep face for a few seconds before she snorted and started giggling. The rest of the people failed to see the humor in the situation. Beral brought a chair back to the table, found a mug on the floor, and poured himself a fresh mug of espresso, full to the brim. Small screens above the doors of the room came alive, indicating that emergency systems were online. The scrolling text listed sections that were off-limits to non-essential personnel, the list was long.

"Anyone have any clue as to what the hell just happened?" The doubt in Beral's voice indicated that he didn't expect an answer.

"As much as you know, maybe less," Salvador replied in a short tone. "Though that was a hell of a noise; some sort of catastrophic engine failure?"

Lin ignored the others, trying to decipher the emergency terminal messages. The bulk of it was security info, what sections had suffered breaches or damage, some of it was info on electrical issues.

After some thought, she had puzzled some essential parts together. "Hey guys, I think someone blew up one of our engines…"

The room went quiet for a few seconds; then, "The fuck are you on about? That's the dumbest." James went quiet when Beral put a heavy, firm hand on his shoulder.

"Be quiet before you embarrass yourself." Turning to Lin he continued, "What does that make you think; sabotage?"

Lin went over her observations in a calm and organized manner; from the type of security measures installed on this class of ship, their placement, the warning systems should they fail, and how that compared to the type of damage she had deducted the ship had taken.

Five or so minutes later she concluded, "So obviously this couldn't have been the result of anything but a man-made explosion in the steering block!"

James managed to look confused and annoyed at the same time, while Beral and Sal just nodded. Sal added, "There's been quite a few mentions of lost transports lately, nothing reported by Kras or Naos, but then again, I hear only independents have been targeted."

James, who had managed to keep quiet for an uncharacteristically long time, was almost vibrating from indignation. "What the hell do you know? We're contracted for Kras, and I've heard nothing of missing ships! A bunch of paranoid loons."

Sal looked at him blankly. "Contracted for Kras? Please, your captain has been feeding you scat. No Kras ship would transport these two." He shot a look at Beral and Lin. "Kras doesn't give enough of a shit to do anything about it, but they sure as hell won't allow their own people to protect fugitives."

James continued to object and kept being berated by Beral. After a few minutes of this Sal made for the corridor with the closest restroom. Lin had a bit of an odd feeling about him, though Sal had weighed in, he had been way less wordy than usual. She'd never seen him let Beral be the one to dominate any conversation.

A minute later Lin found out why she had that feeling about Sal. She had just enough time to see him pull the emergency hatch closure in the corridor; then all security doors slammed shut simultaneously. "What the fuck is happening!" James looked to be on the verge of tears.

Lin answered with a sad smile. "Sal... Sal happened. I think he's who did all this." She looked at Beral. "So what do you think? Slaver, or bounty hunter?"

Beral took Lin by the arm and bent in close, visibly shaken, but still keeping himself together. "We'll probably be boarded, plundered, and killed, or worse within the hour."

Lin nodded. While the other passengers hadn't heard the comment, they were not taking any of this with calm. Two large men were hammering on the main door, shouting at Sal to let them out, a third was getting a barstool to use as an implement.

"Stop being stupid, that's gonna do fuck all!" The large man looked at Beral in defiance for a moment before realizing the truth in those words; he dropped the stool.

"So what now?"

Beral looked to Lin, her response was in a more measured tone than usual. "We don't have access to much from here, but this ship isn't exactly state of the art. With enough time and some tools, I can probably get us out of this room at least"

Beral nodded. "And I have access to the small shuttles. We could make our way to the hangar."

The rest of the passengers seemed happy enough about not having to take charge. A couple of people started rummaging around in cabinets and drawers, producing some screwdrivers, an overcharge device, and a hand-welder. Lin grabbed what she needed and got to work, cutting through an unimportant-looking plain piece of panel; exposing a network node. "I need a few minutes, it should be simple enough." She stared intently at the wiring for a few seconds. "Nevermind." She braced herself and planted her heel into, and through, the panel; the doors opened. Lin grinned at Beral. The giant man smiled but failed at hiding his worry.

***

SAL could hear the doors open, sitting by a screen down the hall. He shook his head. Of course that would hardly contain them for long. He had hoped for a few more minutes to work undisturbed though.

Without looking up, he reached into his pocket with his left hand and grasped a dark metal cube—he could feel the pattern on it squirm under his grip. Just as he finished typing out his communication on the screen, he squeezed the cube hard and let the filaments contained in there flood into him; to anyone who might have observed the scene Salvador faded into nothingness.

The world was a bit muted, but Sal could still hear sufficiently to eavesdrop on his pursuers as he moved to the upper deck. He marveled at the skill of the artificer who had crafted this spell, he'd only used it a few times before, and each time he was stunned at the ingenuity. Kesh was shaping out to be all he had expected her to be.

No one had seen his little trick, he doubted that they would be familiar enough with dark magic to recognize it anyhow. A good thing, he thought. The fewer people who knew of his abilities, the less risk there was of being hindered. Who knows, with a passenger list this long it wouldn't surprise him if there were one or two other casters aboard. Only one passenger was of any value, however. It was quite something to orchestrate this catastrophe for one lone soul, but money was money, and this was the best money he'd ever seen. The hatches of the aft escape shuttles were lined up all neat in the wide floor of this corridor. He bared a panel on the wall, pushed in a long security code into the old-fashioned plasma screen, and proceeded to input a sequence that would have devastating consequences for all of the shuttles but one. Now all that was left to do was wait.

***

ONLY a few minutes had passed before Lin and her group made it to the escape hangar, as it was dubbed. It was strange, they hadn't run into a single person other than those who had been trapped with her in the cafeteria. With all the alarms that were going off, and all of the chaos over the last fifteen minutes, one would assume at least some of the passengers had had the same idea. She knew what this meant; Sal managed to trip a whole bunch of the seals to the living quarters, trapping most in their rooms. Shaking off what little sting of guilt she felt, she cranked the handle to one of the hatches.

The door swung open with a pneumatic hiss. Stale air escaping into the corridor gave away that these shuttles hadn't been getting the protocol-mandated monthly inspections. Lin sighed and jumped into the dark hole. Just as she hit the ground, she heard strangled screams from above.

Sal smiled down at her. "Thanks for joining me. This last part was a little bit hurried but it works." He raised a hand that she'd never noticed was tattooed before now, and the air became a cloud of darkness.

Something clung to her face. She clawed at the strange slick surface, nails slipping, it was sleek like plastic. She was fighting for breath, but it wouldn't come, every breath in just sucked the clinging stuff into her mouth. She tried to poke a hole in it, but it deformed around her fingers. She was flailing as her head spun, she slammed against metal panels. Pain seared through her shins as she fell to her knees. Time felt sluggish and strange, the world was muted and far away. The last light went out as she lost consciousness.

258TH DAY OF 11566 AF

IT was early in the morning, by the hand of the chronograph at least, the sun was close to zenith. Colored dust shimmered in the light; oranges and purples competing as they danced in the sun. The weather was as good as it ever got in City Six, with no rain today, but not dry enough for toxic dust to rise to the degree where it became a hazard to breathe.

The platform where Masan stood was elevated above the rest of the city, and it offered an epic view of the sprawling cityscape; Ushas Mons to the north, rising from the dense mass of metal and ceramic structures that held more than two hundred million members of the general population. Ushas Mons was dotted with large structures, each with walls bordering them, islands on the huge volcano, housing the affluent and powerful. Masan looked at least a decade older than his forty years, hair already graying. His washed-out, wan skin color gave him a slightly ghostly appearance. Today he felt just as old as he looked. He was taking in the often-obscured view as he heard the yacht he had been waiting for approach, a low hum at first, that quickly turned into a scream of powerful jet engines.

He covered his eyes as dust was blown across the platform. Winds were being whipped up by the gigantic golden spear that his visitor was arriving in. The ship was sleek and beautifully polished, a tube with a sharpened knife edge of a nose and small stabilizing wings. The engine exhausts across the body swiveled, pushed the nose up, and in a smooth motion pushed the nose slightly up from the ground as the pads extended. The maneuver was performed at a speed that would have seemed suicidal if it hadn't been for its preciseness. Engines were extinguished and the only sounds from the ship now were clinking from metal adjusting to the temperature and the coolers humming around the exhausts.

The hatch of the yacht popped open on hydraulic pistons. The man descending the stairs was tall, with snow-white hair and a long white leather coat. The man, Frid, turned his iris-less piercing eyes to Masan. "Morning kid, how you've been?"

Masan relaxed. "I'm good sir, I apologize for dragging you into this."

He knew Frid well enough to see through the smile on that perfect pearl-colored face, to the annoyance underneath.

"Ahhh, hardly your fault. We'll get this sorted and I'll be out of your hair in no time. You had my vote of confidence for what it's worth, this is just the council being paranoid." He looked off in the distance for a moment and continued, "Now where is my outfit? Can't have the locals see me like this."

Frid stepped over the threshold and left his ship behind. Masan led him into the tower. They passed over to the small changing room that had been prepared for Frid's arrival.

Some thirty minutes later the regal, almost ephemeral-looking figure had been transformed into someone who wouldn't raise an eyebrow among the residents of City Six. Contacts gave him healthy-looking blue eyes. Some very expensive foundation had corrected the bright white skin to a mid-brown, not too dissimilar from his original skin color. He'd let his white hair stay as it was, bleached or dyed hair wasn't rare on Embla, so it shouldn't cause any issues.

Masan nodded and handed him a purple coat in a synthetic water-repellent fiber. "This should be your size." It was a plain garment other than its remarkable color, but on closer inspection, it was of good make, a garment made both for fitting in, but also for comfort and protection.

Frid draped the coat over his shoulders. "Let's get going Masan, I can't wait to meet everybody."

***

THE path into the stronghold of the Tribe was unassuming. A heavy metal door opened inwards into a long corridor that opened into a massive chamber, what had once been massive shipping crates had been converted to rows upon rows of living space. Step ladders lead up to the upper areas. In some areas, up to six containers had been stacked on top of each other, reaching halfway to the roof of the cave-like space. There was a slightly damp feeling to the air that helped make the sulfurous smell even more potent.

The warehouse was lit with fluorescent panels that provided an eternal daytime to the inside of the cavernous space. Only the individual containers could be darkened. They had been lucky to find this space, previously a home for terraforming and mining equipment. It was both enormous and accessible from the depths of the corridors of City Six, making it difficult to find for the uninitiated.

Masan guided Frid through the maze that was the Undercity to the Tribe's stronghold. He felt like he could almost touch the disapproval radiating from Frid, who was accustomed to living in the constant light of the stations operated by the Council. The inside lighting was not a substitute for the actual light of the Sun. Nevertheless, this was supposed to be a covert base that appeared to be a sanctuary for the cast-offs of City Six, so it could hardly be in a location that allowed it access to real sunlight.

At the end of the rows of makeshift dwellings, the noise hit the two men, a constant stream of music and conversation that dominated the space. The Tribe took in all who needed it and functioned like an artisan's commune. There were always people in the central area cooking and creating. Each small group carved out a home of their choosing among the mountain of shipping containers, but most of the Tribe lived and worked in the central space.

Masan could feel Frid stiffening. This kind of chaos was anathema to Light stations, which were utopias of quiet and clarity, designed for personal contemplation and order.

"If you follow me to the left, you'll find the management quarters. We've installed all of the necessities beyond prying eyes," he told Frid.

Masan continued at an angle across the more open space, towards a container construction much tidier than those close to the entrance. Several boarded-up hatches were visible on the side of this building. Masan caught Frid's eye as he was studying the layout. "Those containers are the reason we're in this space. Shielded by layers of heavy metal and bedrock in all directions, and a path to tap into the power and comm grids. Everything hardlined, and everything shielded."

Frid nodded. "I see that you've created a buffer zone too. I like it, use the civilians here as an early warning system and as a meat shield."

"All standard procedure," Masan agreed, though he felt a slight twinge in his soul at the phrasing.

They reached the reinforced gate of the building and Masan pressed a hand to a pad at the wall. Seemingly he had his palm scanned, but in reality he also activated a complex series of rune patterns that deactivated the early warning system that would have otherwise burnt them both to a crisp when entering.

The reception door opened into a large room, this too built from massive metal containers. It was decorated as a haphazard office and manned by a trusted member of the Tribe, Hissan. Masan nodded at the young man. "Frid, this is Hissan. He's one of the people from the stations."

Frid smiled a warm smile at that. "Ahhh, a cultured civilian then. It's nice to see that we aren't entirely surrounded by barbarians."

Hissan bowed deep at Frid but said nothing. Wise boy, Masan thought.

The two Mages passed through the office and several containers that were used as storage for goods and equipment. This pass-through was used to mask the true interior of this building and keep out nosy members of the Tribe, most of whom eschewed paperwork and order of any kind. A door accessed by a magic-activated key card opened onto a stairwell to the next level of containers, and the noise fell away.

Masan watched Frid's reaction to their secure space carefully. The interior here was a bright white, elegantly furnished, and perfectly lit by omnipresent flat panels glowing brilliantly. The decor aped sterile space stations with elegant and spartan furnishings.

"Welcome to our control center, Frid. It should have all of the comforts of home that can be supplied in artificial light. Consider it your Sanctuary away from the bustle and hassle of the Tribe. Your quarters are this way."

Masan led Frid to the quarters farthest from his own. "Could you allow me?" he asked and indicated at the comm unit on Frid's wrist.

Frid presented the platinum wristband with its deep red spectral projector laying flat over the back of his hand.

"Nice model," Masan noted, and made a flicking motion across his own device, a distinct pinging noise indicating receipt. "You now have admin access to every system. Please tell Sinn if you change anything important though as they're the one that makes everything here work."

"Of course. I'm sure it's all in order."

"The suite contains living quarters and both magical and technical workrooms with access to all of our surveillance infrastructure. Food is available, but I always take at least two of my meals in the central gathering area to preserve appearances as a man of the people."

"Well, that's distasteful, but I understand the necessity. What do you do when you need to work magic for a prolonged period of time?"

"I work minimal magic, to preserve my control for an emergency situation and to slow the effects of corruption on my appearance, as I was instructed by the Council. When I do work magic, I tell the group that I am on a meditation retreat. We have lots of adherents, real and pretend, of the old Earth religions and I often lead group retreats, so this activity goes unquestioned."

"That all seems sound. I would like some time to review your intelligence and get fully up to date on your operatives and infrastructure now that I'm on site. I'll meet you in two hours for a meal with the rest of the Tribe."

Masan knew when he had been dismissed. "I will see you in two hours. Do not hesitate if there's something you need."

Frid already vanished into the quarters before Masan finished his pleasantries. No matter the duration, this was going to be a long project. Masan had gone through phases with this posting, first pride in running an outpost, then dismay when he realized that he had been abandoned far from Light society. It hadn't taken him long to realize that he relished the freedom of living in an uncultured, anarchistic backwater. He never forgot that the Tribe was a front and his stewardship was in service of a greater power, but he also enjoyed living in a place full of diverse magics and peoples without formality. He had worn the mask of benevolent sage for so long that it had started to become the real version of him, the unquestioning soldier left behind when he left the stations.

***

THE area of the Tribe's quarters that was designated as a kitchen and mess was slightly more organized compared to the rest of the compound. It was mid-afternoon, and most had already finished with food and were now out in the city, either on missions for Masan or just doing the rounds, recruiting and begging. Masan liked these moments, getting to sit down with a small group of friends and just feel human for a while. Today he was chatting with some of the younger members, Peanna was one of the newest additions and she'd recently had a baby. The little one had inherited his mother's dark skin and already had a lot of fluff covering his head. Cooing and giggling, he'd gotten past the constant crying faster than any other kid Masan had met, and he'd met a lot of little ones in his role as leader of the Tribe. He'd initially reacted to the fact that the child had a malformation of his hand, it looked wasted and under-formed. Most likely a result of his mother having been both abused and malnourished when she was carrying him; Masan had gotten over it fast, however. Can't blame the little one for things outside of his control. The structures of his guild didn't allow for any physical imperfections in children, but he reminded himself that Embla was quite a different world from the stations, and the majority of Tribe members weren't actually guild members.

259TH DAY OF 11566 AF

MIA was no stranger to tight crawl spaces, but she was less than thrilled to be stuck, completely immobile in this one for hours. It was rare that she and her Apteryx compatriots worked together in the field, but this was a team assignment, and she was the smallest.

Apteryx had been called in to red team security in the corporate city, Speos. Apparently, one of the higher-ups had been waking up with nightmares about insufficient corporate security measures. Though the corporation largely eschewed Mages for tech, the original anti-mage security has been installed by Asio. And who better to test their security than their bitterest rivals?

Information for the op was compartmented, but Mia had known immediately that she would wind up doing the physical sneaking. Peter, Madeline, Madison, and Boris were too large for slipping into tech installations and Sal was too likely to "accidentally" murder the staff on his way in or out. Mia took advantage of her small stature and impressive implants to climb, crawl, or wiggle her way into the tightest physical cracks in people's security.

Mia was unimpressed by their system. Too many people relied on their sensors and shields to detect intruders and not enough people considered the physical layout of their buildings. This corp was no exception. They had focused all of their security on the obvious physical intrusion points sized for adult humans. Mia had used the blueprints of the original city installation to access the sewer system outlet several kilometers outside the city. Now abandoned in favor of better internal water reprocessing, she followed the tunnels into the underground maintenance areas of the building. From there it had been child's play to access the ventilation system and climb to her current post.

Mia has come magically and technically prepared to disable heat and movement sensors in the city infrastructure, but she had only encountered the long-abandoned tech used in the building of the city. It seemed like the corporation had focused on the visible trappings of wealth and security and neglected the ones that really mattered. These were fucking amateurs in comparison to the boys over at Kras on Mars, who had every possible intrusion point rigged with tech and magic sensors, no matter how trivial the conduit or vent might be. Mia could infiltrate there too, but at least it was a challenge.

Mia hadn't wanted to take her physical presence too close to her targets, so she had sent a shadow construct to be her eyes and ears. She was lying face down in the air shaft, eyes closed, letting her implants record the feed of the confidential board meeting going on several rooms over. The corporate blowhards were finally wrapping up their scintillating discussion on food production for the city, so Mia might actually get out of there before she died of boredom, or worse, fell asleep.

Mia keyed her comm to encrypt and transmit the meeting back to headquarters. Technically, she had done her job as soon as she had the intel she had come to record. The corps sometimes sent operatives on suicide missions, knowing that they could get in, but not back out and she wanted to adhere to their playbook. Once done, she turned off her comms transmission, going dark until she completed her exfil.

Intel sent, she cautiously flexed her muscles and checked to make sure her scrubbers had properly prevented any muscle cramps before slowly easing her way back out the way she came. She had a long trek out to safety and extraction.

She had taken detailed photos of the various security failures that had allowed her to access the corp so easily. She figured that today's work would secure Cormac's team a nice new contract to reevaluate the city infrastructure to prevent her from worming her way in this easily again.

It would help the poor executive to sleep better at night, even though Mia knew that nothing could protect them from her. Fortunately, she was the best of the best and very few operatives would be able to replicate her infiltration. She mentally rolled her eyes and continued her slow and controlled descent out of the building.

***

SEVERAL hours later, Mia emerged from the sewers mentally exhausted and dirty. Her suit protected her from the worst of the dirt but knowing that she had been in it was enough to make her want to get clean. Her guild ship was cloaked and waiting for her, just as she had left it. She boarded the vessel, re-keyed the security, and enjoyed a well-earned shower.

Mia didn't have an immediate follow-up assignment, so she had a few weeks to relax between jobs. She figured she would head back to City Six and see what her friends were up to. Maybe, if she played her cards right, Sal might be in the City at the same time. She wouldn't fall so far as to actually ask him if he would be around. Things between them had been off ever since Mia had fucked him and then found out that Sal was incredibly sexually indiscriminate. What she had hoped was an intensification of the bond they had had for years, had apparently just been another sexual conquest for Sal.

Sometimes Mia wondered if he understood that she was the Guild's most likely contingency against him. She wasn't a wet-work specialist like Sal, but no one in the solar system was beyond her reach. She was the weapon the Guild used only in extreme situations requiring advanced infiltration, data extraction, and assassination in one op. The stiletto in the night to Sal's indiscriminate slaughter. They should be two sides of the same coin, but if that wasn't their future… well, Sal should be more afraid of her.

Mia hummed as she piloted the ship back to City Six. Maybe she would torture Sal and maybe he'd be off-planet, but either way, she was looking forward to spending a few days being clean in open spaces.

***

FRID re-emerged from headquarters to the Tribe's central meeting place. He looked unhappy, so Masan assumed his review of the scenario and key players had not gone well.

"You've really let this get out of hand, Masan."

"It was a very nebulous issue, until it wasn't," Masan replied. "How was I to know that there was a Dark Mage here who was trying magic of this level? These Dark Guilds are usually pretty fucking pragmatic. They encourage very reserved use of magic to prevent corruption. Whatever is going on is highly unusual."

"Be that as it may, all of our magical surveillance in City Six went down on your watch. That means that you took an existing deficit in intelligence and turned it into a clusterfuck," Frid replied.

Masan had to concede the point. If he had better intel inside the Dark Guilds, he would already know which mage was responsible. That he didn't was entirely a failure of his team's intelligence apparatus. And now it was compounded by the loss of many of the bugs they had painstakingly placed all over the City.

"We'll find whoever did this and burn him to the ground. And then

I'll head back to the land of the civilized. It's appalling that you don't have household staff here."

Masan knew better than to point out that household staff in a commune of rejects would be extremely suspicious. The Light Guild's space stations were finely tuned machines of tech, magic, and staff. A mage of Frid's stature had his every comfort looked after so that he could focus on communing with the Light. Staying in a lushly appointed suite wouldn't be enough if he had to do any substantial personal care. This was his version of roughing it.

Masan and Frid wandered towards the central kitchen and grabbed food from the people on kitchen duty. They made their way over to one of the long communal tables in a far corner to eat. They dropped the subject of their conversation now that they were among the uninitiated.

Grateful for the break in his scolding, Masan chewed happily amongst the hubbub of the Tribe. He was so focused on his meal that he almost missed Frid looking intently at a nearby table.

"What has captured your interest over there?" Masan asked.

"There's a malformed child. I have never seen one before, especially with so severe a defect."

Masan was stunned into silence for a moment. Who had a malformed child? But then he remembered that Peanna had a boy who had a slightly malformed hand.

"The baby? He has a small disability. It's easily fixable with tech in the future."

"It's grotesque. I can't believe you tolerate that among your people," Frid replied.

The Council of Light Mages placed a premium on physical perfection. They had spent several centuries ensuring that fetuses who had congenital issues were not allowed to reach term. Even now, though rare, a Light Mage carrying a child with any physical or mental imperfection would not be allowed to keep the baby. Nothing could pollute the genetic purity of the Light Mage lineages, even though magic wasn't necessarily heritable.

"Emblan society doesn't view physical perfection as necessary," Masan explained. "It's not uncommon to find people who have compensated for some trauma or birth defect with tech. And since we take in everyone, it would be odd to make a fuss about it. It's counter to the Tribe's mission."

"I suppose you're right. Still, it pains me to be in the presence of such disgusting people."

"Shhhh. You're supposed to be a visiting scholar and minor mage, here to help people with their meditative practice. It's entirely out of character for your persona to be this judgmental."

"You're right of course. Let's move on. I will want to speak with your team over the course of the day if you can arrange to discreetly call them in."

Masan breathed an internal sigh of relief. "That won't be a problem. They have all been briefed regarding your arrival by encoded comm. I'll stagger the recall since they're busy recasting as much of our spy infrastructure as is possible in the short term."

✲✲✲

"THERE are only a handful of Dark Guilds with the power to shift significant Dark Plane energies into the physical realm," Masan told Frid. "Any mage with enough juice to do something like this is either brought into one of the big guilds like Apteryx, Strix, or Asio as a child or moves there when they realize their little guild can't offer them the power and resources of one of the big three. The question is who has enough hubris or indifference to be trying this."

"I read the files you provided and City Six doesn't seem to have any Dark cultists like the ones Tube cleared out a few years back."

"No, the dark guilds on Embla tend to be capitalists, not cultists. They tend to bend only to the almighty credit," Masan replied.

"So that leaves either a solo mage trying to achieve god status, a Guild looking to change its profile in a big way with some sort of world-shattering ritual, or someone messing with powers they don't really understand," said Frid.

Eager to pull Frid's attention away from a crusade against a Dark Cult or immortality chaser, Masan replied, "Maybe we can work out who is doing this by looking at the materials you would need to pull off a spell or spells with that kind of power."

"Maybe… Although if they're working old-Earth Satanist style, they may be chiseling into an old obsidian floor or something and we'll never detect it."

"Let's assume that they're not trying to reconstitute the works of Aleister Crowley. Most of the Guilds here are as modern as the constant corrosion allows. How would you go about pulling the actual light plane into the physical realm, if you wanted to? Of the two of us, only you are powerful and well-read enough to manage such a feat."

"I would need a powerful anchor rune and several strings of interconnected sub-spells with Master Runes in order to achieve something like this. Your average written spell wouldn't have enough magical conductivity to hold magic like this, so it has to be in a physical medium. Steel, stone, glass, or precious metals. Maybe graven stone tablets?" Frid mused out loud. "I would check all purveyors of fine obsidian, dark granite, or quartz. I would also check who in City Six buys precious metals, like gold and platinum. We've seen one or two dark mages with some sort of metallic cube in some recent battles with dark mages."

"Then it's time to put our resources to work. I'll have the Tribe eavesdrop for word of Dark Guilds attempting to make big deals. I'll have our operatives look into the materials for heavy spell work and maybe leave a few surprises for the Dark Guilds to find."

260TH DAY OF 11566 AF

"KESH, do you have the new series of rune tiles ready?" Prior Wallang inquired as he entered Kesh's workshop. He was impatient to try once again and he had an intuition about the new tile set he had asked Kesh to craft. *She's remarkable in her lack of curiosity*, he thought, *or maybe she's just playing a waiting game. She's sneakier than she lets on.*

His apprentice was a clever young woman, clever enough to have realized that she could parcel out difficult runes one by one as tiles, to be assembled into complex spells by more powerful and less technically skilled mages later. She stumbled across this technique shortly after being given access to the workshops as a way around some of her more difficult homework. Given that it was ingenious, and extremely technically difficult to master, Wallang had given her the task of building a rune library, ostensibly so mages could safely test new spells without needing to first expend their energies creating the runes. She might not have been the first mage to approach complex magic in this manner, but he'd never seen anyone be this precise or successful before.

The room was mostly tidy, Kesh was good at cleaning up after herself, other than during active work sessions. Tools and protective gear hung in neat rows above the workbenches on the left immediately inside of the door, and several dedicated stations had been set up so that they'd be ready to jump right into work, crystals, torches, and other gear all in their racks. Over two of the benches holographic projections were slowly rotating, displaying some of the latest designs she'd been working on. The closest one was definitely part of a neural array for battle armor. Wallang made a mental note to inquire about that one at a later date.

He had come down here for a reason. What was it again? Oh right, the theft.

Kesh materialized out of a dark corner. "I'll have them done soon, but I need to talk to you about a Light mage intrusion."

"What?" The mention of Light magic tore Wallang from his rumination.

"One of my new hand-held drills was hiding quite a sophisticated Light magic listening spell. I don't think they got much more than some humming, because I'm always in here alone, but it's unusually clever."

"Is it still active now?" Wallang asked.

"No, I shielded it, dormant but not destroyed."

"Well, that's two odd occurrences in one week." He ran a hand through his beard. Something he often found himself doing when deep in thought or trying to fight off stress.

"Two occurrences?" echoed Kesh.

"I was coming to tell you that Parvana needs a new shadow stalker block."

"She needs what? That thing took me weeks to make! I save all of the designs, but really? It'll take me half a kilo of platinum to redo."

Kesh was a gifted smith, but her work was grueling in its level of detail. The mage cubes were especially arduous as Kesh forced a great deal of runes into a small space. She also ensured that they were deeply graven to prevent erosion. The cubes also had painstaking internal 3-dimensional architecture to accommodate the spells. Wallang was almost as irritated as Kesh by the time wasted in replacing this complex piece of magic, but the needs of Apteryx had to come before their individual needs. This though was particularly bad, Kesh's pieces were extremely valuable, enough so that some people even within Apteryx might be tempted to lose them on purpose.

"Parvana has already faced the Ring due to its disappearance. It was stolen while she was entertaining some particularly attractive gentleman. She claims that it had been shielded and hidden from view, but that in the morning both the man and the cube were gone. We got some images from nearby cameras, but they're relatively poor quality. It is what it is. We'll send some people, they'll collect data from all adjacent buildings, we'll reconstitute the data and find him." Wallang was a bit amused at the stupidity of the whole thing, but he hid it as he could see Kesh fuming.

"That little…"

"Names won't get us out of this. Do you think I like it any more than you? She still needs the block to do her job. Until now the Ring had assumed that Strix or Asio had stolen it to try and copy it and we had assumed that was a fool's errand. They don't have anyone half as good at crafting as you, my dear, and they'd need to disassemble it, probably destroying the runes anyway." Wallang was proud of his apprentice's skills, even though he often wished he didn't have to share them with the whole Guild.

"I'm guessing my little discovery changes things?"

"Absolutely. A little inter-guild espionage is one thing. An interfering Light Mage is totally different." That was all he needed; he was so close to achieving his life's work. Of course, the Light Council's interfering zealots would pop up now and pull his attention.

"I thought Embla doesn't have Light mages." Kesh had been taught the gentle lie taught to all apprentices.

"Heh, we told you so and you believed it? I thought you were smarter than that. We most certainly do. Those Sun-obsessed bastards wouldn't cede Embla to us, or rather, wouldn't admit that it was always ours. Though, they're hardly going to try a takeover. They have a minimal force somewhere to hold the line and make our lives more difficult."

"So, this didn't come from off-world?" Kesh asked.

"There's no way of knowing, although it seems a bit brazen for the contingent here, who are usually pretty quiet. Something is up."

He felt uncomfortable about the whole thing. It didn't smell right. He felt like the coincidence was too much, right when he was getting close. Had Sal fucked up when he acquired the last book? He'd claimed there hadn't been any trouble. He's a sneaky one, investigate it yourself! he thought.

"I'll report this to the rest of the Ring. Hugh and Cormac will want to send teams to sweep all the workshops for other bugs, magical or otherwise." He tugged on his beard hard and grimaced. This felt wrong.

"And get me those tiles! Can't be losing focus at this stage of the work."

"Yes, Prior." Wallang heard the sarcasm in her tone but decided not to make an issue of it. Parvana's fuckup cut into his work too and Kesh deserved to blow off a little steam. With that he turned and left, returning to pondering the exact configuration of tiles that would allow him to find the missing Master Rune. His experiments were too close to fruition to abandon now.

✳✳✳

MEG was bored. Placing bugs, both technical and magical, was within her areas of expertise. But it was time-consuming and tedious.

Masan and Frid had her running all over City Six reactivating all of the magical bugs that she could get close enough to to re-anchor them to the Light. It was nice to get out of her purple robes, she needed to look like a 'respectable' member of society to access public spaces and stores the Tribe would never frequent.

Meg had done the easiest places first and it had taken her days to get to all the little listening spells she had dropped. Fortunately, Masan was a detail-oriented boss, so they kept full records of all of the locations and spells, so they could properly cross-reference the data.

Meg was finishing up with the little spells in some of the shopping centers when her comm pinged with an urgent request.

Tap into the Fusion Forge's network infrastructure by any means necessary. Aim to see all incoming and outgoing orders, especially changes in volume and special requests. Top priority.

The Fusion Forge was the source of metals and custom materials in City Six. They manufactured routine mage resources like gold and platinum, as well as structural metals like the alloys used to build City Six's massive platforms. The use of fusion gave the forge the ability to control the creation of any element out of hydrogen or helium, as long as it was stable in Embla's atmosphere. They even made specific radioactive isotopes if they were needed for industry or medicine. It was an enormous, fascinating operation.

This was going to be a high-tech job if Masan wanted expansive network access like that. Meg had placed listening bugs there before, but the forge was a high-risk zone for her. It was staffed by many mundane mages, who could easily recognize magical runes if they weren't installed with sufficient shielding. They were fanatical about sweeping for external magic that might interfere with the process and containment of the forge. Meg couldn't blame them, she too enjoyed being alive.

Previously, she had stuck to tech listening bugs because the forge wasn't particularly concerned with corporate espionage about their processes. It helped to be a monopoly in a city of hundreds of millions of people. Sensitive client data was another ballpark altogether.

Meg altered course and headed back to the Tribe. She needed her high-tech tools, which she didn't carry unless necessary. Nothing was truly illegal here on Embla, but being caught with equipment like that would bring about unwanted attention. She was also going to need access to any schematics of the forge and its network infrastructure so that she could figure out how to get into the network. With a job like this, it could be anything from breaking into a secure server site to seducing an employee and planting a worm in their tech.

If it was the former, she would need backup. And, if it was the latter, she was going to need a new outfit and some Intel on where to find a gullible forge employee.

She smiled. This was finally getting interesting.

***

MASAN had spent his 'night' hard at work reviewing the files on every Dark Mage who might have had the power and the skill to cause a Light magic eclipse. He rubbed his eyes and figured he'd venture forth from HQ in search of sustenance.

There was a large commotion in the central space. The Tribe had decided on an impromptu celebratory gathering. Music was playing and people sat in small groups.

Frid appeared behind Masan, joining him on his walk over to the party.

"Joyous group, aren't they? It's very... primitive."

"That's the goal. Distract, obfuscate, and hide among the disenfranchised. It's that attitude that makes it so very easy to spy on the Emblans of City Six," Masan replied. "Let me get you a beverage."

Masan returned to find Frid once again watching Peanna's baby intently. He had paper and a stylus in his hand.

"I thought we could make a short list of potential culprits, but I saw you already sent your list out to the team," Frid said.

"What do you need the paper for then?"

"Oh, this and that. I find matter helps me to think sometimes. Go, join your flock. I wouldn't want your leadership to slip."

Masan made his way over to the group telling horror stories about their time in the Guilds, gossiping about everyone's recent doings, and generally having a good time. He made the rounds greeting everyone by name, clasping shoulders, giving hugs, and giving the impression that he was delighted to be in their presence. Normally, that wasn't a stretch, but today the act felt patently false.

As he moved over to greet Peanna and coo over her baby, he briefly made eye contact with Frid. The smile he received was enough to chill a person to their core. Looking right at him, Frid started writing on his piece of paper. Alone and off to the side, only Masan noticed that the paper disintegrated in his hands when he was done.

Peanna's baby promptly stopped babbling, going stiff and blue. She was caught up in her conversation, so it took her a moment to notice. Then, she screamed.

Frid got up and walked back into headquarters, humming without losing his expression of intense satisfaction.

***

KESH groaned internally. Parvana had always been a horny little bitch and losing something as work-intensive as one of her cubes was par for the fucking course. She was going to have to institute a "you break it, you remake it policy" for missing and damaged magic. She was so close with her Masterwork; she didn't want to switch back over to making the cube.

Maybe, she could take advantage of the Prior's forgetfulness and pretend he never told her? Probably not, the Light magic would probably make this unfortunate conversation stick.

Some days she regretted being good at her job. There were some downsides to being the only person capable of making some of her works. Unfortunately, it wasn't possible to die-cast complex magical spells. The caster had to be magically powerful enough to manage the whole spell, which was rare and the reason she had designed the cubes in the first place. By creating each subsection individually and linking the final work together once, she expended a fraction of the magic that would otherwise be needed for the spells. The mage using it still needed the juice for the spell itself, but not the double or triple amounts it would take to inscribe it on their own. The shadow stalker cube was pretty genius, she could not believe they'd given it to someone as careless as Parvana. At least Mia or Sal would have taken good care of her work! They knew the value of their tools. She resolved to make it as soon as she had made some sort of significant progress on her Masterwork.

She only had one more rune tile to make for the Prior's library. She had kept her promise at the beginning of her journey to help him achieve his objectives in ritual magic and he had been as good as his word. She now knew more runes than any other member of Apteryx. She knew the rune tiles were for his Dark Bridge, not the library he claimed to want her to build, but she didn't really care. She got to make some really unusual and rare runes she would never have seen otherwise, so they weren't all that much of an imposition. Honestly, chasing that stupid Shadow Haze across the city was way worse.

Kesh wanted to be free from his oversight. Knowing the runes was only half the battle and she had so many ideas for new spells for mage cubes and battle armor. She was so close to getting her own workshop where she could focus on turning the tools of mage combat into living, breathing art. The Prior kept her too busy to make a full suit of battle armor, so she had contented herself with making the cubes until he had taught her everything he knew. But the Prior only wanted to observe the world. Kesh wanted to give mages the tools to reshape it into something greater. She couldn't do that as long as she was at the Prior's beck and call. She needed to help him finish his project once and for all, to get to her freedom. She knew he wasn't going to let her achieve Mastery until he got what he wanted. Selfish old coot.

Grumbling, Kesh turned back to her bench and started to finish the tile for jēra- saz nauðr. It was a rare, olden-timey rune for Soul. Wallang had dug it out of one of his musty old books, hoping to replace jēra- saz ár with it in something or other. It gave her pretty minimal resistance as she engraved the obsidian tile to fill it with platinum. The sooner she got through everyone else's tasks, she could finally make what she wanted to make.

***

WALLANG exited his study and as he did he stopped to signal to the system to lock it down until he returned. He had never been in the habit of doing so, but lately the guild hadn't been feeling as safe as it used to. As he closed the doors the sound of cogs whirred deep inside the frame that held the black wooden door.

He glanced at his comm and saw that he was running late. He picked up the pace and wound his way through the corridors of the dimly lit structure, and soon he reached the assembly hall.

As he entered, he noted that he was, as usual, the last to arrive. He nodded in turn to each of his six peers, the Ring, as they were collectively called. "Evening friends, I'm very sorry to call a meeting on such short notice.

"I don't think you should apologize, I can't imagine you'd volunteer to meet if it wasn't urgent." The one who had spoken up was Hugh, the spymaster; he was also, to many people's surprise, the friendliest person in this group.

Wallang smiled at his old friend and took his place at the large stone table. "I won't waste your time then. My apprentice found this when working in one of the shops." He placed the small glass-encased piece of gold on the table. It was smaller than a fingernail and glimmered in the low light.

"Illuminate us," said Argent.

"It's a bug, as you can probably figure from the general looks of it, it's magical in nature. Less obvious is the school: It's a Light Mage device."

The room was silent for several seconds before Hugh spoke, "I assume you're certain."

"Of course, I'm certain, neither Keshara nor I are fools. She disarmed it as soon as she found it, and most likely they'll just think it failed. It was cleverly hidden, and I don't think most people would ever have found it."

"That means the increase in electronic surveillance attempts as of late was probably their work too," said Argent.

The Speaker nodded their shaved head in agreement, and their opal black eyes gleamed as they interjected, "They won't leave it at that. They'll try to get other devices in unless they've managed already."

"So we need to increase security," agreed Argent, who turned to Cormac.

"I'll get right at it. Should be able to make a sweep within the hour if I rouse my people. We'll find anything that's been planted, but I'll leave it where it's found and we can form a plan to make sure they don't know we're onto them."

"And you'll increase security?"

"And I'll increase security," Cormac replied in a dark tone. "I know my duties."

Wallang cleared his throat to get the attention of the room. "That's all good, I wasn't actually worried about how to deal with this. What worries me is the why of it. Why now? They tend to keep a low profile, they can't really afford direct confrontation with us here."

Argent now stared at him. "Yes, please, tell us why. The only one of us here that's been dealing in anything new is you. Did you kick a hornet's nest in your pursuits? You've been rather nonchalant about how you get about your materials as of late."

"I hardly think some strong-arm tactics with importers and antiquities dealers would raise an eyebrow among those people."

"No? How do you know you've not been dealing with them, or their agents? While you're not the most violent person in this building or even this room, you scare the hell out of most people who don't know you."

261st Day of 11566 AF

"HAVE I been here for too long?" Masan was staring at the shimmering of his bedroom roof as he posed the question.

Sinn was lying chest down, supporting themself on their elbows to be able to look him in the face. "What do you mean?"

"Frid. I know that he's following doctrine; but doesn't it feel off to you?"

"You mean to ask if you've gone soft?" Sinn grinned.

"Maybe. Is having a bit of empathy really 'going soft'?"

"In the eyes of the Council, it probably is."

"In your eyes though?" Now he looked them in the eyes, pleading for some validation.

"Your empathy is one of the things I like about you. Initially, when I came here, you were so similar to Frid, you sort of scared me."

"But not now?"

"Honey, we both know I'm the scary one in this bed."

"It's true. You're a real monster sometimes."

"And I'm coming to get you." As they said the word they pounced on Masan, biting him on his lip, and then paused to look him in the eye. "Stop it with this navel-gazing. If we do our jobs, Frid will be out of our hair in no time."

***

KESH shrugged on her rainwear and air purifying mask to head into the oppressive sunlight of City Six. The light amplified the heat and the smell of the city, especially during the rain, making surface level transit unbearable when the Sun was up. Adding that to the antipathy that Dark Mages felt for the Sun, it was going to be a trying day.

The problem with being a Journeyman was that you were too useful. Master Mages couldn't trust the apprentices with important errands, but they knew Journeymen were eager to make their mark in the guild and prove that they were suitable for Mastery. This made them willing to undertake the most boring and tedious of tasks. Some of the Adepts had a knack for discovering exactly what you most hated, while being petty enough to constantly use you for that particular purpose. Others were just so entranced by their workings that they had forgotten the tedium of everyday life, to them their juniors were little more than handy tools for menial tasks.

That was the problem with Prior Wallang. He had spent years in the basement of the compound inscribing incantations on the obsidian floors in search of knowledge so esoteric most other Adepts thought he might have gone soft in the head. But he was a Prior and a busy man, at least to his own mind, so Kesh was stuck going to the antiquities dealers, the scriveners, the gem sellers, and any number of random shops in the commons, searching for rare components for Wallang's magic. On a beautiful night, Kesh didn't mind the chance to get out of the compound, but today omnipresent rain left her scuttling between shelter dragging her soaked self from store to store while aboveground. The acid soaked her and she knew the smell of sulfur that permeated the Undercity would last for days. She just hoped she wouldn't stain this time.

The chemist the Prior favored was many levels below the mountain surface. In City Six, nothing was illegal, but psychoactive substances would always have their opponents. The more esoteric, the harder they were to find. There were more reputable chemists above, full of designer drugs, but they didn't traffic in the eccentric products required by some Mages. The shop required Kesh to descend an elevator five levels, walk to the end of a long walkway and take a spindly, almost forgotten stairwell down to UL17. Rain never penetrated these parts of the city, but dirty, sulfurous water dripped from the levels above, pooling in odd corners and rusting the metallic components of the grating. Kesh was sure that one day the path to the scriveners would crumble beneath her feet, sending her tumbling into the even ghastlier levels below.

The chemist was located in a dark corner of a mall marked alternately by fluorescent noodle shops, brightly lit grocers, and heavily shaded shops that peddled darkly mysterious goods to those in the know. The front was barely marked by a faded sign, but Kesh recognized the faded purple book on the door and ducked in out of the throng of people bustling to get meals for their families.

The chemist had always skeeved Kesh out, which was an accomplishment for a Mage steeped in the lore of the darkest planes of this world and the next. Despite the widespread availability of high-tech clothing from Tube and Sphere, he always wore a dark, linen robe that mimicked the robes worn by Mages in long ago fics. Made by hand of natural plant fibers from Sphere, it must have cost a fortune. Kesh didn't like him enough to point out that his affectation was unrealistic, as magic didn't care about clothes, only runes. Mage's habit of wearing long sleeved, high collared clothing had more to do with concealing their rune tattoos than anything to do with the clothing itself. He accompanied his robe of darkness with overly greasy hair, yellowed teeth, and a bad habit of leaving yesterday's food on his person. He would come out and stand too close to her, if she gave him the space to come out from behind the beaten stainless-steel counter that he treated like a pulpit. He was lucky that he was the only chemist with the skill to make the drug the Prior needed or Kesh would have considered lighting his fancy robe on fire just a little bit to teach him some respect.

Kesh stared at the massive wall of pills, searching in vain for the item she required. The place was a maze and the inventory moved frequently. She figured that the clerk did it just to spite his customers and force them to discuss their whereabouts with him. Kesh caved, she was going to have to do this the hard way.

"Do you have the Shadow Haze that Prior Wallang requested?" she asked, trying to start out pleasant before the snark inevitably overtook her. Maybe Wallang's name will hurry this along.

"I'm waiting for a new shipment for the base from Mars. Someone came in last week and cleared us out." The clerk was clearly proud of his big sale, and of inconveniencing Kesh by leaving her empty-handed.

Kesh started in surprise. Shadow Haze was made from a rare Martian mineral containing the fossils of crustaceans from time past and cost a fortune. It was also essentially useless for anyone but certain, very picky, Mages, and Prior Wallang was the only Dark Mage on Embla both wealthy and particular enough to use it. Who else here on Embla would want such a thing? Kesh sagged, both because she would have to come back to this hellhole and because she would have to immediately exit into the disgusting brownish rain. Kesh eyed the shelves of rare drugs, wishing that she had Wallang's freedom to pursue whatever he wanted magically. She could make such beautiful designs for battle armor if she could use drugs like these to expand her magical access.

Kesh steeled herself to loiter just a little longer in the chemists and hopefully safeguard against future supply interruptions. "Can I pre-pay for the next batch that arrives then? You can ping me when it comes in. I know the Prior is eager to get started on his project."

"That's… acceptable," he replied. "You know you could learn a thing or two from the pretty blonde who bought the Haze. She was much easier to deal with."

"Was she now? Another Dark Mage I take it?" Kesh tapped her comm to transfer the credits. Intel on the buyer would probably be worthwhile, Wallang will want to know who's meddling in his craft.

"No, you're all black and boring. You don't bring any light or beauty with you when you're out and about. Criminals, the lot of you. She was a joy in a bright purple cloak. Maybe you should consider a color sometime." He was warming to his obnoxious topic.

"I'll consider it for my next visit. Send me a message when you've made the Haze and I'll be along to get it. Keep in mind that if it's too slow, the Prior himself might show up on your doorstep." Kesh smiled as she exited. I hope the thought of an irate member of the Ring in his shop makes him piss himself.

Apparently in this wrinkly old man's mind customer relations only went one way. She was supposed to make his day pleasant, but not vice versa. Wallang would make it terrifying if he was forced to wait too long. Kesh squared her shoulders, gathered her bags, and set back out into the mall to make the long journey back aboveground, pondering the mystery blonde in purple who would buy the Prior's preferred magical intoxicant out from under him.

262ND DAY OF 11566 AF

PATIENT S.A. was confined in our facilities on the 58th of 11478. The original notes by then facility head Arthur Dean notes "S.A. presented to an emergency room with extreme agitation and multiple lesions on every part of the body including the face. Due to the patient being non-verbal, identity was established using a standard ID scan of a standard implanted insurance chip. S.A. displayed increasing levels of myoclonus, forcing the use of restraints. The emergency nurse pointed out growths protruding from several of the lesions that had not been previously noted. The patient was sedated. Over the course of the following hour, the centimeter length growths extended to over thirty centimeters in length. Some 43 protrusions were counted, distributed across the body of the patient, of particular note was the three growths on the patient's face."

— Monthly patient report S.A., Laden Allen, psychiatrist, 11563 AF

***

IT was the middle of the night or at least as much a middle of the night as you got on this planet that spun slowly enough that the sun wouldn't dip beneath the eastern horizon for another twenty days. The shining clean tower that made up the command structure of the eastern intake was quiet. The only people who had been around in the last hours except for the tower officer were maintenance personnel. Right now, the officer in charge of the night shift, a night shift of one, could see the two other staff out the window working on the floors of the hanger. She was eight hours in on her third twelve-hour shift. It was getting real hard to keep focus.

There was still work to do because there was always more work to do than there was time to do it. There were still ships coming in. The ones leaving weren't really her purview; however, she did need to check every single incoming craft. It was painstaking work, detail-oriented, and it needed to look clean because the registers were public and frequently audited. Some auditors were guild reps making sure their people followed internal protocols, others were there to see what they could glean from their competition. There was a third type, the worst type, her supervisors. Overzealous audits that seemed to be invented mainly to make her life more difficult. It was commonly known that all the flight control officers were taking kickbacks from time to time to falsify incoming logs, but it was also expected that they were good enough to hide it that it would be entirely undetectable. Twice now she'd been caught by her supervisor, and each time the punishment had been to be separated from said kickback. She rubbed her temples, at least he'd been kind enough to inform her how she'd been caught. It wouldn't happen again.

As she flicked through the logs, she contemplated the brain-dead nature of it all. This really could be the job of a simple enough machine brain but then again those were highly regulated and she didn't really want to be made obsolete.

Not very eyebrow-raising. She sipped her coffee, or what almost passed for coffee as looked from one record to another. She'd been trying to cut out the caffeine and this substitute didn't really cut it. She sighed as she decided that this wasn't the day for keeping to resolutions. A few taps on her hand-held control panel instructed the tower system to send her a real cup. A low hum gave away the workings of pressurized liquid running through the prep in the kitchen. Less than a minute later she held a steaming cup in her hand, feeling deep relief. Giving up coffee would have to be a thing for a future time, a time that didn't include twelve-hour shifts.

There was a lull in arrivals, and in her boredom, she let her fingers walk her back in the logs. There was something in there that had raised an eyebrow. She hadn't actually seen the ship, but it sounded a little bit odd. A strange name, something she hadn't seen before, Toxicos. Not a scholar of old languages, she assumed it was just a fancy way of saying toxin.

She looked over the description: black, two-seater, yacht, custom build, City Six build. The description gave away that it was a ridiculously expensive craft, it read as something that you'd normally see in the hands of dignitaries or executives. In this case, it was registered to a guild rep, not even the guild, but the rep himself. She knew that some agents were independently wealthy, but they couldn't possibly be that rich. It must be registered like this to make it easier to hide. In her mind she crafted an intricate story about spies and adventures, that must be it, he's some kind of secret agent for a guild. Something straight out of a spy story. She smiled, having made up this little fantasy she really wanted to see this ship in person.

Maybe the ship would be nothing special, perhaps she was just being silly, but now she really wanted to see it in person, maybe she could validate her sleuthing. She was all smiles as she entered the elevator to dock three.

***

MASAN'S newfound zeal regarding hunting for Dark Guild sabotage since the changes in management had re-energized Meg. It wasn't all bad that Frid was shaking things up. She had been floating along, fulfilling her function and enjoying the benefits of a barbaric planet like Embla, without truly living up to her mission. It was easy to lose sight of her work for the Council when they were millions of kilometers away, physically and mentally.

Meg enjoyed working deep cover ops, but she had definitely been on the precipice of fully assimilating as a member of the Tribe. It was full of kind, interesting people and sometimes it was hard to juggle that with the untouchable, superior being she knew herself to be; especially as her job was to blend in seamlessly with their day-to-day lives.

Frid's arrival had catalyzed a major change in their team's outlook. Meg respected Masan and she wanted his approval, but she didn't fear him. Even though she knew a Master Light Mage lurked under his friendly facade, he wasn't intrinsically intimidating. Frid was intimidating to the point of terrifying. It hadn't taken her long to realize that he had euthanized Peanna's misborn son, in accordance with Light Council doctrine. It was a silent reminder that failure would not be tolerated and that severe punishments awaited those who stepped out of line. Frid expected the same excellence as the Council.

Meg never had any trouble with the Council growing up. She had been delighted to leave her family on Mars and travel to the Light Stations when her magic became apparent. Her family worked for one of the corporations and had been far too busy to really pay attention to her. She had fully embraced the superiority of Light Mages, knowing that they cared about and paid attention to their apprentices. It was the first time that Meg had had standards that went beyond not being an embarrassment. The Council wanted her to succeed and join their ranks. She had risen to the challenge of proving herself worthy of their teachings.

Meg had been a little disappointed to discover early on that she would never be an Adept class mage, but she had been a successful apprentice and journeyman. She had narrowly made the requirements for mastery and supplemented her magical skills with tech skills to make sure that she was as competent as possible. She had been proud to be assigned to work on the City

Six mission because she knew that she was in the stronghold of the enemy.

That most of the enemy populace was in no way in conflict with the Light Council had been a surprise at first. Although there were millions of non-mages on the Light Stations, Meg had always imagined that City Six was teeming with Dark magic. And it was, relative to most parts of the galaxy, but that still meant that 99% of the population were just everyday people trying to make a living. The novelty of being close to the Dark Guilds had worn off when Meg realized that they were more invested in inter-guild espionage than counter-Light magic surveillance. The Dark mages of City Six were secure in their supremacy in this place.

Frid brought back attention to the urgency of their mission. The Dark Guilds here had played them for fools, letting them think that they were toothless criminals bent on profit when they were actually devious creatures focused on eradicating access to the Light plane for everyone on City Six.

Meg had put out her feelers for as many threads of Dark Guild activity as possible. She had placed the taps requested in the Fusion Forge and at the spaceports. Now she just had to do her best to coax her human network into telling her more than they intended.

That was why Meg had been spending her non-Tribe evenings frequenting watering holes favored by port workers and folks who worked in shipping and receiving. She was leaving bugs that could tap into the gossip in those places, so she could look out for unusual activity that smacked of Guild criminality. She knew that if she were patient someone would eventually let something slip.

⁂

MEG had been monitoring her new channels for a week when something finally turned up. Two port workers were sitting in a pub by one of City Six's less popular ports. The conversation revolved around a ship that had just arrived in dock.

"She's a real beauty alright. Fully custom built here on Embla by the design."

"I wonder how much it costs to get something like that made."

"More money than well see in a lifetime"

"Who even owns a ship like that? Must be a Guild ship, eh?"

"It's registered to an individual, not a guild. It's interesting because I could have sworn he was moving human cargo."

"I heard that he got all up in the Tower's face when she asked to have a look at it."

"Mages, eh? Fuck 'em."

It seemed like Meg had found something that might interest Frid after all. She was going to need assistance to pull this off, but she didn't want to tip everyone off until she was sure that she had found something useful. Who should she ask to help? Ideally, she would ask Gere in case she ran into trouble, but he was far too hidebound to run an op like this without clearance and Meg figured she'd need to move fast. It would have to be Kaleb and Freya. She sighed and cued her comm to pull them to a rendezvous out by the hanger.

***

LIN heard the rain drum on the window. A cold metal cuff sat snugly around her ankle as she lay in a cot with her eyes half closed. She had been conscious for a few hours, though she didn't let it show. She'd heard a conversation between Sal and who she assumed was his boss or employer. He had sounded less self-assured than she was used to, more deferential, not quite scraping his foot, but almost. She had only heard parts of the conversation, but from what she could piece together she was now on Embla, City Six to be exact. Should have known from the smell, she thought. This was not how she'd imagined her destination. She had also caught that she was supposed to be moved somewhere in the morning, whenever that was, she didn't know where though. She did know that Sal was supposed to stay with her until she was moved; he hadn't. He'd uttered something like "Sleep well princess" in a sardonic tone before heading out in the rain. Lin couldn't tell how long ago she'd been left here, but she was glad that Sal hadn't reappeared, the presence of the man she once called friend sickened her.

Carefully, to not make any noise, Lin reached down to her cuff, running her finger along it. A mechanical contraption, very sturdy. Convinced there wasn't anyone watching her too closely she dared a glance. She couldn't see runes or anything giving away an electronic system in the cuff, telling her that it was most likely entirely mechanical. She'd always been pretty good with locks, but it had been years since she last tried something like this without professional tools.

Lin smiled to herself, at least he'd been stupid enough to leave her hands free. It's good to be underestimated sometimes. As the thought flashed through her mind, she set to work. The first piece she found was a steel wire that had been used to secure a door of a wooden crate at the head of the bed. With some bending back and forth she broke off a palm-width of the wire. The bed was made from welded metal tubing and the caps were covered with flimsy aluminum caps to make them less sharp. She kicked one of these caps loose and proceeded to attempt to shear off one half of it. She did this by pinning it underneath the leg of the bed and pulling on the far edge. Unfortunately, she didn't have pliers, so her hands had to suffice. It took a few tries and a severe cut on her right index finger. Deep breath, it didn't even hit bone, don't be a wuss. With her tools finished she got to work on the lock. She felt for the pins, counted them. When she was certain of the count, she went on to figure out how to lock them back. Antiquated design, good. Having figured the lock out she quickly raked with some tension, she got five pins in the first try, four in her second, then four again, and then all eight. The lock sprung open.

Lin made her way out from where she'd been tucked, into a corner of what seemed to be a huge shipping container. As she came around the corner of a pile of crates her heart sank. The exit of the container was closed and the light that had been let in was filtered through what must be blast-glass. No chance of breaking through that with brute force, and no exposed locks, hinges, or electronics on this side of the door.

Turning to the containers, she hoped against hope that someone had been dumb enough to leave something in here that would be a useful tool to aid her escape. She found a thin round metal bar tucked between crates; it was a piece sturdy enough to use as a crowbar to open the crates that were stacked throughout the space.

Pain seared through her hands as she slammed the steel bar into a narrow crack in the first crate, and she had to use her whole body weight to make the top of it budge. The crate came open with a loud crack, reminding her that she had no idea who might be around to hear the commotion. After giving her heart time to calm down, and making sure no-one had heard, she pushed the lid off the crate. The motion stirred up a puff of powder from within, and the aroma slammed against her. Cacao.

She didn't let the disappointment of the first crate get to her, she continued with a second box. Tea. A third came open. More cacao. It was the fourth that got her. Coca. She looked around in exasperation. All of the boxes looked identical. They were all labeled with the same print from a shipping company off Sphere. They'll all be the same, nothing here but teas and herbs. She fell back against the wall of the container and sank to her knees, looking at her beat-up hands. Well, that was all a big waste. She felt on the verge of tears when she heard footsteps outside.

"It's in here." It was a woman's voice.

"Are you sure? I don't see any labels," a young man said.

"I'm sure, I can count, you cunt! Didn't you hear what Mark said? Twenty in." The woman again.

"Fine, no need to be an ass."

"Sorry, we're in a hurry. Can you break this lock?"

"Absolutely, it's last year's model."

Silence. Then the whirring of a motor pulling back the bolts of the door.

"Oh, hi there! I see you're halfway out already."

Lin looked at the woman who was smiling at her. The light at her back illuminated her honey-brown hair.

The woman's smile disappeared as she continued, "Well, what are you waiting for? Come on, I don't want to be here when your absent-minded jailer comes back."

Lin got to her feet and almost stumbled as she exited from the raised floor of the container where she'd been kept.

"Be quiet till we've cleared the facility. We're really not supposed to be here, but we've got someone who'll look the other way as long as we're quick."

✻✻✻

THE shuttle to the tower of the docks was just as fast as always, but to Sal it felt like it was standing still. They arrived and the compartment opened with a low hydraulic hiss. The moment he was out of the cramped space he was moving with quick steps towards the central elevators. People who saw the grim, focused look in his eyes sidestepped. The ones who weren't attentive got bumped or shoved out of the way. He passed the line to the elevator, ignoring upset voices. As the gate opened the man who was at the front drew breath to tell him off but changed his mind the moment he looked at Sal. It passed Sal's mind that dark trails of energy licked the lapels of his jacket and, catching his reflection in the elevator door, he saw his eyes swimming with black cloudy tendrils. As he got on the elevator, he calmed his breathing and pushed his channels as closed as he could. Corruption was pushing itself through without him noticing.

As Sal came around the corner a woman appeared. She was standing next to his yacht. She was touching it. An agent of Leanne? She shouldn't have had time to send anyone so fast. Probably a civilian, but better safe than sorry. He pulled enough darkness in to fuel one of his sharper spells before speaking, "Get away from that."

The woman turned, startled, and took a step back. "Ow, sorry, is this yours? I was just."

"I don't care. If you're one of hers, know that I have a razor at your neck. Walk away and I won't use it." The line of dark energy hung in the air just above the woman's shoulder.

"What? What do you mean?"

"Last warning. Walk away. I don't want to kill you."

She raised her hand, he couldn't tell if it was to protest or to get into an offensive stance, and he didn't wait to find out. Her head dropped to the floor with a wet thud.

"You really should have walked away…"

263TH DAY OF 11566 AF

STARING at the screen of her table, Leanne let out a faint whimper of frustration. How could this have happened? Her component was lost in transit right here in town, and of course, after she had signed over the payment to that damned pirate. How could she have been so foolish; she should never have trusted others with any part of the transport. She pulled herself up straight. Focus. The questions now were: how and why had this happened? Her shipment was valuable to her and her alone. Still, some people would steal anything, no matter how low the value. The other risk to consider was the issue of bleeding hearts having been involved. Some people, even here on Embla, had moral qualms about humans as property. She'd heard of these misguided souls setting captives free. It was time for action. In one snakelike flowing motion, she got up, produced her comm from its invaginated hiding space on her wrist, and grabbed a dark green coat from its peg. Before she took a step outside her door, she had gotten her contact in customs on the line. "I need help, any drones you can swing, we've got a manhunt to organize."

***

A small Arrow class yacht was accelerating away from the orange celestial body commonly known as Embla. The craft, painted in a very unconventional "absolute black" was making good speed, far faster than technically allowed in this heavily trafficked part of the system. Inside this very expensive, but slightly odd craft, a clinical lack of decorations gave hints of a pragmatic and clean owner. This owner was Sal, and he was very pale. "Fuckfuckfuck I'm gonna die, fuckfuckfuck." He silently mouthed the words while focusing all his efforts on keeping his craft in one piece. He was channeling more magic than ever before, and still, he couldn't force the acceleration he wanted, though it's doubtful that there was any speed high enough for Sal in this moment. His hands burned as the force coursed through his tattoos. Sweat beaded on his face. The transmission from his friend in the docks still echoing in his mind, "She escaped." The moment he heard the words he had started running. He was still running. He knew if there was any way Leanne could find him, what awaited was worse than he could ever imagine.

Tube was his only hope. What irony, he thought…

He pushed on and on, outward, towards salvation. The sky ever dark felt even darker, and it calmed him. To someone of his talents, the void was bliss. Magic flowed easily now. The further away from the sun, and all the reflective surfaces of the planets, the easier everything was. Looking down at the time displayed on-screen he sighed a breath of relief. He'd managed to get to point one light speed within a few hours, he'd be at Tube in less than three days. He'd heard of very few travelers that had beaten his current pace, and all of those were fully crewed military attack ships. No ships like that on Embla. That horrific old crone couldn't reach him now.

After punching in the sequences needed for the ship to keep course and steady low acceleration he got up, and almost immediately fell over. Sal caught himself on a polished handle, narrowly avoiding smashing his eyebrow on the edge of a cabinet. He realized how much this sprint had cost him. He'd been so caught up in his panic, and the ecstasy of so much magic flowing, that he hadn't noticed. He looked at his hands, cracked lines spread between the lines of his tattoos, black and squirming. A deep cold had set in, if he had gone much longer, he would have done permanent damage. A shudder went down his spine. Running from a fate worse than death to almost incur another.

Sal leaned back in the aft seat of his small, streamlined craft. Touching a panel, he directed the details of a drink. He liked fine-tuning these things each time, hoping to find the perfect flavor. It was something that soothed him in times of stress—taste and aromas we'e good at filling the mind with tangible but non-threatening questions. He needed the distribution right now. Again, he frowned as he chastised himself internally. He'd never worked with Leanne before even though he knew her well, correction: because he knew her well. He knew how far she carried a grudge, and he'd seen the aftermath. The image that flashed in front of his eyes brought a watery feeling to his mouth as if he was on the edge of throwing up. At just the right moment, his system produced a glass with the clear fragrant liquid in its tubular receptacle next to his seat. He brought it to his nose and let the aroma drown out the taste in his mouth and the dark memories with it.

***

LIN raced along behind the purple bedecked woman as she navigated the twists and turns of City Six's undercity. Lin was getting tired, the aftereffects of whatever Sal had done to her had been making her sluggish despite all of the adrenaline in her system. She figured he'd probably drugged her on top of whatever spell or weapon he'd used to knock her out. The woman ahead of her did not let up, descending further and further into the understructures. They had gotten on several elevators, as well as bullet trains; each time Lin had turned to the woman, head spinning with questions. Every time Lin had opened her mouth to ask something the woman, Meg, had hushed her. Now Lin struggled to keep up in the unfamiliar cloak that helped to hide her from prying eyes.

Finally, after a solid hour of running between modes of transport, as well as sections on foot in dark alleys, they arrived at a massive door and came to a halt.

"I'm sorry about that. We kind of took the long way here, but I wanted to be sure that no one followed us. My friends will catch up eventually."

The woman's friends had split into several different parties after one of them had tossed her their cloak. Presumably, they had gone off to provide a distraction and would return when they felt like it.

"Thanks for the save." Lin panted.

The woman opened the door into the largest warehouse Lin had ever seen.

"Welcome to the Tribe. Home to the downtrodden and cast-off of Embla's magical guilds, we give help and a home to anyone in need. I'm not really sure who you are, but you certainly seemed like you were in need."

Meg escorted her to a gathering circle and motioned for her to sit. Lin collapsed gratefully onto a seat. She wanted to take in the weirdness of her surroundings, but she was exhausted and slightly dizzy from the drugs and the pursuit. If the world would just stop spinning for a bit, she would get her bearings.

Meg returned carrying a cup of water and took a seat next to Lin.

"You're safe here. The Tribe is beneath most people's notice. No one cares what we do or where we go. I think they see our joy in being ourselves as a nuisance."

"Thanks."

"You're welcome to stay here as long as you like. I'd love to hear your story when you're a bit less fucked up."

"I'd be happy to tell you. Though I'm not sure I know what's happening.

Why did you help me though? How did you even know where I was?"

"I can only give a partial answer to that. We get information sometimes from our man at the dock whenever one of the guilds does something extra unseemly. Like human trafficking. I despise that sort of thing and so does Masan. Oh, Masan is sort of the boss here. So, well, he sent me both for some humanitarian reasons, but also because we tend to take any opportunity to screw over bastards like that."

Meg took a deep breath before she continued, "I'll show you to one of the containers we keep for new arrivals. You can catch some safe shut-eye and we'll chat when you're ready."

"Container?"

"They're more like single-room apartments really. We don't really know exactly what they're made of but they're almost indestructible and they never rust. Super useful as makeshift living spaces."

"I guess. What exactly is this place though?" Lin looked around to really register the space. The roof was several stories above and supported on regularly spaced metal pillars. A large number of large shipping crates and containers were stacked relatively neatly both close to the entrance of the space, but a similar stack was also piled up much farther in, close to what looked like a series of old boarded-up access tunnels.

"It used to be one of the early industrial storage spaces long ago, you know during terraforming days. These days it's a hideout for the rejects of the guilds, magic as well as craft, though I'd say mages are overrepresented. So do you want me to hook you up with some room where you can recoup?"

Lin considered turning down the offer, now that she was safely away. Sleeping in one of the shipping containers stacked in piles didn't feel quite right. Where am I going if not here? she thought. She didn't know anyone on Embla, she had no way to access her credits; she was a fugitive, and she no longer had her comm. Her implants would boot and prime a new one if she could find one though. This place was weird, but it seemed safe enough. There were lots of people in the central area and they all seemed quite content. Meg had been nothing but helpful since she'd all but fallen over her trying to escape… whoever… had held her captive. She needed time to regroup safely.

"I'd like that," Lin told Meg.

"Then follow me and we'll get you sorted for a nap."

The space she was shown to was a bit strange as an apartment, but in that moment it didn't matter much. There was a bed, and some cupboards that mostly reminded her of all the things that had been left on the Astion. The Astion, I wonder if they're OK. He didn't kill them, did he? The thought cut deep.

The moment Meg was out of sight she pulled back the fabric of her sleeve. She exposed the comm integration in her skin, a centimeter-wide slit with the ability to open or close to allow for interfacing with different models. This unit also had some limited functionality without an external attachment, such as calls and video projection. Right now, she really needed to make that call she'd been dreading. What if he wouldn't answer? What would that mean? That he was dead? Or maybe just in hiding? Damn it Beral, why haven't you tried to contact me? The last thought was desperate, and she knew there might be a hundred reasons.

She touched the skin by her comm, opening a link that could take neural input, and she sent her message: "I'm alive, on Embla, I'm sure that whole thing with Sal was about me. Gods, I really hope you're around to get this.

I got away, and I'll hunt that bastard down. If you're still around after that, and if that doesn't turn out to solve my being wanted, I might meet up with you on the other side.

Before then I'd really appreciate a sign of life you oaf! You're one of my best friends and you're not allowed to be dead!"

Even though she'd dictated the message by neural feed it felt like her voice was catching, those last words had been such searing pain. He's not dead, he's not allowed to be dead! She cursed the signal delay that meant which she had no chance of getting a response in the next eleven hours.

***

MASAN looked up as he saw the entry into Light Headquarters open. He had been puttering around, trying to figure out what the hell to do with Frid while his network worked to find out more about the Dark energies that were skewing the balance.

He was surprised when Meg popped up. She didn't normally come in to see him directly. Usually, she checked in via message or comm, staying with the general members of the Tribe to keep her cover. He suspected that she preferred their company to the other Light mages, but she had never quite conceded that that was the case.

Masan met Meg's gaze and raised an eyebrow at her unusual presence.

"I found someone unusual today," Meg said.

"Someone? Not something?"

"Decidedly someone. I found a woman who was carted unconscious into one of the warehouses by the spaceport by the Dark Mage owner of the Toxicos. The ship is owned by an individual, not one of the guilds, so I made a judgment call, looped in Kaleb and Freya and 'rescued' her."

"Do you think this has something to do with the Dark Mages we're investigating?" asked Masan.

"Honestly, I have no idea. She was too out of it after all of the fleeing and running to get much out of her, but it's not every day you see a solo human being trafficked by a Dark Mage of unknown origin. I sent her to have a nap. I figured caring and compassion would work better than heavy handed inquisition to start."

"Your judgment is usually sound, I guess we'll find out when she's returned to the land of the conscious," Masan replied. "Ping me when she wakes, and I'll make sure to come and greet our newest arrival. Maybe she's a missing piece of our Dark magic puzzle."

"Will do."

And with that Meg departed.

***

THE rain was still pouring. Two figures stood face to face in the downfall, a tall, scarred man, and a young blonde petite woman with almost too perfect light colored smooth skin. In spite of her small stature the man was visibly intimidated as she drilled her green-eyed gaze into him. The smell acrid and fumes stinging the eyes. Adjusting her oddly pristine and dry cloak Leanne repeated herself in a composed tone, "I'm here because I know you must have let her through."

The guard looked her straight in the eyes as he repeated himself, "No ma'am. No-one has left this way today."

Leanne's visage darkened. She had seen the feeds, this was the only exit from the warehouse where cameras had failed, the only possible way where her reagent could have been smuggled out. Her skin tickled as she let life stream into her from microbes, plants, and from the man in front of her. A shard of bone implanted in her arm twisted and turned, as if excited by being awakened. Life flowed through the runes of the shard; some twenty infinitesimal pieces of script interconnected by perfect microscopic cuts. She felt shapes flow under her skin towards her fingertip. She reached out and touched the chin of the guard. Tendrils, not quite plantlike, but almost, poured out along her finger and onto the skin of the man. His eyes widened but he appeared to not make any moves to get away. Leanne leaned in. She could see the scream in his eyes, she'd seen it many times before.

"Are you lying to me?" Her voice was cold as death. A tear ran down the face of the terrified man. A movement like a light nod. "Were they well dressed?" She got a negative response. She always needed to focus to retain her self-control when working this spell; a home brew she was very proud of, but would never share with any other adept. She was a bit saddened by the lack of recognition for all of her advances, but on the other hand she really wasn't one for sharing. The spell had become self-sustaining mere moments after she had begun, her focus was on not letting it progress too fast, not to strip this man of everything that made him human before she had gotten the information she'd come for. The interrogation continued for another ten minutes, with the man now being entirely forthcoming. She was satisfied that she'd gotten all she would. She released the man and he crumpled to the floor.

"Gil! You'll need someone new on this door. This one was defective." She had a slight smirk as she spoke. When she walked away, the corpse had already begun to decompose.

***

LIN curled up in the darkness of the container bed. The cold and dread built as she was left alone with her thoughts. The hour before sleep was always hard for her but during periods of high stress it was hell. She knew she had to sleep but her mind wouldn't let go of all of the things she could and should be doing. A hundred risks and a hundred courses of action spun in her head. Proxima Centauri had been her shot at escaping the unknown person or corp who had put a bounty on her head and now that pipe dream had gone up in smoke. She thought that Sal was her friend, and the shattered illusion had removed any sense of safety or security she might have felt in her flight. How could she trust anyone when it seemed that her judgment was so bad that she had thought of Sal as a friend and not a threat. Now it was clear that she had been his mark all along, no one else from the Astion had been taken. Apparently, her self-professed skills at knowing people and telling lies didn't hold true in this terrible, new, high stakes world she'd entered.

Lin felt queasy and exhausted. Could she trust her mysterious benefactors? Or were they just another step in the life-or-death game of cat and mouse she seemed to be playing with this unknown menace? Lin was sick and fucking tired of running and reacting. She was a goddamn engineer, and she didn't shy away from her problems. She picked up her tools and solved them. Lin had already resolved to turn the tables on her pursuer; eventually she drifted off to sleep thinking up ways to find and confront them, so she could have her life back.

***

A hissing sound of hydraulics punctuated the sealing of the chamber from the outside world. With the sound, a change came over the figure of Leanne. She grew taller, more regal, more notable. The large green raincoat fell off her shoulder as she shrugged, and before it hit the floor a branch stretched out from the wall and caught it. The coat was pulled up to its proper place next to the heavy steel door, held by what looked like a stylish and quite inanimate wooden knob. She flicked a finger, and the lights of her workstations all flickered on. Blues on yellows illuminated the large cave-like room. Vats underneath each light shimmered, some with the clear reflection of water, others with rainbows on tiny waves of oily liquid.

She stripped away the remaining layers of clothes: a collared white shirt, now stained with smears of oily black, crimson, and sickly green. Her pants were sticking to her skin, reeking of blood. With an annoyed grimace, she tugged off the final scrap, her panties, which were now soaked with unidentifiable fluids. Each piece made a damp noise as it hit the floor. Slithering vines were twitching in their eagerness to fulfill their tasks, to keep her home in perfect shape. They had already grabbed the pile and were dragging it in the direction of a gaping maw in the stone floor leading straight into the incinerator. Oh well, a daily wardrobe change is a small price to pay, she mused. The wounds covering her arms, legs, and stomach had already mostly stitched together; the worming of sharp organs calming down. A straying strip of sharp wet tissue had to be forcibly pushed back into the wound it had drilled underneath her breast. She placed a hand on a wooden pillar, the living wood seemed to shudder at her touch, eager to meet her halfway. She felt a surge of power as her constructs replenished what she'd burned through this evening. It flowed through the wood and into her, refilling the emptied stores, and activating one of the many rune-engraved bone shards embedded deep in her body. The wounds on her skin contracted, quivering and they started to fade. The ever-present writhing of her skin subsided to where it was hardly noticeable. If only I could spend all my time in a place like this, she thought. The thought was forgotten as soon as it came. She couldn't afford to waste time. She moved her hand away from the tree and placed it on the edge of one of the reservoirs of oily liquid, sap from the tree that made up so much of the surfaces of the room. Magic surged through the structure and into the liquid, without any resonance or answer from the corruption dormant in her. She directed the energies into the surface that grew still, frozen in place, and she willed the runes to appear.

As she released the control of magic the sap reformed, it swam into the shape of thousands of small dark beads, they grew legs, extended, and started moving. The mat of dark newly spawned spiderlings swarmed towards the exit. She made a motion that opened the door, and within seconds they were gone, out in the city searching for Lin.

264TH DAY OF 11566 AF

LIN flashed awake suddenly. The last time she had come to she had been a captive and her body was not over its fight or flight response. She was still wrapped up in borrowed blankets and alone inside the container. Lin had no idea how much time had passed since she had fallen asleep. For the first time since childhood, she was without any tech or comms to tell her the time. If she was awake, she might as well face the challenge of meeting the rest of the people who had saved her.

Masan considered how best to approach the young woman that Meg had brought in now that she was up and moving. Meg would see to her personal needs and bring her to him for a meal. It had not been even twenty-four hours since she had gone through a major traumatic experience. It wouldn't do to push too hard, but he needed to imply that he had access to the bigger picture, in order to see if she had any nuggets of knowledge to drop in his lap.

He would need the charm of his benevolent father-figure persona, with just enough edge thrown in to convince her that she should be on his side in the upcoming conflict. Assuming she had anything to do with it.

Masan found his mark in the large common area close to the kitchen, where she was having a snack and being friendly with a couple of the younger Tribe members.

"I'm glad to see you're up and moving about. Meg told me about your escapade yesterday. I'm happy you're unharmed."

"Thanks," Lin answered in a guarded tone. Masan could tell that she wasn't going to give him what he needed easily, she was far too suspicious at this point. And probably rightfully so.

"I'm Masan, the de facto leader slash custodian of the Tribe, at your service."

"Oh, well, I'm Lin. Thanks for letting me in."

"So, where are you from originally?"

"What makes you so sure I'm not from here? Isn't that a bit presumptuous?"

"I'd recognize an Emblan anywhere." Masan smiled a disarming smile. "I'm just someone who's interested in your story, and what brought you to the

Tribe in your hour of need."

"Alright... I was born on Mars, but I traveled a lot."

"What made you decide to get off-world? I hear Mars is a lovely planet."

"I was, I mean, I am a spaceship engineer. And I followed the money. I took work where it paid the most. I used to work for a small corp on Mars," as Lin was speaking, it was apparent to Masan that she hesitated a bit too much. Definitely still hiding most details, he thought.

"A respectable profession," Masan mused.

"Is yours not? A respectable profession that is."

"Hahahah." Masan's laugh rang like a bell through the Tribalists assembled for mealtime. "You know you're the first person to ask me that. Emblans just assume that anyone in, or associated with, the Tribe is a quasi-useless degenerate. I would say that my profession, or calling, is to take care of the outcasts of mage society. And I think it's respectable, even though I doubt most of the Guilds here in City Six would agree."

"You're all mages?" Lin asked, visibly taken aback.

"No, most are family members of mages. But we're a fair number of gifted people as well." Masan smiled his most disarming smile.

"And outcasts?"

"You're definitely not from these parts if you have to ask. Let me do my best to explain society here in City Six." Masan leaned back, deep in thought. "This is a mage guild dominant place, unlike Sphere or Mars. All of Embla is. The power, the prestige, and the wealth are all associated with the Mage Guilds who unofficially, officially run the city. There are many powerful Guilds here, but the most prominent are the three Dark Mage Guilds: Apteryx, Asio, and Strix. Those three snatch up the most talented from all across the planet. They take in all children with Dark magical aptitude but, when you're in your early teens you start to have to prove your worth to the Guild, and if it isn't deemed enough, you're 'released'. Sent to return to a family you may not have seen in years, jobless and essentially only trained to be a mage. This is much the same in all the formal ethereal and mundane Guilds." the exasperated look on Masan's face wasn't faked, he really thought the system was deeply flawed, If it could even be called a system...

He continued, "So, this city turns out many half-trained rejects with no viable skills in the tech economy, who may or may not have a home to go back to. The regular folks of Embla aren't always too positive around people who they consider to be trained for murder and mayhem, so a lot of these kids can't just turn around and become shopkeepers or pharmacists. That's where I come in. I give the Guild rejects a home, because I value them as human beings and not just as tools."

"Oh…" said Lin.

"Technically we give a home to anyone who wants a second chance and is willing to work on our collective behalf."

Lin made a face. "You're not like those cult-like maniacs from Naós are you? I can't tolerate that."

"No, we're not religious in that sense. We see people as individuals with skills, some magical and some practical. We help people to maximize what they have to build a community that's full of the joy of being human, not restricted to a hierarchy based on magical power."

"So, you're the resistance?"

"In a way. Most of the Guild mages feel that we're beneath their notice. The few who do care treat us with a bit of pity and sadness that they lose their friends to places like ours, when they don't meet their potential. Occasionally, we scoop up a more talented mage. Like, Frederik over there. He's a fire mage and he left his Guild when they rejected his daughter for Journeyman training. He joined us to keep his family together."

"That certainly caused a bit of a stir, but they can't do much to force people to stay. Mages of his skill are far too dangerous to keep around if they're dissatisfied. Someone like that losing control could destroy everything around them." Masan shook his head. "We resist the notion that we should be judged based on magical aptitude. And of course, we frown on the careers of crime that many mages engage in, especially the Dark Mage Guilds."

"What kind of crime?" Lin asked, her tone keen.

Masan could tell that he had finally found the lure that would keep her interest. She had tried to be nonchalant throughout the conversation, but she definitely showed increased interest in the subject of the Dark Guilds.

"Those guilds do everything from run drugs to assassinations to human trafficking. Although Apteryx doesn't do 'squish' and Strix doesn't approve of drugs. They're centers for corporate espionage, smuggling, and more."

"Sounds profitable. Weird to hear that they have some morals."

"Well, Apteryx hates trafficking because it's messy, not because they value human lives. They got out a couple of centuries ago due to a big mess. Strix just thinks that the drug trade is meaningless and that people should ascend via magic, not chemicals."

"Good to know. How do you know a mage is part of one of those Guilds?"

"If they are children, it will be because they're wearing a uniform. If they're adults, you might be able to tell their magical affinity by their corruption. But you're unlikely to be able to tell which Guild unless they have insignia or feel like sharing."

"Well, then. Feel like sharing? What type of mage are you? How come you ended up here?"

Masan nodded, he'd anticipated this question, and it was one he'd rehearsed the answer to so many times he almost felt like it could be real. "I used to be a Fire mage myself, same as Frederic. I'd even claim I used to be even more powerful. I was careless however, I drew too much in, and it burnt me out. I can't so much as light a candle these days. Suffice to say the guild didn't have much use for me after that."

***

LIN contemplated her earlier chat with Masan. He'd hit all of the right notes about the tragedy of minor mages and the way the guilds considered them disposable. And yet, something wasn't quite right.

Lin had limited experience with cults. Her family had taught her to avoid Naós like the plague back on Mars, so she wasn't very experienced with matters of faith. But, even with their jibber jabber about enlightenment and the very joys of existing, Lin detected cynicism beneath Masan's jovial exterior. Maybe that was what it took to lead a group like this, or maybe he wasn't even aware that he had let something slip. But Lin didn't quite feel right about him. Given her recent experiences with betrayal, she wasn't about to give him her trust anytime soon.

Lin's time with the rest of the Tribe had been relatively unremarkable. They worked together as a community to feed themselves and to keep their lives full. There was lots of music and art to go with a hefty helping of anti-Guild sentiment. Many of the members of the Tribe came by their hatred of the Guilds honestly. They had been separated from their families, their lives focused solely on magic, and then when they came of age and showed no more than marginal aptitude, they had been rebuffed. Sent back to strangers who were unaccustomed to the burden of feeding and clothing them. In some cases, they had nowhere to go, as their families had relocated while they were in school. They tended to ply what little magic they had as part of trades as craftspeople. No one in the Tribe had what Lin would consider a normal job.

Members of the Tribe came and went at all hours, pursuing their various callings. Lin had been surprised to find that begging in public wasn't required of all of the members, even though that was the major impression that the public had of the Tribe. It seemed that the Tribe thrived on underground commerce related to foodstuffs and minor magic, and the begging was more of a recruitment tactic than anything else. It made sure that people in need knew that the Tribe existed and let them find them without finding the Tribe's actual home.

It was that kind of tactical decision that made Lin wary. On one hand, the Tribe was all about raising up the downtrodden. On the other hand, they had serious security precautions, which was odd since the rest of City Six pretty much ignored them.

Lin had been all over the common areas of the Tribe as surreptitiously as possible and had found nothing. There was only one area left, the offices and storage area. Lin hadn't seen very many people go in or out. Most of the Tribe hated structure and organization, probably as pushback against their Guild upbringings. Lin had been told that all areas were open to her, but she wasn't sure if that was true.

She was contemplating her next course of action when Masan showed up in the common area for dinner. Lin tried to pull her attention away from him, but she was still struck by how warm and open he seemed with the Tribe. The people here loved him. There he was kissing babies and complementing the grub like some kind of corporate spokesperson. Why did she still have such reservations?

✲✲✲

MASAN was frustrated by their lack of progress. Meg had managed her little stunt with the Fusion Forge, but there wasn't a lot of evidence of an increase in dangerous black magic in their files. None of the guilds had spiked a sudden surge in precious metal orders. What had seemed like a brilliant idea had been for naught. Though he was sure their little listening device would be useful in the future.

It was hard being away from the Light Archives. The Council was one of the most ancient organizations in the solar system and they had records dating back before the fall. Had he been on-station, he could have easily looked for ingredients in dangerous Dark magic. Here he was limited to the non-restricted sections of the Archive. Well, mostly limited to those, he thought, feeling some slight guilt over having copied a set of select documents he felt uncomfortable about not having at hand. The Council couldn't risk a Dark stronghold like Embla breaching their more sensitive records and research. He was going to have to be clever or ask for more help from back home.

They had tried the quiet, passive routes to information. It was now time to put the human element in play. Masan sent an encrypted message to his team's comms.

"Time to play dirty. Pull in all of your Dark contacts and shake the trees. Use whatever tactics you need."

Maybe they would get lucky and one of their sources would drop a hint into one of the Guilds that led them to the source of the magic.

***

AFTER several days with the Tribe, Lin started to notice some interesting patterns. Most of the Tribe were warm, vivacious people, but a few, including her benefactor Meg, stood out for being much cooler and more aloof. Interestingly, these ice people stayed far away from Masan. She had rarely, if ever, seen them interact. She couldn't decide if it was about them finding Masan's nature overbearing or if there was something more sinister afoot. Many of these people spent a lot of time out in City Six, away from the Tribe. It seemed like they had a lot of business outside the walls of the Tribe.

Lin was causally observing Gere where he was sitting alone at a table. He was a handsome man; she would give him that, but his demeanor was like ice. Her attempts to unearth more of his back story had gone nowhere, as he seemed to barely socialize with the group. He didn't seem pleased to be here, so why had he stayed with the Tribe? Surely, a man of his sheer size could find labor opportunities elsewhere? Lin stayed away and limited herself to the occasional assessing look. Gere never even looked up from his meal.

***

THE warm light washed over the small troupe. The assembly room was the only safe space the Light Mage cadre had in City Six and the one place where they immediately dropped their masks when they walked in.

Gere was rapidly sorting through documents and reports projected in front of one of the brightly lit walls as he talked, having his comm transcribe the relevant notes. He didn't turn away from his work as a comm call came in from Masan. Masan had dialed in his whole team for this conference.

Gere had reviewed the recent reports from the others. He jumped in before Masan had time to mention what the call was supposed to be about, "She's watching us."

The others were silent.

"I kept it cool, but our surveillance shows that she's just a little too interested in Meg, Sinn, and I."

"I wonder what brought about that attention. It could just be sexual or self-preservation, you know, she's a woman alone who has gone through a trauma," Masan replied.

"Not to be one of those people, but she's not behaving like a victim,"

Gere replied. "Her attention is too cool and assessing. She's no wounded bird, sitting there looking for a rescue. And she's not showing any signs of being conflicted about an attraction and trying to fight it. She's trying to figure out what we do."

"I agree," said Meg. "She's been very interested in how we organize, how we make money, who does what. That's not a desperate person looking for aid, that's a person who is systematically evaluating our operation."

"Do you think she's a threat?" Masan asked.

"It's hard to say right now. Her flight and abduction could just be fabrications to gain our trust. But why bother, no one on Embla has ever shown an interest before. And her distress that day seemed very genuine."

"We haven't had much contact, but I peg her for a survivor. Don't let the small stature fool you into thinking she's not as hard as aerospace ceramic," Sinn chimed in. "It's my job to move around our inanimate chess pieces and she hasn't yet gotten too close."

"What do you recommend that we do?"

"Well, Masan. It's obvious that you didn't immediately charm her, the way you manage with most of these people. But maybe that's to be expected for a jittery off-worlder. You're going to have to try harder," replied Sinn.

"Maybe this time, be a little less charming and a little more honest. She strikes me as being perceptive enough to see beyond your façade. And she's jumping at shadows," Meg added.

"I think we should just dispose of her," Gere said, cutting straight to the point. "If we even have to have this conversation, we're acknowledging that we let in a serious security risk. Now's not the time to tolerate potential saboteurs in our midst."

"Let's not be too hasty. She doesn't have comms or funds right now. Maybe it's intentional, but maybe it's as it seems. I wouldn't want to waste a potential anti-Dark mage ally right when we need all the help we can get. Especially if we can use her as an in with Apteryx."

Masan hummed audibly "Yes, yes. I'll give it another go… Now, how about the intel from your sources…"

***

THE two mages sat opposite each other, bathed in bright white light, on each side of a square white table.

Frid looked at him curiously. "So, this girl, you think she's connected to our investigation?"

"Not in a direct way. I think she's of interest to Apteryx though, I'm sure this Sal she's talking about is one of their operatives. More than one of my people has relayed that name to me. It seems like he's a bit of a celebrity among the younger mages there. He seems like a moron to me, but they're all very impressed."

265TH DAY OF 11566 AF

LIN grabbed her coat, in all its purple glory, and wrapped it around herself. It was a surprisingly nice garment. Somehow, it was both breathable and protective. This place definitely needed the protective part, however successful terraforming had been, the place was still very sulfur-rich. A smelly shithole as so many had described it to her in the past. Now, experiencing it for herself she wasn't so sure she felt like that. The place had a strange charm, less reliant on tech, and in spite of its harsh conditions, a lack of protection here meant you'd come home with irritated skin and smelling like onions gone bad; that was a whole lot better than dead from decompression. She closed the big door to the container that she'd been considering home over the last week. Masan was leaning against a wall close to the exit of the cavernous home of the Tribe. He was a surprisingly handsome and put-together fellow for his age, which Lin pinned at between sixty and seventy.

"Ready for that walkabout?" His shout sounded cheery and impatient.

Lin waved and waited to get closer before responding, "Yes, yes, you're in such a hurry one would think I was the senior of the two of us."

"I can't help but feel a bit insulted. I don't look that old do I?"

Lin smirked. "I'm sure you look young for your age." She sold it with a wink.

"I think you're probably right." This time his voice gave away something tired. "Did you know I've been here running this show for more than fifteen years ?"

Lin felt somewhat surprised. "Oh really? I had no idea!"

"Ahh yeah. I came over here. From Mars. Back in eleven five five one. Built this to have something resembling a family."

Lin hesitated. Family wasn't something she had a good framework for. She nodded and smiled as she passed the old man and went for the door. "Come on, slowpoke. It's time to go."

As they wandered the narrow walkways Masan kept quizzing her on her history. "So, Mars? It's a good place to live, I lived there myself for many years. Most people I know wouldn't trade that for life in the void, and definitely not for Sphere."

"I never said I lived on Sphere"

"I may be old, but I'm not stupid. Following the money means work on Sphere, probably either for a local outfit, or more likely one of the large corps. Kras, no?"

Lin sighed, "Fine, got me, yeah I worked for Kras. To the point though: most anyone I knew on Sphere wouldn't have left for anything short of being chased out of there."

"I guess this just tells you that I socialize too much with mages and not enough with the rest of the world."

"Really? How's that? I mean I know Sphere doesn't have a lot of mages, but I figured they were just less visible there."

"No, no, there are way fewer of us there than anywhere else. There's some sort of bad vibe there that non-mages seem to be entirely unaware of. I mean you guys must be or it wouldn't be the most populated place in the system."

"So, you guys refuse to go there?" Lin asked.

"And those of us born there tend to leave as soon as they can."

Lin was deep in thought about the implications of this and missed a step as the metal grating dropped a few centimeters. She stumbled but caught herself on the railing. She shrugged it off and gestured at Masan that she was alright. She then continued as if she hadn't just almost twisted her ankle, "Weird. You don't know why?"

Masan smiled at the feigned casual attitude. "Not really. I know people who have tried to figure it out. Really, mages have been trying to crack that for millennia, but nobody has been successful as far as I know."

Lin was mulling that over as she walked. Hm, no mages on Sphere. After the assault by Sal, she regretted having left Sphere. "So, how severe is this thing, this 'bad vibe'? Does it mean mages would refuse to go there?"

"You mean, if you had stayed, would you have been safe from Sal and the likes? No, probably not. As I said, it's just a bad feeling, it isn't actually that would stop a mage who's going there with a purpose."

"I see." Lin felt heavy, as false hope left her. A moment of forgetting that it was on Sphere they'd first come for her. I wonder if that bounty hunter was a mage too. She racked her memory but couldn't remember anything that would have indicated that. She realized that she could at this point get back to Beral, it seemed clear to her that whoever had sent those people after her knew she was on Embla, meaning a call to an old friend couldn't give anything away. Maybe the investigation back on Sphere had brought up some info on why she was being targeted, or who had put out the bounty.

***

A beautiful building, with numerous high spires in a black that never stained, stood alone on a small hill some few kilometers from City Six. A callback to architecture of a time long since forgotten, some thought early Martian, others thought even older. The architect had been so old, so massively old by anyone's standards, that it was impossible to say where he had found the art that had inspired him. It was a masterpiece, though the beauty of it was grim and overstated. There was a courtyard of statues of trees, each one as black as the towers around them, with sharp nail-like branches. The courtyard had a dome covering it, not made of physical matter, but a thin film of magic that cleansed the air of any vile smells, and burned away any impurities from the raindrops falling. Kesh looked up to the shimmering filament, daydreaming of the day she'd have an office to retreat to; she was also eating a particularly tasty sandwich, it was a good day. She knew it was almost time to head out to inquire about today's duties; but time was still hers for another entire, she looked at her wristwatch, five minutes.

***

MASAN smiled a lot as they wandered through the undercity. He knew he needed to put this woman at ease, she was inexperienced around mages, and naturally very hesitant after what had happened with her supposed friend, Sal. He knew he'd heard that name before in the context of Dark Mages, he just couldn't remember where. He'd gotten too many reports on the Dark guilds over the years to remember it all. He needed to get some upgrades to his implants, maybe a visual memory database. Frid would probably kill him if he knew how much he'd strayed from the path. Masan smiled inwardly at this, he would never say it out loud of course, but knowing that Frid would disapprove was almost the exact reason why he'd gotten augments in the first place. The fools back on their station and their obsession with purity. It wasn't as if all of those mages dead from corruption were in any way pure.

"We're here," Masan exclaimed. "I think you'll like Histel, they're a techie just like you.

"So why would a techie know anything about my abductor?"

"The Dark Mage spies and assassins are some of the most prolific customers among those that sell top-of-the line augments. Particularly the big three here on Embla seem to have decided that any shortcuts to be more efficient killers or infiltrators are worth the cost. Your friend Sal seems like the type to go for high-end stuff."

Lin eyed the boutique in front of them. A bright screen with sections fallen into darkness spelled out the name Histel's Hideout. The rest of the storefront was in no better repair than the sign, yellow dirt staining the edges of the door and windows, and cracks in the glass.

"Really? This place?"

"Yeah, really, this place," Masan answered with more than a little bit of sarcasm in his voice.

***

"SALVADOR? Oh, that Sal, yeah, I know him! Fantastic lad; he never leaves without having found something to purchase. You know him? From where?" Histel said.

Lin looked like she was going to be sick, so Masan stepped in front of her hoping that Histel hadn't noticed. Masan offered, "Just a friend we met out traveling the system."

After a few pleasantries, Masan motioned for Lin to exit ahead of him, once on the walkways he leaned in conspiratorially.

"Please keep that little interaction to yourself. Particularly around Frid."

"Oh, why? I thought the two of you were thick as thieves."

"Oh, of course we are." Masan grinned. "He's just a bit peculiar. He really doesn't like augments. It's a religious thing or something."

"So, you and he aren't from the same religion?"

Masan hesitated a moment, damn, that was a dumb choice of words. "One could say that," he volunteered. "It's not exactly right though. We're both fire mages, and we both come from the sort of guild that has slightly sectarian-like overtones. I grew out of it. He didn't."

266TH DAY OF 11566 AF

THE purple robe felt overwhelming, but Lin tried to embrace the anonymity that it afforded. The residents of City Six paid no attention to members of the Tribe attired in their signature robes, assuming they were cultists so far gone that they were beneath notice or import.

It was a clever disguise and Lin was impressed with the cunning that it displayed. She wasn't sure how she felt about the Tribe yet, but there was obviously much more than there appeared to be on the surface. By embracing the ascetic hedonism of religions past with their strange chanting and dancing the Tribe displayed a public face of utter frivolity. It seemed to mask a much more serious inner core of people working against the influence of Dark magic here in Embla.

Lin was out today to check the layout of the city and see what its tech looked like. The majority of the Tribe were Emblans born and raised, so they were not exactly the most tech-savvy group in the galaxy. Lin had lived and worked in high-tech, high-surveillance space stations all her life, so her knowledge of facial recognition, spy software, and telecommunications monitoring was much more advanced. She wasn't sure how many of those systems were in use on Embla, especially as the climate and profligate use of magic meant that most Guilds relied on magic, not tech for surveillance and security. Whether that was to her advantage was yet to be seen.

Lin wasn't alone in her travels. It was extremely rare for members of the Tribe to venture out alone in regalia, so she was accompanied by three colorful, cheerful people with marginal mage talents who were mostly there to project an image of cheerful dilettantism. They checked out shops, cooed over outfits, and asked passersby to sing and dance, masking Lin's searching and assessment with their over-the-top behavior. Lin didn't know if the behavior was real or fake, but she suspected mostly the former. They certainly seemed happy enough and never once dropped their facade.

Lin was wary of the spaceport, but it was the most likely a location for high-tech gear, so they moved through the lower layers of City Six up to the far edge of the mechanical surface. On the way, Lin saw very little in the way of tech other than battered and most likely non-functional business security cameras, probably purchased from a charlatan who convinced the shop owners they were resistant to the elements before disappearing with the money before they began to malfunction.

Lin wished she had equipment to check for listening bugs and other transmitting devices, but the Tribe didn't seem to possess anything of the sort.

At the spaceport, Lin saw real surveillance cameras. Housed in rune-embossed casings and covering the majority of the spaceport area, these cameras were clearly maintained by both techies and mages to function in Embla's corrosive environment. Lin realized that the security was close to seamless, and the corporations likely paid to keep full tech surveillance up and running to protect their import/export concerns.

She danced in circles with her friends at the gate and quickly ascertained that Embla had real customs and immigration controls. Bribery was certainly part of the game, but it seemed harder than expected to slip a person through the port. Either there was a secondary landing site or Sal had been much better connected than Lin realized. Lin was growing more and more concerned that it was the latter. Why was she important enough that a mage would join the hunt for her? She doubted that she wanted to know the answer but knew that it was imperative that she found out.

Lin and her party continued their meanderings through the well-to-do surface districts, begging for coins, singing, and dancing. Not for the first time since arriving on Embla, Lin cursed growing up in a place where everyone wore their corporate allegiance openly for both pride and protection. The Emblans wore whatever they wanted under uniform gear designed to protect from corrosive rain. They were both so externally drab and personally individual that it was hard to discern their occupations. The mage guilds didn't like to advertise their members when they were about their day-to-day business and Lin didn't know enough about mage accouterments to tell a powerful mage from a marginal talent wearing a permanent piece of assistive magic. Her new friends might know, but now was not exactly the time for such a discussion.

Lin smiled and suggested they head home. She couldn't do much more without acquiring some monitoring tech that she could likely find in the lower city. She'd just have to convince Masan that she needed it badly to check the less visible tech here on Embla.

***

MASAN leaned back in his chair. He'd finally gotten a report from Freya on ways to get the intel he needed on Apteryx, and he was in luck. The Prior had been his best guess for a culprit since they narrowed in on that guild, a stone-cold killer turned philosopher and a member of the Ring. That man had always had nefarious plans, Masan just hadn't been able to figure any of them out before now. Now he knew the Prior had a weak spot, and that weak spot was wandering the streets not far from Lin. *The fates are finally in our favor,* he thought.

Apparently, the clerk at the Prior's scrivener had an axe to grind with his Journeyman, Keshara. Freya hadn't filled him in on all of the details, but it hadn't taken her more than a little sweet talk to clear out the Prior's favorite tools and get an earful about his uppity assistant. Privately, Masan thought that Kesh had the right of it, because the clerk was downright oily, but a source was a source.

The upside was that Keshara left the safety of the Apteryx fortress often on missions for her Master. Freya's little caper with the drugs meant that Kesh had to go back to the scriveners to pick it up. Seems the clerk had found some excuse to justify why he couldn't deliver, just to inconvenience the girl. It was a petty revenge on the Mages he envied, but today it would help Masan get closer to the Prior and his objectives.

He keyed his comm and sent a message and an image of Keshara.

"Caleb, you're to redirect to these coordinates. We've got a high-value target and we can leverage Lin. This is Keshara Arabris, Journeyman Mage and a known associate of Salvador. Convey as much information as you need to Lin. Hopefully, the fact that she isn't a Mage means she can get a lot closer, maybe even inside of the compound."

The wait for verification that they had found the girl dragged on. Masan caught himself pacing again. A full hour had passed by the time Caleb verified that they had found the girl.

Masan sat down and placed his hand on the glass table, which lit up to show the interface controls of the local system. He keyed himself into the comm systems of Caleb and Lin.

"I hear you found the Mage. Lin, I think you're the best person for this. Caleb, I'm afraid, would probably be made as a Mage in a heartbeat, and Apteryx are a suspicious bunch. I doubt he could get anything of use out of her."

"So, you're suggesting what? I thought we were just supposed to gather some info. I'm not exactly a master spy."

"What I'm suggesting is: make friends with her."

Lin was silent for a few seconds before responding, "Make friends? With a Dark Mage? With a friend of Sal?"

Masan adopted his best paternal tone of voice. "Try to compartmentalize, forget those things as well as you can, and chat with her. You want to find out what the hell they're doing right? If you don't, I don't know how I can help you get out of the trouble you're in. We need to know, so we can find a way to stop them from sending more bounty hunters." Masan hoped that Lin was naive enough to think they were somehow here for her sake.

There was another brief pause before he got an answer, "Alright, I'll do my best. But if she figures me out and kills me, it's on your conscience."

Masan smiled to himself at the last comment. Feeling guilty over dead civilians was something he was far past at this point. Out loud he said, "You'll do great!"

***

THE area she'd been led into was crowded. Lin was having some trouble staying at an appropriate distance from her target. She wanted to approach the girls, but not yet. She needed more information. This was not a normal person but another Dark Mage. While the Tribe was showing her that there were plenty of normal people among the Mages in general, she had a hard time thinking this was true for the Dark Mages. Maybe I'm just biased because of Sal, she briefly thought. But she brushed the thought away, no, there's something rotten about them. Dim red lights illuminated the path ahead, the type of light that indicated a part of the cycle where most were expected to sleep. Lin thought this area seemed just as busy as the waking part of the cycle, however, she kept being brushed up against by strangers with no sense of personal space.

267TH DAY OF 11566 AF

CORRUPTION comes in many forms, influenced by both the shortcomings of the wielder as well as by the spells of origin. In mild cases, it can be resolved over time or healed. Over a certain threshold though, the effects can be assumed to be permanent or even progressive.

The element of origin, particularly the element being channeled, has a great impact. Each of the eight elements is a separate and distinct entity, both figuratively and literally.

Light is a creature of order, of shining singular purpose, horrible and beautiful. Darkness slithers and coils, corruption for corruption's sake, the allure of the chaos at the end of time. Life is forever striving, crushing, recreating, reorganizing, an element of myriads of parts, eating itself and all the rest. Death, the calm, serenity, the sterile desert who's choked all who drew breath, and will do the same to all who will, the force that always prevails.

Air, the ethereal of the material, the pump that fuels all but death. Fire, which consumes without life, at mercy to others when young, but pulsating seemingly forever in its mature form, all is one from flickering flame to furious star. Earth, the cool, the source of all life and thereby all magic, unassuming but never yielding. Water, all that flows, the tiniest of streams to the greatest of maelstrom.

— Lectures for the Young Accepted, Loram Sam of the Flame, High Mage of the First Temple of the Flame, 11567 AF

***

MEG strolled through the densely packed neighborhoods of the undercity, anonymous in a black rain cloak and mask. The goal was to look purposeful without looking rushed, just another Emblan about their business. The mask blocked most of the sulfur smell from the water dripping down from the more affluent areas of the city, but clouds of fumes and fog gathered around cool spots, and sulfurous water pooled in any crevice without drainage. Plants engineered for low-light environments spilled out of balconies above, shadowing neon lights.

Meg was on her way to her designated surveillance post. Caleb and Freya would also be out in the neighborhood, floating specs in the crowd, ensuring that their quarry couldn't slip their digital net with magical interference. Freya had scoped out the various shops and restaurants on her initial missions to buy our the Prior's drugs and she had identified a few places suitable for mid-length surveillance of the street. Of course, she and Caleb had picked the most active spots first, so Meg was on her way to the least exciting site.

A glowing sign proclaimed the sale of psychedelics, a popular amusement for the populace of City Six. A doorway led up a flight of stairs from street level to a cozy-looking café style space. Psy dens could be a combination of a pharmacy, a café, or an opium den. Meg had never seen one prior to arriving on Embla, psychoactive substances were frowned upon on the Stations. An amusement for lesser minds was the commonly held opinion.

The psy dens allowed you to pick your drug of choice, a tablet or a tea, and provided cozy seating with full VR integrations for your comm, to allow for guided, immersive experiences. This psy den wasn't classy, but it was cozy and well-traveled by the locals. In fancy psy dens, each patron got their own room to preserve their privacy with a full set of amenities. Here, there was a more communal layout, with chairs arranged around a room full of semi-private nooks and crannies. Many patrons preferred to make chit chat with their friends or attendants while drinking their tea, before moving to a chair when the drugs started to hit.

Meg wasn't here to make friends, so she found a seat with clear access to the stairwell and plugged her chair into a false port on her comm. Eschewing human interaction, she ordered from the integrated menu. She needed to be here for several hours, in case their intel was incorrect, so she picked a slow synthetic drug in tab form. It was easier to fake taking a tab, and she wanted a chair, not a trip. The attendant silently dropped off her order with a small glass of liquid to wash it down.

Just my luck to get the job of being high in a cozy chair.

Meg disliked the inactivity of being stuck in one place and she was at least 30 seconds from intervening on the street. But, she was the surveillance specialist and the most experienced at monitoring multiple feeds in real-time, to provide Freya and Caleb instructions if they needed to act and could no longer monitor the feeds themselves. Meg wriggled herself into a comfortable position and focused on her feed from several cameras that were placed on the block.

I'm in, she sent to Freya and Caleb in their group chat.

Caleb: Do you think she's up for this? She's practically defenseless out there.

It was obvious that he thought he would be a better choice.

Freya: It's a conversation, not a battle, Caleb.

If anyone knew it was her. She was much better at gaining people's trust. Caleb could never entirely shed his haughty opinion of himself, and that only worked on a very specific subset of people.

Meg: We're here to make sure that Keshara doesn't slip our grip, even if Lin can't manage this. Keep your eyes and ears open and half a thought on the feeds. This is mission-critical intel.

Caleb: If it's so mission-critical where are Sinn and Gere?

He never learns, does he?

Freya: Sinn literally looks like *magic* and Gere will scare the locals.

Meg: Let's keep this professional. Sinn will review this if something goes awry. They'll be mad if we're debating orders and not doing our jobs.

That shut the two of them up, at least temporarily.

Freya: The clerk assured me that Kesh will be here this afternoon. She's always prompt. The Prior needs his supplies.

It took another hour before anything of note happened. Meg lounged and watched. The cameras were purely tech devices that were unlikely to trigger a Dark mages' senses, as many shops had them for protection.

Freya: She's on her way. She's wearing her Apteryx cloak, you can't miss her.

The first camera in the area picked up Keshara as she made her way to the shop.

Caleb: I guess she wanted the authority of her office?

Freya: The clerk is a weirdo and a self-important prick. He bought dumb blonde and eager hook, line, and sinker like it was his due. I imagine he's afraid of her and lashes out because he knows the Prior's beholden to him in a small way.

Meg: Makes our jobs easier. I'll send Lin into play.

The camera Freya had planted in the shop showed Keshara mid-negotiation with the clerk.

Meg keyed a message to Lin. It's time. She watched in real-time as Kesh stowed her tiny package in a pocket and began to search her pockets her mask to leave.

Lin entered the shop, shucking her mask and hood. Kesh looked up at the new entrant, seemingly a bit shocked that there would be another customer present.

Lin caught her eye, smiled brilliantly at her, and began to speak. Kesh smiled back and Meg breathed a sigh of relief. Only an hour more stuck in this stupid chair.

***

KESH pulled Lin into a fluorescently-lit noodle shop. She couldn't bear the press of the masses anymore and the noodle shops of City Six were relentless in their homogeneity. It was a good place for an anonymous conversation and perfectly timed to prevent them from getting too hangry and forgetting themselves. Kesh wanted to be able to get up close and personal and look Lin in the eye while she talked to her, in no small part because she was unexpectedly as charismatic as she was intriguing.

They sat at the counter and Kesh ordered them two house specials.

"Trust me, you have to try Embla-style noodles at least once while you're visiting our less-than-fair city."

Lin looked skeptical but didn't protest. She raised an eyebrow and said, "I'm surprised you have such strong food preferences. I thought all you Guild Mages stayed in your isolated towers and ate what you were told to eat." There was a careful balance between sting and charm in her words.

Kesh was saved from answering by the arrival of the steaming noodles. She carefully added hot sauce and chilis to her bowl and picked up her chopsticks.

Lin watched her methodical application of condiments and couldn't help but jab her again. "Aren't you all spies and assassins, off doing dastardly deeds for the rich and powerful?"

Kesh couldn't help herself, she turned and laughed in Lin's face. "Is that what you really think Dark Mages do? Skulk and loom and kill people? Whether or not we want to?"

Lin started, taken aback by Kesh's obvious amusement at her expense. Something flashed in her eyes at being the butt of the joke. "Well everyone knows that you are taken from your families young and taught in great secret. I also know firsthand that Dark Mages are infiltrators."

Kesh paused and considered how to respond. She slurped some noodles while thinking. How much to say without giving the game away?

Out loud she replied, "Both of those things are true, but they don't add up to all Dark Mages being soulless assassins. I think you've been watching too many drama reels." Kesh figured she didn't need to mention that her best friend was probably the finest 'assassin' in the system. "For the schooling, magic is dangerous. More dangerous than the public realizes or even wants to know. Not just to other people, but to the Mages themselves. Corruption will erode your sense of self and turn you into an empty channel to your power.

"We're sent away from home to live in supervised environments, so we can't hurt ourselves or others before we have control over our abilities. Parents aren't equipped to handle even bound, nascent Mages. And, unless they're also Mages, they don't understand the temptations of corruption. Living at school means never being alone where you can get out of control without immediate help."

Lin looked a little bit surprised, so Kesh pushed onwards. "We're trained for our magical aptitude, whatever form that may take. For example, I'm a metalsmith. I make magical items for everything from protection against bad dreams to combat cards for Battle Mages." Kesh omitted her work on battle cubes and armor. The Ring considered the cubes top-secret, and she had never told anyone the extent of her plans to re-envision battle armor into a tool for magic amplification that went way beyond using it for destruction.

Lin cocked her head, intrigued. Something about how the hair fell across her face, just barely touching her lips made Kesh feel flushed. This was why it had been so hard to just walk away when Lin had first approached her. In spite of the other woman being quite a bit older than her, Kesh couldn't help but to feel spellbound when Lin gazed at her.

"I won't lie to you and say that we don't make excellent spies and assassins. We're all trained to defend ourselves, especially because lots of the public shares your opinion on the evils of Dark Mages.

"But it turns out that the involuntary make really bad field agents. And the guild is a business before anything else. They can't afford botched jobs or journeymen with vendettas coming back to try and harm the guild. So, you only train to be a Dark operative if that's the best use of your affinity and temperament." There that was the politest way to explain that you only became a killer if that was where you found personal satisfaction, or in some cases, joy.

Lin started a sentence while Kesh was contemplating some of her bloodthirstier colleagues, "So the Dark Mage who came after me…"

"A Dark Mage came after you? Why?" Kesh was chocked at this. Was this why she cornered me? Why she so desperately wanted to get my attention… Not romance but information gathering, Kesh's shoulders sunk ever so slightly at the thought.

"I'm not sure, he referred to me as components and kidnapped me off a freighter."

Kesh cocked her head, considering.

"Well, you couldn't be a component in dark magic. We don't have a great affinity for the biological, outside of crafting implants. That's a fact that's pretty easy to verify on the Net if you care to do so. Are you sure it was a Dark Mage?"

Lin didn't look convinced, "If not one of you, then who?"

"Apteryx is the best, but far from the only Guild with the reach. And we're not big on human trafficking. Too many squishy moving parts. The other Dark guilds are more alright with that sort of operation, but I don't see what they'd want you for unless they're holding a grudge. My lot tend to be better at intelligence and paramilitary operations like security and protection."

"I'm not sure that I believe you…"

"Well, you don't have to. But our guild makes most of our money from the security business, with magical tech coming in as a close second line of revenue. You can ask around, but the Ring's dislike of squish and mess is pretty well known."

Both women turned their attention to their bowls. Lin's head raced, wondering if Kesh could be trusted to tell her the truth about the Dark

Guild. She didn't seem particularly concerned that what she had said would be reported back. To be honest, she seemed very matter-of-fact about the whole thing.

Lin propped her chopsticks on her empty bow, just as Kesh finished her food.

"You were right about the noodles. I'm not sure how I feel about what you've just told me."

Kesh shrugged. "Just keep in mind that being a Dark Mage is as much a job as it is a calling. We're people, not nefarious bad guys in a strip. If you have more questions, you can always send me a message".

She put a scrap of paper with her number on it on the counter.

"Noodles are on me. Think about what I said."

Lin pocketed the number and headed back out into the dim lights of the undercity. She would certainly be doing a lot of thinking.

268TH DAY OF 11566 AF

THE hallway stretched out in front of the young man, dark and oppressive. The black stonework of the walls and roof looked as if there were no gaps between each plate or brick laid down, the patching fused to a shiny ceramic finish. The sides of the hallway were lined with pillars in a similar black stone holding small artisan creations under domes, each with a plaque describing the object. The space was one of strange and ancient architecture.

Foreign to the young man who was making his way through the darkness, he was someone who'd spent his childhood years on a brightly lit station, clean and sparse, and after that in the ramshackle of the Tribe. He'd never spent much time anywhere that wasn't brightly lit and built from steel sheeting. He'd definitely never been comfortable in dark spaces. It wasn't his first time infiltrating a Dark Mage compound, but the other ones had been minor guilds or workspaces. Places that only ever saw the presence of at most a handful of Mages, and plenty of other workers and civilians. Those places were very low on security, where detection could be shrugged off with an excuse of "I just took a wrong turn" or "I thought you guys were open to the public." This place, however, was littered with hidden security measures. He'd made it past the gates using a spell of confusion, and he hadn't let go of his cloaking spell since he passed the threshold. He knew however that his efforts only worked against passive attention, it wouldn't fool anyone who was actually looking for him, and it wouldn't be able to divert attention if he was the only person in the room. It was a spell that worked by avoiding the attention of others rather than actually making him invisible.

Right now, Caleb really wished he'd managed to get true invisibility working again. After the punishment, he'd been careful to avoid those spells and the fury of his superiors. Now, he didn't know if he could even get them to work again; magic required just as much skill and practice for channeling as it did for crafting the runes. He'd shrugged it off as an unnecessary skill, as he was good at glamors. Of course, that was before the days where he was required to enter spaces where detection might mean death.

Sweat beaded on his forehead as he moved fast but quietly. He paused before exiting the corridor to look around the corner. The walkway continued forward across a large open space that he realized was the garden. It should've been bright as the sun was close to zenith that night, but a dome of Dark energy covered the sky here. He wondered at the ingenuity that had gone into creating that dome so that it wasn't visible from outside of the complex.

***

THE two Mages stood above the charred corpse. The older woman poked the arm of the figure with the toe of her boot and the blackened limb crumbled with the slight touch. "Was that really necessary, Blaise?" She shot the young woman in apprentice garb a sideway glance "He'll be real difficult to interrogate now."

The girl was crying but trying to keep her composure, "I... I'm sorry Master Kiste. I didn't think. It's the only spell I had prepared that would have done anything to him."

Kiste's eyes narrowed. "You could have just alerted us or clubbed him down. What's wrong with you lot? Who thinks something like this is appropriate as a sole defensive spell? Do you know what defensive means?"

The girl broke down sobbing, turning away from the man she'd killed and from her disappointed master.

"Get out of here but expect Argent to send for you tomorrow. If it were up to me, I'd have that tattoo dug out of your skin the old-fashioned way, but your rector might allow you to use a laser if you're lucky."

***

THE door slammed shut, sending a boom through the room, shaking the glasses of the mages around the horseshoe-shaped table. The Speaker sighed demonstratively before having a sip of their wine. "I wish you'd be more careful with the door, old man. It's done you no harm, and neither have my eardrums."

Wallang shared the sentiment but held his tongue. Cormac's having to take the brunt of this and I really don't think there's much he could have done, he thought.

Cormac shrugged and took his seat, pouring a glass for himself from a gold and glass decanter. He cleared his throat. "Let's get to the matter at hand. I've got a busy day because of this mess."

The Speaker nodded. "Well, now we know that it's not some irrelevant petty matter."

"True, that's some risky behavior," Cormac said.

Argent was tapping a finger against the stone table, giving away more of her emotional state than usual. "What the hell were they thinking? Breaking in, couldn't really end any other way."

"It could have if your students were less quick on the trigger," Kiste shot a sharp look at the rector.

"Oh please do shut up, she's a kid," Argent replied.

Cormac sipped on his wine, and spoke in a low serious tone, "If they're willing to send someone in, there's a real issue here. They're looking for something."

Wallang felt deeply uncomfortable, he didn't like having to explain himself, but it was getting to be ridiculous, "I'm starting to suspect it's about me."

All eyes turned to him, and it was the Speaker who inquired, "Oh really, something you haven't told us, old man?"

"Some of the work I've been doing is from old times, really old."

The Speaker continued, "I don't see how that would infuriate them this badly."

"The critical information I found was in something called 'secrets of the enemy'."

"God damn it, you're using their tomes now?" Hugh looked furious.

"It might be written by a Light Mage, but all the information was stolen from one of our old temples, right after the fall. The bastards stole our secrets."

"Our temple? Embla never had those," Hugh asked.

"You misunderstand, they stole it from Earth."

"Right after the fall? You're joking I hope."

"No, the author tells the reader that the crystals the work is based on were found on Earth circa 5 AF."

"So whoever wrote this is even crazier than you." Cormac offered.

"It would seem so; they supposedly lost a lot of people hunting for this."

"And how did you get this?" Argent asked. She didn't sound like she was anticipating an answer she'd like.

"I found the location of this work myself, but to procure… Ehrm, Sal helped me out."

Hugh sighed. "So not only did you steal Light Mage property, but you also almost certainly had one or more of them killed in the process. Pure genius."

"Oh really, quit it with the holier-than-thou attitude. None of us are as careful as we should be, old age in this business breeds a foolish type of bravery. At least we have a better idea of the why, I just wish you'd told us earlier, Wallang," Argent said.

"I know, I wish I had too. It wasn't my best moment and I'm sorry. I was really hoping it wasn't anything that would incite anything like this."

The Speaker continued, "The next step for us needs to be a show of force, but we don't even know what enclave this is, or where they're located. I doubt this is something that's being organized from any of the stations. It smells like a local op."

"Almost certainly, I've run into several of their agents here in the city in the last few years. I've been able to clock them but not tag them. Was never able to find a base of operations," Cormac said.

Wallang felt annoyed, both at himself but now also at Cormac. He's the one who's supposed to protect us when on home turf, how can he fail so miserably? Wallang thought. Out loud he said, "So no retaliation is possible at the moment."

"Not immediately but we can put the word out, we never really hunted Light Mages in City Six before, could be entertaining."

The Speaker smirked, a twinkle in their eye. "A rat hunt so to speak."

"I think you're being far too insulting to rats," Hugh offered.

The Speaker raised a hand. "So we all agree? We'll mobilize the agents we have in town for this purpose?"

Each person in the room in turn gave a thumbs up, indicating their vote.

They spoke again, "It's decided. Cormac, you're of course in charge of this. Please don't make it too messy, we don't want to start a war, just make an example."

"I'm a professional, am I not?"

***

MIA was surprised to get an urgent message asking her to report to Hugh when she arrived back at the Apteryx campus. She thought she was on R&R for the next few days since she'd had a pretty busy schedule recently and a tired Mage was prone to making mistakes.

Orders were orders so she reported directly to Hugh's office once she made it through the City. She barely made it through the door when Hugh rose and said, "Come, I have something I want to show you. We held it until you returned."

Silently, Mia followed after him as he took her to the entrance to the mountain workshops. Just inside there were horrific smells and a charred body.

"What on earth happened here?"

Hugh sighed. "One of our more foolish apprentices encountered an intruder at the door."

"Encountered seems like a mild word." Mia cocked her head to the side as she examined the carnage.

"Blaise is in a great deal of trouble over this, for not exercising even a modicum of common sense."

"I take it she fireballed the intruder?" It seemed like the most likely spell.

"Yeah, sadly she's an artificer, not an infiltrator or a battle Mage. She took care of the problem in the worst possible way. When I asked her why she didn't call for help or try to restrain the intruder so we could question him, she just looked at me blankly and told me that our enemies must die."

Mia put her head in her hand. "For the love of … Why do none of our artificers understand that we're intelligence brokers and strategists before we're assassins?" It was starting to be a practical, as well as an intellectual, question.

Hugh looked pained. "I'll be discussing that with Rector Argent and

Artificer Hira later this week. For now, we'll have to deal with the shitty hand that we've been dealt by an overzealous apprentice."

They left the scene of the crime. Mia had seen and recorded it for reference, so there was no longer a point in standing in the smell.

"What do we know about the intruder?" Mia asked.

"He's a young man, and he avoided routine detection wards on the boundaries for long enough to make it to the workshops. The few bits of magic he was carrying that weren't barbecued suggest that he's a Light Mage."

Mia stopped and stood still for a second. "Well, shit. You're positive he's a Light Mage?"

Hugh paused, waiting for her to catch up. "No, and thanks to Blaise we didn't get to see his magic or question him. But, the workshops have received some equipment with Light magic bugs recently. It's certainly worth further investigation."

"Yeah, I can see that."

Hugh pressed on, "This is delicate. If we're wrong about his origin, I don't need to start a cataclysmic Light Mage hunt by all three Guilds. I need a deftly handled, detail-oriented inquiry into his provenance."

"Understood, sir. Was he picked up on any of our surveillance, or did he just pop up here?"

"The analysts are looking at it now, but it looks like he avoided detection until inside the mountain and then either glitched or deactivated his shielding. Which is when Blaise detected his presence and fried him."

"Has she been questioned? Are you sure he's not a boyfriend or an enemy of hers she 'accidentally' flamed?" It would hardly be the first time an apprentice had killed a lover 'by mistake'.

"All of our apprentices and journeymen are accounted for. She's not covering up murdering one of our own. But you're free to question her yourself. She's in holding and being a right little bitch. Maybe a visit from the shadow assassin will help her see sense."

"Alright then sir, she'll be my next stop. Can you ask the analysts to send me any info on the tech or magical surveillance as it comes in? It might help to narrow his path down."

"Yes. Mia, this is a strictly need-to-know investigation. Report only to me or members of the Ring. We do not need to start a panic."

✲✲✲

STEAM filled the air, thick enough to have streaks and whirls of fog, perennials lined the waterline of the natural pool. The cave wall was far less polished than anything found in the compound that sat hundreds of meters above; rocks of all colors and dimensions jutted out from the space in chaotic patterns.

Wallang's skin was rosy from the heat, creating a stark contrast to the dark patches and strokes that covered his body. Some patterns were tattoos, others the constantly swimming Darkness underneath his skin. An expensive price to pay, but power and knowledge were worth anything, for what else was there to be had in this limited existence? Leaves of the closest bush brushed against his cheek as he was startled awake from his introspection.

Argent slipped into the water next to him, ripples spreading from her smooth legs and their intricate spidery tattoos, many of which Wallang himself had helped design. The ripples propagated across the pool of the hot spring, reflecting the dim light of the illumination screens above. Wallang let his lower half sink down into the hot water, assuming a sitting position, as he watched his old friend find a comfortable spot across from him. Argent was only slightly younger than him, but she had suffered far less corruption, and she'd always been keen on repairing whatever she could. Even though she was in her sixties her body didn't look a year over forty, and while she was covered in magical runes, the only glaring sign of her corruption was the reflective black swirling through her eyes. She'll outlive us all, he thought slightly bitterly.

He nodded a greeting at her, and took a deep breath, letting himself float back to the surface. "I see you needed some down-time too?"

He couldn't see her from this position, but he could tell from the tone that she was smiling as she responded, "Not down time, we live and breathe our work don't we? More like, this place allows me to think more clearly."

It's a good point, Wallang thought, the same reason that I like this place. Out loud he said, "Sure you're not just checking up on me?"

"Now why would I do that?"

"I'm really sorry about the chaos, I could hardly be blamed for Sal's methods."

"Don't apologize, what you did led to the death of quite a few Light Mages. How could that be a bad thing?" She sounded more callous than usual, almost delighted.

"I mean, yeah they're our enemies, I don't feel bad about losing some of them, but it's not like we had them killed on purpose."

She didn't respond, and Wallang adjusted his position slightly, moving up against the stones behind him, finding a comfortable position that let him observe his friend. She wasn't wearing her glasses, which was rare even here, and she had her head turned in his direction. It was odd, it felt as if she was watching him through those black dead mirrors that used to be her eyes. Something felt really wrong about the whole scene.

Argent smiled at him. "Now, how's that work going? Your big project? I so want to see it completed."

He was confounded, she never asked about his project, and she knew he didn't like discussing it. "It's going forward, the last book, the one that was so hard won has gotten me really close."

She nodded in a stiff manner, looking even stranger. Almost like a doll, he thought.

"If you need any help, I'm always with you, always on your shoulder, always in your soul." The last words echoed through every fiber of his body. He jerked, twisted, and panicked as water filled his nostrils, as water stung his eyes. He threw out an arm, getting a hold of the stony edge of the basin. He dragged himself out of the water coughing. When he looked out through the dusky room, over the water there was no one there. What happened? Did I fall asleep? Did I just panic because I inhaled some water? Even in his thoughts that sounded hollow, that had all felt far too real.

***

BLAISE had clearly had a rough night; she was curled up in an ugly blanket with her back to the door when Mia entered holding.

"Go away. I didn't do anything wrong!" she shouted as the cell door clanked open to admit Mia.

"Well, that's entirely untrue and, worse, you know it," Mia replied evenly.

Blaise rolled over at the sound of a female voice and paled when she saw Mia.

Mia had played up the intimidation factor in her appearance. She was decked out in her stealth suit and armed to the gills with throwing knives, regular knives, and her rarely-used sword. The suit gleamed with dark runes, as did many of her knives. She held her platinum shadow cube loosely in one hand. When you were pocket-sized, you sometimes needed the trappings of your profession to get people into the correct headspace.

Blaise was defensive and thinking like a schoolgirl. Mia knew that a defensive teenager would say almost anything to get out of trouble; to get to the truth, fear would be the only useful tool. She needed the girl to cooperate because she needed every detail. Mia had no mandate or permission to hurt her. Blaise didn't know that and could use a solid dose of real-world consequences for her actions. Treason is a good pain point, she thought. Mia would give Blaise the impression that the Ring thought she was a traitor who was culpable for the intrusion and that her life was on the line today.

"Sit up and stop telling me shit that even you don't believe, Blaise. You're a goddamn Dark Mage, not some little techie schoolgirl."

Blaise gaped at her dumbfounded.

"Well, that expression might be the first honest thing to have come out of your being all day. Come with me."

Blaise got to her feet and followed Mia to an interrogation room, which was only slightly less cramped. The room was usually reserved for interrogations of serious offenders, true enemies of Apteryx. It was a room that had been the last thing many unfortunates had ever seen, and it had the aura that went with that fact. Blaise looked like something the cat had dragged in, more than slightly dazed.

"Sit. We're going to have a nice chat about your future right now."

"I didn't…"

"Blaise, this will go so much better if you don't lie to me. I don't want to compel you, but I will if there's no other choice. You will not enjoy compulsion magic." Mia actually wasn't great at compulsion magic, but Blaise didn't need to know that. And Hugh would certainly find someone if she decided it was necessary.

Blaise swallowed and shut up for the moment. Apparently, the fact that her protests were falling on deaf ears had finally kicked in.

"Why did you let your boyfriend onto the compound, Blaise?"

Horror bloomed in Blaise's eyes. Apparently, she had been so busy mentally casting herself as the hero in the story, that she hadn't considered that she could also be the villain.

"I dunno what you're talking about!"

"Blaise, I have the dead carcass of what was once a very attractive young man. Only you saw him, and you killed him in a fashion so gruesome that it's like you were trying to prevent his identification. Try again."

"Oh my night, oh my night, I don't have a boyfriend, I didn't know him."

Mia pulled a knife off her bandolier and started playing with it. Twisting and turning it so it gleamed in the light.

"Blaise, he evaded every camera on the wall and several inside the campus. He could only do that with help, so… Why did you let your boyfriend onto campus?"

Mia enjoyed watching Blaise's self-righteousness crumble before her very eyes. She didn't get to interrogate people often. She usually just went through their lives until she found what she needed. But it was kind of fun to screw with Blaise. Especially as her lack of foresight had gotten them into this mess.

Blaise started sobbing.

"I don't have a boyfriend. I don't leave campus enough to know anyone out there."

"Are you sure Blaise? We all have lives and families before we come here. If he's not your boyfriend, then are you spying for another guild? What did Asio or Strix offer you in exchange for letting him in?"

Blaise was panicking, bawling, and hyperventilating.

"I didn't... I wouldn't... I would never... Please."

"You seem very out of sorts for someone who claimed to have done no wrong a few minutes ago. You're still insisting you didn't let him onto campus?"

Blaise sobbed, "I didn't let him in. I found him by accident."

Mia put the knife away. "What do you mean, you found him by accident? Breathe first, girl, you're going to make yourself sick."

Blaise took a deep breath and then offered, "I snuck into the Journeyman workshop late in the cycle. I just wanted to see what was in them. Kesh always makes such cool stuff and I just wanted a peek."

"Well, that's starting to sound a lot more like the truth. Continue."

"I was down there for several hours just looking at the equipment and some of the work in progress. I didn't touch anything dangerous or valuable, I just wanted to see."

Mia cringed internally, sometimes the Guild proscriptions against eagerness backfired in the most spectacular ways. Since they couldn't seem eager in class, Apprentices let that out in other less productive ways, like breaking into places they shouldn't be outside of teaching hours.

"Alright, so you were just looking at the Journeymen's workshops in the pitch dark, late in the cycle. I guess that explains why you were alone. When did you come across the man?"

"I was exiting the workshops from one of the side stairs and hugging the wall so none of the Journeymen or Masters who were working would run into me. I was supposed to be in bed. I was listening to make sure I couldn't hear footsteps as I hugged the wall to get to the exit, so I could go back to the dorms."

"Alright, so you were sneaking. Were you using magic?"

"No!"

Blaise seemed overly defensive, so Mia pressed her further, "Remember what I said about honesty? It is a very poor idea to lie to me." Mia resumed playing with her throwing knife to emphasize her point.

Blaise gulped and tried again, "I might have been using a small fade-away spell. Nothing too major, I just didn't want to get in trouble for being out past curfew."

Mia could see Blaise realizing how ridiculous that sounded now.

She dropped her head onto her stacked, facedown palms.

"I had done it before and it always worked so well," she mumbled.

"Face up kiddo. Okay, so you were using an active cloaking spell when you reached the entrance. What then?"

Blaise tilted her head, searching her memory. "I was hugging the wall, headed to the door when I saw something wrong in space."

"So, you fireballed it?" Mia wanted to push her to see how illogical her choice had been.

"No. I originally thought it might be another apprentice, so I froze and waited because the disturbance was between me and the door."

Mia pressed her, "Why not turn around and get help?"

"I thought it was Dex, okay? And then we both would have been in trouble."

"So you waited?" Mia asked.

"Yeah, and then it seemed like the distortion blipped and an unfamiliar boy came into view."

"So, you fireballed him?" Mia really wanted her to see just how much consideration had been given before she fireballed the man.

"No! I don't just fireball every random person I come across." Blaise was getting defensive again. It was time to pull her back to the facts of the situation.

"What then?"

"He did something with magic, and I might have. . ." Blaise trailed off into another mumble.

"Don't mumble, what happened?"

"I squeaked." Blaise's face was the picture of misery. Dark Mages did not squeak at danger. Mia was capable of taking out a room full of people without a single sound on her part and Blaise knew it.

"You squeaked? Like a mouse?" Mia knew she shouldn't antagonize her, but shame was a good learning experience.

"Even if he belonged, he shouldn't have been doing magic."

"You were doing unapproved magic."

"Well, erm…"

Mia was enjoying watching Blaise's need to be a goody two shoes war with her desire to be in the right.

"Just continue." Mia was finally tiring of stringing Blaise along; it was time to get to the point.

"It was our magic and when I squeaked he turned towards me aggressively and fired up a light spell."

Mia confirmed, "And none of us would have done that."

Blaise agreed, "No, no dark mage would have lit up the entryway. And my spell was pretty weak, it couldn't withstand the light. He saw me and started moving in my direction."

"So, then you fireballed him."

"I panicked and it's my only defensive spell."

Mia cocked her head to the side. "Fireballs are not defensive spells. I'm going to need a better reason."

Blaise looked shifty and uncomfortable, she started playing with her hair and looking away.

"Well, my name is Blaise and I'm kind of a nerd? My classmates were making fun of me, so I found the scariest fire spell I could find and tattooed it on myself to shut them up. You know, so I could blaze."

Sweet, sweet night, protect her from the idiocy of apprentices. Had she ever been this foolish?

"Alright Blaise, that is literally the dumbest thing I have ever heard."

"Kiste wanted to cut my tattoo off." Blaise looked at Mia with a desperate look, as if she was begging to hear that they'd never do anything so horrible.

"I'm still considering it, but since the spell clearly works, let's work on your future judgment." Mia thought her calming words were probably not going to end up untrue, but then again it wouldn't be nearly the cruelest punishment she'd heard of inflicted.

Blaise perked up a little at the thought that she might actually have a future beyond this conversation.

"Why are we all so upset about the fireball spell?" Mia asked in her best instructor voice.

Blaise looked confused. "I killed someone?"

"You can do better than that, Blaise. You stumbled across a magical intruder. What does someone like Hugh or I want to know about that?"

"Who they were and what they wanted in Apteryx?"

"Correct. So why is what you did a problem?"

"You wanted him alive?"

"Ideally, yes. We always want enemies alive for questioning. But if your life is at risk, I'm not telling you not to kill people. What else is wrong there?"

Blaise just sat there looking confused for several tens of seconds, Mia could practically see the cogs in her brain spinning.

"I torched him completely," Blaise said in a rush. Illumination dawned on her face, finally. "Oh shit, I destroyed him and everything he was carrying."

"Exactly. Look, the priority for intruders is to remain safe and contain them until they can be captured by our security teams. If your life is in imminent danger and you have to kill them, ideally kill them tidily so we can go through their stuff. Right now, I have a man-sized pile of soot with no identifying features, no forensic evidence, and very limited clues to his Guild or motive."

"Shit. I didn't think..." Blaise sat back in her chair, defeated.

"No Blaise, you didn't think. And you're lucky that this time you lived through the experience. Next time you will not be so lucky. Now we are going to go over your encounter with this stranger until I am satisfied that I know everything you know and some things you didn't even know you noticed."

"Okay."

"And then you get to face the Ring disciplinary committee. Help me here and I will try to make sure you don't have to start your apprenticeship over again." Mia gave her best reassuring smile, trying not to scare her further.

"They won't kick me out, will they?" Blaise sounded small.

Mia allowed herself her first real smile in the conversation. "Kid, that fireball was idiotic, but it was powerful as hell or you wouldn't be in this much trouble. So, no they won't turn you out. But I expect you might be reconsidering your area of specialty."

***

KESH didn't enjoy having dramatic problems. She preferred the chill of metal and the heat of her workshop to the vast majority of people and most who knew her knew that. Sure, she had friends and even some lovers, but no one would call her a people person. She firmly believed it was better to be alone than to be bogged down in relationshit with others.

This mess with potential Light Mages in the City and Lin's sudden appearance in her life was an unwelcome interruption. She had just been trying to do her job and keep the Prior happy until she finished her Masterwork. If only Lin wasn't quite so alluring. Kesh smiled internally, even when interrogating her about magic.

Kesh hated games of manipulation and subterfuge. She sucked at cards and party games. She didn't enjoy feeling like she was in the middle of one of the novels she had loved as a kid; full of adventure. She thought she had given all of that up to have her craft.

But now, this mess with missing drugs, suspicious cultists, charred Mages in the fortress, and damsels in no small amount of distress was drawing her in. *Should I tell the Prior everything and walk away? Should I notify the Ring that Sal has finally fallen to his corruption? Will they even care, given their profligate use of magic? What if Lin's abduction was Apteryx business? Can I put aside my growing interest to protect the interests of the Guild?*

Kesh liked magical problems with engineering solutions. Substitute a rune here, use a different alloy or tool to alter the flow of magic. Her art was full of subtle manipulations to get the desired result. But now she was faced with a complex interpersonal problem, and it felt like she was standing there, magic-less, with nothing but a sledgehammer.

If she was going to get to the bottom of this and figure out who to tell what, she was going to need assistance. And, she could think of only one person to ask, and the problem was that that person was far too close to Sal for comfort.

***

MIA had been out working on some top-secret infiltration project, but she should be back this week. Kesh hadn't seen her around the fortress, but she knew that Mia had a hidey hole or two in the city where she could decompress away from the Ring's watchful eyes.

Kesh cued her comms and messaged Mia to see if she was around. She was in luck, so they arranged to meet for coffee in an out-of-the-way spot in the Undercity.

"You look good, my dear. Did you get even sparklier in my absence?" Mia laughed as she hugged Kesh hello.

They had a long-running joke about Kesh's love for bright golden jewelry, given that Mia was intentionally as nondescript as she could make herself.

"You know a little gold here, a few gems there. The perks of making, not using, battle magic," Kesh replied. "How was the mission? Are the cubes working for you?"

Mia smiled at her, flipping through the menu, looking for something tasty. "They work well, and they let me carry more conventional weaponry and fewer spell sheets. Plus, they're much more stable to cast. It has been a big save in terms of energy and corruption." Mia pursed her lips as she reflected. "It's too bad you didn't know how to make them when we were first getting tattoos as teenagers, I could have saved a lot of real estate on myself."

Kesh considered, "It's nice for some spells, but I'm pretty sure you don't want to be separated from your basic shield and last-ditch offensive spells."

"You're right, as usual. This way you can make me even more cool stuff to use." Mia's eyes sparkled with the possibility. "I hear you found a Light bug in your workshop."

"I hear you got to check out the charred corpse of a Light Mage in the entryway. Yuck."

"Yeah, this job always takes me to the best-smelling places." Mia pulled a face at the thought. "I scared the ever-loving shit out of poor Blaise when I interrogated her about it."

"She's just a kid! You probably shouldn't scar her forever before she's a Journeyman," Kesh replied. Then she leaned in and asked, "Did you find out anything useful?"

"Only that Blaise has a hell of a fireball and no common sense. It looks like he was a Light Mage, but Blaise was uninvolved. She was mostly just sneaking around trying to be the new you."

Kish sighed. "I wish... Then I could become a Master and make you really cool toys and Prior Wallang could stress her out." She buried her head in her hands in dismay. Blaise wasn't old enough to be a Journeyman anyway.

"I doubt it," Mia replied. "I'm pretty sure her punishment will be re-training with Cormac's teams for a bit. She's got some power."

Their conversation was interrupted by the server taking their order.

"So, what's the game plan for dealing with the Light Mages? I got stuck making Parvana a new cube, in lieu of doing something more useful."

"That little bitch. So, freaking careless." Mia shook her head. Kesh loved that she didn't have to explain herself. Mia hated Parvana more than Kesh, she had botched more than one mission with Mia early in their training.

"Hugh's got his ear to the ground, and we have teams combing the city. Looks like I'll be around for a while until we find the source. Maybe we'll get lucky, and he was a solo operative, but my spidey senses tell me otherwise."

The waiter returned with their coffees, giving them a small break in the conversation. Kesh figured that Mia was in a good enough mood for some light probing about Sal.

"Will you be seeing Sal while you're in town?" Kesh asked as innocently as possible.

Mia narrowed her eyes. "No. He's an asshole and off planet right now."

Mia and Sal had a long history, most of which involved Mia worshiping the ground Sal walked on. Kesh knew it hurt her friend when she grew up and realized that Sal was an unequivocal narcissist, who was only out for himself.

But she needed to check that they hadn't patched things up when Kesh had been buried in her own work.

"He is an asshole," Kesh agreed. "Maybe one day the Ring will let you stab him a bit when he fucks up."

"Why are you so interested in Sal anyway?" Mia asked. She knew Kesh was up to something.

"So, I have a problem. And it definitely involves Sal, and it may or may not involve the Ring," Kesh told Mia.

Kesh laid out the details of Lin's kidnapping and subsequent escape.

"Well, we have now confirmed that you are the least stealthy Dark Mage in all of Embla. You got found out by a non-mage civilian running errands. I told you it was too much sparkle."

"Look, I know. Low profile, inconspicuous, all that jazz. I'll ask for help with my stealth technique later, but for now, just help me out."

"Are you sure this chick is who she says she is? All you know is that she's a supposed fugitive in more ways than one. You're taking her at her word, Kesh, with no idea how good that might be."

Duplicity wasn't Kesh's strong suit unless she was trying to hide staying up all night in the workshop.

"Sal is one of our best operatives, she could be trying to discredit him or turn him over to a competitor or one of the Corps. She could be trying to get you to doubt our leadership and soften you up to join another Guild. You know how much those vagrants would love to have a real mage, not just a marginal talent. Your skills are unique and valuable, you should be more careful who you tell about them. Especially with dead light mages in the fortress."

Kesh moaned. She had totally forgotten all of her skepticism in the face of Lin's pretty face and horrible predicament.

"If I wanted to trap you Kesh, a pretty damsel in distress is exactly where I'd start. You're nice and sheltered in your workshop and you wouldn't even see the betrayal coming." Kesh took a moment to respond, so Mia pressed her case. "Look Kesh, the guild doesn't like to set little kids up to think of themselves as great mages because praise of that sort usually comes with life-threatening overconfidence. But you are something unique. The guild hasn't had a spellwright as creative and productive as you in a long time. And your battle cubes and spelled wearables are slowly making their way out into the world. We may try and keep them secret, but Strix and Asio know we have something unique and it wouldn't take them that much sleuthing to find the source."

"I'm not sure what you're saying."

"To the other Dark Guilds, you're a valuable commodity. One that's worth luring away or outright stealing and putting to work for them. And that's the good news. The bad news is that other Guilds, like the Mundanes or the Lights, will perceive you as a threat and they might try to eliminate you."

Mia was ruthless, but she wasn't wrong. The info in Kesh's head was very valuable and she was a much easier target than the Prior. He had been a battle mage for decades before dedicating himself to his arcane studies. Kesh had never really considered herself as a target for inter-Guild warfare. Even when she had found that Light Mage listening device, she had assumed it was a generic pass at espionage, not something sinister directed at her.

Mia continued her lecture, "You need to take better precautions. I know Wallang has you out running all of his errands and you probably think that being Apteryx is enough to keep you safe here in City Six, but your anonymity is running out. And your distinctive golden halo isn't helping matters any."

Kesh felt her dismay rising. Mia saw her panic and tried to soften the blow. "Look, I'm not saying that this girl is lying. Darkness knows that Sal has been getting more erratic over the years. But you need to protect yourself and make sure that she's on the up and up. Especially before pulling in the Prior or the Ring."

"What do you think I should do?"

"First, consider carrying something more than just a shield spell. You make some of the most powerful stealth and battle magic out there, you should be armed with more than just a couple of small spells in rings. Second, stay in public and try and feel this girl out. Maybe there's more to her than meets the eye, or maybe she's exactly as lost and confused as she seems. If you can figure her out, maybe you can figure out why someone wants to use her to get to you."

"You think she sought me out?" asked Kesh.

"You told me she came up to you in public, that's right out of Parvana's playbook for her marks."

"Ew, you make me sound like a honey-trapped idiot."

Mia gave Kesh a stare indicating that she was on her last nerve. "Kesh, she had to be there in the first place. We don't have very good intelligence on the Tribe. Mostly because no one has really bothered. But maybe that should change."

Kesh's panic continued unabated. "Will you tell the Ring?"

"Tell them what? Kesh met a pretty girl who belongs to the Tribe who told her Sal kidnapped her off a spaceship. That sounds like a fairytale, not an actionable piece of intelligence. Look, I'll be around chasing Light Mages all week. Try to get more out of this Lin person. And then if you have something useful, we can go to the Ring together."

Mia took a sip of her coffee.

"Now, let's talk about something more fun. Did you hear how the Ring is planning to punish Parvana?"

***

THE sun was filtering down through the clouds, tinting the cityscape in a pleasant orange glow. The greenery that climbed across everything that wasn't a recently cleared walkway helped create an atmosphere of peace. It was hard to believe that hundreds of millions lived here. It was still very early in the morning, and the city hadn't woken up yet.

A few others like her were taking in the sun and lounging in the parks. The scenery reminded Lin of her old place on Sphere, the apartment she had to give up when she realized it did nothing but remind her of loss. She took a deep breath, this was not Sphere, this was somewhere fresh. Sure people were after her, but that couldn't last forever, could it? The chaos of the last few weeks had shaken her out of a stagnant headspace. It was of course terrible that she was on the run from who knows what, but at least she's not stuck doing the same thing day in and day out. Maybe if she found out who was after her she could start over somewhere new, maybe here, there was that adorable mage. Not enough on her own for sure, no one was, but she definitely made Embla seem a lot more attractive than it had otherwise been.

***

THE shadows were long in the glassed-in garden. The space was occupied mostly by plants that cleared the air of the unpleasant smells of Embla and allowed the guests at the many establishments here at Yasaga Tower to enjoy some fresh air.

Lin hadn't spent much time in the shopping districts due to the omnipresence of surveillance tech in these areas. She very much doubted that her pursuers had given up. Kesh had however reassured her that none of the cameras here worked. Lin learned more and more each day she spent in City Six what power the Dark Mage guilds wielded. Most high-profile centers of commerce were apparently under the protection of one of the guilds or another, this one belonged to Apteryx, Kesh's guild.

She sat alone on a railing high above most shops and restaurants, on one of the highest walkways. She liked being able to see what was coming. The artificial wind fanned the long leaves of the blueish-green vines that wound around every metal structure here. The air was filled with fresh scents, freshly brewed spiced teas mingling with flowers and baked goods. Beyond the glass stretched City Six, gleaming towers interspersed with the greenery of the massive gardens, shadows of the extremely slowly setting sun lighting the metal and plants in a high contrast way that was unlike anything on Sphere. Curious, she thought, Mars hadn't had a natural cycle in millennia, and Sphere never did. It dawned on her that in a few cycles, she'd experience the first natural sunset of her life.

She almost kicked off the railing as someone touched her shoulder.

Kesh grabbed her and held her tight for a second, to make sure she wouldn't fall. At least that's what Lin figured it was, either way, her heart went from beating fast from fright to beating hard due to other feelings.

When it was clear Lin wasn't at risk of falling, Kesh let her go and climbed up next to her. "Hi there, you're very far off today. First time you don't see me coming from a mile away."

There was something strained in Kesh's voice. "You seem a bit off. Is everything all right?"

"Yeah. Uhm. No, maybe not." Kesh looked at her feet intently. "It's just, I don't think I should really bring up guild business outside."

"No? The things you've told me so far aren't guild business?"

"Not really. I mean it's not exactly a secret what we do, neither is the ins and outs of our magic. Today I'm more bothered by politics."

"Politics… You don't seem the type." Lin wasn't sure she meant it; Dark Mages seemed like they were all very good at seeming to be something they weren't.

"I'm not, I mean I guess the stuff going on isn't my business, but I can't help to feel like it is," Kesh sputtered. Lin wondered how she had found either the least or the most devious Dark Mage in the whole city.

Lin smiled reassuringly. "If you're going to share you should just share, stop beating around the bush."

"I'm sorry. I guess it doesn't matter if you know, just please don't tell anyone." Kesh took a breath before words started pouring out. "You see, there's been signs of spies for a while. It's pretty normal that, spies I mean. But I haven't ever been in the middle of it before. It almost feels like this is directed at me somehow. First, they bugged the shop, and now that Mage, that poor Mage, he died on the way down to the Prior's study. Right as I was leaving there. Am I being paranoid?" Kesh hadn't really stopped for breath during that entire utterance, Lin was a bit impressed that the Mage hadn't fainted.

"I don't know if you're paranoid. Is there a reason someone should be after you?" Pay no attention to the man behind the curtain, Lin thought to herself.

"I don't think so," admitted Kesh. "But it's strange, isn't it?"

"That there was a Mage you didn't know in the compound?"

"I don't think you understand. It was a Light Mage and one of ours killed him."

"You killed him? What in the hells?"

"Intruding in a guild house isn't an everyday offense Lin, anyone in this city knows that that's something that is likely to get you killed. Light, the building isn't a house, it's an enormous magical fortress that has stood on that mountain for 11,000 years. It doesn't have a 'strangers welcome' sign."

"So, he wouldn't have been there unless he had something extremely pressing…"

"Or the devil on his heels so to speak."

"Sounds like you're afraid of this devil," Lin inquired.

"You bet I am. If there's someone here pushing Light Mages to suicidal missions something is seriously wrong." Kesh sounded genuinely afraid, and Lin felt some of it spill over.

"And you think it's about you? I mean I guess I was after you so to speak, but I just wanted information."

"I guess it sounds silly. But if it's not about me it's about someone I'm close to. Maybe the Prior or Mia," Kesh said. She leaned against Lin, as to borrow some mental fortitude or calm.

"I take it they're more prone to getting in trouble?" Lin asked.

"Definitely, Mia is one of the best spies I know, but that means she's both got a lot of competitors looking at her sideways and a lot of enemies she's burnt."

"And the Prior?"

"I like him a lot, but I'll admit he doesn't always play nice."

"You mean he kills people, don't you?" Lin only suppressed the loathing in her voice to the slightest degree.

"Not himself, but he's got a tendency to use some rather blunt tools" Kesh avoided eye contact again.

"You mean Sal don't you?" Lin's voice was ice in her throat and she had to steel herself to keep her eyes from tearing in rage.

"I'm sorry, yeah, him; and others like him."

"Little better than Sal then. I can see how he finds enemies." Sal's name was enough to make Lin furious. It's not Kesh's fault that Sal is a monster, she thought to calm herself. She took a deep breath.

"He's nothing like Sal. He'd never do what Sal did."

"No, if he sends that psycho after someone what's to say innocents won't be collateral? Sal didn't seem to have any problem killing people to get to me... Beral... And the others, I still haven't been able to reach them."

"I'm really sorry. I know. Maybe you're right. I don't think the Prior ever does that on purpose. There's something not entirely right about him."

"You mean he's sick?"

Kesh continued in a softer voice, more insecure, "Sort of. Sometimes corruption does things to the minds of Mages, particularly those of the ethereal elements. I'm always careful but even I sometimes feel it." Kesh was fidgeting with the leaf of a vine hanging from its planter above.

"You're starting to make magic sound like a disease."

"Sometimes I think it might be. It's very useful, but I don't think we understand it nearly as well as we should."

"I thought your people had been doing this for thousands of years."

"Tens of thousands, but think about it, how much do you know of the tech on earth before the fall? Or even about the building of Sphere?"

"I get your point. A lot has been forgotten."

"Or buried on purpose."

"The corps have a tendency of doing that yeah..." Lin shook her head, remembering all those times she'd been asked to shred documents and files after an assignment or build.

"The guilds are the same. Apteryx is supposedly one of the oldest, but coups have entirely replaced the leadership several times. This is actually some of the things I'm working with Wa... eh I mean the Prior, on."

"History?"

"Yeah, in a manner of speaking. He's trying to recover some very old knowledge that everyone thought was lost."

"Maybe he's not entirely irredeemable." Lin failed at keeping the doubt from her voice.

Kesh frowned. "If he's irredeemable, am I not that too then?"

"Do you really feel OK with people dying for your history project?"

"No! I'd never…" This time it was Kesh's eyes that just slightly teared up.

"See. That's my point." Lin placed an arm around Kesh's shoulders and pulled her close.

269TH DAY OF 11566 AF

MIA'S conversation with Blaise hadn't yielded very much in the way of concrete intel. Unfortunately, Blaise was on track to be a damn powerful Mage and she had been far too successful in incinerating the man in the foyer.

Mia had confirmed that he was a Mage though. He hadn't appeared on any of the tech surveillance on the compound or triggered any of the magical wards. He appeared to have sprung up in the entrance to the workrooms fully formed. And that took a Mage of some skill. Just apparently not enough to avoid getting flambéd by a 16-year-old girl after unveiling in the hallway. Had that been on purpose? Or had his magic failed in the Dark?

Mia couldn't be sure that he was a Light Mage, but it seemed unlikely he was a Dark Mage. Blaise was far from the first apprentice to sneak in shadows and a skilled Dark Mage would have known she was there. Mia knew that the Masters had definitely seen her sneaking as a kid, but politely ignored her given the extent of her efforts. Sometimes they had to pay the price for good apprentices by not being able to keep tabs on them all.

He could have been a mundane Mage, but Apteryx really didn't have ongoing difficulties with any of the likely factions. They had a good relationship with the fire Mages who headed the Fusion Forge and did a fair amount of business with the Earth, Air, and Water Mages who specialized in local food production and acted as engineers and artisans. There were barely any Life Mages of that caliber around, so that left a Death or a Light Mage. Mia wouldn't assume that a Death Mage was out of the question, but the grandiose or powerful ones tended to migrate to Earth; the locals were mostly medical practitioners. The process of elimination left a Light Mage.

That was a problem. Light Mages tended to also be reclusive, preferring their stations by the Sun. Mia had run into a few working espionage and assassination jobs on Tube and Mars, but they usually left the Dark Mages of Embla alone. The planet's light and dark cycle was inhospitable to Light Mages who would probably rather be anywhere in the solar system than Embla. But, the two planes were inimical to each other, so a baseline of antagonism existed there at all times, even without a concrete conflict.

Could Kesh's new inventions have sparked their interest? Mia couldn't believe that Parvana had been clueless enough to lose a battle cube. Really, they should have knocked her back to journeyman for that. Too bad she was one of their best close contact operatives.

Mia's forte wasn't human intelligence. She didn't seduce people and cultivate relationships. When she wanted to know something, she went and got that information the stealthy way. Now, she just needed to know where to look.

Mia suited up donned her rain gear and headed to the perimeter of the Apteryx campus. If she couldn't identify the dead man, maybe she could find a point of ingress onto the campus. There really shouldn't be a way in, Mia thought. She left the campus by the main gate and considered the geography of the place. Apteryx was designed to have a single main gate for everyday traffic and a rear helipad for deliveries. Both of these locations were heavily guarded with combat-trained Mages present at all times. No sane human would try to sneak past those guards.

Two sides of the compound faced a road and two sides backed onto other estates. Mia wouldn't come in from the road-side either, there was too much traffic from the Guild and the surrounding estates. The heavy greenery would show the person's movement over the high walls too clearly. Not to speak of the ward that stretched across the sky of the fort, that one had been crafted a long time ago but remained as deadly as ever. Mia assessed the first of the two adjoining properties from the road. The first was an estate that belonged to a Fusion Forge executive, a fire Mage by training. This site was extremely secure, with extensive tech and wards. If Mia wanted to break into Apteryx, she wouldn't do it from an equally fortified area, unless it belonged to an ally. Mia doubted that the Fire Mage would risk his business, and life, by allowing a Light Mage to access the grounds. And his business was too fraught to allow anything other than routine personnel onto his grounds.

The second estate was the more likely point of access. It belonged to an old Emblan family that had fallen on hard times but managed to retain their valuable property. The tech surveillance was just for show and Mia doubted that they had had Mages renew their wards recently. It was probably an unnecessary expense. Mia figured that they were counting on Apteryx's security to keep that wall secure. And what was the worst that could happen? A few Apprentices might try and fail to sneak out.

Mia returned to the Apteryx campus to examine the inner wall. The wall was eight feet high and built of magically imbued stone with laser-enabled movement sensors capable of discharging a high-voltage electric shock to anyone dumb enough to climb it. The wall was clear of foliage on the Apteryx side, forcing anyone who breached it to cross empty ground to reach the gardens. On the other side, the foliage had grown out of control. There were no trees large enough to act as access points, Apteryx would have strongly objected to the owners, but there were a lot of large bushes and ferns creating ground cover. Mia shed her rain cloak, activated her suit's infrared control, and engaged her invisibility shields. She climbed up to the edge of the wall using traction gloves. She stopped and touched the flat stone wall below her, and she moved her hand forward until she felt resistance. The shield stretching above her and across the whole courtyard flickered barely visible. A deadly sheath kept Apteryx safe inside its deadly embrace, but something was wrong. A few meters to her right the shield looked out of focus, the regular dark strands looked frayed. She walked closer, careful not to actually touch the shield. She sat down on her haunches, as she moved her hand close to the shield the runes that bound it in place appeared, two of them looked incomplete, ages of acidity had worn them down ever so slightly; in spite of the expert craftsmanship that had gone into building the structure and inscribing them. Mia carefully moved her hand forward across what should have been a boundary of acrid death, but she was able to move through only sensing a tingle. She slowly edged her way through the faulty ward. She came out unharmed on the other side of the shimmering barrier. What a massive fuck-up. Whoever that Mage was, he had intel on this breach and we had no idea, Mia was furious at the thought.

She planted her foot heavily on the outer edge of the wall and leaped, over the sensors, and landed in a crouch on the other side. Her implants had cost a fortune, but they allowed her to safely jump and land over a distance of several stories. It had come in handy more than once and Apteryx had been glad to front the cost for their top stealth infiltration agent.

On the other side, Mia moved slowly to make sure she didn't trigger any security measures that she didn't know about. Generations of Dark Mages had left generations of nasty traps; sometimes those traps weren't good at telling friends from foes. She figured the Mage had waited here for the correct time to move. He had been clever, there were no footprints or obvious rookie mistakes, but there were some subtle signs that the otherwise neglected flora had been shifted.

Mia examined the bushes carefully and she found disturbed soil. Just under the surface, she felt fabric, as she fished it out of the earth she smiled. She'd recognize this ugly piece anywhere. A bright purple that was only ever worn by one group in the City. Mia didn't know what the Tribe had to do with Light Mages, but now the real hunt could start.

270TH DAY OF 11566 AF

CASE Report: Fire Mage

The subject was found in the center of a blast pattern that took out the entire floor of a Kras Corporation Office building. He lay in a perfect circle of undamaged floor. The subject appeared to have a terrible, weeping sunburn. On first examination, his body had expelled so much fluid that he had fused to the carpet. Emergency responders noted that the body was still expelling steam upon their arrival at the site. They did not attempt to touch the body as it was glowing with a red light internally upon close inspection. Attempts to remove the subject from the carpet were hindered by the fact that his internal organs had liquefied, and his skeleton had charred so badly, it no longer retained any structural function.

The subject was later identified by Kras Security as Alfred McKintock, age 37, a Fire Mage who had worked in the employ of the Fusion Forge, crafting complex alloys for spacecraft. It is believed that he was attempting to kill his supervisor, Able Packard, who had recently fired him after a longstanding disagreement over workplace safety. No one who survived the attack recalls the event that initiated the attack, but several employees report that Mr. Packard fired Alfred in a rage after he tried to explain that the current budget cuts were unsafe for workers. Justinium Treble, the Director in charge of Aerospace Manufacturing, was unaware of the feud, likely due to intentional ignorance. He has long distanced himself from day-to-day operations feeling they were beneath his status.

Mr. Packard was a business executive with no previous magical or forge-related experience who was transferred from Sphere to implement budget cuts in the department. A non-Mage, he had no way of defending himself from an irate employee.

Formal recommendation:

Terminate the employment of Justinium Treble

Ensure that the chain of command for the Fusion Forge has specific experience with both magecraft and materials manufacturing.

Require replacement Director to conduct routine team and individual meetings to better monitor the interpersonal relationships of his team.

— Martina Heathmoor, Kras Corporation Investigator, Mars, 11427 AF

***

KESH was sweating by the time she was done with work for the day. Remaking Parvana's shadow cube was costly in time, power, and corruption. Kesh could feel her skin writhing as black vessels grew and retracted in her skin, mimicking blood vessels in a distorted abstract way. They also danced in her sclera, expanding and retreating to her black irises. When she was a kid, Kesh couldn't wait to have her eyes go black like a real Mage. Now, she looked at the visible signs of her corruption with a dawning horror.

It was one thing to take on corruption to make boundary-breaking spells or change your perception of the world. It was entirely another to feel it robbing you of your youth and vitality just to do a job for an ungrateful ditz.

Kesh sighed. This was the price for being a Guild Mage. You had wide latitude to make the most of your skills, but when the Ring called you answered. Or else. You could leave the Apteryx fortress, leave the City, even leave the planet, but you didn't refuse a direct order. You kept your reservations and objections to yourself, and you did your job no matter the personal cost. Guild history was littered with stories of people who thought they knew better than the Ring and paid the price with their lives.

Kesh wondered what Sal was thinking, taking side gigs for profit outside the Guild. Everyone did a few small favors. They all made compromises and concessions to grease the flow of commerce for Apteryx and themselves, but kidnapping and human trafficking had been out of the purview of Apteryx long before Wallang ascended to the Ring in his twenties. That was a business for Asio and Strix.

Thinking of Sal immediately brought up thoughts of Lin. Kesh smiled. Lin was a beautiful, inconvenient, vibrant problem. She pulled Kesh outside of her little world of metal and magic and propelled her out into humanity. Most Mages were plotters, climbing up the Guild hierarchy on the backs of their less talented and political colleagues. Success in Apteryx required a strong plan for the future and eyes in the back of your head for the dagger that was coming for you. Sometimes literally. Kesh had never met anyone who lived as fully in the present as Lin.

Here she was, thousands of miles from home, thriving when she should have been terrified. She'd found a home, friends, and even a little work for the Tribe. She was able to make the best of a situation, free of the confines of anyone's expectations but her own. It was terrifying and liberating just to be in her presence.

Kesh could use a break and a stiff drink. She hoped Lin would be willing to have a drink and overlook her dark tendrils. Still smiling, she keyed her comm and called Lin.

"Fancy a drink?"

***

THIS particular bar was rapidly becoming Lin's favorite. Just well-lit enough not to feel seedy. Clean glass interior. Interesting colors everywhere, red and purples set in glass architecture, reflecting spotlights, acting as prisms, and casting rainbows of light slowly moving across the surfaces of the room. It was made to invoke feelings, joy, wonder, and maybe some love and affection too. Kesh had pointed it out to her during their first evening, but she'd only actually entered a day later. As if called by the thought, the girl walked through the door, with her gold jewelry dotting her black hair. Lin admired her for a moment before waving to catch her attention. Kesh's black eyes were glistening in the light sweeping across her face, and Lin was struck by her incredibly long lashes. There was something about this girl she found very enticing, maybe her wires had gotten crossed though, maybe she was mistaking the adrenaline she felt from being around a dark mage for other, more affectionate feelings. She did have a tendency to mix danger and excitement with attraction.

As Kesh made her way over, Lin followed her with her eyes. When they were face to face Kesh smiled at her and sat down.

"Are you trying to make me nervous? Looking at me like that," Kesh said.

"Maybe, it depends, I wouldn't want to make you uncomfortable, at least not all too much," Lin teased. "A bit nervous can be good though. It seems to make you blush, and you're very cute when you blush."

Kesh shook her head. "Hah, now I know you're messing with me, you can't tell if I'm blushing."

"Oh, I can definitely tell." Lin smiled a confident smile. "Blushing is more than color, you know. I can tell by the way you breathe and move."

Kesh smiled. "Really? You're incorrigible, I thought we were here to talk about something serious. You told me it was important."

"This isn't important?" Lin feigned a sad tone but smiled. "You really ought to be nicer to me. Didn't you hear? I'm a damsel in distress."

Kesh laughed. "Sure you are. I guess you're a bit tougher than I first thought. You must be if you bounce back this fast."

"I wouldn't say I bounced back, but I can't just walk around feeling sorry for myself, and I won't squander an opportunity to flirt with a beautiful woman if I get it."

Now Kesh was definitely blushing. "So you didn't ask me here because something came up?"

Lin smiled and shook her head. "No, this is what I'd call an ambush date." She paused. "Now, if you want to, we can discuss all serious matters, but I'd much prefer we'd just hang out and chill for a bit. I'm tired of everything being so serious all the time."

"I guess that's fair. It's been a bit too much lately." Kesh put on a big smile. "So, what do you normally do on an ambush date like this?"

"Well, first I'll get you a bit more comfortable around me. Jokes and flirting and the like."

Kesh seemed to have recovered from Lin's initial offensive, and now she smirked at her. "And what if I'm already plenty comfortable?"

"Then the hard work is already done, and we can get to the part of the evening I really enjoy."

"Tell me more, oh genius at social machinations." Kesh cocked her head and grinned to underscore the lighthearted sarcasm.

"You're mocking me, but see, it's working!" Lin smirked and Kesh gave a small laugh.

"It's true. How do you manage to be so composed when the world is so chaotic?"

"I don't know. I mean, my life has always been a bit screwy. I went into officer training really young, but when I lost my mom that went down the drain. Lots of fighting, lots of getting into trouble. I was relatively well-behaved, but somehow I always made friends with the worst of the worst; meaning while this is the first time I'm at the pointy end of a situation like this, I've seen similar shit happen to friends more than once. I've even helped resolve a few grim situations. Turns out Kras trains their people better than most, the first fight I ever truly lost was to Sal, and he fights even less fair than me."

"So you're saying you deal with stress well because you're full up on trauma? That's pretty messed up." Kesh's tone became more serious as she contemplated Lin's bravado in the face of danger.

"Probably is. Don't really know any other way to be." Lin smiled. It was always difficult to explain her mentality to someone who hadn't lived with the threat of violence or death. What Kesh was saying was true though, she knew that. Having seen friends die over petty squabbles; having to kill to protect other friends when they probably deserved all that was coming their way. It had left Lin a bit cold. She didn't really remember if she'd always been like this, or if it was the result of loss after loss.

***

LIN swiped her pattern across a reader and the cost of the dinner, drinks, as well as a room on the third floor, were tallied. *I need to say thanks to Masan for whatever stunt he pulled to get my funds unstuck,* she thought to herself and smiled.

"What are you grinning about?" asked Kesh.

"Nothing at all, beautiful. Just happy to be in your company is all."

"Incorrigible!"

"You don't know the half of it." She flashed a grin at Kesh as she brushed her hand against the inside of her thigh. A half-choked moan told her that she was doing something right. "I guess I could always show you just how 'incorrigible' I can be."

She grabbed Kesh's wrist and pulled her in tight, her own back leaning against the wall of the hallway. She let her breath just slightly tickle the neck of the young Mage, and she heard another slight moan. *This would be fun.*

Two minutes after their public display of affection down in the bar, the pair were in the room. Kesh had let Lin lead the seduction, something she was very much enjoying. It was a big change from Beral, but she always enjoyed being in charge with women. *I really hope he got out okay.* The thought flashed in her head for an instant, but she pushed it away for another time. It would do no one any good if she let her anxieties ruin this evening.

It seemed that Kesh had sensed Lin's momentary hesitance, as she grabbed her face, pulled her close, and grabbed her lip between her teeth. "Am I not interesting enough?"

Lin was in the moment again, she smiled a cold superior smile. "Oh you definitely are, and uppity to match. I'll need to teach you to behave."

She grabbed Kesh's neck with her left hand, moved her towards one of the four pillars that cornered the suite, and pushed her against it with just enough force to make the young woman show a slightly pained expression. Lin moved her other hand up Kesh's side, sliding her black blouse up, exposing her chest. As her skin caught the light in a way that made it look slick and reflective, Lin felt something warm and fuzzy inside her chest. *She's adorable!* While the thought had a giddy note to it, she didn't let that show. *Stern and matronly is what we're going for.*

Kesh let out a giggle as she was tossed onto bed. A moment later Lin was straddled on top of her expertly undressing her without letting her slink away. Kesh kept giving her smiles in between her feigned expression of distress. As Lin got her panties off, Kesh saw her opportunity and dove up to steal a kiss. Lin laughed in delight before pushing the younger woman down hard into the mattress. "So sneaky! If I had ropes, I'd tie you up."

***

KESH giggled at the thought of being tied up. She didn't think that she was naughty enough to need restraints, even if she was wriggly. She was enjoying being pinned down by Lin.

Kesh writhed underneath Lin, rubbing her full length up and down the beautiful light skinned body, relishing the heat and the pressure. Their skin slid against each other, warm, soft, and slightly slick with sweat. Kesh grasped Lin's earlobe with her mouth kissing and nibbling it. She licked up and down the long neck, listening to Lin pant and moan in sync with her movements.

Lin leaned back and used her position to her advantage, pressing a knee between Kesh's legs to let her rub against it. Kesh moaned, pressing herself against the leg, the warm compressive feeling of the body above her and the pressure letting her mind let go of everything else. Her hair sprawled all over the pillow as Lin's hair curtained their faces, all Kesh could smell was the scent of her gorgeous partner.

Lin took control, taking Kesh's nipple in her mouth and tracing circles around it with her tongue. She sucked and licked and lightly nibbled until Kesh squealed at the pain-pleasure boundary.

"Please, Lin. The other one," Kesh begged, wanting a moment of respite.

Lin swapped nipples, keeping the first one pinched in her one hand and now tormenting the next nipple with her teeth. Kesh was so wet and ready, she felt close to screaming. Rubbing herself against Lin wasn't enough sensation. She needed more.

Sensing her frustration, Lin reversed her position kneeling over Kesh's face and bringing her face between Kesh's thighs. Kesh was once again squished into the mattress, as Lin began licking and kissing her inner thighs. So close and yet so far away from Kesh's ultimate goal.

Kesh mimicked Lin's frustrating actions, kissing and licking her inner thighs. She refused to give in until Lin caved and gave her what she wanted. Lin gave her no choice though, sliding her knees apart and all but smothering from above.. Kesh gasped a little as moisture flooded her mouth and she gave in. Lin moaned and finally decided to give Kesh the same attention.

She started to lick up and down, slowly, building up momentum as she went. Kesh had long since focused in on Li, sucking to keep up constant pressure. Lin begun moving in a more determined manner, setting her nerves on fire. Kesh tried to breathe and lick and suck at the same time. She heard a panting, mewling sound and realized that it was her own voice. Swept away in the sensation she kept at it, ignoring the tension in her neck and jaw as she tried to make Lin feel as good as she did. She leaned into the pulsing sensations that were building. She could sense that Lin was close, as she was grinding into her, pushing for more and more pressure. Hold on, wait for Lin.

Kesh was barely there anymore when she felt Lin moan loudly with her release. That set Kesh over the edge and she let herself be swept away by the waves of pleasure as her whole body quaked. She saw darkness and stars, as she was overcome with pleasure. Lin has collapsed above her, pinning her heavily into the mattress.

In her daze, she felt Lin roll off her and snuggle up next to her. She rolled to put her head on Lin's chest. The last thing she heard before she passed out was, "Goodnight sweet girl."

271st Day of 11566 AF

LIN checked the time again. It hadn't changed since the last time she checked. She drummed her fingers against the cot, dangling her feet off the weirdly high bed. What if Kesh hadn't really liked that? Was I too aggressive? She had seemed to like it, but what if it was one of those things that seemed fun in the moment but awful in hindsight? Damn it... Can't sit here all day. Wait a few hours and then contact her. Yep, that's the plan.

Lin scooted her butt off the cot and landed with feigned confidence in her stance. Look it to feel it. She grabbed her heavy coat under her arm and got out of her container-constructed apartment. In the distance she heard laughing, several of the Tribe members were hanging out in the central area. From the loud voices, Lin figured there was alcohol involved.

As she walked over to the group, which on closer inspection held many familiar faces, her comm buzzed her. She looked down to see a message pop up on the semi-translucent screen. It showed a small heart. I didn't scare her off! As she came into the central part of the complex, her expression immediately gave her away.

Aman winked at her and raised his glass. "You look happy Lin! Something nice happen?"

"It seems I'm less awkward than I thought. Got anything to drink that isn't alcoholic?"

Milani, who was already close to the refrigerators, gave her a thumbs up and her head disappeared into the closest of the massive cold boxes. "We've got plenty of ciders here, most are non-alcoholic, or there's something called 'Misery's Breath'. I think Masan imports those, but I don't really know what they actually are."

"One of those sounds good, let's see if the old man has any taste."

Milani returned with a small stack of cold drinks, she handed two to Aman who was drinking something called 'Ambrose's Nectar', which looked a lot like beer. She handed Lin her drink. "So tell us, what's this victory over awkwardness?"

"So, there's a girl I've been seeing..."

"I see, and I take it from today's mood that it's going well?" Milani smirked at her.

"It seems like it. I thought I had screwed up, but nope, I think she really likes me in spite of everything."

Aman, who was refilling his glass from the garish flask, interjected, "What did you do to her that made you think she wouldn't like you?"

Lin went over things in her head for a few seconds and realized the list was quite long. "Well, it's not just the one thing. I think I was pretty shitty in a lot of ways. She's a Dark Mage, and well, you know I had some issues with those."

"Well yeah, but that's to be expected after what you went through."

"It still wasn't right that I took that out on her."

"You can't have been that bad if you started the day with this amount of bounce in your step."

"Maybe she likes mean girls," Aman said with a smirk.

Lin gave a small laugh at that. "She better, I'm not very good at pretending I'm anything but." Lin realized she'd been sitting with her bottle in hand but hadn't actually tasted it. She took a swing at it and heat flared up in her mouth. It was as if the drink was hot and cold at the same time, and it tasted way too intensely of mixed fruits and berries. It wasn't bad enough to spit out, but it was a supremely strange mixture. Looking at the label she found that it was a list of concentrates. No water added, just ten different fruit concentrates, several of which were well-known allergens. What the hell is wrong with you Masan?

Act III

273TH DAY OF 11566 AF

KESH always found talking to Lin very soothing. She had an engineer's mindset that was oddly in line with the way Kesh viewed magic. Despite the seeming limitations of runes, Kesh believed that there was always a way to get magic to come together the way you wanted it to. You just had to find the path of least resistance through the runes to give it form.

Kesh realized that she had made an error in imitating the rune sequence for her bracer. If she truly wanted a universal solution to corruption, she was going to have to find a way to source the spell through multiple anchor runes, one for each branch of magic. The spell needed to pick up the magical energy and funnel it into the anchor runes until it found purchase before shunting the energy off-plane to close the channel. Kesh figured that the easiest off switch came from the opposing element, so the magic needed to flow from an open anchor rune, into an opposing anchor rune to shut off the stream.

She tested the bracer in a minimal version using only Light and Dark anchors. The Light anchor rune fought her tools every step of the way and she wound up having to significantly magically augment the plasma cutter with her magic, but she was finally able to set it as the terminating rune in the chain. She carefully sent a small stream of her magic into the trap spell that directed any incoming or ambient magic to the Dark anchor rune then funneled it into a Light anchor rune.

The bracer immediately cut off the flow of Dark magic. She couldn't even intentionally push opposing magic into the Light anchor. The trap spell was configured to catch all ambient magic that contacted it.]It was fascinating and she reeled from the fact that she couldn't even contact the dark plane with the Light anchor in place. She was cut off from the Dark plane.

Kesh pulled the bracer off and tried to re-access the Dark plane and it was as easy as breathing. The magic only extinguished as long as she was in contact with the trap spell.

Kesh smiled, the effect was awful, but it worked! Now, she just needed to alter the volume of incoming magic that triggered the trap spell, so that it could be worn by a practicing Mage without activating indiscriminately. She pulled up her research on detecting when a Mage had their channel fully open, so she could direct the spell to trigger only when the Mage attempted magic at three-fourths of their capacity when the risk of damaging corruption and becoming an inanimate channel for their plane became a risk.

Kesh hummed as she worked, creating a braided cuff with a central trap spell and eight channels for each of the magical sources. This way the main channel spell could send magic into the correct dead end for the Mage wearing the bracer. Now she just needed to find another powerful journeyman to test the bracer at scale.

She figured she could also make bracers specifically for Dark apprentices, so their magic didn't need to be sealed, as hers had been. They could wear protection against overwhelming their abilities to keep themselves, their classmates, and their teachers safe.

Oh well, time for a different type of fun, she smiled as Lin's face entered her mind.

***

KESH hummed under her mask as she traversed City Six. The day was full of sulfurous smog, but her mood only improved as she descended the towers to the Undercity. Kesh traversed high-end shopping centers full of gleaming tech and fashion that gave way to smaller, independent stores and restaurants full of comfort food for busy workers. She could smell chilis and garlic and she smiled at the memory of her first real conversation with Lin at the noodle shop. I had forgotten just how much better sex makes you feel, she thought. Kesh was ignoring the fact that that feeling might be just a little more in favor of her mission for today, visiting Lin at the Tribe.

Kesh had intentionally worn a nondescript outfit for this adventure. She had chosen a universal black rain cloak and mask, to blend in the Undercity. Lin had invited her to visit her home at the Tribe, and Kesh had to admit that she was curious. Mia had told her to find out more, so she figured it couldn't hurt to visit them on their home turf and see what it was like. Kesh had heard more rumors and suppositions than actual facts about them over the years.

Lin hadn't been able to give her an exact position over comm, so Kesh was meeting her in a nearby market. That way Lin could escort her directly into their little compound. Kesh was surprised at the depth of their home. The market was full of produce stalls overflowing with greenery, decorative plants that helped to scrub sulfur from the air inside apartments, and slightly worse for the wear tea shops. Kesh had rarely been this low in the towers and she routinely went all over the city looking for esoteric materials for the Prior. At this rate, they might even be on the actual ground of Ushas Mons.

I knew they were outcasts, but I didn't think that they had taken it quite so literally, Kesh thought to herself. If I had to walk this far every day to get from home to work or shopping, I'd certainly have a chip on my shoulder.

Kesh knew that she was spoiled living in a fortress on the actual peak of the mountain, but she'd never really processed that anyone really lived on the edge of the City's existence like this. Most Sixers lived in Towers that were reasonably well maintained and far from the sulfurous buildup of the base. In her naiveté, Kesh had assumed that these low levels were all but abandoned.

Kesh took a turn next to a small fruit market to see Lin standing waiting for her. There wasn't any ambient solar light in the Undercity, but Lin's brown hair gleamed in the fluorescent lights of the market, revealing its red undertones. When Lin saw her she gave a mischievous smile and wink and waved dismissively to the vendor she'd been in conversation with. She always moves in such a composed way, Kesh thought. A moment later she was in Lin's arms and got a kiss that filled Kesh with happy tingles. I'm such a sucker for this girl!

"How was the trip down?" Lin asked.

"Uneventful, although this may be the lowest I've ever been in the city," Kesh replied. "Where on earth is this place? It's seeming more and more like a secret lair out of some vidfic."

"Oh, you haven't seen anything yet, come with me."

Lin expertly navigated them through the maze of stalls, to a stairwell to descend even further down. The vibe was definitely more industrial and less sleek than the areas of the city Kesh usually frequented. The community had not bothered to fight the effects of sulfur on the building's surfaces and fixtures. Greenery ran over rusted metal and stained plastics creating the illusion that the plants were taking over the buildings.

"It's a maze, but you get used to it. I think the Tribe's space is a remnant of the original terraforming of Embla. I had to have my comm record the path, just to be able to go in and out on my own."

"That's intense... Why so complicated?" asked Kesh.

"I think that when you live on the fringe you take what you can get. And this way no one bothers them."

"Except the smell…"

"Spoken like a true upper-tier brat," Lin teased, smiling at Kesh. "They live on the same planet as you and not everyone can have a 15,000-year-old obsidian fortress to call home."

Kesh broke out in a smile of her own. "I suppose it's true. Don't knock the place, it's a really nice ancient castle."

Kesh had been busy chatting and sneaking little looks at Lin, so she snapped back to the present when they came out into the strangest place Kesh had visited.

"Welcome to the Tribe," said Lin. "My home away from Sphere or something. Come, you should meet Masan."

There was a fire burning under a makeshift chimney in the middle of the cathedral-sized room. Around the fire lounged a large group of Tribe's members, most of them in their casual dress, but a couple still swaddled in their signature deep purple.

Kesh nudged Lin with an elbow as they walked toward the group. "I never figured out, what's up with the color you all wear?"

"You don't like it?" Lin teased. "Seriously though, I asked the same question when I arrived. It seems like it was just a coincidence. This place had been used for industrial storage, of fabric. Apparently, Masan is very frugal." She made sure she put enough emphasis on the word that it was clear she meant cheap.

Kesh giggled much harder at the joke than it deserved, and that made Lin smile widely.

Lin walked ahead of her, tugging on her hand. "Come, even Frid has joined the gang!"

Kesh hurried along, feeling a bit juvenile for half running indoors; Lin is the one tugging on me and she's supposed to be the more mature one! The thought made her smile even wider.

There were some twenty people gathered in the center of the space. The smell of sulfur had abated inside, replaced with the delicious smell of something cooking. Lin started introducing her to everyone, but the names disappeared as soon as she heard them. She was normally quite good at names but even she had her limits. Lin had gotten to most of the people around the fire and sprawled on soft seating on the floor nearby. As Kesh was getting accustomed to the foreign atmosphere, she noticed someone new. A beautiful young woman, with long blonde hair, and emerald eyes that looked quite magical in the proverbial sense, had entered. Lin waved in a soft manner at the girl and spoke, "And you, I don't know. Hi, welcome to the Tribe, I'm Lin."

The woman, or girl, Kesh couldn't make up her mind about her age, responded in a much huskier tone than expected, "Hello Lin. Lovely meeting you."

There was something in the look in her eyes when looking at Lin, something that made Kesh deeply uncomfortable. The same seemed to have occurred to Lin as well, as she moved on in an awkward manner, without saying anything further and forgetting to introduce Kesh.

Lin recovered her composure almost immediately and smiled at the only two left to introduce, "Last but not least, these two gentlemen are our hosts, Masan and Frid."

***

LEANNE watched the foursome move towards the rooms at the back, what she figured were the quarters for the leaders of this strange guild. She'd been aware of the Tribe and their secret ties to the Light Mage council; how could she not, their satellites had terrible encryption. She also knew that the Dark Mages didn't have a clue.

The second before the door shut behind Lin, Leanne had an ugly realization. She could feel that something wasn't right, the mannerism of Frid and Masan had changed the moment they had seen the Dark Mage enter. They'll use Lin as leverage against that Mage, the thought struck her like lightning. At that same moment before the door closed behind them, she saw that Lin had also had a similar feeling. With a deep boom, the door sealed behind the group, and Leanne could no longer see her longtime objective. Rage welled up. This Frid wanted Lin, a dirty Light Mage! He has no right! The thought was like fire spasming in her chest. She looked around, closed her eyes, and she felt the space. Twenty-two souls present. That should do it. Life magic didn't need to be destructive to the source, life could be a conduit for the magic, allowing it to flow into this plane. With time Leanne had learned, however, that life in peril was a much stronger source. Right now, she needed everything she could gather. Frid was extremely dangerous, and while she doubted he was at her level, he had the advantage of home turf. *I can even the odds.* Leanne rose to her feet, lifted her arms, and a multitude of thin glistening roots shot out of her, a full twenty-two of them. They all found their marks, and the screaming started. Leanne smiled as she felt energy envelop her.

No need to hold back. The ground close to the doorway where her quarry had entered tore open with a deafening crack, and tendrils of green and black poured up and tore the large metal door off its hinges. It twisted, and the metal screamed from strain as magically fueled roots assaulted the container. Leanne couldn't see exactly what was happening inside the containers, but she could feel the metal as if the roots were part of her. In seconds she had destroyed the first container and felt the resistance of a second reinforced barrier. She screamed, furious, and the slithering mass of oozing wood retracted before slamming into this barrier as well. A force that could grind rocks to dust tore through the metal. The door itself was ripped from its place as the walls around it buckled. Leanne let the mass she had let loose calm, let it flow towards the walls, and create a pathway for her. She walked towards the crater she had created, hardly noticing that the people she'd been drawing her magic from had collapsed and were now drawing their final breaths. No need for them anymore, she thought as she pulled even more power from the roots she had lured into the space. As she walked, she let spell after spell etched in implanted bone start their work. She grew taller, she felt muscles flex and stiffen, and her eyesight became sharper. Her mind began splitting. To most having their mind torn apart would be intolerable, but Leanne had learned to embrace that strange pain. In moments she was more than just one, moving as two. Murder, yes, time for murder. The thought was cold and grim, and it echoed in her skull. It was followed by a jubilant feeling; there was something dark and warm and rewarding about cleansing the world of Mages.

***

THE rubble was weighing on Lin's chest. She was pinned on her side behind metal and stone. She could see out, but she didn't know if she could call for help. Her ribs ached and her lungs felt as if someone had inflated them to twice their normal size only to let all the air out again. Breathing was a struggle. She tried to move her legs. They wouldn't move more than a few centimeters, but they didn't feel broken. Her right leg felt wet though, drenched and sticky. She figured she must be bleeding but she couldn't get to a position where she could see properly. She was lying on her left arm, but her right was free. *I can probably dig myself out.* The thought was accompanied by a much darker thought, *What if that was an attack, what if I was spotted?* She calmed herself and tried to listen for anyone else. *Where is Kesh? Is she alright?*

A second passed and then another. Suddenly she saw it, the thing that must have caused this. Lin winced as she recognized the face of that young woman she'd seen with the Tribe minutes ago. Long blonde hair and big eyes, but now the features looked as if they were painted on a frozen mask, and the woman's body looked inhuman. *It? She?* The thing was taller than any human she'd ever seen, and its limbs were all wrong. Its clothes had torn and its feet had elongated to terminate in large black claws. Its fingers were like the legs of a spider, impossibly long and glistening like metal in the low light. The whole creature looked wet as if covered in oil or murky sewer water. It was moving closer, towards the opening in the side of the room that had been torn open. It hadn't noticed her yet. Lin made her breath as silent as she could, stiff from fear. The creature moved slowly and deliberately, scanning for something, and suddenly found a target. It launched itself with impossible speed, crossing some twenty meters in a heartbeat, grabbing a man from the floor; Masan. With a strangle grip of thin, sharp fingers it pushed Masan up against the back wall.

It spoke, "Where is she?" The sound was strained and guttural.

Masan was dazed, but conscious. He struggled to speak but couldn't get the sound out. The creature grabbed his arm with its free hand and slammed him into the wall with even more force.

"Where?" Louder, angrier. Lin couldn't see the face of the thing from this angle, but it didn't sound human.

Masan managed a whisper, "I don't know, didn't see."

The thing paused for a fraction of a second. It pulled its hand back, extending her razor-sharp digits as a spear, shoulders tensed and the arm moved forward in a motion clearly intended to impale the Mage's face. Just as the blow fell, before hitting flesh, a flash of light surged through the air. The arm was sliced clean off and only graced Masan before falling uselessly to the ground. The creature howled. It slammed Masan into the wall, leaving a deep indent in the metal, and a bloodstain where Masan's head made impact, before letting him fall to the ground.

It turned in the direction the flash had come from. Its movements were quick and snakelike, nothing like what would be expected by a lumbering giant. It got low, on all three, claws ripping apart steel and concrete as it rushed towards Frid. The large man, the Light Mage, Lin realized, stood at the end of the room, bleeding from wounds on his head and shoulder. Before the creature reached him, he'd raised his hand again, and searing light, like threads, weaved through the air. The threads cut the creature over and over, slicing chunks of flesh off, thick black fluid pumping out of wounds, he severed the remaining arm, a piece of its strange human face, and its leg. The creature howled as it collapsed; wiry, bright-burning white threads kept cutting into it through the spasms. Finally, the walking horror had been reduced to nothing more than pieces of flesh without any remnant of life in them. Lin saw Frid cautiously approaching the remains.

***

KESH froze in confusion as the monstrous construct entered the container, tearing off a corrugated metal wall. Her eyes saw the magical construct, but her brain struggled to perceive the sheer magnitude of the magic she was witnessing. This proved to be a terrible idea because she should have been getting out of its way, not wondering how it was made and how much power it required. Debris came at her, stinging her body with pieces of metal. When Kesh finally moved out of the worst of it, her brain continued to work on the problem that was the construct. It wasn't typical of Dark Mages who preferred to animate metal constructs or shadows, not living tissue. It could be a golem made by an Earth Mage, but it was too moist, too sticky for their liking. This belongs to a Life Mage, Kesh realized.

Kesh didn't get more time to assess the creature before she was stopped in her tracks by a laser light show, the likes of which she had never seen before. Kesh got down low, managing to find a spot mostly concealed by the masses of rubble. First discs, then beams of light, shot out from one of the men, Frid, chopping the construct to pieces. He's not a Fire Mage. Shit. That kind of beam-based shit-show was exactly the kind of thing favored by Light Mages. Was she the only honest Mage in this whole damn place?

I am not going to die today, I'm not dying! What would Mia do?

Darkness flowed through cracks of rock and into her body, she could feel the tingle in her feet and legs as invisible tendrils made their way into her. The darkness brought runes alive, it activated her personal shields with a quick pulse. Her hands fumbled, searching in her rain cloak pocket for the spells she had brought. She pulled the stack of plaques out, only to find that the plastic sheets had been torn when she was hit by the debris. Shit. Shit. *This is why I invented metal freaking cubes in the first place.* She had an offensive tattoo, but it was far too slow and too powerful. She might be able to take out one of these Mages, but there was no chance it'd be fast enough when facing a group. *Do I want to get into a fight with adepts? Dying in my first real battle.*

Kesh cast about assessing the battle and then saw Lin under the rubble. She immediately abandoned all hope of getting off a spell of her own as Frid continued the onslaught against the creature. *I'm a Dark Mage in a Light Mage place, we need to get the fuck out. Run, run to fight another day.* Keeping an eye on the increasingly choppier creature Kesh activated an obfuscating shield and made her way over to Lin.

***

KESH reached out and touched Lin's shoulder letting her into the field of the spell and motioned to her lips indicating that she should stay silent. The light vs monster battle lit up Kesh as she grabbed Lin by the shoulders and heaved. As she pulled and worked her weight back and forth, Lin helping by trying to wiggle herself free, they managed to get loose. Masan was hulking and struggling to breathe some forty meters further in, and it didn't seem like either he or Frid had seen them yet.

The moment Lin was loosened she started running, ignoring the pain shooting through her leg. She had a grip around Kesh's wrist, feeling her golden bracelet under her fingers. She kept low, and moved quickly; she didn't need to look around to know that Kesh was doing the same. In moments they had cleared the containers, another few seconds and they'd reached an entrance to an access tunnel. She'd only briefly explored this before, but she knew there was a small hatch that exited several stories above. She pulled the grating covering the tunnel aside and stared upwards, but when she put weight on her right foot it almost gave out. She looked down to realize that she'd been cut deeply in her calf muscle. Adrenaline had masked how bad the injury really was.

She continued up the ladder more carefully, avoiding putting a load on that leg. Outside Lin turned sharp left, she'd noticed a narrow metal ladder, a fire escape during her walks with Masan. *Masan, that dirty treacherous asshole!* Only when she got up to the ladder, which was buried behind scrap metal and trash, did she look behind herself for long enough to see the shaken expression on Kesh's face.

Lin kept her voice down. "We're okay, we'll be okay, but we can't stop yet. Whatever that was, it might not be dead, and if it is, those two will be after us. Up! I'm right behind you." She motioned for the ladder.

Kesh didn't hesitate. She had to do an awkward jump to clear the trash. She headed up as fast as she could. Lin jumped up after her.

The duo continued up and up. Lin lost count, but they must have passed at least ten stories before Kesh opted to get off the ladder and onto a walkway.

"This way." Kesh motioned in a direction that Lin figured was vaguely towards the mountain. Kesh started at a quick pace and seemed confused for a moment when Lin couldn't keep up. Now she finally seemed to realize the extent of the injury.

"You're bleeding!"

"I thought you'd seen that."

"No, I did, but I didn't know how bad." Kesh got closer and gasped when she saw the tear in Lin's leg. "How are you walking?"

"Practice. I've maimed myself more than once while working on repair jobs."

"We need to stop the bleeding."

"We do, I'm starting to feel faint." Lin realized the truth of the statement as the words left her mouth. The world was a lot less colorful than usual, and her peripheral vision was starting to go away.

Kesh got to her knees next to her and took her robe off. She was dressed in an expensive-looking, red jumpsuit made from synthetic silk. Lin felt a twinge of sadness at the destruction of such a beautiful garment as Kesh ripped one of the arms off at the seam. Wrapping the wound only took Kesh a few moments, and she did it with a lot of force, almost making Lin pass out from pain rather than blood loss. As soon as Lin managed to collect herself, she motioned for Kesh to continue and they walked on, now with Kesh supporting some of Lin's weight.

There were few pedestrians on this level, but there were no shops or gathering places, only dwellings. It wasn't an easy place to find an inconspicuous spot to deal with a wound this large. After a few blocks, Lin grabbed Kesh's arm to slow her down, and she indicated to a passageway that led to an adjacent path. When they'd gotten into the shade and shelter of the alley Lin finally felt calm enough to speak. "What the hell was that? I get that it was magic, but what the hell?"

Kesh leaned against a wall. She was rubbing her hands as if she was cold or she didn't know what to do with them. "I... I don't know. It was magic, but I haven't seen something like that before. I think Life Magic, but that's rare. It could be mundane magic. It was powerful, usually, we can't really sense magic from other schools, but whatever that was it warped everything around it. Then, well, apparently your friends in the tribe are Light Mages." The last words were sounded out slowly, with both fear and contempt.

"I get it, you don't like Light Mages. After this, I can't say I do either."

"No, you don't get it. They're not like us, not like any of the other Mages. They embrace corruption, they've made it a religion or something. They hate the rest of us, especially Dark Mages. I don't know what they wanted, but I'm sure they used you to lure me in. Maybe they wanted to kill me. Mia told me I might be a target, she thought your target, and I guess she was half right."

"Why would you be a target?" Lin tried to keep her expression confused, which worked because she was confused. She knew that Masan had wanted her to target Kesh, but she thought it was to help her find Sal and figure out the cause of her abduction and bounty. Even knowing she'd been used against Kesh, it stung her that Kesh had distrusted her enough to bring her up in this way with a friend. *She was right you bitch! You were a threat to her, sort your shit out!* Her conscious thoughts had to fight her emotions.

Kesh hesitated for a moment, it looked like she was blushing, or at least like she was very uncomfortable. "Well, they tell me I'm rare. Both Mia and the Prior Wallang keep saying so, but I never really believed them."

"Prior Wallang? His name is Wallang?" Masan and his people had been after a Wallang. She just hadn't known that he had had anything to do with her or with Kesh. It seemed she had been right to question Masan's motives. He had used her as a pawn in a game he hadn't even acknowledged existed.

Kesh raised her eyebrows. "Yeah, why?"

"I never heard you use his name, only title. I've heard the name before when Masan was talking to one of the older Tribe members. Something about Wallang being a likely suspect. I didn't hear more; I didn't even know Wallang was a Dark Mage."

Kesh nodded, "Well, maybe they weren't so right then, if it's about him this makes sense. If they were interested in the Prior, they must have heard my name. That's why you got that reaction when you introduced me. They might have wanted to get to him through me."

It was as plausible a reason as any. Lin hadn't really considered if Kesh had been merely a step on the path of her quest for vengeance and safety, let alone what she was to Masan's plots.

"Alright, I guess. Maybe. Could you go back? Why the hell would they want this Prior of yours?"

Kesh quietly leaned her head against the smooth metal wall for a few stretched-out seconds, seemingly thinking it over. "For a while, for months I guess, maybe even longer, something has been happening at the Guild. The Prior has been pursuing some research for years now, but he's getting close to finding the solution. I've been helping him. Maybe they somehow felt what he was doing, or maybe they somehow got a spy into our guild."

"Sal?"

Kesh sighed. "He's not usually around often enough to know about something as private as the Prior's work. I don't think he'd stoop as low as to sell us out. Sal is a mystery. I don't think he'd sell the Guild out, but I didn't think he'd be in the human trafficking business either. I can think of very few ways to find out and they all involve asking the Guild for help."

Lin touched Kesh's shoulder. "I'm sorry for bringing you there, I promise I had no idea."

"I know. We should go. Stay close and I will try to force my shields to cover you too."

Just as they turned around to leave the alley Lin gasped and flung a hand up to stop Kesh. A familiar face passed only meters ahead of her, scanning the crowd. Lin turned around deliberately, but not in a sudden way so that she wouldn't draw attention. She took Kesh's hand and walked towards the direction where they had entered this alley.

"What's up?"

"That girl is a Tribe member, I've seen her almost every day, but I can't remember her name. She's not in purple. I think she's looking for us." She talked at a low volume but not a whisper, and she didn't break her pace. She had absentmindedly produced her gun and was now holding it hidden in the folds of her heavy purple robe.

The two walked on and on. Small markets and blocks of apartments gave way to areas of implant clinics, then a district full of repair shops. They shifted levels regularly, moving between blocks, always towards the mountain. Exactly where they were going Lin hadn't figured out yet. They couldn't go to Kesh's guild. What if Sal was there? What if the Tribe was there waiting? What if that thing was there waiting? Lin shivered, a cold went through her and chilled her to the bone. She felt nauseous.

***

LEANNE fell back hard against a container wall. The stream of pseudo-consciousness from her construct had been cut off in flashes of searing light. She could feel the cuts as if they'd been inflicted on her rather than this thing she made. *That man is no ordinary Mage. What the hell was a Light Adept doing here? They wouldn't send someone like that for no reason.*

Thinking was hard, pain shot through her limbs, and her implants felt like they were on fire. She'd managed not to draw too much on her storage, but the trauma of her second body dying always had a brutal effect. It was like her soul was sling-shotted back into her body, taking all the pain she'd just incurred with it. She looked at her arms, there was bleeding but not too much.

She couldn't leave like this. These barbarians couldn't be allowed to get their hands on Lin. She belonged to Leanne, she'd made her, and she would have her. Leanne straightened herself and took a deep breath. She could feel life still surging, brewing all around her, but not enough. *I guess we're doing it the hard way.* With a muffled grunt, she focused her mind inwards, explored her own depths, and found the shards she'd implanted in herself pulsating with power. She drew from several of them and made it surge outwards into another piece of bone, this one inscribed with a favorite spell of hers. Anchored with obala-ūruzsól, it gave a low hum as the piece started fighting the sinew that she'd grown to hold it in place. As the other runes came alive, she could feel the surface of the implant deform. Pain shot through her arm as black, steely legs dug through her muscle and skin, blood and pieces of flesh pumped out of the large gouge that was forming. The hand-sized creature formed on the surface of the bone piece, a bubbling black mass that hardened as it took shape. The razor-sharp legs extended out of Leanne's arm, cutting a path big enough to drag its swollen pear-shaped body out.

In a few excruciating seconds, the spiderling had been birthed and made its way to the floor. Let's see how those miserable creatures deal with this one. The spiderling skittered away towards the spot where Leanne's last creation had been destroyed moments ago, as Leanne herself turned towards the exit. Time to be off. Leanne calmed her breathing and counted the seconds to make her mind come to a point of calm that would allow her to reel in the energies she'd allowed to move according to their own volition. Life was hers to control, she would not be controlled by it. She moved towards the exit as fast as she could, keeping to shadows and behind pillars of the now relatively dark structure. Her assault had ripped apart a lot of the electrical infrastructure, it had also cratered the roof in at more than one point. The darkness and piles of rubble were now helping her keep hidden.

As she exited the building, her head flashed in agony. Losing a construct always came with a lot of side effects. This one was worse than most, she'd used a sliver of bone in its making. Her need for more components was more apparent than ever. She steadied herself on a railing and limped down towards an elevator. She needed to get the hell out before that Light Mage realized that he hadn't actually killed a caster, but a sending.

This time Leanne didn't have nearly as strong a connection with her construct, but she could still hear and see the general surroundings of the spiderling. As soon as she was fairly sure that Lin and her friend had managed to get away in the commotion, she gave it a nudge, telling it to attack. A heartbeat passed and then the Light Mage that had destroyed her last creature was screaming in agony. She smiled.

✷✷✷

THE lights of the back room flicked. The shifting of soil and stone that had resulted from a gigantic root crawling through the facility and slamming through walls had disrupted several power lines. Masan had been forced to swap the grid to their barely functioning backup generators. He didn't dare let his guard down for long enough to cast and hold any unnecessary spells. He needed his reserves and concentration in case another attack was forthcoming. He moved across the floor with purpose, making sure his pattern was sound. He drew the last rune with five short strokes of a brush coated in a silver colloid suspension. As he got to his knees above Frid, he was reminded of the bruising on his own neck and collarbones, his hair was caked in blood from a deep gash on the back of his skull. A problem for later. Healing spells were not his specialty, but he'd manage. Frid was not being a good patient, with a constant scowl on his face, distorting the many deep bleeding cuts. Masan thought he could see both bone and sinew, but kept the concern hidden.

"Please Frid, you need to relax! If I make it fuse like this, the skin will become distorted."

Frid nodded slowly, and assumed a neutral face, letting all emotion drain from sight. "Fiinne." His voice sounded deeply strained, as he barely managed to hide the pain of speaking through his mangled features.

Masan pushed Frid's head down gently with a finger to the forehead, to have him lie entirely prone on the cold steel floor. He took a last look at the spell that he'd drawn across the metal floor, silver settling on the stainless steel. No mistakes. Masan touched a spot on the wall and the entire room lit up like a sun for a moment, reservoirs hidden for emergencies let free. He guided the power through the large pattern on the floor, and from there into Frid. The lines cut open by the spiderling fused as if the skin around them were clay, the tissues moved in subtle ways to find the exact shape they'd formerly held. Seconds of tense focus passed, and Masan started breathing again.

"Give me a mirror," Frid's voice was harder than Masan had ever heard it.

"One moment."

"Now!" Frid's eyes burned with radiant fire, hinting at him being filled with magical energy in spite of not channeling a spell.

Masan shivered and moved to a cabinet at one of the walls. He produced an antique silver mirror that he used when applying makeup. He handed it to Frid.

Frid looked himself over from every angle. Masan could swear that time had stopped, then Frid exclaimed, "Fantastic work! Better than new. Now let's burn this fucking city."

***

WALLANG was in his workshop pacing unconsciously around the circle of rune tiles inset in the floor. *She should have been back long ago. It's not like her to be late.* Wallang suddenly realized he'd been walking back and forth, and he made himself stop abruptly. He sat down. *I shouldn't rely on her for so* much. It makes me weak and puts her in danger. He was certain of the latter, but he didn't entirely know how he knew this. Lately, he'd had a lot of feelings that something would happen, and they were right eerily often. He got back to his feet and stalked out the door of his workshop. Maybe she's just lost in work.

***

KESH cursed the fact that she had never been interested in spycraft or combat operations. She made the best offensive magic the Guild had seen in centuries, but she'd never had to fight her way out of a dangerous situation. She wasn't even carrying any of her own work. She was just going to have to hope that she could make the best of her tattoos. She was pressed into a small alleyway with Lin out of sight, where they had ducked to evade members of the Tribe who were no doubt searching for them.

Lin was tiring quickly from her injury and Kesh was trying to keep her on her feet by resting often. Kesh was also beginning to feel some small traces of corruption, as she tried to push a spell designed to cloak one person to cover two people. Cold pain was spreading out from her shield tattoo, when she inspected the pattern she could see black crawling out in places where it shouldn't, it looked like the tattoo was leaking out or spreading. She realized that her only options were to release the spell or permanently destroy the tattoo. She brought out her torch and rapidly sketched a much larger shield pattern on the wall next to her, it was always so easy with larger surfaces. That solution would work for now, but that spell wouldn't be able to cover them once they moved. They needed something mobile, something to keep them invisible for the whole trip. Surveillance might be hard here, but Kesh knew that this close to a hideout these people would be tapped into every camera, and have a layer of magical eyes on top of that. Dark magic should be safe enough, Light Mages were generally really bad at detecting it, or at least so she had read.

Kesh could feel Lin breathing beside her, trying her best to hold still.

"You don't have to tense Lin," she whispered. "The shield will mask small motions, so it's not a problem if you have to shift your weight or scratch an itch. We'll be here a while, so you might as well be comfortable."

"Can we talk?" Lin asked.

"The spell doesn't do much for noise, we'll be fine if we keep our voices down. We're lucky that this is a loud district."

Kesh thought furiously while Lin finally relaxed at her side. It was terribly bad luck that the Tribe was at the very bottom of City Six, while the Apteryx campus was in the open air at the very top. She and Lin needed to traverse the majority of the city in order to get to safety. Kesh considered the best way to leave a message for Mia. Maybe she could help them if she knew they were missing.

"We need to figure out where we are in the City. I was so busy running that I wasn't keeping track of the districts, I know I saw implant clinics a while back. I'll assume the Tribe knows this warren of walkways like the back of their hand, so I'll try to cover us with magic until we reach an area I recognize. We'll just have to aim to go up and hope that it will bring us to an area I know better."

For once, Kesh appreciated the fact that the Prior made her scramble all over City Six on errands. Her mental map of the city was far from perfect, but she had visited most of the districts. In her panic and desire to put as much space as possible between them and the Tribe, she had forgotten that her implants carried a full map of the city. Shaking her head, she accessed it to figure out where they needed to go.

Realizing that they had made good progress in their journey, Kesh said, "I think we've waited long enough. Help me find a piece of wood or metal in this dumpster."

"What do you need?"

"I need to make the shadow spell portable. Right now, the runes are burned into the wall, so they won't cover us if we leave. I need a relatively solid medium to hold the spell, so it doesn't erode while we move."

"Okay, is the spell big enough to cover us while we look?" asked Lin.

"I may have overdone it a bit, so this corner might have a shield for months," Kesh replied distractedly, eyeing the contents of the dumpster.

Kesh and Lin turned to the dumpster and hunted until they found a piece of scrap metal about the size of Kesh's hand.

"It's not pretty but it'll do. Remind me to make myself a cube if we survive."

Kesh sat on the ground and took a deep breath, centering herself. She felt Lin sit beside her, resting her injured leg. She continued breathing until she entered an almost meditative trance. The Darkness could fight you if you started to work on a spell while agitated. I am a professional. I do this every day, she told herself. Then she got to work etching the shield runes into the metal with her torch.

The magic flew through her like it had been dying to escape into the world. The scrap metal was less perfect than her usual materials, she could feel the imperfect crystalline structure melting for the runes. It didn't take long before she had a full shadow shield up and ready to go.

"It's time. Let's get somewhere safe."

***

KESH and Lin had slowly made their way out of the Tribe's immediate district with great caution. They had risen several stories and Kesh was beginning to think that their surroundings looked familiar. Kesh saw a mall up ahead full of cheap clothing. Lin was still wearing the heavy purple garment of the Tribe. While protective it might prove dangerous if they lost the shield for any reason.

She pulled Lin into the shadow of another dumpster and said, "I'm going to leave you here with the shield. We need to ditch that purple coat of yours, so you look like a Sixer, not a lost Roman Empress. Wait here."

Kesh ducked into the mall, looking for someone who sold outerwear. She found them a few shops in and rifled through the racks until she found a dull, green, waterproof robe with a large hood. It was a bit big for Lin, but better to be hidden and a bit sloppy. She paid for the coat and hurried back to Lin.

"Here, put this on."

Lin shed the purple coat and put on the dull green one. While large, the hood hid her face and the dull green was anonymous in the dim light of the Undercity.

Lin smiled a weak smile, plastered on a pale face, "Let's get going to that castle you brag so much about."

They turned to get going, not realizing that Kesh hadn't been as subtle in the mall as she had hoped.

***

MIA shook her head and grimaced. That girl was well on her way to giving her a stress disorder. She had warned Kesh that she might be a target for the ongoing incursions into Apteryx and Kesh had ignored her as usual. Oblivious kid! She might be my age but she behaves like a damned apprentice at times, while she had harsh words for Kesh she did feel for her; Kesh had never had to get used to the risks of fieldwork, it was really the fault of the Ring for not preparing her properly.

Luckily, Mia was a good enough friend to entirely ignore Kesh's privacy. A spider had been clinging to Kesh's garments for days keeping Mia apprised of her whereabouts during this mess.

The connection with the construct had just lit up like crazy. Mia couldn't tell exactly what had happened, the information from the sending was limited. There was a violent incident involving magic, and Kesh was still alive; Mia couldn't get more out of it.

Mia suited up into her gear, finished the ensemble with a protective and obfuscating rain cloak, and hit the streets of City Six. The spider was now only a faint tracking beacon, so it wasn't about to give Mia a nice clear visual or signal of Kesh's whereabouts. She used the feel of it to get a general direction far in the lower levels of the city and took off after it. Normally, Mia would wind through the crowds and try to blend in but making her way inside wasn't going to cut it today. She was going to have to take the direct route.

Mia found a likely tower in the correct direction and looked for one that had external scaffolding. She quickly climbed onto the rig, probably for cleaning or repairs, and started climbing and sliding down the poles to drop as many stories into the lower city as fast as possible. Mia's strength was dramatically enhanced for this type of free climbing and her gloves had a nano surface that allowed extremely strong grip on concrete and rebar to make it easy for her to get into and out of buildings the creative way. If she had to, Mia could free-climb a smooth stainless steel air vent or external wall to get where she wanted to go.

Mia dropped over twenty stories in a few minutes by slide hopping the tower, before returning to the scaffold walkways. Her spider was still giving a faint signal in the area, but not moving dramatically, so she looked around at the neighborhood.

If I were Kesh, where would I go to feel safe? Mia asked herself. The logical answer was up and in the direction of the guild. But, if she couldn't go up for some reason, where else would she go?

Kesh ran a lot of odd errands for the Prior who loved everything magical and obscure. She was familiar with some of the City's speedier shopping districts. Mia checked her map of the city and sure enough, there was a nearby shopping tower that Kesh might have visited before. Mia used her small stature to duck and weave through the press of people, focusing on the spider and looking for hiding spots.

The shopping center specializes in clothing. What was Kesh trying to do there?

The spider had definitely stopped, and minutes ticked by. She likely wasn't carrying the materials to cast any form of offensive magic and she carried a minimal amount of defensive magic. She also refused to geolocate her comm because 'she never went anywhere'.

Mia headed into the center looking for any trace of Kesh or hints of ongoing violence, but there was nothing. The shops ran out on the 45th story, so Mia hit the walkways searching for cover.

"I swear I saw the Dark one, she was buying some threads."

"Well, that isn't doing us a lot of fucking good now is it. They vanished. Again."

Mia swiveled in the direction of the profanity. She didn't recognize the voice, but she moved towards the voices, so she could hear better. Dark one certainly sounds like Kesh. She didn't want to take the time to cast an invisibility shield, so she pulled out a knife in one hand and her battle cube in the other. After today, I will make Kesh train to carry one of her own lightforsaken cubes.

Mia rounded into an alley in the scaffolding to find two purple-cloaked goons swinging bats in the space, trying to see if there was anyone present with a shield. She recognized a small disturbance in the light of the area, the tell-tale signs of a shadow shield to a Dark Mage. Mia stepped out of the men's line of sight, pulled out her shadow cube, and sent her shadow to join the magical shadow in the corner.

The shadow merged with the magic, showing Kesh holding out her hand, ready to cast an anti-matter spell, and another girl, Lin, holding a gun, ready to fire on the men if they didn't turn and leave. The thugs were looking in the direction where Kesh was hiding, allowing Mia to come out of the darkness at their backs silently. She considered her options for a half second, then knifed the first one in the neck, severing his carotid artery; she then swiveled around and put her knife in the other man's kidney. The first man dropped like a stone, spewing blood everywhere. The second collapsed in a kneeling position, frantically trying to locate the knife.

"I wouldn't touch that knife if I were you. It's the only thing keeping you alive right now," Mia told him.

Impressively, the girl hadn't lowered her gun or fired at her prematurely. Mia applauded her and Kesh heaved a sigh of relief, as Mia dropped her shield entering their view.

Mia extended her hand. "My dear, if I wanted you dead, you'd be dead. I'm a professional. I'm Kesh's friend Mia."

Kesh came around the girl protectively.

"Lin it's alright, she's a friend."

"Thank you, I really don't have room for more enemies right now." Lin holstered her gun and took her hand, grimacing.

"It's good to know your limits," Mia smirked.

"How did you know we were here?" Kesh asked.

"Do you really want to know?"

"Probably not. But we'll be discussing it later," replied Kesh.

"Oh, I bet, but probably with me and the whole light damned Ring." She turned to Lin. "Well, Lin it's nice to meet you and it seems you're in need of a medic. Let's patch you up and get the hell out of here."

The injured man decided to croak at them at that minute.

"Do we need him?"

"No, he's not in charge, just a flunky for the Light Mages," Lin answered.

"Good." Mia jerked her knife back out with a gush of blood. She cleaned it on his clothing and put it away. She swapped her battle cube for her shadow cube and focused, quickly dropping them into an invisibility shield.

Kesh relaxed a bit more as she felt the shield go up, letting all her magic drop completely. The spell in the cube was much more complex than the one she'd jury-rigged on the fly and it would do a better job of protecting them all.

Mia pulled a medic pack out of her cloak and said, "Lin, sit. I'll bandage you for now and we'll head home shielded. I can't wait to hear this story."

274TH DAY OF 11566 AF

KESH breathed a sigh of relief when they exited the city's substructure. This district was wide open and there were no vertical levels of structures, just solid mountains underfoot. This area had avenues, not tunnels, corridors, and walkways. There was more space and more surveillance. She and Mia helped Lin to the gates of the Apteryx compound.

The black fortress loomed above the wall separating the compound from the street. It was surrounded by a no man's land of protective obsidian, deeply graven with spell traps for the unwitting and unwary. It was as good at keeping apprentices in as it was at keeping intruders out.

Kesh turned to Lin, who was taking in the brutalism of the Apteryx fortress. "I understand if you want to leave and try to fade back into the city, but I think you will have a better fighting chance if you stay here with us."

Mia wisely decided to stay quiet for this part of the conversation.

Kesh could see Lin considering her options, but her exhaustion won out. Lin's shoulders dropped and she replied, "I'll come in for now. Better to be alert inside a fortress than stranded alone outside."

Kesh and Mia deactivated the spell field so they could cross the shiny surface to the entrance. As they entered the compound, Mia told Kesh, "You need to report this to Prior Wallang and the rest of the Ring immediately."

"Are you sure that's the best move?"

"When this was a case of Sal being mixed up in an abduction, it was acceptable to keep private, but we just saw a highly skilled Light Adept battle it out with a completely unknown Adept. And, we confirmed that the Tribe is a cover for a serious cadre of Light Mages. At this point, the issue is too existentially serious to keep from the Ring. For all our sakes. Not to mention we just walked up to the fort's main door with a bleeding woman. We need the big guns."

Lin broke the silence. "I feel like there's something you're not saying."

Kesh wrung her hands and stared at them as she fidgeted. Mia saved her from having to reply by explaining, "Lin, that was the opening skirmish in a major Mage war. It's not just Apteryx who will respond. All three Dark Guilds will go on high alert and hunt the Light Mages down like dogs. They're too dangerous to be left alive."

"What about the other Mage?"

Kesh answered, "Well, we can safely say she's not on their team. I have no idea why she intervened, but anyone who can marshal trees into weapons and make autonomous constructs is as terrifying and dangerous as Frid and Masan. That's the kind of thing that will kill you with corruption if you are not extremely powerful and skilled. She might be a Life Mage and if so, the Dark Guilds might just leave her be. We don't have a feud with the Life Mages, and she saved our asses, so we'll see what happens."

"You seem more scared now than you were back there."

Once again Mia took pity on Kesh. "The Ring is made up of seven Mages who are each as powerful as Frid and the lady Adept. I'm guessing that Wallang and Kesh kept a lot of this from them. That Kesh told him and he didn't pass this along might help, but she's supposed to prevent his absentmindedness, not exploit it for personal problems. If she's lucky, they'll delay punishing her for her secrecy until after they've eradicated the Light Mages."

"What will they do that's so bad? You're clearly very useful."

Kesh swallowed grimly. "I have no idea, this is exactly why I'm so scared."

***

THE room was as dark as the sun outside the large, tinted window permitted. The screens of the security station were running at minimum intensity, and low music with a heavy bass was playing. The tallest of the three figures at the table, Ocron, put down his chip with a shit-eating grin. "I guess that's game then. Really sorry to take your hard-earned creds."

Spelaeus rubbed the bridge of his nose to fight off a brewing headache.

"You really aren't though." The headache was largely caused by Oc being such an absolutely terrible winner.

Rea smiled at S. "At least we're done, we don't need to listen to his goading anymore."

"We're getting to the gloating phase though," said S.

Oc waved his arms defensively. "I would never!"

"You would, in fact, you always do," Rea teased him.

"If you mind it so much you really shouldn't lose so often."

"Eh, you're not the worst, and with the introduction of twelve-hour shifts I don't know how we'd stay sane without some fighting."

"Did either of you figure out why Cormac's been so pissy lately?" interjected S.

"First of all, I'd never call him that; because I'm not suicidal. But yeah, I heard a student killed a spy inside the guild," said Rea.

Oc's face became a lot more serious. "Inside the fort?"

"Yep. Figured you'd heard."

"Jera!" whispered Oc.

"As we've been asked to keep an eye out for Light Mages I'm sure you can figure out what sort that was."

"So some of his other people screwed up and we're stuck paying the price," said Oc

"Hmmm, not exactly. I checked the logs. You and I were on duty when that happened."

"No kidding. Oopsie."

"Oopsie indeed. I'm sure we'll eventually hear all about Cormac's opinion of that, I'm guessing we haven't faced any consequences mostly because they can't spare the manpower right now."

"You're thinking we're about to be suspended."

"Corporal punishment seems more likely," said S.

"Shut up, S."

"Yes, do shut up, S. We don't need you gloating either at the moment."

"Hey, the light is on."

"Oh, I guess we should pay attention."

Rea flicked her wrist and the screens next to the window came alive. They displayed three women, one of whom was being half-carried by the other two.

"Isn't that Mia?"

"And Kesh. I'll go and help, you call for help, the third one is injured."

Rea was already on her comm, reporting what she was seeing to Cormac.

***

KESH was quaking when she went into the chamber of the Ring. The Ring, of course, didn't have a boardroom or a meeting room. They had a giant fancy-ass obsidian chamber where all seven sat in a horseshoe around the person that had been called in for judgment.

Kesh had never been there before. Her youthful indiscretions had primarily been limited to being told off by the rector and the rector alone. After she'd become a Journeyman and started working for Prior Wallang, she really hadn't had any issues with discipline. She'd been too busy losing herself in her work.

The scrutiny she felt now in front of these seven made her miss the times in the rector's office. This was a million times worse; having Lin and Mia there with her didn't help. She felt exposed like she was a little kid again, she did realize that in reality, she was a Mage who might have inadvertently set off a war. Whenever the Light and Dark clashed the results were horrific.

Kesh was bolstered slightly by the fact that Prior Wallang was present. Surely the fact that she had told him about the bug spells, Lin's problems, and her abduction, would mean something; maybe even afford her some leniency.

That was probably beyond him. She hoped she wouldn't be punished for helping him because she had only been doing her job. And technically, he'd never really told her what he was trying to do. Kesh was clever enough to guess that he needed esoteric runes for something. You know, maybe slightly more nefarious than usual, but that didn't necessarily equate to her knowing exactly what he'd been up to. She couldn't have known he'd done something to piss off the Light Mages.

Kesh realized that her internal monologue was rambling. She took in the panel of Mages around the table. Hugh and Cormac, the most security-minded of the Ring, sat to the left of the Chairman with Prior Wallang rounding out the male end of the Table. Argent and Hira sat to the Chairman's right. Argent looked calm and composed, as always, but Hira looked fit to be tied.

The Speaker was looking at Wallang when they spoke, "So you were proven right I take it?"

Wallang nodded. "It seems so. It also seems we underestimated the threat this group poses. Kesh, explain the situation."

Kesh was spiraling as she waited; so much so that she almost didn't hear the first thing that she'd been asked. She looked up to realize that now the Speaker, the chairperson of the Ring, was staring down at her waiting for an answer.

"Ehrm. Yes. I've been seeing Lin for a while now, and she told me about this man, Masan. He had been pushing her to investigate me."

"She was investigating you?" asked Hugh. He leaned forward towards Kesh, as he spoke.

"Yeah. So, Sal has been doing side deals." Kesh winced internally as she said it, but she tried to keep her composure. From their expressions, the Ring didn't seem entirely surprised.

"Of course he has. Have you met the man?" said Hira. Hira punctuated her rhetorical questions with an elaborate hand gesture.

"Don't be shitty," said Cormac. He leaned back in his seat.

"Please, I'm just trying to explain what happened," replied Kesh. She shifted nervously on the spot. It was overwhelming to the focal point of this much attention.

"I'm sorry, go on." the Chairman waved at the rest of the Ring to give her back the floor.

"Masan and his people helped Lin get away from Sal."

"He took her hostage?" asked Hira. She seemed almost smug.

"Yes, but no. It seems he planned to sell her," Mia interjected.

"That fucking bastard. I'll kill him this time," said Cormac. He slammed his hands on the table to punctuate the sentiment. He seemed almost ready to rise and go looking for him when Hugh replied, "You might not need to, nobody has seen him for weeks."

Wallang interjected, "Not since the night Lin was rescued in fact."

"He better pray he's dead," Cormac grumbled curling his hands into and out of fists repeatedly.

"So, Sal kidnapped Lin, the girl here, right? How does this matter to us? No offense of course." Argent gestured at Lin dismissively. It was just like the rector to ignore the men and get straight to the point.

"If you'd let me speak… Lin was rescued but wanted to find out why she'd been taken. Masan pointed her in my direction, knowing that I knew Sal. We now know that wasn't the whole reason. Lin told me about all of this after a few days. Seems she figured out I wasn't the enemy," Kesh explained.

Lin took over, "Masan, the leader of the Tribe, wanted me to look into Dark Mages. After I was abducted by Sal off a moving ship, I thought that your guild or one of the other dark guilds here was responsible for kidnapping me. But, it seems like Masan was really just using my naiveté and my fear against the Dark Guilds. Probably because a Mage would have been more suspicious. He tried to get me close to Kesh so I could learn more."

Kesh jumped back in, "We went back there, to the place where Masan hangs out with his Tribe, I guess a lot of them are really his guild. I just wanted to know how he knew me; I didn't think he was an actual threat."

"But he was?" asked Cormac. It was like watching a caged panther, waiting to pounce. Kesh hoped that she wasn't going to be the recipient of his next actions.

"He and at least one other person there are Light Mages. They knew that I knew the Prior, and I think they were about to interrogate me."

"Why didn't they?" asked Hugh. He had already put on his look of strategic contemplation.

"There was an attack. They seem to have been making a lot of enemies."

"I'm not so sure. I think she might have been after me," said Lin

"Possibly. Either way, the attacker was a Mage. I think, a Life Mage. It was incredible, I've never seen constructs like that, and she almost brought the entire structure down on us." Kesh was slightly awed as she recalled the giant construct.

"So, an Adept I take it?" asked the Chairman.

"I've never seen an Adept do anything like that. She killed everyone in seconds. She brought literal tons of matter barreling in. I... I have no idea where she came from or why she interfered on our behalf. We're lucky to have made it out alive and I know that they're still coming for us," Kesh finished.

"I think we've heard enough. Kesh and Lin you're dismissed. It looks like we're going to have a lot to talk about." Wallang's voice was much colder, and more authoritative than Kesh was used to.

"Mia, give us a few minutes but wait for me outside. I'm sensing an increase in your workload," said Hugh.

***

THE Ring turned as one to look at Wallang. The darkness of the room grew noticeably heavier and denser, the small light at the center struggling to stay alive.

"Your protege has found herself in quite a bit of trouble, and I sense you have something to do with it," said Argent.

Wallang waited patiently for her to get to her point.

"We've overlooked your esoteric experiments for some time. But since none of us have recently done anything that would have provoked the presence of a Light Battle Mage here on Embla and Kesh is up to her eyeballs in this, now would be the time to unburden yourself," she concluded. She tapped her fingers on the table as she spoke.

"I may have taken my recent experiments too far. But I'm not entirely certain how they relate to the Light Mages." Wallang kept his posture loose and relaxed. He would not show these vultures any hints of weakness.

"Tell us anyway," replied Hugh. "Especially as you've dragged an untested journeyman into your 'experiments'."

Wallang formed his hands into a trial, acquiescing to the question, "I have been trying to access the Dark plane to examine our world from outside the confines of our physical existence. It has required old and forgotten magics, rare runes that I found in my research. Kesh has been making rune tiles from old texts for me to test, as part of a large library of tiles that can be used for complex incantations."

"How is this different from all of the guilds we've crushed? The cultists that would have us worship some fictional mad god" interrupted Kiste. This was her first contribution to the conversation. She seemed a little agitated by the news.

"I wasn't trying to let the Dark in, I was trying to let myself out."

"The semantics are unimportant, you've been opening a massive channel between our world and the Dark."

"Yes…"

"So you've triggered a magical event that was large enough in scope to raise the hackles of Light Mages," Kiste hammered away at him mercilessly.

"Kesh had identified a Light listening spell on a tool recently, and we reported it. But, I hadn't realized it was part of a specific offensive."

"I can confirm that they reported the Light spell," added Cormac. The change of topic seemed to have calmed him a little.

"And Lin?" Cormac asked.

"We don't do people," Hugh flatly pointed out, with some sense of regret that it was one of the few trades eschewed by Apteryx.

"Well, Light Mages know that, and Emblans know that, but a techie from Sphere who was just kidnapped by a Dark Mage from our Guild doesn't know that. The dim bulbs took advantage of her ignorance and sent her after anyone in our Guild that she could get her claws into. Kesh just happened to be in the wrong place at the wrong time," Wallang said.

"Kesh was hardly an accident; this was targeted and you know it Wallang. They were after you and you gave them an in when you kept sending your closest confidant out as an errand girl," said Argent. She punctuated her language with firm gestures.

"You're probably right. Too many coincidences. I do regret that I exposed Kesh in this way, she's rather naive, especially given her high value to the guild," Wallang opened his hands in surrender. He felt some regret, Kesh was really one of the most interesting Mages to join Apteryx in years, she should have been better prepared.

"We're going to have to take care of Kesh's naiveté. She can't be allowed to hide in her workshop away from the real world any longer," said Cormac. "In her current state, she's a serious security liability."

"Well, I think that's going to have to wait until we've dealt with the Light Mages. It's also not just Arabris who's a liability. We've been far too relaxed in how we train our artificers," said Hugh.

"Record it anyway, I don't care if she's traumatized, she's not getting off without consequences for this one," said Cormac.

"What of this mystery Mage?" asked Hugh.

"Kesh and Lin have told you as much as they or anyone knows. I don't know who this woman was or what her interests are," Wallang replied.

"Do we really think she's a Life Mage? They've become extremely rare of late," queried Hira.

"Well with skills like the ones Kesh mentioned, maybe we just found out why they're so rare. We knew someone had been cleaning house among them, I propose that it was some internal conflict. Either way, she helped them out, so she's no friend of the Light," Kiste pointed out.

"I don't think she's relevant for now," said the Chairman. "Whatever her motives, she isn't our opponent in this fight if she saved Kesh. Hugh, catch us up, what can we expect now that they know they've been made?"

"It's a bad sign that there's obviously more than one of them and that they seem to have had quite a substantial foothold in City Six," said Hugh. "One dead, two mauled, and several more at large is a big problem."

"Apparently, we were deceived by the frivolous nature of the Tribe. It's a pretty astounding intelligence failure," said the Chairman.

Hugh and Cormac looked at one another.

"All our intel said that they had some minor talents who were Guild rejects and a couple of full Fire Mages. They seemed to want to be left alone. We'll rectify this oversight going forward," said Hugh.

Wallang roused from his reverie, "Light Mages usually confront their problems head-on. They're not exactly known for surgical precision. Scorched Earth and nukes are more their style."

"It's too much to hope that this Life Adept will have dissuaded them," mumbled Hira.

"If they're alive, and it sounds like they are, they won't give up until they've either solved their problem or we've eradicated them. The Council doesn't permit failure," said Cormac. "If they targeted Kesh, it's Wallang they're after. They'll keep at it until they're dead, or he is."

"Then we're going to need backup. Let's send a team of our people to assess the primary scene down at the Tribe and send all of our intel to Asio and Strix, except what Wallang here has been up to," ordered the Chairman.

"They'll want to know what started it," warned Cormac.

"Tell them the Light Mages wanted something Kesh made. It's plausible and they'll be too worked up to ask too many questions right now," said Hugh.

"We'll recall as many of our people as you can, lock down the apprentices and journeymen, and let's check all of our fortifications. Cormac, Hugh, I want all of the available intel all the Dark Guilds have on high-ranking Light Adepts, maybe we can figure out who we're dealing with. I'll go let the heads of Asio and Strix know that we have a problem," said the Chairman. "This is about to get ugly."

***

FRID sat in one of the silver and glass chairs of the innermost offices, back against the wall furthest from the door, "So she made it back to Apteryx?"

Masan, who had been walking in circles while reading through logs on a data slate, looked up at him, "Unfortunately. It was inevitable though. It's a big city and we only have five operatives we can really trust."

"I'm sure five will be enough. I've seen their files, and I trained Gere myself. I will have that little shit, and I will have her master's head."

"I'm not sure a direct assault is wise..."

"The time for your sneaky bullshit is over! What results have you managed? It's only by pure dumb luck you have any clue as to whom we're after." Frid's eyes burned with an internal flame, rage making his corruption stir. "No, we'll go in hard. They won't be expecting it. They're expecting us to be weak and skulking because they forget who we are. I'll remind them."

Masan hid his fear, adopted a hard face, and nodded "Very well. I'll send out the word and we'll gather everyone at the post closest to Apteryx."

***

LEANNE felt a tugging on her mind. A spiderling had found something. She leaned back and let her senses wander along the thin thread of magic that extended from her across the streets, drains, and roofs. She traced the little creature's route. She found it a few kilometers away, tucked into a dark corner of a cheap, scarcely furnished room. There were six occupants. The tall one that had destroyed her other constructs was standing in the middle, palms on a table, addressing the group. His voice was cold and low, and Leanne had to strain herself to hear what was being said.

"Two hours? That means, at most, they've talked internally. No external people will have been mustered."

"We're still only seven against a couple of hundred. Walking into their fortress seems very foolish; remember what happened to Caleb."

A tall, androgynous figure was the second speaker. They sounded detached.

"Caleb was the weakest of you. No great loss. The majority of their numbers are artisans, politicians, and the like. Apteryx has gotten soft they may only have some forty or fifty battle-trained Mages on the planet, and most of those will be on assignment."

"Not only that. Remember that they're Dark Mages, we're each worth two of them in battle," rumbled a large, muscular man.

The man Leanne knew was called Masan raised a hand, "None of that, Gere. Overconfidence can kill the best, and we know there are at least seven or eight adepts among them. It doesn't matter how old or out of practice they are, assuming that they aren't dangerous is borderline moronic."

The large, burly man stared at him in defiance but kept his tongue. Masan continued, "We'll follow Frid's orders, obviously." He nodded at the tall icy man. "But, we'll do this in as safe a manner as possible. We need to go in soon.

It's only a few hundred hours till sundown and the power shift that comes with dusk is not in our favor."

Frid wandered over to a worn stuffed armchair and sat down. "Agreed. Freya is the least conspicuous of us, so she'll go in first. Our surveillance tells us there are only a handful of guards, but that might have changed in the last hours. Go in unseen, find their numbers, report, and then we breach."

Leanne had heard enough. They'd be going in within hours at most. She needed to beat them there. She didn't think Lin was their target, but if this other girl was they'd both be on the chopping block. They can't have her! Her mind rebounded as she was all of a sudden entirely in her physical body again. Leanne calmed her mind as much as she could. Maybe these Mages shouldn't be her enemies. They were after some Dark Mages, not her Lin. This was the time for diplomacy.

***

THE sky was now as clear as it got on Embla, with pillars of light filtering down through the clouds. The apartment in front of Leanne's tall figure was only three levels below the top of the city, and close to the edge of the mountain. It was only a few blocks from the fortress that was the Apteryx guild house. She knew that the cameras had already alerted the group inside, but she still knocked on the steel door with a heavy hand. Two seconds passed before the door swung outwards exposing a brightly lit studio apartment. She could only see five of the seven Mages, luckily two of those were the leaders.

She stepped in without waiting for an invitation, the tension in the room was intense enough to taste. She knew that every person in here had already prepared spells that could turn her into fine dust if she made a suspicious move.

"I'm really sorry about your face," she said with a solemn face and nodded at Frid. "Heat of the battle and all. I get carried away."

"I only have two questions: Why are you here, and do you really expect to walk out of here alive?"

"I'm here because I've learned that we're not necessarily at odds, and we both have a better chance of getting what we want if we put our differences aside. As to whether I'll walk out of here alive, that's a dumb question, I haven't exposed myself here." She smiled and gestured slowly with her hand to Gere as he looked as if he was about to strike her down. "No need for that. I'm just saying that this isn't my actual body."

Frid looked at her curiously. "This is a construct? I've never seen anything remotely like it."

"I've had a lot of time to practice my craft. That's actually why I'm here. I didn't intend to harm you in my attack, but I was afraid you might harm my components."

"Components?" asked Masan.

"The girl you call Lin. She's mine, and I'd raze this planet for the sake of keeping her."

"Wait. What do you mean? She's just a girl, she's not even a Mage."

"There's nothing 'just' about her. She's of my blood, and I need my blood and my bone."

"That sounds rather horrifying." Masan looked even paler than usual.

"I'm not here to be lectured on morals by isolationist fascists. My point is that you don't have an interest in her. I don't have an interest in your Dark Mages. Right now those Mages are in the way of me collecting what's mine. The only thing left here is for you to decide if you want to fight both me and them, or if you want my help to fight them."

Frid gestured to Gere, who had gradually moved closer to Leanne, to stand down.

"I see your point. I've also figured out who you are, I sent a query to our archivists since last we spoke. You've got a checkered past."

"If you know of my past I take it you've already made up your mind."

"Of course. I'm happy you came to me. I'd be honored to work with you, but please refrain from messing with my face again. I have entertained some very violent fantasies targeted against you after that incident."

"Of course. I'll play nice."

"Then come in properly, sit down, and have some tea. Let's reassess our plans."

A few minutes passed before a second Leanne was at the door, and she was quickly let in. Once inside the mass of meat that had been impersonating her seemed to melt into nothingness, leaving a set of three intricately carved shards of white bone on the floor where it had stood. The process left a faint scent of flowers. After collecting and pocketing her shards, Leanne sat down on a white divan close to the kitchen alcove. Sinn, with their unreadable face and beautiful eyes, came over with a cup of steaming tea before the meeting continued.

***

FRID was looking out through a window where sparse light was filtering in, "We breach as one. My shields are near impossible to get through, so as long as you all stay close to me we can cross no man's land unharmed."

"Unless they meet us face to face there," Masan offered. He didn't like the idea of facing a full cadre of Dark Mages while his most powerful ally was occupied with shield duty.

"They won't, we're too few for them to realize the threat, and they'll expect the first layer of automated defenses to weaken us enough for an easy finish when we get to the wall.

"The wall might have posed a problem originally but, Leanne; we've seen what you can do to structures, think you can handle that?"

"If you make sure I get there without shadows shredding me, I can open that up for you." Leanne smiled, Masan didn't believe for a moment that she was worried about the shadows.

"Freya is our scout after that. She won't be noticed unless there's some really extreme circumstance. She'll update us on the exact positions of the enemy," said Frid.

Freya nodded and sipped her tea. "Understood. I'll stay alive and keep you alive."

"Leanne, will you assist Gere in clearing a way through the worst, so that Masan and I can focus on the search?"

Gere loudly cleared his throat and swore at this.

Masan grabbed his shoulder. "Would you come here for a moment?" He told the man as he led him into the adjacent room.

"What do you want?" It was clear from Gere's tone that she knew exactly what Masan wanted, he just didn't like it.

"Reel in your attitude. We don't want that woman as an enemy."

"She's nothing. A piece of shit Life Mage." Gere made a spitting motion but didn't actually spit. It was not a thing done in the presence of a superior of the guild.

"You think Frid would let 'A piece of shit Life Mage' live?"

Gere paused at that.

"I saw the same reports Frid saw. That woman over there is a god damned walking genocide, and Mages are her favored victims. We're not 'letting her' do anything."

"I don't understand."

"You don't need to understand. Just remember that she has managed to scare both me and Frid. If she can manage that you can manage to be polite, no?"

"Yes sir." It seemed to Masan that it finally had dawned on the brute of a man; anyone that made Frid nervous was worthy of some respect. Or if not worthy of it, still unwise not to fake it, Masan thought.

"If the two of you are done gossiping, maybe we can get on with it." Leanne's smile looked genuine, but there was a mocking note to her words.

Images from Light Mage recon troops flashed before Masan's eyes. Images of piles of bodies. Image after image, guild after guild. The last ones were some fifty years old, pictures of the corpses that remained after the last known Life guild had been annihilated. He forced a smile. "Sorry for the interruption. Yes, let's get on with it."

***

MIA had never raided a Light magic stronghold before and wasn't sure if she was or wasn't hoping they were home. Infiltrating the Tribe's command center was a daunting task, made no less easy by the fact that it stood alone inside an incredibly brightly lit, cavernous space. There was no creeping in the shadows. They would have to mount a full-frontal assault across the open space.

Fortunately, Mia wasn't alone in this task. Hugh had sent her to back up a cadre of Cormac's battle Mages, who were supposed to clear the area for traps. Mia thought the likelihood of traps in the open space was low; after all, this place had held families with small children only 25 hours ago. Nevertheless, she was a thief and infiltrator, not a battle Mage, so she appreciated not taking the role of cannon fodder. Sometimes, it was nice to have a team.

Once Cormac's folks had cleared the way to the inner sanctum. Mia came into the pile of containers to open the door. Unfortunately, the apprentice who had barbecued the Light infiltrator had taken all of their personal effects out in the fire. Fortunately, Sal had stolen a lot of documents from Light Mages for Wallang over the years, so they knew the entrance would likely need tech as well as magical input to open. She wasn't worried about that, she still hadn't run into a door that could stop her.

The tech component went pretty quickly, encryption only required patience and their tech had plenty. Mia needed to figure out what kind of magic was on the door. If it was her spell, the wrong type of magic would cue a lock-down and wipe everything in the place, so she needed to be careful.

Then, she had an alternate thought. Light Mages were egotistical and superior. What were the chances that they had warded the walls against intrusion? After all, this was a secret fortress inside a secret lair. The entrance was disguised against the people who lived here, not other Mages.

Mia threaded her way back outside. She painted a magical detection spell on the roof of the container. And waited to see if they had warded all of the points on ingress.

When it failed to detect magic, she smirked.

"I need one of you bruisers to come over here and drill me a hole in this roof. We're going in through the floor."

The battle Mage made quick work of the floor, while Mia braced internally and called up a shadow, sending it through the breach.

Better safe than sorry. She wasn't putting her head through until she had checked the lay of the land. Mia funneled the small corruption to her skin, allowing another millimeter to fade into shadow.

The shadow checked the facility, finding living quarters and some offices, but no sign of internal fail safes.

"Alright, who wants to go first?"

***

THE search didn't turn up much. The terminals had been remotely wiped. The team grabbed the hardware to see if they could reconstruct anything, but Mia wasn't hopeful.

Mia was more interested in the personal effects of the Mages. They had gone to great lengths to conceal their appearances. Mia found makeup for skin, contact lenses, and all sorts of clothing, designed to help them blend in.

Kesh and Lin would know what the Master and Adept looked like, but they still didn't have a full head count.

The building had living quarters for six Mages, but there could have been more housed out with the rest of the Tribe. Based on the makeup and clothing, Mia didn't think that there were more than ten Light Mages on the team.

There weren't a lot of magical spells or artifacts in the fortress. Mia found stacks of straightforward bugs and trackers, but not a lot in the way of devices like her cube or jewelry. The Light Mages must be carrying them as tattoos or on their person. She sent images and her observations back to the base by encrypted comm. That fit with the reports from Kesh about the magic they had used.

Mia had been instructed to look for traces of a Life Mage, but there were none to be found here. Life Mages tended to ooze and this place was so pristine that Mia wondered if they were incinerating dust. She was a little let down, but she figured that the Guild would let her track down the mystery woman soon enough.

"All right, split up and head back to base."

"Do you want us to run counter-surveillance against tails?"

"There's no point now, they know that we know that they're coming for us. And the Guild campus isn't hard to find. Just stay safe on the way home, this could just be a pretense for an ambush."

The battle Mages rolled their eyes, indicating that they didn't need to be told. But Mia just didn't want her ass on the line to Cormac if this unfruitful endeavor caused them to drop their guard. There was a whole team of Light

Mages somewhere in City Six just itching to kill them to get to their goal. Mia was too good at hiding and sneaking to be caught on open ground and she hoped the team was sensible enough to do the same.

***

APTERYX had exploded into a flurry of preparations and fortifications. The compound had always been fortress-like, but the full range of defenses was rarely deployed. They had stepped up their wards and perimeter security after the incident with the infiltrator, but that was nothing compared to the new security teams at all of the entrances, the enhanced wards on all of the buildings, and the requirement that all Apprentices stay on campus.

Kesh had been instructed back to her workshop to generate battle tablets for the security teams. These were less complex than the cubes or autonomous constructs she usually made. She had made individual master runes so she could emboss spells onto thin sheets of metal for simple explosion and trap spells. She didn't have time to make more cubes as they were too complex, but they knew that the recipients in range had all been urgently recalled.

The three Dark Guilds had coordinated to blanket the city in strike teams, for the event that any of the Light Mages step out of their hideout, or if they were to be outed by an informant. Their presence was no longer secret. The Guilds had issued bounties on any Light Mage, dead or alive. And what the Dark Guilds wanted, they got, especially in City Six.

Kesh knew that they had sent teams to all of the incoming ports to check for potential reinforcements or supplies for the Light teams; as well as to keep any suspected Light Mages from leaving. Retreat was no longer an option for Masan and Frid, even if they had decided that they were outgunned. The Guilds would accept no less than their heads, preferably on stakes.

Kesh knew that she shouldn't be viciously contemplating their impending demise, but she had looked into Frid's eyes and understood that he had intended them dead. He was a true believer in the Light and he considered her an abomination. He had been perfectly willing to use Lin to trap her, so he could trap Wallang. He had made it clear that he would kill anyone who got in his way.

Kesh wondered how badly his ego was hurt by having his ass handed to him by a bunch of magical constructs. With their luck, his narrow survival had only made him feel invincible and increased his fervor for the cause.

Kesh wasn't in charge of security, but she wondered how on Earth he believed himself strong enough to reach Wallang. Beyond the fact that Wallang was one of the most powerful living Dark Adepts and no stranger to battle magic, he operated out of the very base of their mountain fortress. Frid would literally have to go through the forces of the whole Guild to reach his workshop and stronghold, as it was at the base of the spiral deep in the mountain rock. There were tiny air shafts, but they were warded and alarmed against intrusion and far too small to traverse for anything larger than a mouse. No construct that small could contain enough runes to generate anything nearly powerful enough to harm Wallang now that he was prepared.

Frid would have to be truly mad to fight his way through the full forces of Apteryx to get to Wallang under the current circumstances. And yet, no one here doubted that the Light Mages would come, and soon. The Ring had centuries of experience dealing with Light Mage strategy between them. They seemed sure that the Light Mages would try a head-on assault, and she didn't doubt them.

Kesh wondered what it was like to be raised with that kind of magical fervor. Apteryx emphasized caution and incremental gains over grandiose magic and made sure that their apprentices understood their mortality and the dangers posed by corruption. In contrast, Frid had so much corruption that the loss of his carefully applied makeup had revealed a completely alabaster skin tone, despite obviously having started as a dark-skinned man. It seemed that the Light embraced their corruption as a badge of honor and it spoke to a level of fanaticism that was rarely seen in Dark Guilds.

Kesh wished that she wasn't stuck doing busy work, even though she intellectually understood that this was her best contribution to their defenses. She had proven that she was entirely unsuited to combat scenarios. Still, she knew she was being punished with this drudgery, and the Ring was hardly done with her yet. There would be a reckoning after the danger had passed.

Kesh's mind wandered to Lin, wondering what would happen to them after the fight was over. If they made it that far. Lin was convinced that the mysterious Life Adept was after her. Is she going to run again? It was after all how Lin had first reacted to being hunted, and that was even before she had any idea who was after her. If it was someone like this, it was double the reason to run.

Kesh stood up straight, *this is not how I'm spending an evening like this.* If she was going to seize the night, she should kiss pretty girls and ignore this busy work to finish her Masterwork. Even if, she would only prove to herself that she could. At least then she would be remembered as a genius, not just an unaware fuckup.

Kesh tidied her bench and went in search of Lin and dinner. She could work all night to finish her bracer, but it would be easier after some nutrients and attention. Maybe Lin would have some comforting words in the face of all this danger, she had survived this long and Kesh had no doubt that if she could make it past Sal and Frid with no magic, then she could weather the coming Light storm.

***

AS he opened the thick metal door of his armory cabinet, memories came streaming back. Wallang's youth as an active agent had been a strange time, it almost felt like he'd been a different person back then. So focused on winning, on being the best at what he did. He still carried a lot of scars from that time, the earliest corruption and the massive amount of augmentation he'd gone through to be the best. Today some of that will be of use again, he thought as he inspected the shimmering dark armor set hanging on its hooks.

It would still fit, even if it was a bit loose over the shoulders. He was still a very large man, but he was nowhere near the form he had been in back then. He stripped naked and took out the lower part of the set, a chained series of leather-like straps that enveloped his things as it shifted in texture from soft and bendy, into its active steel hard form. He could feel the needles digging to find their subdermal interfaces for a few moments; after which the heavy garment turned from a piece of clothing he wore to an integrated part of his augments. These metal pieces of his old life that he still kept repairing over and over as the Darkness ate at them. He'd used to think it was just an affectation, an unwillingness to let go of his past completely, maybe there was some premonition of this time of need behind it. He let a slight amount of dark energy flow through the interfaces and into the anchor runes. He felt the echo from the armor, it was as if he'd never taken it off. Fully functional.

The next pieces were the greaves which were the only pieces of the armor lacking direct interfacing, though an intricate pattern of a defensive spell covered them. The armored coat was next. It felt alive as it welcomed him back, digging its needles into the length of his spine. Finally, he picked up his gloves. While all pieces had spells inscribed, these gloves had served as the instrument of destruction back when he was regularly deployed. He had never been deployed when there wasn't an expectation for spectacular destruction. Putting them on now made it feel like destruction was inevitable, but this time it was here, among the people he respected, some of which he loved. Memories of mangled bodies invaded his mind. *No, not here, I will stop them and there will be no collateral,* he felt a deep conviction that he was right. He'd never felt this right in his life. He knew deep down that his experiments had changed him greatly since last he wore this. Sometimes he even felt like he could recognize that grandiose tone in his thoughts, the one he often found in the writings of old corrupted masters. *No, not me, I'm still myself.* With that, he deeply drew in the darkness around and underneath. The force was funneled through all sixteen anchor runes at once and the armor came alive fully. The echo he felt now was deep, and a complex mixture of magic, drugs, and nanites filled his bloodstream.

275TH DAY OF 11566 AF

REA stared at the monitor in disbelief. Seven figures were approaching in a haze made up of something similar to fireflies. *If they're this overconfident, they'll walk right into no man's land and be ripped apart by our traps.*

She keyed in the code for a general alarm and patched the feed to all visual displays she had access to in the facility. Radio was down, but they hadn't managed to screw up any wired communication.

The room behind her had been rearranged to have a series of barricades behind which lines of battle Mages crouched; she'd alerted them the moment the figures on the screen had appeared. Cormac was hovering over her shoulder smiling.

"So, we're dealing with idiots? Wonderful, we'll be done in time for afternoon coffee." His voice didn't sound as joyful as his words.

"It doesn't sound like you believe that..."

"Let's just watch, but no, I don't think they're as dumb as they seem."

Oc, who stood a few meters closer to the gate, behind a makeshift barricade, smirked at this. Rea didn't find it as amusing.

The seconds stretched on as the group came closer. Rea could see their faces, severe expressions and eyes darting.

The Light Mages triggered the first trap, three shadows flashed into existence and invisible edges slashed at the closest of the Mages, at the man with flowing white hair. Rea saw the trace of faint light weave flash into existence just as the edges found their marks to no effect. This was followed by the man making the slightest of gestures and a blinding white light melting the shadows to nothingness. Cormac didn't even blink at this, and Rea understood what he'd meant.

She'd never fought a Light Mage, but she'd been told that they were one of the most dangerous opponents you could find; now she saw why.

The audio surveillance picked up the man stating, "Go," and the group went from a casual walk to running at full speed. Trap after trap sprung, explosions and constructs appeared one after another, and each was extinguished with ease. Rea felt sweat form on her palms. *How do they think they'll be able to get* in the front? That gate was built to withstand a nuke she thought. The thought was answered within seconds.

A woman took the front, she moved ahead, and the rest slowed their pace. Rea was struck by the strange ethereal nature of the face on her screen, the woman looked like she was daydreaming about something nice, not charging across a battlefield. When she was a few meters away from the gate the demeanor of the woman changed, her face distorted to a grim mask, inhuman and ceramic looking; she became taller, and her fingers grew into blades. The horrific creature made a sweeping motion toward the sky, and the entire room shook. The half-meter-thick, indestructible gate was torn out of the wall and sent flying across the room as huge, semi-metallic, organic-looking trunks flooded in. Rea heard screams and her ears were ringing from the boom of tons of metal hitting stone. Oc was lying unmoving in the rubble, and Rea couldn't tell if he was breathing. Spelaeus and two others were already there clearing the debris to move the injured, five armed battle Mages were flanking them with guns and spelled gloves aimed at the churning madness of magical roots at the entrance. Rea crouched down behind the nearest pile of sandbags with her rifle aimed at the entrance. The twisting mass of organic matter was spreading out to leave an opening and then it became still.

The moment the silhouette of the first Mage appeared in the gaping hole, the Dark Mages opened fire. Conventional weapons fire was interspersed with crystalline projectiles and the ripping of the air by dark blade arcs. The first of the offensive force to enter was not the monstrous woman, but the man with the flowing hair; his hand stretched out in front of him producing a radiant shield that burnt everything thrown his way; magic, lead, and uranium alike.

Cormac roared as he charged the Light Mage, his battle armor seemed to make every shadow in the room flow in his direction and the floor darkened under his feet each step. Black fire flowed like oil from both hands as they came down towards the Light Mage's head. The man was dazed by the blow and staggered to his knees, but the fire didn't penetrate his shield, and he still kept enough focus to fight the incoming projectiles. Before Cormac could land another hit, the monstrous woman was on him; she moved far faster than her giant size should allow, and her claws cut straight through Cormac's shields, his battle armor, and his left arm leaving it severed below the elbow. His pained cry was silenced when the woman's left fist slammed into his chest hard enough to send him flying into the stone wall on the opposite side of the room. Rea stared in disbelief at the battered and bleeding shape of her master.

Only a few seconds had passed since the breach and there were already mass casualties. She raised her rifle and flooded the anchor rune with Darkness. The gun spooled up as uranium shells were encased in shells of Dark energy increasing their penetrative power several-fold. She hadn't opened fire yet, she was waiting for any type of opening. The five other Light Mages came into sight silhouetted in the light, and Rea pressed the trigger aiming for the closest one, a young woman in white crystalline armor. The first burst of bullets crashed against the armor without much effect but the second burst found its mark below the edge of the helmet, Rea saw sparks fly as the super dense projectiles shredded the magical shield meant to protect the Mage's neck. Blood poured in a violent gush and the woman staggered backward. The man behind her caught her and, in a fraction of a second, he had cast a spell that closed the wound. The man holding the wounded Mage had seen where the barrage had come from, and his eyes met Rea's. The spear of light that flashed from his outstretched hand ripped into her with searing heat; her shield crumbled and frayed, her armor melted and every nerve in her body exploded in pain, her last thought was, I hope some make it.

***

"WHO the hell," the words coming from Freya's mouth sounded slurred.

Masan lowered her to the ground as he replied, "She's already dead."

Freya's eyes seemed to come into focus, and she got up to sit, steadying herself on her hands. "I'm alright, let's go."

Masan turned to go in again and in a moment Freya was on her feet, she stormed into the building, blinding light flooding through every offensive spell in her armor.

Masan moved quickly, but by the time he'd made it across the heaps of rubble and roots conjured by Leanne, Freya was already inside. Every reserve she had must have been fully opened, she had passed beyond Frid and Leanne's methodical ingress. She ripped the helmet of a young man and a stream of melted metal flowed from her hand into his armor. Before that first one had stopped screaming, she discarded him and moved to her next victim.

Bullets and dark energies were deflected by her armor while she wielded conjured blades of liquid metal against her foes. She cut them down one after another, each slash burning away shields rapidly, each Mage felled in a few strokes; while their spells and bullets seemed to have no effect. Masan could see the corruption spreading across her body, cracks of the skin, showing through the semi-transparent diamond surface of her armor. Light glass shredded her insides, while she grinned ecstatically.

Masan's attention was diverted as he came under heavy fire, two men who had taken refuge behind a line of sandbags were firing at him with automatic weapons, while a third was building a spell that seemed aimed at him. Not waiting to see what sort of terrible magic was worth this slow of casting, Masan raised his arms in their direction and activated perb-fehureið the anchor rune just linked to a single other rune, both etched on the armor of his arm, inscribed in the diamond surface. The second rune of this deceptively simple spell was perb-naning a great rune. A torrent of light shot across the room and caught the man trying to cast his spell, in a heartbeat the man had been erased from existence. Without letting his focus go, Masan redirected the beam towards the gunners. Not even ashes remained when he released the spell.

As the hyperfocus required to channel a great rune left him, a relative silence filled the room. Those three had been the last men standing. Leanne had returned to a semi human-like-stature and Frid had released the active shields he'd been maintaining around all of the other Mages. Masan's attention went back to Freya, she was on one knee at the far end of the room. Meg and Sinn ran to her and got to the floor, laying her carefully on her back. Masan joined them and he could see that Freya had let far too much magic flow through her.

He looked to Sinn. "Will she recover?"

"With surgery, we could remove most of the shards. But I don't think that's the worst."

Freya looked pale, and she tried to find Sinn with her gaze. "The bullets, I was shot."

Sinn removed Freya's helmet and inspected her neck. "Your work, Masan?"

"Yeah, she was bleeding badly, needed to stop it."

"Are the bullets still in there?"

"Fuck."

Sinn produced a blade from its scabbard at their waist. "This will hurt," they said, but they had already started cutting.

Masan knew there was nothing more he could do for Freya. He turned to Frid, "One of us down, but I think the original plan should still be in motion."

"Absolutely. You and I enter the subterranean south of here. Gere, you take Leanne and enter through the northern stairs."

Gere nodded, and he motioned to Leanne. The two of them were out of sight before Frid continued.

"Sinn, you and Meg cross the courtyard and you'll go down on the other side. Get going as soon as you've stabilized Freya."

Sinn was already standing up. "That won't be necessary. There's too much radiation damage, the tissue of her neck is almost melted. They've modified their rounds, they act as critical fissile material. I'm afraid there's nothing I can do, she's unconscious and she won't wake up again."

Masan felt the weight of the statement, but Frid didn't blink.

"Then you should already be going."

Sinn touched Meg's shoulder and the two of them exited the same way as Gere had just left.

Masan touched his bracelet comm to open a channel to the other groups, "Gere, Freya is permanently down, the rest of us are proceeding. We'll meet you at the bottom floor."

***

APTERYX bustled with activity as preparations for a manhunt were well underway. Built 14,000 years ago as a fortress, the building had numerous safety features designed to repel everything from orbital bombardment to a ground siege. All Apteryx personnel in City Six had been recalled and reassigned to contribute to the manhunt for the Light Mages.

With her lack of field training Kesh wasn't sent out on the streets looking for Intel. Slightly disgraced from walking into an outright trap, she had been assigned to work on spell preparations for the security group. Kesh could use all of the spells that she crafted, but she didn't exactly have the finely honed reflexes to use them in a stressful situation. In combat, she was probably about as useful as poor Blaise.

Lin, who had volunteered as a runner despite her injury, rapped on the door to her workroom. "The rector requests your presence in the South stairwell."

Kesh appreciated the change of pace. Usually, she wanted to live in her workroom, but today it felt more like a prison than a refuge.

"What does Argent want? And why is she sending you? She could just buzz me," she asked Lin, giving her a quick kiss.

"Something about Apprentices. Also, comms aren't working properly. They started acting up almost ten minutes ago. Wide-range radio band blockers all over the city. Optical and direct electronic communication is working though." Lin sounded a bit worried, and Kesh didn't blame her, something was about to go down.

The apprentices had been confined to quarters since the Guild had swung into battle mode. They may be a harsh organization, but the Apprentices were their future and far too unskilled to risk in combat. They were as likely to take out themselves or their Guildmates by overextending themselves and becoming corrupted. No one needed to finish a difficult battle only to have to turn around and mourn children.

Kesh and Lin made their way around teams hauling long-range spy equipment and cameras through the labyrinth to the stairwell.

Rector Argent was waiting for them. "The Apprentices have been confined to their wing, but they're getting restless, and the threat becomes more imminent with every hour. I need to move them to the workrooms below for safety and I don't want to have to chase stragglers. Please come with me, so I can get them all moved at once."

She led them up the stairwell to the dorms in the South wall.

"Not a problem, Rector," replied Kesh. "Are you expecting anyone in particular to be difficult?"

"No, but the youngest are terrified and the oldest feel excluded from the fight. I don't have time to hold hands right now, I need them safe so I can armor up and help Hugh and Cormac organize the troops."

"We'll hound any stragglers and prevent anyone bold from trying to slip away."

They entered the dorms to find 28 sets of eyes turned towards them.

The rector clapped her hands. "Follow me. Bring your sleeping gear, clothing, and something to keep yourselves busy. This could be a long wait. You had best be prepared because there will be no returning until the Light Mages are neutralized."

The kids did some grumbling, but they seemed prepared. Argent led them back to the stairwell.

"Wait here while I check the dorms for anyone trying to hide out," Kesh told Lin.

Kesh pulled out her lamp and fired it up. It would dispel any diffraction or illusion spells that the older Apprentices were using. They didn't stand up well to bright, direct light. Kesh walked through the rooms, checking closets and under beds. She found only one teenage boy who had tried to hide out to go help the combat teams.

Kesh walked right up to him in the closet, smiled, and said, "If you're not good enough to hide from a lamp, you're not ready to be out there. Get going."

He grumbled but complied and scampered to catch up to the main group. Kesh knew that he would tell his friends about his valiant efforts to fight on their behalf as soon as he was out of her sight.

"Teenagers…" Lin smiled.

They traced the group down the stairwell 10 stories underground to the emergency bunkers. Argent was counting heads as the students came in the door. "26, 27, 28, and Dex makes 29. All accounted for. Thanks ladies, you can get back to your other tasks."

Kesh and Lin turned to head deeper underground, back to Kesh's workshop.

"What's next?" Lin asked Kesh, sending her boredom and restlessness.

"Did you know that I can use any spell I can create?" Kesh grumbled.

"I had kind of guessed, but I wasn't sure."

"I'm as talented as any battle Mage, hell more, because I made their combat spells."

"And? I didn't think you wanted to be out on the front lines?"

"I don't, but it's infantilizing to discover that no one thinks I'm even competent enough to ask." Kesh was fiddling with one of her cubes, twisting and turning it in her hands.

Lin looked at Kesh. "Why not do something about it then? Practice more active spells, upgrade your self-defense?"

"That's an entirely practical suggestion." Kesh pouted.

"Do you want the Guild's respect or to whine about the lack of it?"

Kesh sighed. "I want their respect. But now's not a great time to start changing, people really do need their attention on our 'friends' from the Tribe."

"Make a plan for after then, surely the teams in the City will track them down soon, then you can..."

Lin was cut off as two huge beings ran around the corner. Kesh recognized the woman as the Life Adept from their earlier encounter. She was followed by an enormous Light Mage in full battle armor. Kesh had just enough time to open her mouth and start turning to Lin before the ceiling came crashing down. Kesh and Lin jumped to avoid being hit and the roof came down between them, trapping Kesh further down the spiral than Lin, on the wrong side.

Kesh looked at the cube in her hand, but it was a shadow cube, a tool for a spy, nothing more. It wouldn't lift the tons of rock barring her way. Kesh did what she often did in times of duress, she channeled Mia, what would she have done in this situation? Kesh spun off a shadow to watch Lin and cut the incoming Adepts if they came too close. Then she broke into a run for the next staircase to go save her lover.

Fuck, fuck, why didn't we realize they might launch a direct attack? she thought as she ran. The shadow told her it was already too late. Lin was unconscious and tossed over the woman's shoulder like a piece of meat. She was arguing with the man-mountain. Kesh changed course and headed deeper into the fortress, sending the shadow to find Mia and send her to the blockage after the Mages.

Somehow, they had been overtaken in their stronghold. She headed to her workshop as fast as her legs would carry her; she was going to need a better weapon.

***

FOOTFALLS echoed through the corridor of the ground floor as Hugh pounded the stone tiles with his bulky metal boots. In contrast, Mia didn't make a sound as she darted along behind him. The hulking figure of the Adept ahead of her had her cautious, the destructive power of Hugh being just as dangerous to allies as foes. Both of the Mages were stained in blood, all of it from fallen Dark Mages. How did we underestimate them like this? The thought came with a deep knot in her chest and a flood of regret. She had been on her way back when the comms went out, and the sight on her return had almost destroyed her. So many friends dead, these Light Mages were absolute monsters.

Now, some of them were wreaking havoc in the Northeastern subterranean floors, right in the section where the apprentices were supposed to be sheltering.

The two Mages entered the spiral staircase, Hugh hardly slowed down, but rather used the smooth stone wall to redirect some of his momentum. Sparks flew as the steel of his shoulder-guard repeatedly slammed against stone. Mia activated a stim infuser to clear her head and allow her to increase her pace even further. The world was painfully sharp, her mind dialed in to the pinpoint that was their target; save the children, kill the Light Mages.

Hugh came to a lumbering stop in front of the door of the 11th subterranean floor. "They're here, the stone is damaged, runes disturbed." He swung the door open, and he adapted a battle stance as he moved at a fast walking pace, his right hand raised. Mia could smell ozone from the conduits the Adept had opened. Dark coils licked the edges of the runes of his armor. Far ahead in the darkness, Mia saw shapes move, the drugs and her ocular implant allowed her to resolve the figures.

"It's the Life Mage and one of the…" She reacted just in time to dive below the fiery lance that the hulking Light Mage had flung in their direction. She had no time to warn Hugh that the Life Mage was carrying an unconscious Lin.

Mia had dived into an alcove by one of the workshops, the smell of singed hair was intense and the flash of light overwhelmed her optics for a moment. Looking up she was relieved to see that Hugh had managed to shield against the worst of the blast. Within a heartbeat, the juggernaut of a man had picked up speed and he was now halfway to his target. Black matter took shape in Hugh's hand and as he swung it ahead of himself it unfolded like an impossibly long whip. The air whined at the motion, it was the sound of fission, a dark energy that ripped apart anything it came into contact with.

No light shone in spite of the insane energies being unleashed. Mia knew the spell, but she'd never thought she'd see it used.

The whining exploded to a roar as absolute darkness met a Light Mage shield, as it ripped the shield apart, as it ripped right through the leg of the Light Mage.

Mia rushed towards the fray, letting her own channels open as much as she dared, letting her Darkness flow through spells of concealment and confusion. To any opponent, she'd be a blur of dark shapes, impossible to pin down. She had been slowed down by the surprise firestorm, and she was desperately trying to come to Hugh's aid.

The woman, the Life Mage, somehow deflected the dark matter whip. She posed it back with slivers of gloving force, streaming from her free hand. She had brought the large man to her right enough room to get out of the way to move backward, avoiding getting his leg entirely severed. Before Hugh could react, the Light Mage dove to the ground, slamming an armored glove on the stone.

Whatever the magic was, it was devastating. The floor and walls of the space lit up along cracks, bright as the sun at its zenith. Narrow streaks of molten rock met the rushing Dark Mage mid-stride, his shield being ripped apart; his armor held, in most places, but radiant white flowed into his helmet, through the cracks of his visor. Mia's heart sank as her Master screamed in agony.

In what Mia could only imagine was blind pain-fueled rage Hugh raised his arms towards the roof. The moment crystallized in Mia's eyes, a second stretched to minutes. Darkness flowed through every inch of the space, the inside of every object and creature acting as a shaded place, fueling the three master runes inscribed in the Dark Adept's heavy battle armor. Mia wanted to shout, to stop him, but there was no time. A tidal wave of dark destructive power, of ripping tendrils made from materia prima flooded across the hallway, over the enemy Mages, over Lin. Absolute darkness obscured whatever horror had destroyed everything ahead.

The moment was over and Hugh collapsed face forward to the floor. The air stank of fire, blood, and ozone, a stench so overwhelming that Mia almost fell to the ground herself. She forced herself forward, the body of Hugh was crawling with corruption, stretching in her direction as she neared. She kept a wide berth, avoiding any contact with the vile slithering mass. She wanted, needed, to make sure it was over. She couldn't imagine the enemy Mages had survived that, but she had to see.

There was no trace of the male Mage, but where the Life Mage had been there was a crystalline cocoon. It looked like the foam from which amphibians spawned. The translucent matter was falling away, melting. Mia jumped to the side as black steel spikes shot out from the mass in her direction. The Life Mage was still alive, she'd managed to shield both herself and Lin from the attack. Monster Mia thought, Hugh died to kill you and you dare to live? The woman looked confused as she got up on her left knee, Lin lay collapsed at her side. Mia realized the woman looked smaller now, and her clothes were writhing, and soaked in blood. Hugh bought me a window, her corruption has her off guard, with that thought Mia dove low, and pushed herself flying, every augmented muscle pushed to its limit, dark energy flowing through the blade in her hand. The Life Mage reacted swifter than Mia expected, but in her dazed state, she turned in the wrong direction, towards one of the many hazy doppelgangers Mia had conjured. The mistake bought Mia the fraction of a second she needed, and her blade found its mark. It ate through the woman's neck as if it was made from jelly. The blade in Mia's hand cut with precision and effortlessness. The Life Mage's head fell, and her body collapsed.

***

SINN and Meg sprinted across the courtyard, heading into the far stairwell. Sinn sparkled in the Darkness of the fortress, a dazzle of light penetrating the black. Meg glowed with the fluorescence of a firefly. They were both casting light spells to penetrate any low-level dark shield spells and try to boost their other magic.

Halfway across the courtyard, a giant ball of plasma hit the ground next to them, forcing them to take cover.

"They're attacking from the upper stories!" yelled Sinn. "Shields."

Meg focused on her shield runes, spinning out a web of light to protect from incoming projectiles. Sinn examined the windows facing onto the courtyard, looking for their attacker. The golden glow of the sunset worked more in their favor than in the Dark Mages.

Sinn began to cast lances of light methodically at the windows where the attack had likely originated. They heard no response to the attacks.

Then another ball of plasma landed on Meg's shield, overloading the edges and causing it to shut down. Meg took a deep breath and recast, layering copies of the spell to give Sinn space to work.

Sinn had swapped to glowing, explosive balls of light, sending them into the upper levels of the fortress like heat-seeking missiles.

Antimatter bombs, tiny but deadly, rained from a third wall. Their pursuer was either moving rapidly or there were multiple attackers stationed to protect the courtyard.

"Can we make it to the far wall?" Meg asked Sinn. "We're outnumbered and outgunned. They have better cover and what seems like superior numbers."

"Hold shields and we'll try to make it to the walls," Sinn ordered. They spun out their own diffuse prism ahead of them, bouncing light all over the courtyard to dispel any weak traps.

The two Light Mages ran for the far wall, anti-matter bombs and plasma taking out layer after layer of shields. The last shield winked out of existence as they entered the far door.

Sinn recast their protective spell again, lest there be a trap in the hall. They moved along the corridor, sending laser beams through the gloom to open the way.

They hit the stairwell at a run. "Up or down?" Meg asked Sinn. "Should we find the bastards who attacked us out there?"

"Down. The less Light, the greater their power, they will have retreated into the basement of the fortress."

"Aren't they trapping themselves?" asked Meg as they followed the spiral staircase down.

"No, they're hoping to trap us where they're strongest. They don't need to retreat in the stronghold of their power. Hit them with your strongest spells, if you don't kill them immediately, they have the upper hand."

The pair came out of the stairwell into the gently sloping floor of the workshops. They opened each door, searching for anyone hiding in the corners. They were so engrossed in their search for human-sized prey, that they didn't see the tiny spider who had attached itself to Meg's shadow, following their every move, tracking their progress through the fortress.

***

FRID stalked towards the stairwell, his white hair flowing in his wake. His pale irises burned with hatred for the Dark and those who tarnished his soul with their very presence. Every rune on his battle armor glowed with a pale blue light, piercing the gloom of the fortress. Masan followed in his wake, his battle armor glowing a gentle gold.

They took the stairwell down as far as they could. They encountered minimal resistance on the way, as Frid cut down two Dark Mage guards with laser pulses on the move. Their charred, bleeding corpses made the stairwell stink of iron and fear.

The stairwell came to an end and Frid and Masan paused. Masan cast a mirage spell, making their presence wink out of existence so they could scout the floor for Wallang. The pair exited, looking for signs of Dark Mages on the lowest floor.

A brief flicker of colored motion caught Masan's eye. "There!" he whispered and pointed to Frid. "Was that Lin?"

The two men moved slowly in that direction, following the flash of color. It was indeed Lin, dressed unlike a Dark Mage in a silver and blue synthsilk jumpsuit and heading rapidly down the hallway. She ducked into a workshop, obviously looking for someone.

"How did she get away from Leanne?" Masan asked Frid.

"Don't know, doesn't matter, we'll kill her and move on."

"And pick a fight with that monstress?"

Frid nodded as he plowed ahead, "As much as I like a good fight, you might be right. I guess it's not her time yet. Let's see who she's looking for at least. We can bundle her up for Leanne if nothing else."

Masan and Frid each activated their shield spells moving towards the door. Masan called fire to his hand making sure he wouldn't be caught unaware.

They opened the dark wood door to the room to find a cluttered office with two women inside.

Lin stood behind a table, pointing a gun at them. Kesh, eyes fully black, stood in front of her holding a ball of energy that seemed to eat Light.

"Welcome to Apteryx," Kesh exclaimed in the same breath as she released the barely contained anti-matter directly at Frid.

The spell splattered against the shield, but managed to shatter it. He retaliated with spinning whirlwinds of scorching light. Lin had ducked behind the large desk and well-aimed bullets flew at the Light Mages.

Masan let energy flow into a pattern he didn't use often, but the perfect one for opponents with guns. A wave of heated energy flowed forward, through the desk Lin was hidden behind.

Lin screamed and threw the melted piece of metal that was boiling the skin from her palm. He pushed outwards again, this time throwing a bolt of air and heat, exploding the desk and throwing Lin hard against the far wall. The girl collapsed bleeding and unconscious. Fuck, I hope she's not dead, Masan shivered at the thought of having to deal with Leanne. He hoped that if she came too she would stay put and stay out of the rest of the fight, assuming of course that she was still alive. He didn't want Frid to turn his uncontrollable rage on her. He turned his focus back to Kesh. While the girl was only Journeyman, she was presenting more of a fight than Frid had counted on. He was always an overconfident bastard. Hadn't their own intel indicated that she was a hell of a spell craftsman?

Kesh was now surrounded by a whirlwind of shadow, deflecting Frid's Light attacks and slowly peeling off to eat away at the new shields he'd erected. Dark fire, antimatter bombs, and pulses of pure energy shot from the cube in her hands, pinning both Light Mages in the doorway. Kesh's figure was barely visible through the veil of shadows. Even with all of this Masan knew it was a futile struggle on her end. The only reason she was still alive was that Frid still wanted a word before killing her. Even with all her power, even with all the handicaps imposed on the Light mages in this arena, she was no match for either of the Light mages and when facing both of them it was almost laughable that she tried. She was on the verge of catastrophic corruption at this point, Masan hoped Frid could subdue her before she accidentally offed herself.

Masan focused on shielding both of them, putting up layer upon layer of shields to protect them while Frid focused on offensive magic.

Frid was grinning widely. "Give up child! You don't have anything more to dig into and we both know it!"

Insults never won a duel, just finish this already! Masan stayed on task and tried not to wonder why Wallang's prized pupil was here alone, without him.

Frid's magic sent blazing light from each of his fingers, cutting through the shadow whirlwind. As they chipped away the shields, Frid was slowly working his way from the door towards Kesh, one step at a time.

It looked like the Dark Mage was getting close to breaking through the shield, but Masan realized Frid had been putting less and less focus into his defenses. Light poured out of Frid as he let loose the reserves he'd held, patterns that Masan recognized lit up. He dodged just as Frid flung a huge burning projectile of plasma. The thing washed over Kesh, ripped her shield, stripped skin from her arms, and left a gash across her face. Blood coagulated the moment she was hit, and the wounds took on a black cracked look immediately.

Frid advanced over the prone woman, who was glaring at him as tentacles of black magic played under her skin. He gathered the neck of her garment in his fist, hauling her up to his face.

The light in his eyes whirled and flickered as he growled, "Where. Is. Wallang?"

***

THE tiny spider sent minute pulses of magic to its controller, who followed the Light Mages at a careful distance. Mia was too drained by her assault on the Life Mage to launch more combat magic, but she had found these two moving cautiously, but assuredly, through the workshops. They were getting perilously close to the stairwell, to the apprentices, so Mia had looped in Argent and Parvana to lay a trap for them.

Just a little bit further now...

***

KESH stared down the massive white Mage. Closer, come closer... Frid was the greater danger and Kesh couldn't take him in a head-to-head fight. He needed to be neutralized and she wasn't too proud to feign defeat if it meant putting an end to this unfeeling monster.

Her face burned. Her left arm felt strange, the feeling of pain that was too intense to reach the brain. She stopped herself from looking at it.

As Frid growled at her about Wallang, she reached into her pocket and pulled out the prototype for her Masterwork. Hold him off and Wallang can finish him. The bracelet clapped shut around the towering Mage's wrist with dark tendrils licking the skin around it. As Kesh felt the energy pass through the lock, she drew a sigh of relief.

The hatred in Frid's eyes gave way to confusion as his spells dissipated. Confusion almost immediately turned to rage and his fist came down on Kesh's face with force that shattered bone.

***

MASAN looked on in horror as his superior landed blow after blow on the woman's face.

"Enough, we need her! Stop!" His words did nothing to slow the torrent of violence. "Please! We need her. She's our best leverage against the Prior!" The words were a half-truth. Masan didn't shy from violence, but that girl was no threat at this point.

Frid was snarling as the blows kept falling.

"She took my magic. I will end her!" Frid had straightened his back for a moment to answer but used the momentum from the motion to follow up with a kick toward the woman's chest, causing a sickening cracking and wheezing sound. Frid grabbed a heavy hammer from the workbench next to him and raised it for a finishing blow.

Not again! I can stop him, I could calm him, if I just had a moment. Masan let Light flow into him and through an amulet hanging on his chest. Light and air weaved through the air and enveloped Frid's whole figure, freezing him in place.

"What the hell are you doing?" The words had hardly left his mouth as Lin came screaming towards him from where she'd been tossed moments ago. Brandishing a long artisan's blade, she came down on the helpless figure of

Frid. The blade flashed as it sunk into his neck. The two figures crashed to the floor as Masan lost focus and released his spell. Frid was making a gurgling sound as he tried to stop the blood from pouring out of the gaping wound.

Lin had already moved away from the Mage's body to Kesh's.

***

THE world felt blurry and confused. Lin was on her knees, blood everywhere. She was clamoring to Kesh, feeling for a pulse, not daring to breathe herself. There! I saw her breathe. And a pulse. Lin finally remembered they weren't alone. Masan was standing only feet away. She looked at the man she had thought to be a friend, not knowing what to feel. He was a liar and a threat, but he'd saved Kesh. Why did he do that? She wanted to ask, but the next few moments exploded again. Masan opened his mouth to speak, and at the same moment, Lin saw Wallang enter the room from behind the Light Mage.

Lin had been disturbed by the appearance of the Prior when she first saw him, but now she was doubly so. His features were distorted in a grimace of rage, black smoke emanating from every crevasse of his wrinkled skin. He roared. Black gloves with intricate metal inlays turned from a garment into a storm of flames that seemed to radiate darkness. A flood of flames engulfed Masan whose body was flung hard against the wall past where Lin and Kesh lay collapsed. The roaring and the flame and intense eye-watering stink of ozone filled the room.

Lin tried to get to her feet, shouting at Wallang, "Stop! Please!"

Without the old man seeing her, his eyes burning with hatred and the flames eating all the light of the room; flames flowing in a liquid stream slamming into what Lin could only imagine was Masan's corpse. "Please! It wasn't him! He tried to stop it. He saved her!" With those words it finally looked like she got through to Wallang, the man blinked and pulled his fire back. Smoke and tendrils of darkness still licked the edges of the metal of the gloves, waiting to be released again.

"What did you say?" The man now started taking more the form of his normal human self rather than some horrific avatar of death. "You want me to stop?" There was still plenty of rage in his voice.

Lin managed to get to her feet, supporting herself on a workbench. She had to fight her nausea not to throw up. "He was trying to stop the other one,

Frid. He betrayed them. He saved Kesh." As she was talking she dared a glance at where Masan lay. The body was burnt in places, but not destroyed as she would have expected. A silvery light, like a finely weaved net was visible around him, it was flickering in and out of existence, like an electric light that wasn't entirely in contact with its lead. In the places where she couldn't see any of the flickering light the burns were horrific, some bone deep. "Is he dead?"

Wallang looked at the body and shook his head. "No, not quite. He'll recover if I don't finish the job." Lin felt a shiver at the tone of his voice.

Lin remembered what had happened moments before and got back on her knees next to Kesh's body. "Would you please calm down? I need help, she needs help." She looked at Kesh, at her girlfriend. Please don't die, her thought was desperate in tone. "Can you help her? Can you heal her?"

Wallang sat down on his knees next to them. "I could, but my healing has always been fast and efficient, never tidy. I think it's better if one of the others does it; otherwise, her nose will always look like that." The ironic tone of voice seemed to have a sad undertone.

He got up again, stepped over Frid's corpse, and walked over to the body of Masan. Lin had imagined Wallang to be a frail old man, in spite of his size, but now he lifted the Light Mage by the collar of his jacket as if he was handling a small child.

He pushed the Light Mage up against the scorched wall and shook him as he shouted in his face, "Open your fucking eyes! Come to, you bastard!" Nothing happened for seconds, then something seemed to dawn on the old Mage. "Very well. Lin, I'll give you a visual aid to why Kesh wouldn't like my healing." Lin saw Dark tendrils emerge from the Mage again, this time from the metal wires on the arm of his strange leathery coat. She saw intricate runes made of twisted copper go from their metallic sheen to an oily black, and she saw a ghostly aura extend across Wallang's arm and embrace the Light Mage he was holding up.

Masan opened his eyes, and he screamed. The deep flesh wounds of his arms and legs were closing, turning from a weeping red to something that looked like a weave of black flesh. Bones that had been exposed were covered in new thick scars. Through the process that felt like an eternity, but in reality only lasted for a few seconds, Masan was writhing as if he was on fire again.

Wallang turned to Lin without letting go of the wailing Light Mage. "Take Kesh and go towards the council chambers, I saw several artificers back there taking care of the injured. I'll deal with this."

Lin was still disoriented, she was certain she had gotten a bad concussion. She still realized that Wallang was right, he couldn't leave Masan, and Kesh needed urgent help.

She grabbed Kesh under her arms and dragged her out of the room, almost stumbling over the feet of Frid. She exited right and continued towards where she'd seen the council just hours earlier. The corridor seemed so impossibly long now, it felt like Kesh was now twice her normal weight. Lin tried to walk straight and fast, but she stumbled over and over, she bumped against the wall, and she fell. Before she'd gotten the weight of Kesh off herself, she heard running coming towards her. She fumbled, trying to reach for her weapon, realizing that she'd lost both gun and knife in the earlier fight. Looking up she felt the tension leave her as it was someone she recognized, the woman called rector. With the tension and panic releasing, so did her consciousness.

***

BLACK cold stone rose all around; perfect seams with a glassy appearance made the whole place look and feel as it was molded, rather than built. A warm puff of humid air welled up, enveloping the two Light Mages in a sulfurous odor that was otherwise far less prominent in this fort than anywhere else in the city. Sinn leaned with their back against a doorframe, panting lightly. Their normally pristine skin had been seared by some dark magic. Their left arm dangled, seemingly useless, at their side. Meg held the rear, magic pulsing through runes of her left arm and a sleek plasma rifle in her right, aimed up the round stairs.

"Why aren't they coming down? They have us outmatched. What are they waiting for?"

"Probably for me to faint, to leave a single easy target to take down."

Meg didn't turn but her voice was filled with scorn as she replied, "Anyone who thinks I'll be easy will learn otherwise."

"And anyone who thinks I'll go down from something like this likewise." Sinn's voice was pained, but Meg could also hear an iron focus in there.

Meg snuck a glance back at her superior in time to see tattoos flaring, energies hot enough to burn off most of Sinn's remaining clothes seared through patterns. The electric charge made Meg's hairs stand on end and pungent ozone freed the air of any other smell.

As the Light fell away, Sinn was already massaging the new clean skin and muscle of their left arm. "There we go, now you take the front and if these idiots dare come down after us I'll torch them."

Meg moved past them, careful to scout around the corner before stepping into the corridor, now acutely aware that the Dark Mages had been far more prepared for an assault than they had anticipated.

She saw from the corner of her eye Sinn's comm light up. Masan's voice was low and strange, it sounded broken, "We're down. Frid is dead, I'm not going to make it back, please get out." The communication was down again as fast as it had come in.

Sinn had stopped in their tracks, their hair hanging in front of their face, obscuring their expression. "We need to leave." The voice was cold and controlled. Meg couldn't imagine what was going on in their head.

"But, Masan's..."

"That's an order!" Sinn roared. "We go back, same way as we came. Move fast, don't take care: take aim."

Sinn turned on their heels and went back towards the stairwell they'd exited less than a minute ago.

***

WALLANG looked back at the miserable excuse of a human that he was dangling by his neck. Wallang's muscles were bulging from a multitude of battle spells weaved into both his armor and his skin. The power of his old battle suit made him feel fifty years younger and filled him with a rage he'd not experienced in as long.

"You will open your eyes and you will talk to me, right this moment, or I'll crush your skull."

Masan opened his eyes, looking more present than he had any right to be. "Fine." His voice was slightly slurred but carried anger rather than the pain and confusion Wallang had expected.

Wallang lowered the man to his feet but didn't let go of him. "I have triggered an explosive spell in this glove, if any magic except dark is channeled right now, you'll be a head shorter."

Masan tried to nod. When he couldn't, he volunteered: "Understood. I won't try to kill you."

"Now, what the hell is all this about? All of this for a few dead archivists?"

A flash of confusion passed over Masan's face before he managed to hide it, "I'm not sure who these archivists are. We weren't informed."

"No? What in the hells are you doing here then? It's me you're after, isn't it?"

A weak nod.

"So explain yourself."

"We figured out that you were targeting us. The spell. Some magic you're working on to separate Embla from the Light."

Wallang felt his rage build for a moment, but then the irony of the thing became too much, and he let the rage run off him to be replaced by a tired chuckle. "You think I'm making some weapon against you? It had hardly even registered to me that you had an outpost here."

"Well, someone in your guild is!"

"Come with me. I'll show you, it's not like you can copy my work anyhow. Just know that I haven't released that spell."

"Yes, yes, I get it. If I'm bad you'll blow my head off. Sounds like you would have made fast friends of Frid if Lin hadn't cut his throat."

***

MASAN stared at the runes covering the floor in horror.

"Do you realize what you've done?"

"Better than you do, I'm sure. What do you know of dark magic?"

Masan opened his mouth to answer, but Wallang continued, "It started quite innocent." He walked over to the bookshelf that now occupied a far corner of the massive room. He reached for a blood-red book, bound in synthetic leather. "I had heard of a spell that had never been completed. One that had eluded the greatest Mages through the ages. It was said that the one that came closest lived so far back that we didn't even have their name on record. I didn't know anything about this person. I only knew that if I could be the one to do this, I'd live on forever. A legend larger than anyone else, at least among the Dark Mages." He flipped through the large book, eyes staring through the pages, looking into the distance unfocused. "The purpose of the spell was really not that important originally. I knew it was an effort to open a permanent gate to the dark plane itself, but the implications didn't matter much to me. The important thing was that my old master had tried and failed. All of that scorn and ridicule would be disproved. I'd be able to walk into the eternal night with my back straight, and I'd spit that bastard in the eye." He looked slightly defeated as he stood there in the corner, flicking through a book, a pretense at reading. "It was naive and juvenile of course, and that petty motivation only carried me so far, but it carried me far enough to find a new purpose. The dark plane is more than we're taught. It's alive. I know it now, it's been guiding me for so long and I didn't even realize it. It's longing to be free, and I can make it so. I'm much more than some petty student trying to one-up his teacher. I'm a herald."

Masan gave him a dark look. "I hope you're done. You're proving my point. You've been doing this for a long time, do you not recognize the signs of corruption in your thinking? You sound like more than one Mage I've known in their last days; just before they go and burn themselves out, or cause such corruption that they die." His face softened and there was some sympathy there. "I really need you to listen to me now." The Light Mage looked around. He walked over to the desk on the other side of the room and grabbed one of the clean crystals from its rack. He pulled back his sleeve to reveal a slot in his lower arm and inserted the crystal.

"I thought you lot didn't allow augmentation?"

Masan looked up at the old Mage with scorn. The massive amount of data being transferred through his central neural implants made it hard to speak. "That's none of your business, I'm tired of listening to old men with more power than sense. Wait till I'm done, and I'll show you what you've been doing."

***

A storm began on the South American continent. Upscaled IR images found one sole person at the epicenter. According to earlier intel, the location was a large Death Mage temple. No other inhabitants were detected in the images. The figure of the Mage remained frozen in place for the duration of the storm. There was a detectable drop in temperature extending 15 meters around the Mage. High-resolution upscaling shows that the cold, measured at absolute zero, emanated from a rune pattern inscribed in stone.

Note: The exact runes are preserved in an accompanying set of crystals. The original upscaled photos were unstable and corrupted the drives they were stored on within minutes. CAUTION: A tech working on transferring the files suffered severe necrosis as a result of direct contact with media containing a record of the spell. Extreme caution should be used when approaching any of these files.

The storm began at 22H local time, July 11, 3045 FE. The intensity continued to build over the next few hours. Initially, there were minimal signs that the source was magical in nature. Four hours after the storm began IR imaging revealed severe loss of life in the vicinity of the epicenter. This observer notes that this is most likely the point in time when the spell became self-sustaining. IR detection showed life being extinguished in a rapidly expanding radius, accelerating at 400 meter-seconds squared. The last signs of life on earth expired four minutes after the spell became self-sustaining.

While IR could no longer detect life on the planet, other spectra continued to show movement that was not a result of weather or other natural phenomena. The mass of dead matter rapidly re-assembled into seemingly animate constructs. Observations collected in the five months that have passed since the cataclysm show no decrease in activity on the surface. No manned expedition on record has yet to successfully return from the planet.

Report on orbital footage. Station 11. Sealed records. Day 149 0 AF.

***

"I'VE seen what's on those crystals. All adepts of Light magic have. We're shown that file if we have enough aptitude to ever hope to pull something like it off. This pattern." He gestured across the floor of the cavernous room. "It's almost identical. I don't know how you did it, but you've managed to create the best approximation of a Dark magic version of the spell that devoured life on Earth. The day that marks the end of the last age, that's what you've been working towards."

The old Dark Mage looked at his work as if it was the first time he saw it. "I... I thought I was building a bridge. I thought I was increasing our power. I never thought it would." His voice trailed off as if he didn't quite know what to say next.

"You didn't think? If you did all this, you must have felt it. I've felt it. Close to the sun, when we do our greatest work. I've felt the will that pushes against this world from the other side. I don't know your Darkness, but if it's anything like our Light you'd have to be a suicidal idiot to have felt that presence and thought: 'Let's open the door for it'."

Masan was flustered, so upset he could hardly breathe. He was sharing some of the closest-held secrets with a Dark Mage, but this fool was powerful enough to succeed. He had to be let in, he had to learn the horrific truth. "They're there you know. Every one of the eight schools has them. Magic is just a sliver of their breath breaking through the fabric of space-time. Eleven millennia ago a Death Mage let one of them in, and you've been attempting to do the same."

***

AT first, it was a tiny spec on the monitor, the promise of safe harbor and old memories brought back to the surface. Sal hadn't spent much time in the cockpit since he got to cruising speed, but now he couldn't find the peace of mind to be anywhere else. Constantly checking his gauges and screens. The feeling of being the prey rather than the predator was a hard one to shake, and completely foreign to him.

He'd known of Leanne's network for years and he'd worked side by side with some of her agents in the past. He'd seen how she rewarded failure. A shiver broke him out of his navel-gazing and back to the present. He gestured to his system to initiate handshake protocols with Tube, knowing it'd take close to an hour before he got an answer. It was a busy place, but he had priority over any nonessential landings.

As the taxi pulled away, and bands snapped in place to secure landing pads of the yacht, Sal breathed deep in relief. Safety, real safety. No matter how mad a pursuer, she'd never put her foot here, and he'd be on the next ship out when one took off, the guild had a lot of pull here. After you made the jump from Tube, there's no way back, and this was exactly the charm. Now all there was to do was make a few calls, get his tags, and ticket, and wait.

277TH DAY OF 11566 AF

KESH and Lin lay in the grass in the middle of the courtyard, mostly hidden away by both live trees and the eternal stone trees that decorated the courtyard. Next to them were all the necessities for a calming afternoon; wine, cheese, and newly baked bread from the closest bakers. Now the two women were digesting in silence and casually snuggling. Lin felt at peace for the first time in weeks. She ran her fingers through Kesh's hair, and the smell of lavender washed over her. Kesh was too adorable, doubly so due to how unaware she was of this fact. Lin leaned in to steal a kiss but was surprised by a noise and the two bumped their foreheads together from the startle.

Kesh sat up, leaning on the palms of her hands. "Damn it Mia, should we have put up a do not disturb sign?

"I found him," Mia said. She didn't sound excited.

Lin knew instantly that she was talking about Sal. "You're going after him?"

"I'm not sure yet, I haven't told the Ring yet."

"You're telling us before them?" Kesh sounded confused.

Mia nodded and smiled a sad smile, "I used to love the man, but the things he's done are things I can't forgive. He betrayed and used me, and I thought I had dealt with that. But now I know he was also going against the codes of the guild. He's a traitor on every level."

Lin leaned forward, with her face over her cup of coffee, taking in the smell to ground herself. Talking about Sal hurt. "So, you're worried they'll send someone else and rob you of your chance to kill him?"

"I don't want to kill him… But someone needs to do it, who better than me?"

Lin chuckled. "I wouldn't mind taking a stab at it."

Kesh smiled an unconvincing smile at Mia. "They'll punish him, isn't that enough? They might even kill him, and even if they don't, I'm sure you'll never be in a position where you have to work with him again."

*****

THE room was lit by a single flame in a lantern above the middle of the council chamber. The six surviving members of the Ring all looked at the young Mage who had just entered; a silhouette against the light let in from the corridor behind her. The light lasted only for a brief second before the door slammed shut and returned the room to relative darkness.

MIA held herself steady as she waited to be spoken to. It was long since the Ring had relied on this degree of formality. Mia figured the shift wasn't likely to be temporary considering the damage they'd been dealt.

"Good evening, Mia." The Speaker's voice was as cool as always.

"Good evening, Speaker. I'm honored to be before you."

"We've got an assignment for you. We need haste and discretion."

"Always Speaker."

"As you know we have an empty seat, we need to fill it."

Mia's heart missed a beat before she realized they couldn't possibly be talking about her. She had nowhere the seniority to be offered the spot.

"What do you need from me in regard to that?"

Argent leaned forward to take over from The Speaker "We're aware that you're close with Salvador. It's time we had someone bring him home."

Mia felt the blood drain from her face "You can't mean you're considering…"

"We're not considering," the Speaker said coolly. "We considered it. It's been decided."

The other members of the ring all gave nods in approval. The group of older Mages had never seemed as intimidating as in this moment. The atmosphere of Apteryx had never been this formal, and it had eroded some of the walls one could have expected between the leadership and the members, it seemed the walls had been re-established.

"But he went against our codes, our rules." Mia felt bewildered. *Sal is a traitor and they're talking about giving him the highest honor!*

"None that matter." Argent offered.

Cormac continued, "Indeed, it would even seem that we might need to re-evaluate some of those codes. The weakness we displayed during this assault was farcical. Salvador will right some of that weakness." He sighed. "Either way, we didn't bring you in here to discuss the merits of his appointment, we were hoping you had the capabilities to bring him in. Were we wrong in our assessment of you?" Cormac sounded both tired and irritated.

"No, sir. I can do what you need me to do. I will do it." Mia kept her voice as solid as she could, though her internal voice was railing against the madness of it all. *It's not that I can't, I already know where he is. He just doesn't deserve to come home!*

"Then get to it." Cormac's voice had softened a bit, but she couldn't tell if he was just getting tired. The man might be the sturdiest person she'd ever met, but a procedure replacing a whole arm with a neurally linked prosthetic put most people out of commission for months.

She kept her thoughts to herself and bowed before turning to leave.

The door closed behind her and Mia wandered off along the empty corridor, once she had rounded a corner she let her back fall against the wall and she sank to her haunches. Her head was spinning. *I'm a good agent,* she thought. But at the same time, she knew she couldn't be. She couldn't help them get that bastard back, she couldn't let them get him back. *Fuck.* She couldn't let anyone see her like this. She quickly got up again, composure regained. *I need a plan. I won't let them do this, but I can't have any trace leading back to me.* Then a thought dawned on her. She'd been tracking Lin's calls the last few days, and there'd been frequent messages to Tube. The location of the elusive Sal. *If Lin has a contact on Tube; she's the one person who wants that bastard dead more than me.*

***

THE apartment was small but well-equipped, the fully stocked bar behind its glass doors displayed flasks from the best distilleries in the system. The single room was right now mostly occupied by the retractable king-size bed, which in turn was occupied by a very tired Sal.

He'd been running for a week, and he'd spent a lot of his energy doing so. While his ship was one of the fastest in the system, it required a huge amount of skill and magical power. In retrospect, he might have overdone it. While Leanne was vengeful, she was probably distracted by the hunt for Lin right now. He still didn't want to be anywhere within reach once she remembered who'd lost the girl in the first place. Luckily Hugh had entrusted Sal with the master passes for their hideouts through the system, including this one. *A privilege I'll miss once I've passed to the other side of Tube,* Sal thought bitterly. He reached for his glass half filled with Safran, a saffron-flavored liquor he'd found at the back of the cabinet. The strong flavor and full sweet smell was a momentary escape each time he sipped it. In those short moments, he wasn't about to leave his entire life behind, he was entirely in the moment; then the glass was empty, and the moment was gone. Sal sighed, another day before the next ship was to leave, he just wanted it over with at this point. *Once I'm there, new adventures await, and this time I'll be wiser about who I do business with.*

Two days had passed, and Sal was impatient, but more out of boredom than fear. Waiting mode was a very real thing and he found himself incapable of starting any productive work, not knowing if he'd be called to head out at any moment. Instead, he wandered the gardens, spending much time admiring the starry sky. This far out even the sun was barely more than a really bright star. It was a relief to leave everything behind. He'd saved up enough valuable material to barter for the royal treatment for the rest of his life, even out there, in a new system where no old structures or alliances would hold.

As he was pondering this, he heard footsteps behind him and a low rasping voice. "I told you it was him, saw him on the feed, I told you."

As Sal turned, he saw Beral's familiar face. He didn't see the knife though. It punched straight through the bottom of his jaw up and up, it didn't stop before it got wedged on the inside of his skull. The world went black for the very last time.

Epilogue

WALLANG paced the corridors heading to the very top of the fortress. He hadn't climbed these staircases in years, chasing phantoms in the depths where the Sun's light couldn't penetrate.

He watched the sun setting over City Six, sending them back into night for so many cycles. He could feel the energetic change in the atmosphere as the Sun slowly sank before the horizon.

His objective had been thwarted. Not by power or lack of skill, but by pragmatism. He didn't want to turn Embla into a wasteland like Earth. He shook his head and turned back into the fortress, he needed a drink. Badly.

Heads turned when he entered Ambrose's place. It had been too long since he'd enjoyed any of life's simple pleasures, like freshly brewed beer and company. The host looked intimidated by his presence. Wallang often forgot that he now wore his corruption externally, a visible reminder of his power and his lifelong work as a Mage. He would need a new life's work. Or at least a project to focus on.

Wallang ordered the house lager and sat in a large booth, staring off into space.

Kesh deserved to pass on to Mastery and forge her own path. He had been keeping her from her future. It would be a while before she was done "retraining" as her punishment, but when she did she would finally be able to create without limits.

Maybe she would even travel a bit with her young lady. That girl and her life were a mystery. Last Wallang had heard, she was planning to return to space in hopes of tracking down the rest of her bloodline. They'd never found Leanne's body and one could never really be sure if a Life Mage was dead. Unless they were properly burned to cinders, like the young man who had infiltrated Apteryx. Lin had a long road ahead of her to find out why she had mattered so much to the Life Adept.

Wallang took another sip of his beer and murmured to himself, "What really matters anyway?"

He continued in his head, I could end this planet tomorrow. Take away every living being on this planet, open a door so wide that the Darkness would pour forth into the system until the void of space has been replaced with absolute black.

Wallang felt the tendrils of his corruption curl and move as he thought that. It felt like he was hearing a sound from a great distance, like cackling.

Suddenly, the noise came to an end. Someone had put a hand on his shoulder. Wallang looked up, expecting to see the server, but instead, it was Ambrose.

Ambrose smiled down at him, his expression open and his pleasure at seeing him evident in his body language.

"My dear friend. How have you been? Can I join you for a drink?"

"Of course. As long as you promise not to tell me, I told you so," replied Wallang.

"Well, that sounds like a hell of a story."

ABOUT THE AUTHORS

Elle and Fiona are scientists, entrepreneurs, and dreamers. Fiona is a Canadian PhD in biomedical engineering who reads obsessively and uses her spare time to knit and crochet. Elle is a Swede, a chemist, a lover of weird science, and equally weird art. They live in Canada with their two world-ending cats: Hel and Fenris.